SEDUCED BY PASSION

Billionaire Island Brides

Book 1

ANA E ROSS

Cedar Trees Publishers

Also by Ana E Ross

Billionaire Brides of Granite Falls Series

The Doctor's Secret Bride

The Mogul's Reluctant Bride

The Playboy's Fugitive Bride

The Tycoon's Temporary Bride

With These Four Rings: Wedding Bonus

Beyond Granite Falls Series

Loving Yasmine

Desire's Chase

Pleasing Mindy

Billionaire Island Brides Series

Seduced by Passion

Consumed by Desire

Destined to Love Her

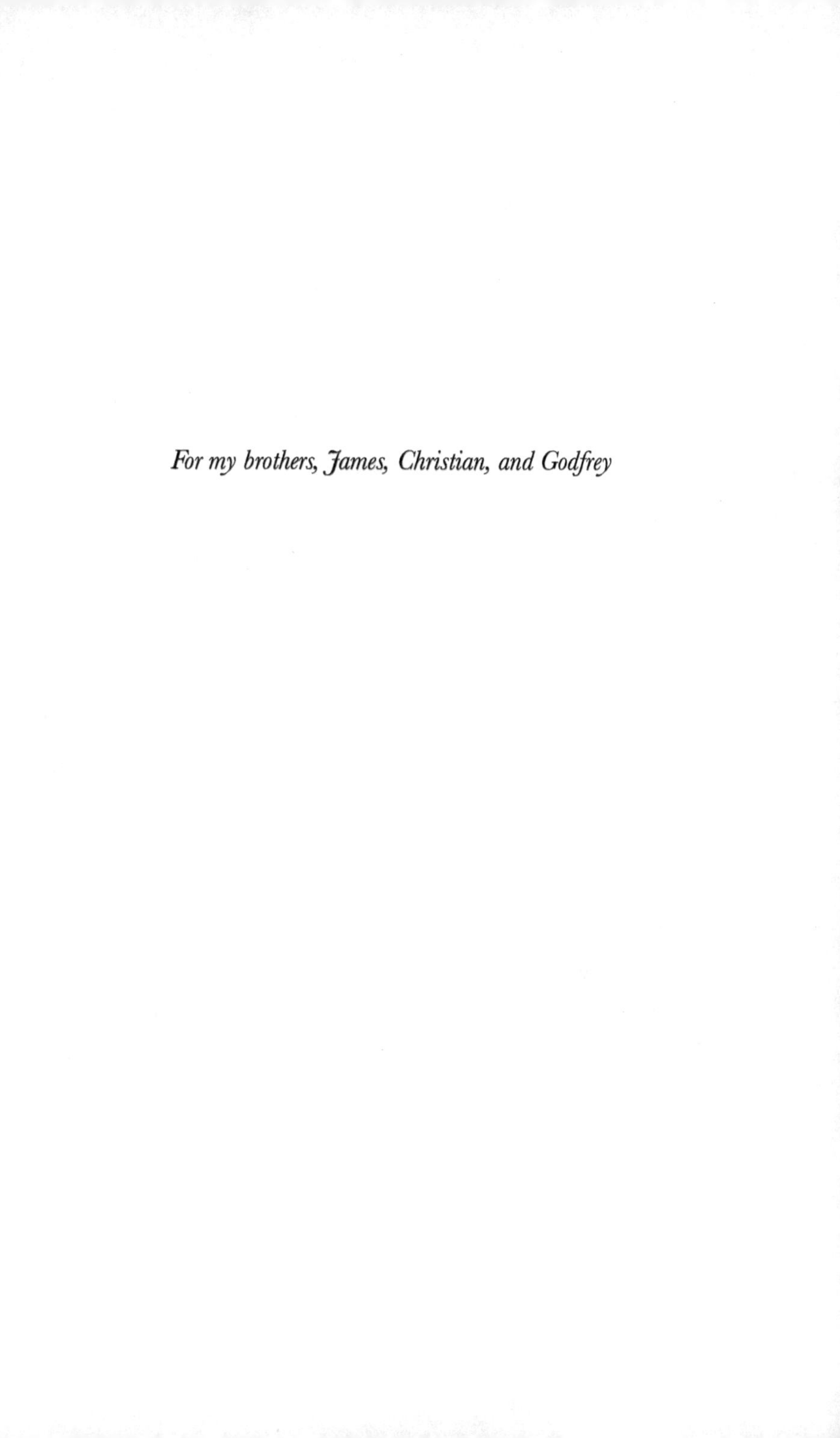

For my brothers, James, Christian, and Godfrey

When you are joyous, look deep into your heart and you shall find it is only that which has given you sorrow that is giving you joy. When you are sorrowful look again in your heart, and you shall see that in truth you are weeping for that which has been your delight.

Kahlil Gibran, "On Joy and Sorrow" from The Prophet

Part I

THROUGH A GLASS DARKLY

Prologue

HERE TODAY, GONE TOMORROW

Raph sat in the tan leather chair, staring at the naked woman in his bed, her auburn hair fanned across her face. He'd awakened not long ago to find her snuggled against him, her smooth leg slung over his, and her arm over his chest as if he was hers to claim. For the last ten minutes, he'd been debating whether he should ask her to leave, or if he should just walk down the hall and spend the rest of the night in one of his guest bedrooms.

He'd found her at The Painted Lady, perched on a stool, picking at a Caesar salad, and scrolling through her phone with a half-empty glass of Chardonnay beside her plate. He'd needed a drink—maybe two—and the familiarity of his favorite downtown bar after another sixteen-hour day at G3. She'd been attractive enough: polished and professional, with manicured nails, a black sheath dress and ivory blazer, and classic black pumps.

She was a pharmaceutical sales representative, she'd explained after he'd slid onto the stool next to hers and signaled the bartender for his usual Macallen, neat. She had been in town for a convention and was supposed to be heading home to Miami in a few hours, but the storm raging outside, bringing heavy rain and dangerous winds, had grounded flights across the Bay Area.

She was just searching for an affordable hotel room, and was starting to think she'd have to beg the manager to let her sleep behind the bar, she'd said.

To ease her pain, Raph had bought her another drink. Then another. And by the end of the night, she was writhing and moaning under him in complete satisfaction.

Now, watching Brittany—*or was it Bethany*—asleep in his bed, Raph felt the familiar hollowness that followed these superficial encounters. Sure, the conversation had been easy enough, and she was just his type: here today, gone tomorrow. But she was only meant to be a temporary distraction, and now that it was over, he wanted her gone from his apartment and the controlled solitude that had become his sanctuary.

Rain hammered against the floor-to-ceiling windows—the storm that had grounded flights still raging over the Golden Gate City, a relentless drumbeat that matched the dull throb in his head. He glanced at his watch and wondered what his mother would think of him—throwing a woman out in weather like this at three o'clock in the morning.

Raph sighed heavily and wiped his hands down his face. That sliver of decency he'd been unable to completely snuff out over the last few years wouldn't let him stoop so low. He'd sleep in the guest room, of course, let her have his bed until morning, then send her on her way with coffee and a polite goodbye.

Raph pushed himself up from the chair and was halfway to the door when he heard his phone vibrating on the nightstand, the soft sound barely noticeable against the muffled howling wind outside. Quickly grabbing it, he moved to the windows on the far side of the bedroom before answering, his voice barely above a whisper.

"Rapheus, is that you?"

"Dr. Constantinou?" Raph's heart began beating double-time. He pressed his free hand against the cold glass as he listened to his grandfather's doctor—his words both a source of comfort and pain.

"Thank you for calling, Dr. Constantinou— No, no, don't apologize about the time, you were right to call me first. I'll let them know. We'll be there as soon as we can." His hands were shaking as he hung up, and his mind was already making a list of everything he needed to do before flying to Santorini. First and foremost, he needed to call his pilot, then his brothers, his mother, Declan…

"Hey you." The woman's voice made him turn. She'd propped herself up on one elbow, her hair tousled, the sheet slipping to reveal the soft curves that had seemed so appealing a few short hours ago. "What are you doing out of bed?"

"Hey, I just— I have a—" *What the hell am I doing?* The call had him frazzled—he didn't owe her an explanation. Raph took long strides across his room toward his walk-in closet. "I need you to leave," he stated blankly, leaving little room for misinterpretation. Throwing her out wasn't his first choice, but after Dr. Constantinou's news, it was the only option.

He watched her expression shift from provocative to alarm as he crossed the threshold.

"What? Now?" she asked as he pulled on a pair of black sweatpants folded at the edge of a divan.

He reentered the room and stood beside the bed, looking at her with what he hoped resembled a remorseful smile. "Something came up last minute."

"Must be something important," she muttered with sarcasm.

"Very important. It really is," he added, bending to give her a consolatory kiss on the forehead. "I'll book you a suite at The Ritz-Carlton."

Her eyes widened. "The Ritz-Carlton? Are you serious?" She sat up fully, the sheet pooling around her waist.

"Is that not okay?" he asked, turning his attention to his

phone still in his hand. *Is she really going to argue with an offer like that?*

"No— I mean of course it's okay, I just… It's the middle of the night and you want me to get out of bed and go out in this weather?"

"Don't worry, I'm texting my driver now. He'll be in the garage in five minutes, no need for you to get wet." *At least not on my account…*

"Raph, I thought…"

"Look B, I'm sorry to push you out so unceremoniously, but I've got some really important calls to make." He lowered his phone, sat on the edge of the bed next to her, and rested his hand on her leg, brushing it with his thumb. "Believe me when I say I wish it wasn't like this, but it's one of those things that really can't wait. I have to get going. I'll book you a suite for two nights —just in case your flight is still delayed tomorrow."

"Oh, Raph, you really don't have to do that."

I'd buy the whole damn hotel if it would get you out of here faster. "It's my pleasure. My 'thank you' for such a great night."

She smiled bashfully, her skin flushing, reminding Raph for just a moment why he'd sat next to her in the first place. She was beautiful, and interesting—he'd give her that—but he'd wanted nothing from her beyond sexual gratification.

He cupped her chin and kissed her pale lips—brief, practiced. "This was fun. Thanks." And with that, Raph stood and walked out of his bedroom, his finger swiping through his contacts, his heart and mind already across the Atlantic with the man who'd been more like a father than a grandfather to him.

Behind him, he heard the rustle of sheets and the pad of bare feet on hardwood. Soon she'd be gone, and he'd be alone again.

Just the way he preferred it.

Chapter One

HIS RA

Raph scowled at the six-foot, three-inch man staring back at him in the bathroom mirror. Fatigue had settled in pockets under his sleep-deprived eyes, and a black, five o'clock shadow covered his olive skin. He always took great pride in his appearance, but with the circumstances of the last week and a half, especially the last few hours, grooming had been the furthest thing from his mind.

Bending under the weight of sadness and unease, he turned on the faucet, splashed cold water on his face, then threaded his wet fingers through his rumpled hair, pressing the black strands against the collar of his white shirt. Lifting a clean towel from a stack on the counter, he dried his face and eyed his reflection again. He still looked disheveled, but at least he felt somewhat refreshed.

He exited the bathroom and, ignoring the hum of voices coming from the living room, he headed toward the large oak door at the end of the hall. As soon as he opened it, the smell of ammonia and antiseptic flooded his nostrils and the sound of air being forced through congested lungs filled his ears.

Swallowing the lump in his throat, Raph walked over to the

bed and gazed at the ninety-three-year-old patriarch of the Giannopoulos family sleeping in the middle of the bed. His wraithlike body was propped up by pillows on either side, and his skin was so pallid, he was almost indistinguishable from the white cotton sheet beneath him—a stark contrast to the towering man he used to be.

His name was Andris Sebastian Giannopoulos, and he was Raph's beloved *pappoús*.

Andris was more than a grandfather, though. He was the man who'd made Raph feel safe and protected as a little boy. Raph remembered the feelings of security when his grandfather held his hand, of excitement when they flew kites on the beach while waves lapped at their feet and the wind tugged at their clothes, and of contentment as they solved jigsaw puzzles together.

Solving jigsaw puzzles was Andris' favorite pastime, and of his three grandsons, Raph was the only one who showed interest in his hobby. He loved the challenge of creating beauty from chaos, but that wasn't the only thing that had kept Raph sitting and sifting through thousands of identical cardboard pieces for hours, days, and sometimes weeks. It was his love for his grandfather, and the joy he got from spending time with him. He hoped that, over the years, he'd given the old man as much love and joy as he'd received from him.

The flap of the white linen window curtains moving in the cool evening breeze brought Raph back from the past, and into the dread of the dimly lit room. Wiping the tears from his eyes, he eased his body down onto a chair beside the bed, reached out, and methodically brushed the gray, wrinkled brow, just as Andris had brushed his when he was a little boy in need of comfort. And God knew that he and his brothers, Neo and Tele, had needed a whole lot of comfort when they were children.

Even though they had outgrown that need, their grandfather still piled it on every chance they gave him, until two years ago when he suffered a stroke that robbed him of his ability to speak and his mobility on the right side of his body.

The family had placed him under the care of the best doctors and therapists money could buy. Then two weeks ago—after many small incremental improvements—Raph and his brothers had gotten good news from the doctors. Andris had regained his speech and was asking to see his family. It was the miraculous breakthrough they'd all been praying for, and they'd immediately flown to Santorini to be with him.

For the past week and a half, Andris had been talkative as he visited with his grandsons, his great-granddaughter, Petra, and their extended family. Everyone thought he was surely on his way back to a full recovery, but a few days ago, even though his speech was still strong, his body had weakened, and he'd developed a severe case of pneumonia. This morning, his doctor had warned the family that the infection and his old age would claim him before the next sunrise. It was as though his grandfather had fought his way out of his prison of silence, just to bid his family farewell.

Raph's brothers, his niece, and the children and grandchildren of Ilaria, Andris' late sister, had said their final goodbyes this afternoon. Raph's mother, Jordan, was expected to fly in from New York this evening to say her goodbyes to the father-in-law who had accepted her into his heart and loved her like she was his own daughter.

Even though they had all traveled back and forth between the U.S. and Santorini to visit each other, Raph wished he'd spent more quality time with his pappoús over the last ten years. But he'd been too busy turning G3 into the billion-dollar real estate development giant it had become. In his twenties, he'd thought he had all the time in the world to do all the things he wanted. It had taken Andris' stroke for Raph to realize the importance of family over business, but by then it was too late. He'd been misguided, stupid, and focused on the wrong things in life.

After the happy, tearful trips down memory lane this afternoon, Andris had asked everyone, except Raph, to leave. He wanted to have a talk with him, but he'd been so worn out from the visiting that he'd fallen asleep shortly after the room had cleared.

RAPH STILLED as his grandfather's hand stirred against his thigh, and his eyes fluttered open.

"Raph… Raph…" he whispered, looking around the room until his eyes focused on his grandson's face.

"I'm here, Pappoús." Raph resumed caressing his brow.

"The clock. You'll take it with you."

Raph wondered why, of all the possessions Andris had amassed during his ninety-three years on earth, that forgotten clock was the first thing he mentioned upon awakening. It was as though he'd been dreaming about it. "Yes, Pappoús, I will take the clock with me."

Raph looked at the seven-foot-tall grandfather clock ticking away in the corner where it had been since he was thirteen years old. He had been here in Santorini when his grandfather had it moved from an outbuilding on the estate to his bedroom. His mother had remarried that same year, and he and his brothers were looking forward to spending the summer in Greece to get away from their new stepfather, but Andris had asked Jordan to send Raph two weeks ahead of his brothers

Neo and Tele had also wanted to leave early, but Andris had insisted that Raph came alone, with a promise to take each of them for one week every summer from then on—a promise he'd kept until his teenage grandsons had become too busy with friends, girlfriends, and eventually business, and began spending less and less time with the old man.

That summer, Raph and his grandfather had traveled all over mainland Greece to places he'd never been before and hadn't been to since. It had been nice not to have to split his attention with his brothers for two whole weeks. Then, two days before Neo and Tele were to arrive, his pappoús had brought him into this room and asked him to help him clean the precious family heirloom for the very first time.

While they'd carefully laid out the pieces and polished the carved eagle standing guard on top of it, Raph had felt as if his grandfather wanted to tell him something important. But every time he started a sentence, he would get tongue-tied as if he couldn't find the words to say what he wanted to say.

Raph had never seen his grandfather at a loss for words until that day. He remembered the firm grip of his grandfather's hands on his shoulders, and the urgency in his voice while he made him promise to take the clock to California if anything should happen to him—to make sure it stayed in the family.

He grimaced at the thought that he would soon be the unenthusiastic owner of that monstrosity, but a promise was a promise. "I'll take the clock," he said again to set his grandfather's mind at ease.

"Thank you." Andris gave him a faint smile, then said, "It's my fault, *to mikró mou gio.*"

Raph's hand stilled on his forehead. He gazed into the fading brown eyes. "Your fault for what, Pappoús?"

His grandfather swallowed and took a few shallow breaths. "Everything. Your father and *Yaya*. They died because of me."

Raph stared at him, baffled. Why was his grandfather blaming himself for their deaths? Is this why he'd asked to be alone with Raph? Alarm quickened his pulse.

Pulling a tissue from a box on the nightstand, he wiped the tears that slid from the corners of Andris' eyes. "Pappoús, Yaya and Baba died in an accident. It wasn't anybody's fault. It was—"

"It's more than that. It's everything. It's Cleon. It's Giannport. It's… It's…" Andris' voice trailed off as his lungs fought for air. "You're not listening to me. You're… You— You're not hearing me!" Andris' frail body began shaking in the bed as he succumbed to a coughing fit.

"It's okay, Pappoús. It's okay," Raph said as he placed his hand on Andris' shoulder, trying to calm him down. He waited for him to catch his breath. "Pappoús, you gave Giannport to Cleon after Baba and Yaya died because—"

"*Óchi.* Óchi." Andris shook his head in frustration. "He knew something. He took it."

"You mean by force?" Anger churned in Raph's stomach at the thought that Cleon, his estranged cousin, had coerced his grandfather into abdicating his forty-year position as CEO of Giannport Vineyard & Wineries. Andris had helplessly watched as his company was sold off, vineyard-by-vineyard, until it all but ceased to exist. All that remained was one dilapidated vineyard in Aetós, the launching pad for the Giannopoulos wine-producing empire that was once the most successful in all of Europe.

"If your father had lived, he would run Giannport. Pass it to you, Neo, and Tele."

Raph could not argue with that fact. His father, Xander, who'd loved the wine making business, would have taken over Giannport years ago, and Raph's mother, who was one of the few female sommeliers in the world, would have helped him run it.

But as fate would have it, Xander and Kerena, Raph's father and grandmother, died in a car crash not too far from the family estate in Santorini when Raph and his brothers were six-years old. If things were different, yes, he would have been coached and prepped to take over Giannport, but there was no going back. "If Cleon stole the company from you, I will make him pay, Pappoús. I swear!"

"Óchi! Leave it alone. Doesn't matter now. Waste of time." Andris tried to clear the phlegm from his throat. "Promise me you'll leave it alone."

Raph frowned. Why would he say that his cousin had taken the company away from him by force in one breath, and then in the next, say that it didn't matter, anymore? Of course, it mattered. *What was he afraid of? What was he hiding?* "I promise, Pappoús," he said, even as he knew in his heart that he could not just forget it.

His grandfather let out a deep breath and relaxed into the mattress again as Raph continued to soothe his brow with long, gentle strokes of his thumb.

"You are head of the family now, Raph."

The implication of that responsibility weighed heavy on his heart. "I know, Pappoús."

"Take care of your brothers and your mother and little Petra. Find the right woman and fall in love."

"You know me, Pappoús, I wouldn't know the right woman if she punched me in the nose." Raph laughed to lighten the grim aura in the room, and to keep himself from saying exactly how he felt about women and love.

"You'll know her when you feel her. When you dream about her."

"You mean when I see her?" Raph asked with a questioning frown.

"*Óchi.* You don't see love. You feel love. Experience love," he whispered on a smile. "She might not be the most beautiful woman you've ever seen, but you will know she's right when you feel her in your heart, and when you dream of her, *mikró mou gio.* You must carry on the Giannopoulos bloodline," he said, before closing his eyes and lapsing into silence.

Raph was only older than Neo by five minutes, and Tele by seven, yet his brothers had always looked up to him. They had allowed him to lead the pack, even when they were children. And, it was understood by all, that once their grandfather made his earthly exit, Raph would become the *de facto* patriarch of the Giannopoulos family.

As for carrying on the family bloodline, Tele had already grown his little branch, and he was sure that soon Neo would settle down and plant a few seeds of his own. Marriage and a family were not in Raph's life plan.

"*Neró*," Andris whispered in a voice, much weaker than it had been a few minutes ago.

Raph took the glass of water from the nightstand and helped him take a few sips through the straw. When he'd had enough, Raph replaced the glass then held his waning gaze. "I love you, Pappoús," he said in a choked voice, needing him to hear it one last time. "I wish we'd spent more time together during the years before your stroke."

Andris' eyes flashed gently. "We had our moments, *mikró mou gio*. More moments than many people get with their loved ones. You and I solved so many puzzles together." His thin lips cracked on a crooked smile. "You brought me so much joy."

Raph pressed his lips together as wrenching knots formed in his belly. "You brought me joy, too, more than you would ever know, Pappoús." He wiped his sleeve across his eyes and nose.

Andris squeezed Raph's hand. "You were always my favorite."

Raph grinned through his mounting pain. He knew his grandfather told Neo and Tele the same thing, but he also knew the old man held a tad more fondness in his heart for him. He tightened his fingers around his grandfather's. "I know, Pappoús. And you've always been my favorite grandpa."

"I know your heart, *mikró agóri*. I know what you gave up."

Raph's eyes narrowed to slits. "What do you know, Pappoús?"

Andris simply smiled, then said, "I want you to do something... something for me."

"Of course. Anything for you, Pappoús." He fought to suppress the grief spreading through his gut with each passing second.

Andris' brow knitted, and he beckoned Raph closer. "Take us to Aki… Aki—li—na, Rapheus."

Raph stared wordlessly at his grandfather for a second. "Where? What—"

"Will you take us, me and Yaya?"

"Yes. I will take you and Yaya to Akilina, but—"

"No one else is to know. Not your brothers. Not your mother. Only you must go. Promise."

"Yes, Pappoús. I won't say a word. But, what is Akilina? Where is it?" he asked, curiosity and surprise warring in his mind.

Andris' eyes darted around the room with a burning faraway look. "I… Island. Carib… bean. My *Ra*."

"Your Ra? What is a Ra?"

"My birthplace."

Raph drew back in confusion as he tried to absorb the information his grandfather just dumped on him. He took a deep breath and hoped his voice would not portray his alarm. "You're saying you were born on this island in the Caribbean? I've seen your birth certificate, Pappoús. You were born in Aetós. You were born here in Greece." He paused, again wondering at his grandfather's state of mind. "Are you getting your facts mixed up, Pappoús?"

"Óchi." He shook his head and tightened his lips in frustration. "Óchi," he said again.

"I'm sorry, Pappoús. I don't mean to upset you. I'm just trying to understand what you mean—what you want me to do."

His grandfather's eyes darted around the room again, causing an eerie feeling to skitter up and down Raph's spine. What, or who was he looking for?

"My baba. He was promised. To another. He fell— They fell…in love. They eloped. To Akilina," Andris said, pausing after each sentence while his chest rose and fell, and the crackling in his breath grew louder.

Nausea rose to Raph's throat as he realized that his grandfather was struggling to take his last breaths. "Pappoús," he whispered. Tears raced down his face and landed on his hands, both clasped around his grandfather's. "Pappoús…"

"I'm sorry, Rapheus. I'm so sorry. I didn't tell you. I— I wanted to… I— I—meant to. But then I…" Andris closed his eyes tightly and pressed his lips together as a lone tear slid from the corner of his eye, rolled down his temple, and into his ear.

Raph's stomach cramped at the sadness and regret he'd heard in his grandfather's voice and the turmoil on his face. "What, Pappoús?" He shifted on the chair, his body tightening with urgency. He wiped a hand across his nose. "What did you want to tell me?" He needed to know.

Andris' eyes brightened and moved around the room as though he were following something, his gaze tense and alert. When his focus zeroed in on a spot above Raph's head, a chill enveloped Raph, and he had the feeling that a ghost had passed through him. The hairs on the back of his neck stood on edge and goosebumps covered his skin. But he did not feel panic, only a quiet acknowledgement of the existence of things beyond this world.

In that moment, he knew that his father's and his grandmother's spirits were in the room. Raph pressed his lips together to bite back his sob. "Pappoús…"

Andris' gaze drifted to Raph, and he managed a faint smile. "Akilina. Raph, take us to my Ra."

"I will, Pappoús. I will take you to your Ra." Tears blinded him. Knowing it was the last time he would gaze into his grandfather's eyes, he hurriedly dried his tears on the sleeve of his shirt.

"Thank you… Rapheus." Andris' gaze shifted to the portraits of his son and wife on a table at the foot of his bed. They had been placed there after his stroke so he could see them without having to strain his eyes. He took deep shallow breaths—breaths Raph knew were his very last.

"Pappoús..." His chest felt heavy as lead, and his breath solidified in his throat.

Andris squeezed Raph's hand. "Xander. Kerena, *agápi mou*," he whispered, and with those final words, his lips sealed together on a smile. His grip relaxed around Raph's fingers, and his brown eyes shimmered in the bedside light one last time before his lids closed around them.

And there, in the quiet of the home where he'd lived all his life, Andris Sebastian Giannopoulos peacefully died. For twenty-seven years, he had grieved in silence for his wife and son, hardly speaking of them, even to his grandchildren, because his pain was too deep, the wound of loss, still too raw. But now, he was with them, and finally at peace.

The grandfather clock chimed seven times, tolling out the evening hour.

"*Antío*, Pappoús. *Se agapó*." Raph leaned over the bed and pressed his lips to his grandfather's cool forehead. Still holding his frail hand, he dropped his head on his chest and wept, regret for not spending more time with him stabbing at his broken heart.

Chapter Two

THE LETTER

R APH WAS STILL SITTING at his pappoús' bedside when he felt
Neo and Tele's hands on his shoulders. He'd been so lost in his
sea of grief that he hadn't even heard them enter the room. He
lifted his head and stared into the faces that resembled his, and
although the sorrow in their green eyes mirrored his, Raph felt as
if he needed to say the words. "He's gone," he whispered in a
broken voice.

They crouched down beside the chair and hugged him as
they looked upon the body of the man who had been a surrogate
father to them since they were six years old.

"He's at peace, now," Neo said, wiping his eyes. "He was
never the same after Yaya and Baba died. He'd been longing to
be with them for years. I think he was holding on, just for us."

Tele shook his head slowly. "Losing the love of your life is
bad enough, but losing your only child at the same time is the
worst thing that could happen to anyone. The pain of losing
Helena is still so unbearable at times. Even though I have Petra
who reminds me of her, sometimes I wish I had died with her."

"Telepheus Giannopoulos, don't ever let me hear you say
such a horrible thing again! Ever!"

Raph and his brothers turned as their mother entered the room. Even though he wasn't the one who'd tested the fates, when he saw the shock on his mother's face, Raph felt as if it was his fault. He had always taken the blame for his brothers when they got in trouble as children. Even to this day, they willingly stepped aside and let him take the fall. He was not taking the fall today. Raph stood and nudged Tele in the side. "Go to her."

Tele met their mother at the door. "I didn't mean it, Mom," he said. "It's just too painful when I think about her, and when I look at Petra— She looks so much like her mother. It brings back too many memories, especially of that day."

Jordan clasped his face in her hands, wiping at his tears with her thumbs. "You think I don't know how it feels, my baby boy? I know your pain. Not a day goes by that I don't think of your father. I miss him with everything in me, but I never once wished I had died with him."

Tension swirled in Raph's belly as he thought of that fateful day his father and grandmother died. Jordan and Kerena were on their way out the door to meet some friends at a restaurant in Oia. But at the last minute, Rapheus had come down with a stomach bug, and Jordan had decided to stay home with him. Instead of letting his mother go alone with the family driver, Xander had driven her to her lunch date in his brand-new Ferrari.

Raph had always wrestled with the possibility that if he hadn't gotten sick, his mother and grandmother would have left for the restaurant earlier with the driver, and his father would not have been taking the steep curve at the same time as the produce truck coming from the opposite direction. They'd died instantly, and the old man who'd been driving the speeding truck succumbed to his injuries the following week.

He swallowed the rising panic in his throat as he recalled hearing his mother's blood-curling scream echoing through the house when the police had come to give her the news. Still weak with fever, he'd jumped out of his bed and run into the living room to find her standing by the door screaming her husband's name at the top of her lungs with Neo and Tele holding onto her, and his grandfather on his knees, rocking back and forth, his face buried in his hands, calling his wife's name.

No one had needed to tell Raph what had happened, and his little heart had broken in two as he'd rushed to his grandfather and thrown his arms around him.

"I might never know why fate took my darling Xander," Jordan said.

Raph sucked air into his lungs as his mother's voice yanked him back from the abyss, and the despair of the "what ifs" that have plagued him all his life.

"I often wonder why he didn't live to watch you grow into the wonderful, successful men you've become. But," she continued, glancing over at the bed with tears streaming down her face, "I'm grateful Andris was here. He was a wonderful grandfather to you."

"Yes, he was," Neo said.

"The best," Tele added.

Jordan slowly walked over to the bedside, took Andris' thin wrist in her hands, and stroked it tenderly. "I wished I'd made it in time. If I'd known you only had a few days left, I would have come as soon as we heard you were better. Forgive me." Jordan placed her lips to his forehead. "Thank you for helping me raise our precious boys. I could not have done it without you. Give Xander my love… Tell him…. Tell him…"

As he watched his mother struggle with her grief, the wall of ice around Raph's heart thickened. He had witnessed three members of his family suffer the loss of a spouse—his grandfather, his mother, and his youngest brother—a crippling burden Raph had no desire to carry for the rest of his life.

"Tell him that I miss him every second of every day. I will

miss you, too, my dear Baba." She pressed a trembling hand to her mouth.

With a groan erupting from his throat, Raph pulled Neo and Tele over to their mother. They wrapped their arms around each other and wept for the souls who had departed decades ago, and for the one who had joined them tonight.

As their cries waned, Jordan pushed out of her sons' embrace. "Our lives will be very different without him," she said, drying her cheeks on her silk sleeve.

"Our lives changed two years ago when he had his stroke," Raph said. "At least then, we had hope that he would recover. But death is permanent. He's not coming back." He pressed the tears from his eyes with the tips of his fingers.

"Yes," Jordan said. "Andris is gone forever, but he left you behind to continue the Giannopoulos line. The thought of it dying with him brought him so much anxiety," she said, gazing hopefully at her sons. "It was very important to him that it continued."

"It was one of the last things we spoke about before he slipped away," Raph said. "He told me to find the right woman and settle down."

"Did you tell him you would?" his mother asked, the hope in her brown eyes growing brighter.

"Of course, Mom. I wasn't going to disappoint my dying grandfather."

"I've already done my part. It's yours and Neo's turn," Tele said to Raph.

"I'm pretty sure Pappoús knew he was barking up the wrong tree," Raph stated. "He was just doing his duty."

"It's much more than that, and you know it, Rapheus." Jordan placed a hand on his arm. "Your grandfather was serious about the family lineage." She walked over to the family photos and studied them for a minute before turning back to her sons.

"You know you are named after three brothers in the Giannopoulos lineage, right?"

"We know, Mom." They rolled their eyes at each other.

"When Andris found out I was carrying triplets, he was over-the-moon and insisted on naming you Rapheus, Neopheus, and Telepheus, even though your father and I had already picked out your names."

"What were you going to name us?" Neo asked, clearly to appease their mother who loved to tell the story they had all heard a million times already.

She laughed and tucked a strand of dark hair behind one ear. "Since Raph was the first, he would have been Xander, after your father. You, Neo, would have been Yiannis. And Tele would have been Zeno."

"We were to be the XYZ babies? Really, Mom? Sounds like an algebra equation to me." Tele chuckled.

Neo raised his hand in the air and pretended to write on a whiteboard while drawling in a nasal, monotone voice, "Good morning, class. Your challenge today is to solve for X, Y, and Z. You have ten minutes."

Despite the pain in his chest, Raph couldn't help laughing at Neo's spot-on imitation of their tenth-grade algebra teacher, Mr. Donahue, but he quickly sobered up as he thought of the sad fate of their namesakes.

Raph, Neo, and Tele had been named after three brothers whose parents, Thaddeus and Amaryllis, had fled to England to escape the Ottoman invasion and occupation in Greece. Once there, they'd started a shipbuilding company. But in 1688, after a flood killed his entire family, Rapheus returned to Greece where he expanded his family's business.

Giannport Maritime dominated the shipbuilding industry, and in the mid-nineteenth century, one of Rapheus' descendants branched out into the wine making business. Giannport Vineyards and Wineries had produced some of the best wine in Europe for over a hundred years, until Cleon took it over from Andris.

"Yaya! You're here. You came." Petra ran into the bedroom and dashed toward her grandmother.

Jordan scooped her up into her arms. "Petra. *I mikrí mou kóri.* I've missed you so much."

"I missed you, too, Yaya." Petra wrapped her arms around Jordan's neck. "I waited and waited for you to come every day."

"I know. Grandma had to work, darling."

"Are you coming home with me and Daddy? Are you coming to my ballet recital? Did you pencil me in, Yaya?" she asked, causing everyone to chuckle.

"Do you know what that even means?" Neo brushed a curl from her forehead.

She scowled at Neo. "Of course, Uncle Neo. It means you write somebody's name with a pencil in your book. Uncle Raph already penciled me in. Right, Uncle Raph?" She grinned eagerly at him.

"I wouldn't miss it for the world, darling." His heart drummed with love for his niece, whose sweet smile reminded him too much of her mother.

Petra turned and gazed at her great-grandfather. "Can Propappoús come, too?"

Stillness descended on the room as the adults glanced warily at each other. It brought back unpleasant memories for Raph, as he was certain it did for his brothers, who were only two years older than Petra when they'd lost their father.

Raph walked around the bed and took Petra from his mother. He wrapped his arms tightly around her little body. "Propappoús is sleeping," he said, stifling his own cry at the stark reality. Now was not the time to tell her that he would not be waking up. "Would you like to give him a kiss before we say goodnight?"

"Okay, Uncle Raph."

Raph held her as she kissed her great-grandfather for the very last time. "Good night, Propappoús. Sleep tight. Don't let the bed bugs bite."

The adults glanced at each other, and with tears running down their faces, they approached Andris' body. One by one, they kissed and bade a final goodnight to the man whose smile and voice and warmth they already missed.

***

SAN FRANCISCO, California...

Raph filled his mug from the full coffee pot and took a day-old chocolate croissant from the glass jar on the counter. Leaving his kitchen, he walked through his living room where the early morning sun filtered through the glass walls, and down a long hallway lined with ancient Greek artifacts and paintings he had collected over the years.

In his home office, Raph bit into his croissant and took a sip of hot coffee. He was just about to sit down at his desk and open his laptop when he heard the clicking of high heels on his hardwood floor.

Damn, he'd forgotten about the one-night stand he'd picked up at a bar last night. He braced himself for the impending encroachment.

"Oh, there you are, Rapheus," she said. "I've been looking for you. Your place is so big, I didn't think I'd ever find you."

He swallowed his mouthful of croissant, turned, and offered her a pleasant smile. "Hi, um——" *Shit,* he'd forgotten her name. Was it Lisa, Linda, Leslie? He peered at her over the rim of his mug, waiting for her to supply her name.

"It's Lara," she said, disappointment edging her blue eyes.

Raph was used to that look, and it didn't faze him, not one

bit. She was attractive, sexy, in her tight little red dress and black stilettos, and he'd had a good time with her last night. But play time was over, and he just wanted to be left the fuck alone. He had things to do.

"Right, Lara." *The ER nurse.* She had approached him last night at the bar across from G3's headquarters in downtown San Francisco. He hadn't been looking for a pick-up, just a couple drinks to ease the tension. She wasn't shy, and after she'd offered to make the scowl on his face go away, he'd thought, what the hell. A soft, warm body in his bed and a rosy pair of lips against his skin was a much better way to forget about his pain than bourbon or Scotch could ever do.

"You wake up early," she said, advancing into the office. She came to stand so close to him that he could smell her perfume. Last night he'd found it appealing, but this morning it made his stomach churn.

He'd been up for three hours already, and had split the time between his gym, his rooftop pool, and a long, cold shower. He gestured toward the stacks of folders on his desks, projects that had been backing up for the past four weeks since he'd left for Santorini. "Work."

Her eyes roamed around his office before they zeroed in on the coffee table that sat between two brown leather sofas. "That's a pretty vase," she said.

Raph's jaws tightened as his eyes followed hers. "I had a good time last night, Lara, but I do need to get to work."

She pouted and placed her hand on his chest. "Well, I don't have to be at the hospital until later this afternoon. I was thinking we could get some breakfast before I leave." She used the same sexy smile that had convinced him that getting laid was more fun than drinking alone last night.

And it had been, but the night was over and she was becoming a nuisance. Raph took a step back, breaking contact.

He set his half-eaten croissant on the rim of his mug. "I'm really not much of a breakfast person, Lara. And I really do have a lot of things to take care of."

"Maybe another time then." She batted her eye lashes at him.

"Sure, maybe another time." Raph picked up a notepad from his desk and handed her a sterling silver pen.

"My driver is waiting downstairs," he said, as she wrote down her name and number. "He'll take you wherever you need to go. The elevator is just down the hall to the right." He took the notepad from her, and gave her a peck on the cheek. "Thanks again, I had a great time."

"Sure. Bye, Rapheus." The look in her eyes told him that she understood he would not be calling her.

As she clicked her way toward the elevator, Raph dropped his weight into his brown leather chair. He ate his croissant and sipped his coffee as he stared at the urn on the coffee table.

The gold-leafed porcelain urn was inspired by the Lekythos vases used by the ancient Greeks to store oil for funerary rights. This modern interpretation, with its elegant silhouette and yellow and blue mosaic snaking its way around the narrow neck, had held Kerena's ashes for twenty-seven years. Now, it held Andris', too. Raph's mother had chosen it, and a matching one for his father. That one, she kept on a bureau in her bedroom. She refused to let the love of her life go.

The grandfather clock in a corner of his office chimed, drawing his attention away from the vase, to its gold pendulum, swinging back and forth behind the beveled glass door.

Made from dark wood with a wide sturdy base, the long-bodied timekeeper sported a magnificently carved eagle perched on the top surface, its wings spread as if it was about to take flight. His grandfather had told him that Thaddeus Giannopoulos had built the clock in England, and ever since, it had been passed down to the eldest son in his direct line.

Repaired and polished through the ages, it had been keeping time in the Giannopoulos family for hundreds of years. In Raph's opinion, the clock should have been retired a few generations ago.

As much as he didn't want the family heirloom, he felt he had to honor his grandfather's wishes and bring it to California with him. It was among the very few items Raph had brought from Santorini.

Feeling like a caged animal, Raph got up and walked over to the wall of glass behind his desk. He massaged the crick in his neck as he watched the cars disappear into the fog on the Bay Bridge. It's been three weeks since his grandfather's death, and one week since he'd come back from Santorini, give or take a day. Saying goodbye to his grandfather had been mentally and emotionally taxing, but having to deal with his relatives at the memorial had made it more—well, unbearable.

Andris' last will and testament was short and simple. Apart from a small fortune in trust for Sebastian, his sister's great-grandson, he'd left everything he owned to his three grandsons: a few properties scattered across Europe, including the Santorini family estate, two yachts currently on lease in the Mediterranean, and stocks in various global companies.

Raph wished he'd instead left the answers to the questions that plagued him. How did his great-grandparents, Arsenios and Giulia, end up on an island in the Caribbean? Why did Andris' birth certificate reflect that he was born in Greece if he said he wasn't? Was Ilaria born in Akilina, too? Had his grandfather ever visited the island again?

Raph balled his hands into fists as he paced between the clock, the coffee table, and his desk, the shock and curiosity he'd been feeling since Andris dumped the information on him, giving way to anger and frustration.

How was he supposed to just continue with life as usual with this mammoth family secret in his head? It wasn't fair, nor right, that he should have to bear this alone. Why did it have to remain a secret, anyway? Neo and Tele deserved to know, and he deserved to have their support.

Raph stopped behind the sofa and stared at the urn. "Why, Pappoús? You had ninety-three years on this freaking earth, and you waited until you were on your deathbed to tell me about all of this? Why bother mentioning it at all? Where the hell am I supposed to find the answers?"

"Knock, knock."

Raph turned his head to see Declan Ashbrook, G3's Chief Operating Officer, walking into his office with a manila envelope in his hand. He'd called Declan earlier to tell him he would be working from home today. He wasn't in the mood for a suit and tie or pretending that his world was alright, nor did he want to hear condolence from people who didn't know anything about his grandfather or the mess he'd left him.

"You didn't tell me you were coming by," he said, walking over to his desk. "Is there a problem?"

"No, no problems. I was on my way into the office when I realized I didn't have the Graystone Mall file. I have to go over some specs with the team today. I think you might have grabbed it by mistake last night."

"Oh." Raph dug through the stack on his desk and pulled out a green folder. "Yep, I did. Here you go." He handed it to Declan. "You know you could have just printed off another copy, right?"

"I'm thinking of the environment, Raph. Every wasted sheet of paper and empty ink cartridge add to the problem. Haven't you heard the seas are rising? I don't want to wake up one morning floating on my bed in the middle of the Pacific."

Raph laughed at the image Declan painted. But all jokes aside, G3 did everything in its power to cut down on waste. "You realize you wasted gas coming here," he pointed out.

"Oh hell, Raph, we can't have everything." Declan groaned.

"Speaking of having things, I bumped into your one-night-stand coming off the elevator," he said, setting the folder on the edge of the desk. "She seemed a bit peeved. Weren't you able to get it up?"

"I got it up," Raph said without emotion. "She wanted to stick around and have breakfast."

Declan laughed. "Poor girl. I'm sure she'll be pining after you for weeks."

"I doubt it."

"Well, I hate to pile more onto your plate, but a currier was on his way up with this so I saved him the trip." Declan handed the envelope to Raph.

Raph's heart skipped when he recognized the name of the law firm in the upper left corner. He placed it on his desk.

"Aren't you going to open it? I'm not familiar with that firm."

"You wouldn't be. It's from Andris' lawyers. It's the paperwork for transporting his remains to Akilina. I've been expecting it." He dropped wearily down into his chair. "I don't think I can handle it today."

"You have enough on your mind with all the questions he left you with. Too bad there's nowhere for you to find the answers."

He leaned back into the chair. "To be honest, Declan, I'm not sure I want any answers. They might be worse than the questions. Maybe that's why he waited until he was on his deathbed to tell me. Maybe the truth scared him."

"You've never shied away from answers before, or any truth for that matter," Declan said, crossing his arms. "Sometimes we just need to step away from everything to clear our heads. Maybe you need a vacation to grieve your loss properly, then the answers might come easily."

"I just had a four-week vacation."

Declan scoffed. "That was not a vacation, Raph. You took off to be at the bedside of your dying grandfather. You were the executor of his will; you were responsible for his cremation, the memorial service, and for closing out his affairs. That's a lot of stress. And since you came back, you've been working harder than you have in years. Why don't you take some time off? And don't say you can't abandon G3. You know that I'm capable of holding down the fort when you're away."

"I need to get everything in order for my trip to Akilina."

"Which isn't until next week."

Declan was the only person Raph had told about his grandfather having been born on the island and that he'd requested his ashes be scattered there. "You know as well as I do that I don't take vacations."

"You think you're invincible, Rapheus. But one day you will crash and burn. I just hope it won't be too late for you to bounce back. Even your grandfather understood the value of leisure. Before his stroke, he used to travel all over the world."

Raph frowned as he evaluated Declan's last statement. It was after the accident that killed his wife and only child that Andris had started buying up properties around Europe. Raph could only speculate that he'd been trying to escape his loneliness, and the memories that lingered at the estate in Santorini, where he'd heard the horrible news.

Declan arched one brow and tapped his chin with a finger. "From what I've heard, Akilina is a beautiful, laid-back place. I could come along to make sure you don't spend the entire trip working. We can slip in a little sun and rum on the side."

"This isn't a fun trip, Declan."

"But it could be, Raph. You stopped having fun since..." Declan's voice trailed off when Raph sent him a dagger stare, daring him to say her name.

"You know what I mean," Declan said. "Yeah, you go through the motions of chasing and catching women, but you don't seem to get any fun out of it. It's just so animalistic—unemotional. But that's nothing you haven't heard before."

I had fun last night, he thought on an inward smile. Lara had helped him forget his sorrow for a couple of hours, but then morning had come. "If you want to go to Akilina so badly, you are welcome to take off when I return."

"Come on, Raph. It's never fun chasing women alone." Declan leaned against the desk and eyed Raph comically. "Remember the good old days?"

Raph smiled at his best friend's attempts to cheer him up. Declan and Raph had been roommates since their sophomore year at UC Berkeley. The first thing Raph had noticed about the witty, math geek, was that once he set his mind on something, he stayed on it like a dog on a bone. He and his brothers hadn't even thought twice about bringing Declan onboard as COO at the inception of G3 when they were all still undergraduates. It was the smartest move they ever made where the company was concerned.

Raph knew that Declan had played a leading role in catapulting G3 into the multi-billion-dollar corporation it was today. He was also aware that several companies had flirted with his top man, offering him outrageous salaries and perks, but Raph never felt threatened by their plays of seductions. He knew it was more than money that kept Declan at G3. "Another time, Dec," he said. "There's something I need you to focus on while I'm gone."

"A takeover?" Declan rubbed his hands together and smiled like the Cheshire cat at the prospect of a new challenge.

"It's about my cousin, Cleon."

"Oh. Are we killing him or simply maiming him?"

"We're burying him."

Declan raised an eyebrow. "Alive?"

Raph chuckled. "Of course. There's no other way to do it. I'll put a file together and get it to you by the end of the day."

"I'll be waiting with swords drawn. You know how I love to slay your demons for you."

"It's why I pay you the big bucks." Raph felt a stab in his gut for going against his grandfather's wishes, but it was a matter of principal. Dirty business never sat well with him, especially when it came to his family. Cleon would not get away with stealing his grandfather's company. Not as long as Raph drew breath. The bastard was going to pay for whatever it was he'd done. He glanced up at Declan, forgetting he was there for a moment. "You got the Graystone Mall file."

"Yep," Declan said with a grin. "I guess that's my cue to get the hell out. Catch you later, boss." Declan tucked the folder under his arm and walked out the door.

Deciding to bite the damn bullet, Raph opened the parcel and pulled out a note addressed to him in his grandfather's handwriting. It was dated March 15, 2018, two months before Andris' stroke.

My Dear Rapheus,

As you must have already learned from my lawyers, I wish to have Yaya's and my ashes scattered at Aetós on the island of Akilina in the Caribbean. I don't know if you know of it, but more importantly, I don't know if I will have the courage to tell you about it before I die. The thing is, Raph, I was born on that island.

I hope you will have it in your heart to honor my dying wish, whether or not I have told you the truth. When you do get to Akilina, I want you to stay in The Davenport at Jewel Beach Resort. It's where I stayed when I visited the island.

You should have received another envelope in this package addressed to Xiomara Davenport. Please deliver it to her as soon as you arrive. When you get to Akilina, don't be afraid of what you learn. Follow the light that leads you to the truth.

I hope you find love and happiness, mikró mou gio, because when all is said and done, love is the one thing that will defy all odds and stand the test of time.

Se agapó me óli mou tin kardiá.

Your loving pappoús,

Andris

"WHAT THE HELL?" Who the hell is Xiomara Davenport, and why was his grandfather writing to her? Raph turned the parcel upside down and shook it. The transport papers for Akilina fell onto his desk, along with a small, light blue envelope. He picked up the envelope, his eyes widening at the words scribbled across the front: *Xiomara, i mikrí mou kóri.* My little daughter.

Raph dropped the envelope on his desk and eyed it as if it was a cobra about to strike.

So that was it. His grandfather had a love child named Xiomara Davenport. She lived on Akilina. Was that what Cleon had on him?

Raph threaded his hands through his hair, tugging until pain shot through him, confirming he wasn't dreaming. This was real. He dropped back into his chair like a sack of potatoes. Sweat broke out on his forehead. He swallowed to soothe his dry throat, then opened his laptop. His fidgeting fingers hovered over the keyboard for a moment, not certain if he wanted to know, but then his curiosity got the better of him, and he typed 'Xiomara Davenport' into the browser bar.

Desire and intrigue consumed him as her picture appeared on his screen. She had smooth, golden-honey skin, a diamond-shaped face with a heart-shaped mouth, and red lips—slightly parted on a smile. She gazed back at him through a pair of dazzling, chestnut-brown eyes, framed by long dark lashes and soft-angled brows. A thick curtain of black hair flanked her flawless face and cascaded down her slender shoulders. Dressed in a silver gown, she looked like a goddess who'd emerged from the Caribbean Sea behind her.

Good God.

Butterflies fluttered around in Raph's stomach as he stared into her seductive eyes that seemed to call to him, enticing him.

He closed his eyes and shook his head, trying to reject the debilitating feeling of losing control, of losing himself, his thoughts, his mind.

You'll know her when you feel her.

But how could he be *feeling her* this way, if she was his grandfather's love child?

Damn it, Pappoús.

Chapter Three

DUPED

AKILINA...

Xiomara's heart was overflowing with pride as she walked through the lobby of Jewel Beach Resort, waving at guests reclining on the sofas and chairs intimately arranged around pots of towering palms and beige Corinthian columns. She greeted guests coming out of the boutique swinging little gift bags in their hands, and those on their way to the restaurant, tempted by the delicious smell of JBR's famous breakfast buffet wafting through the air. Her stomach growled, reminding her that all she'd had today was a cup of coffee and a coconut tart she'd swiped from the kitchen on her way to the daily meeting with her department heads.

As she neared the concierge desks where guests waited to be checked-in and attendants toted luggage in and out of the lobby, Xio found it hard to believe that this hotel that had been in her family for generations, had almost come to ruins under the negligent management of her half brother, Fitzroy.

For five consecutive years before their father died, the global travel magazine, *Sand and Sun*, had named Jewel Beach the number-one destination resort, not only in the Caribbean, but in the world. It had been an achievement that her grandfather and father, Malik Davenport, had been working toward their entire lives.

But nine years ago, Malik suffered a heart attack, and within the hour before he died, he named his eldest son, Fitzroy, as CEO of Jewel Beach. Fitzroy's only job was to keep JBR running smoothly until Xio finished her MBA at Princeton, after which point Fitzroy had promised their father to hand the company over to Xiomara. But instead, he'd turned their father's legacy into a playground for himself and his free-loading friends.

Between Fitzroy's negligent management and the destruction caused by Hurricane Julie six years ago, by the time Xio took it over, JBR was crumbling under the weights of low to no reservations, struggling restaurants with unqualified chefs who'd replaced those who had resigned, badly damaged swimming pools, termite-infested roofs on the great house and some of the villas, and a host of other problems.

When she'd seen the condition of the resort, Xio had wondered if her father's decision to grant Fitzroy the chance to prove himself was rooted in guilt for divorcing his first wife when Fitzroy was still a kid, and for the deterioration in their relationship after he remarried.

Like all little sisters, Xio had looked up to her big brother, hoping to have a relationship with him, but over time, his behavior had destroyed that possibility. For years, Fitzroy had manipulated her into asking their father for money to buy something she wanted, and then he would take the cash from her. Twenty dollars here, fifty there, a hundred… Her father was so trusting that he never seemed to notice that she didn't have the items she was supposed to buy. Fitzroy would even talk her out of her allowance.

When she was eight, her parents had gone on a European vacation, and had given Xio the green light to have a slumber party with the staff's supervision. She had games and movies picked out, and had even been allowed to order whatever food she wanted from JBR. But while she and her friends were at the pool, Fitzroy had shown up with his own group of friends. By the time Xio and her guests got back to the house, all of the snacks and food had been eaten, and there were empty beer bottles littering the house.

Xio had called her dad in tears, but Fitzroy had refused to leave, and the staff, who were afraid of him, couldn't be of any help to her. Her friends had all called their parents to pick them up early, and Xio was left alone in the house with Fitzroy. She'd started hating him that day. But she was still a little girl who wanted the love of her big brother, and after a while, she had forgiven him.

Their relationship took a major dive after he walked into her sweet sixteen birthday party, high and drunk, and started a shouting match with their father that escalated into an exchange of physical blows in front of the most respected and powerful people in Akilina. Xio had never been more embarrassed in her life. Even after that scene, she'd still hoped her brother would change, but he had only grown into a bigger lying bastard who thought he was entitled to everything, just because his last name was Davenport.

Fitzroy got full access to his trust fund the same year their father died. And in addition to wrecking JBR over the five years he was in control, he blew all of his money on sports cars, women, liquor, drugs, and lavish vacations. Xio had found the cars to be the biggest waste of money since there was nowhere to go on their small island. When his trust fund ran out and his opportunistic friends started deserting him, he sold the fifty acres of land their father had gifted him at birth to keep them around for a few more months.

When Xio returned from Princeton to take over JBR, like their father had intended, she'd had to spend two years fighting with Fitzroy to step down. He'd finally named his price to not only vacate his position, but to also leave the island to get out of her hair.

Xio had weighed the options of parting with the family business, or with the fifty acres of land she had also inherited upon her birth. In the end, she had chosen to sell her land.

It had been four years of uphill battles, but she had managed to place JBR back on the Caribbean's twenty best resorts chart, and she was determined to make it number-one again. All departments were performing above expectation and projections, and the senior managers who'd been skeptical of her ability to make JBR a success again were finally giving her the praise she deserved.

Xio credited most of the income to The Davenport, a five-bedroom luxury villa set on nine acres of flowering gardens, orchards, and a dense forest with private stables and paths that led to a beach, studded with royal palm trees. The villa was a sanctuary within Jewel Beach Resort, and with its own dedicated staff, two swimming pools, a spa, and an unbeatable view of the bay in Anacaona, Akilina's main city, The Davenport brought in $20,000 per night. Hiring a new marketing team when she first regained control of JBR was one of the best decisions Xio had made. With their social media savvy, they had made The Davenport one of the most sought-after stays in the Caribbean.

"Ms. Davenport!"

Xio turned to see a gray, curly-haired couple waving enthusiastically from a sofa.

She hurried over, her mouth split in a wide grin. "Mr. and Mrs. McGregor. How are you?" she asked, sitting down on the chair across from them.

"A little sad, as you might expect," Mrs. McGregor said. "We don't want to leave."

"I feel your pain." Xio placed her palm against her heart. It was moments like these she appreciated. "It's been a pleasure having you with us."

"The pleasure was all ours, Ms. Davenport." Mr. McGregor smiled. "I'll be telling all my friends back in Burlington about your little treasure of an island, and the exceptional service and staff here. You surpassed our expectations in every way."

Xio was beaming. It was exactly what she needed to hear.

Mrs. McGregor chimed in. "We try to take a trip at least twice a year since we retired. We've been all over the world, but this," she said, sweeping her hands around the lobby, "this is one of the best vacations we've had."

"I'm glad to hear. The best is what we aim for."

"You've got it," Mr. McGregor winked at her.

"I think the Thursday night bonfires on the beach were our favorite. They made us feel young again. Didn't they, dear?" Mrs. McGregor gave her husband a coy smile.

When he blushed, it left no doubt in Xio's mind what she meant.

"The nights are so magical here," Mrs. McGregor added.

They certainly are, Xio thought, recalling watching the couple dancing around the flames to the rhythm of the live steelpan band.

"It's Thursday. Maybe we should stay one more night," Mr. McGregor teased his wife and pulled her against him, kissing the top of her curly head.

"You know we can't," she said, smiling into her husband's flushed face.

The McGregor's had initially booked for one week, but a day before they were due to leave, they'd asked to extend their stay for two more weeks. All two-hundred rooms in the main house had been full, and another couple who'd booked the same room in advance were due to arrive on the day of their departure. Xio had offered to upgrade the McGregor's to one of JBR's private cottages, but they had politely declined and, citing their age, had asked to stay in the main building.

Taking her father's advice about bending the rules to make

her guests happy, even if it might cost in the short run, Xio had instead upgraded the much younger Millers to a cottage. They'd been so ecstatic about the unexpected upgrade that before they left, Candice Miller, who turned out to have a huge following on social media, raved about the resort and wrote about it on her blog. As a result, the reservations were rolling in.

Two couples had already booked JBR for destination weddings, and a Hungarian skincare company had emailed Xio's office about hosting a retreat at the resort the following year. As of a week ago, that little cottage, with a nightly rate three times higher than the McGregor's room, was booked solid for the rest of the season.

"We really wish we could stay` longer." Mrs. McGregor said, "But our fourth grandchild, and second grandson, is due next week. Our Sarah won't forgive us if we miss it."

"Congratulations!" Xio declared, sharing in the happiness she saw on this couple's faces. This was the kind of experience JBR was all about. "Wait here one minute. I will be right back."

Xio hurried toward the nearest boutique. In the children's section, she flipped through hangers on a rack and picked out a white new-born onesie with a map of Akilina and the words 'Jewel Beach Resort' printed on the front. She walked behind the register, folded it into tissue paper, and dropped it into a small gift bag. The price of this little onesie, she thought, as she hurried back to the McGregors, was nothing compared to what they'd spent during their extra two weeks on the island.

"This is a little something for your grandson." Xio gave the bag to Mrs. McGregor.

"Oh, this is so generous of you." She clasped it between her hands before placing it into the carry-on tote at her feet.

"I hope you come back to visit us again."

"We have decided to make Akilina an annual vacation spot," Mr. McGregor said. "We already booked our room for the same time next year, so you will see us again."

"We'll bring the whole family next time," Mrs. McGregor added.

"Wonderful! I look forward to it." Xio's heart bubbled over as she shook their hands.

"Thank you for everything," Mrs. McGregor said.

"You're very welcome. Your ride to the airport is here," Xio added, as a van pulled into the courtyard and an attendant began loading their luggage that had been sitting on the curb.

"Unfortunately." Mr. McGregor stood to his feet, then helped his wife up. He placed a green cap with the word *Akilina* and an embroidered eagle on his head, then picked up his wife's tote.

"This is Josef," Xio said, as a young man made his way over to them. "He'll assist you to the van, and make sure you are comfortably settled. I hope you have a wonderful flight and get home to Vermont safely."

"Thanks again, Ms. Davenport. You take care now." Mr. McGregor gave her a big grin, took his wife's hand, and followed Josef out to the courtyard.

Xio was blissfully happy, wrapped in a silken cocoon of euphoria when she finally headed toward her office suites. Olivia, her best friend, and personal assistant wasn't yet back from her meeting with the seafood suppliers.

She left a note for Olivia to check in when she returned and ascended the flight of stairs to her office on the second floor. She opened the door and let out a sigh as she took in the beige, coral, and gray decor with floor-to-ceiling windows and doors overlooking the resort and the blue sea behind it.

Xio kicked off her heels and made her way across the tiled floor to her desk. Easing into the comfort of the oversized black leather chair that had been her father's, she stared at a picture on the corner of her desk of the two of them. It was taken on move-in day, during her freshman year at NYU. He'd been so proud of her then. She hoped he was just as proud of her accomplishments with JBR now, when everyone had thought it impossible. She could finally relax, just a little, after functioning on the edge of a debt precipice for four long years.

"I did it, Daddy" she said. "We're back in business, and I promise to make ours the best resort in the world again. I'll make you proud." Reaching out, she traced the outline of her father's chin with her fingertips, smiling as she remembered sitting on his lap and playing with his beard.

She pulled back and killed the sob in her throat, wondering if the pain of losing her father would ever go away. Whether or not, now was not the time to succumb to the memories. She had to stay in the present and focused on restoring JBR. Despite the increase in revenue for the past few months, she still wasn't out of the woods yet.

She knew her father would be upset if he knew where she'd gotten the money for the renovations. Her mother had told her that she was taking a risk, but at the time, Xio didn't have any other options. Four years ago, JBR was in such bad shape that banks were reluctant to give her a loan. Those that did, offered them at shockingly high interest rates—evidence, she felt, that despite the Davenport name, they had little trust that she could reverse the damage Fitzroy's negligence had caused.

"It has been difficult without you, Daddy. I did what I thought was best. Things are looking up now, though."

Xio swiveled around and studied the paintings of eight Davenport men hanging on the wall—all former CEOs of the first hotel ever built on the island. And one day, when she passed the baton to the next generation of Davenports, her portrait— JBR's first female CEO—would hang next to her father's.

"Xio! Xio! Are you there? Pick up, *gurl*. Pick up!"

At the alarm in Olivia's voice coming through the speaker on her desk phone, she pressed the intercom button and spoke. "Olivia, what's the urgency? Who died?"

"Somebody's about to, depending on your interpretation of death."

Xio bit into her bottom lip. "What do you mean?"

"Mr. Stamer is in the waiting room. He's demanding to see you."

"Which one?" she asked, already knowing the answer. Olivia was not fond of either of the Stamer men, but only one of them could throw her into a frenzy.

"The old leathery one."

Xio let out a long groan. "He knows, doesn't he?"

"Judging from his pompous-ass attitude, yeah, I'll say the ground lizard knows everything."

Xio dropped her face into her hands. Olivia was right. The mere fact that Samuel Stamer had come calling without an invitation or an appointment meant he'd discovered what his son had done for her, and he'd come to make her life miserable. How? She did not yet know. The man was sharp and ruthless and created chaos for anyone who crossed him. The thought of being in his line of fire scared her. Her confidence immediately turned to panic of the worst kind. Her chest tightened with anxiety as a myriad of bad scenarios played out in her head.

"Your schedule is already tight for the day," Olivia said.

"Yeah, I know." Xio slowly lifted her head and glanced at the opened calendar on her desk. She had meetings with suppliers and event planners into the evening, and with Stamer now about to invade her space, Xio knew this was going to be a crazy day. She wished she'd made time to meditate this morning.

"I can move your schedule around, ask Amara if she can meet about the Garcia wedding later today," Olivia said, penetrating her wishful thoughts. "Or better still, I can make him schedule an appointment and come back another day when you're ready to see him."

Xio bunched her hair in her hands and let the strands fall back across her shoulders. She sighed deeply. "I never want to see him, Liv. But putting him off would only prolong the inevitable. If there's one thing my father taught me, it's to face my problems head-on the moment they arise. The longer they fester, the worse they get."

"That is so true, girl. It's best to get it over with."

Xio bit into the right corner of her bottom lip. "Hold all my calls and don't let anyone up here. Don't need my dirty laundry out there."

"You got it. Don't let him bulldoze you."

"Yeah," she said with a lilt in her voice, her gaze going back to her father's picture.

"And don't forget, you're meeting your mom for lunch in an hour. You want me to send him up now or make him wait a few more minutes?" Olivia asked.

Xio glanced at the gold Tag Heuer watch on her wrist—a gift she'd received from her father when she'd completed her first year at NYU. She might be able to squeeze in fifteen minutes of meditation before lunch to reset if she got rid of Stamer quickly. "Send him right up." She ended the call.

"Well, Daddy," she said, glancing at her father's picture, "this is a true test to see what I'm made of as I face off with the most insufferable man on Akilina."

Even though she was expecting it, Xio jumped at the firm knock on her door. Despite the boost of confidence she'd gotten from Olivia, her stomach still rolled with nerves.

Remember who you are, Xiomara.

At the sound of the second, louder knock, Xio slowly rose from her chair, walked over to the door, and slid her feet back into her shoes. She needed to look the part—the epitome of professionalism—when she engaged the devil. She arranged her hair over her shoulders, took a deep breath, and opened the door.

"Mr. Stamer. What a surprise. Please, come in." She forced a smile at the average-size man with cold brown eyes encased in a web of crows' feet, neatly cut salt-and-pepper hair, and a mustache to match. His jaws were working overtime on his usual wad of chewing gum.

"Ms. Davenport, is it really a surprise, though?" His voice was infamously emotionless as he strolled past her and looked around the office, eyeing everything in sight.

When his beady eyes settled on the picture of her father on her desk, Xio's stomach tightened.

It was no secret that Malik Davenport and Samuel Stamer, president of Akilina Bank and Trust—the oldest financial institution on the island—had been lifelong professional rivals. Since her father died, Stamer had been set on overtaking Jewel Beach Resort. He'd tried to purchase it from Fitzroy, who, thankfully, had enough loyalty not to sell his family's legacy to his father's rival.

"Please, have a seat," she said, closing the door and pointing to the beige leather sofa. "Can I get you a drink, a Magua perhaps?" she asked, knowing the local guava drink was one of his favorites.

He waved her offer aside, sat down on the sofa, and placed a brown leather-bound folder on the glass table in front of him.

Xio took one of the club chair on the other side of the table. "What brings you here, Mr. Stamer?" she asked, crossing her ankles, and clasping her hands on her lap.

He held her gaze and chewed on his gum, then said, "Ms. Davenport, let's not beat around the bush, eh. You know why I'm here."

Xio nodded. She would not insult his intelligence by pretending ignorance. "You found out that Trevor gave me a loan from your bank."

He stroked his mustache and nodded slowly. "Yes. The problem is that every loan, especially those as large and favorable as the one you received, must be approved by me."

"Well, shouldn't you be talking to your son about that?" she asked defensively. "I didn't go to Trevor. He came to me knowing that I needed a loan for repairs."

"He has always had a soft spot where you are concerned. That's for sure."

Xio would beg to differ, but there was no point. Despite their families' rivalry, she and Trevor had been friends since they were in grade school. She'd liked him, and even trusted him as they'd grown up together. He'd been supportive of her and her younger siblings, Akilah, and Malik Junior, after their father died. Six years ago, when she returned from Princeton, Trevor had started pursuing her romantically. She'd kept him at arms' length at first, but he'd eventually worn her down with his affection and persistence. The next thing she knew, they were engaged. But just as she'd begun planning their wedding, she'd found out that he'd been sleeping with someone on the side, and had gotten her pregnant. He'd broken her heart.

When Trevor approached her with the loan offer, three years ago, she'd refused, but then he'd actually gotten down on his knees, something he hadn't done when he'd proposed, and begged her to let him help as a way to make amends for hurting and embarrassing her. His only stipulation was that they had to keep it from his father who would not have agreed to such generous loan terms. Xio imagined that Samuel had ripped his son a new one when he came across the contract. But Trevor's decision to keep his father in the dark had nothing to do with her.

She cleared her throat. "To tell you the truth, Mr. Stamer, I don't know why you're here. I haven't missed any payments, and based on my profit margins, the size of the installments will increase in six months, per the contract. She glanced across the room at yesterday's reports on her desk, and the pride she'd felt before he arrived began to flow again. "Trevor's offer made good business sense. So of course, I took the deal."

"I'm all for making good business choices, Ms. Davenport, but not when fraud is involved."

Xio straightened up in her chair, her hands fisting on her lap. "Fraud? What are you talking about? I didn't commit any fraud?"

Stamer unbuttoned his gray suit jacket, leaned forward, and opened his folder. He pulled out a stack of papers that were stapled together and placed it on the edge of the table closest to her. "One of my loan officers found this buried at the back of a cabinet. While going through it, he realized that the assets and value of your establishment had been gravely inflated at the time you applied for the loan."

Xio read her name and 'Jewel Beach Resort' typed on the top sheet. "What do you mean inflated?" she asked, switching her gaze to Stamer.

"See for yourself. Page eight lists the value of JBR's assets that you provided." He sat back, chewing on his gum with a sly grin on his face.

With trembling hands, Xio picked up the file and flipped to page eight. The bottom fell out of her stomach. The figures were three times as much as what she remembered providing. "This is not my contract," she said, shaking her head vehemently. "I did not give anyone these numbers. I—"

"But you did, Ms. Davenport. Your signature is on the last page, isn't it? See for yourself."

She did not need to. "This is not what I signed off on," she repeated, dropping the stack of papers on the table like it was a hot iron. "Somebody fudged the numbers after I signed it."

"Xiomara, are you accusing my son of committing bank fraud?"

"Ms. Davenport, to you, Mr. Stamer!" she spat out. No way in hell would she allow him to get informal with her while accusing her of bank fraud. She knew exactly what he was doing, and she was not going down without a fight. "Either Trevor, or somebody else at your bank changed those numbers."

"I don't understand why anyone would put themselves in jeopardy by committing such an egregious act. People go to jail for such crimes." He picked up the file and weighed it in his hand as if it was a trophy he'd won. "You have a copy?"

"Of course, I have a copy." Xio got to her feet and walked over to the row of silver filing cabinets behind her desk. She opened the one where she'd filed the contract and yanked it out, flipping to page eight as she returned to the sitting area. The nerve of this bastard to come into her office and accuse her of...

Xio came to an abrupt stop as she stared at the column of numbers on the asset page. They weren't the ones she'd provided and signed off on. The file slipped through her numb fingers and landed on the floor. She collapsed into her chair.

"From your reaction, I'll assume the numbers in your contract match those in mine," Stamer said.

Xio's gut wrenched as her mind whirled back to last week Friday when Trevor had shown up at her office, unannounced. Olivia had already left for the day, and Xio was getting ready to do the same, but she had felt obligated to tolerate and entertain him because of what he'd done for her. They'd shared a drink, and again, he'd apologized for hurting her, and asked if she would give him a second chance, which she'd of course declined. He must have switched the file when she'd gone into the bathroom to change for her kickboxing class at the resort's gym. He knew that she went to that kickboxing class after work on Monday and Friday afternoons like clockwork.

She glared at Stamer, the fact that she'd been set up quickly dawning on her. She should have known that Trevor could not have offered her that loan without his father's consent, as Stamer had so gleefully pointed out. Desperation to save her family's legacy had made her blind and vulnerable to them. And now here she was, trapped in their plot to steal her family's business from under her.

People go to jail for committing such crimes.

Xio swallowed the panic rising to her throat, and forced stability into her voice. "You and Trevor set me up with that loan. You changed the numbers after I signed it, and you sent him here last Friday afternoon to switch out the file."

Stamer stared at her as if she had two heads. "I don't know what you're talking about, Xiomara. Was Trevor here last week?"

Xio shot to her feet, her panic turning to fury. "Don't screw with me, Samuel Stamer," she said between clenched teeth. "You and your son inflated the values of my assets after I signed the contract. You're the ones going to jail for committing fraud. Not me."

He laughed as if her threat was water rolling off his back. "Come on, Xio… Ms. Davenport. Nobody is going to jail." He left the sofa and picked up the contract she had dropped and placed it on the table. The corners of his eyes crinkled, reminding Xio that with Stamer, there was always an ulterior motive. "Not if we work together," he said, confirming her worse nightmare.

Pressure built in Xio's chest and slowly moved upward, tightening around her throat like an iron fist. Fearing she might slap the arrogance from his face, Xio walked to the verandah door and stared out at the deep blue waters of the Caribbean Sea.

Being indebted to Samuel Stamer was tantamount to selling your soul to the devil. Under his directive, Akilina Bank and Trust approved loans at historically high rates, and God help those who fell behind in payments, as first-time borrowers often did. He had swindled vulnerable, elderly widows and widowers out of their properties through his snaky dealings, and tied the hands of ambitious young people who lacked credit and couldn't get loans from other banks, destroying their lives before they had a chance to live it. There was little anyone could do, since he could hire the best lawyers on the island. Plus, Stamer always had his ass covered. Nobody was ever able to prove in court that he'd done anything illegal, even though there were always quiet rumors that he had. Her father had had the wisdom not to put one penny of his money into Akilina Bank and Trust, because he didn't trust Samuel Stamer.

But it wasn't him she'd trusted. It was Trevor. Was Trevor an innocent pawn in his father's plot, or was he a willing partner? After he failed to buy Jewel Beach from Fitzroy, had Stamer told Trevor to marry her as a plan B? If that was the case, Trevor cheating on her made perfect sense. He never loved her. He was just using her to do his father's bidding. Now this—blackmailing her—was what they'd resorted to after the engagement fell through? Like father like son. Why hadn't she seen this coming?

Swallowing her anger at herself and at the father and son with whom she'd unwittingly fallen into bed, Xio turned around to find Stamer standing at the bar across from her desk with a glass of water in his hand. She knew what he wanted, what he had always wanted, but she would force him to say it. She wanted to hear him say that he was about to defraud her of her family's business, so when the topic came up again, he couldn't say that it was all in her head, that she had misinterpreted his intentions. Her father had taught her that assuming her opponent's intentions would put the burden of proof on her back. "What do you want, Mr. Stamer?" she asked in a very calm voice.

He emptied the glass in one draft, set it on the countertop, and raised his arms as if he were already the king of her hotel. "Jewel Beach has been a profitable resort for decades. I respect and applaud your father for putting it on the map." He took a fleeting glance at the wall with the certificates of excellence Jewel Beach had received over the years. "But Malik did a stupid thing when he handed it over to Fitzroy. He offered a pearl to a pig, and the pig trampled on it, because he's incapable of appreciating the value of what he'd been given."

No argument there.

"Don't you agree?" he asked her.

Xio tossed him a dagger look, then walked over and stood behind her chair, her hands curling around the wooden back. She agreed with everything he said, but at the end of the day, Fitzroy was a Davenport, and as rotten as he was, she would not lower herself and speak ill about him with their enemy. "What do you want, Mr. Stamer?" she asked again in a flat tone.

"Oh, yes." Stamer came back to the sitting area and faced her from behind the sofa. "I admire what you've done in two years, Ms. Davenport. I believe that under your management, Jewel Beach will be restored to its former glory." He paused. "But this is business. I didn't get to where I am by doing favors for everyone and their grandmother."

Favors? No, you just steal and trick and commit fraud. Xio saved her breath as she knew he would deny it. Stamer was a narcissist, and he would never admit to any wrongdoing.

He folded his arms and toyed with his mustache as he looked her up and down. "You and Trevor were a couple once. I think you should reconsider giving him another chance now that he divorced that little side piece of his. Marry him, give him fifty-one percent control of Jewel Beach, and we'll call it a win-win." He dusted his hands.

Xio eyed the counterfeit contract on the table and her blood boiled like a volcano on the verge of eruption. It was all clear now. Stamer had sent Trevor to entice her into getting back together with him, and with instructions to plant the doctored contract if she declined.

Xio clenched her teeth. She wanted to slap somebody, kick something. Fight! She tightened her hold on the back of her chair, willing herself not to pick it up and hurl it at his head. "Are you out of your goddamn mind, Samuel Stamer? I wouldn't marry your deceitful son if he was the last man on the planet. You are two of a kind."

"Fair," he said with a nonchalant shrug. "Trevor hurt you, and I understand that some things cannot be forgiven. But with that being said, Xiomara, you might find becoming a Stamer much more palatable than the other two options."

Xio's body shook from the force of her lungs pumping air rapidly in and out of her body. She waited for him to lay out options two and three.

"You'll sell me Jewel beach, I will forgive your loan, and toss in a couple hundred thousand, just for old time's sake. You won't be able to say I left you with nothing, now."

His insult further infuriated Xio. The Davenport alone pulled in much more than what he was offering to 'toss in'. She could throw that information at him, but she bit her tongue. Business was a real-life chess game, and when her queen was backed into a corner, she knew not to react, but to let her opponent get comfortable in his own self-righteous gloating. And just when he thought he really had her, he would slip up and make a mistake that she could use against him.

Xio bottled her rage and seethed inside while she watched Stamer walk pompously over to the bar. He spit his gum into the wicker waste basket, fished a new stick out of his pants pocket, unwrapped it, and slid it into his mouth while walking back over to her.

He gloated at her, obviously thinking that her silence and her inaction meant defeat. "There is a third option, Xiomara. It is the least favorable of all, but I will have to alert the authorities of your dishonest business dealings. You will end up in prison for bank fraud."

"Then go ahead." Xio tossed her head back in defiance. "Alert the authorities. Nobody would ever believe I committed fraud," she said, watching a trickle of saliva slide out of the corner of his mouth before he licked it away. *So disgusting.*

"Oh, Ms. Davenport, you can't prove that you didn't. Desperation, my dear, makes people do desperate things. You were desperate to save your hotel. My bank was the only one that was willing to take such a huge risk on JBR. My son felt sorry for you and was trying to make amends, but you took advantage of him."

He paused to get a response out of her and when she didn't flinch, he continued. "Your sister and brother are too young to take over, and your mother doesn't know anything about running a resort. If you should go to jail, Jewel Beach would fall into disarray again. Which would be a real pity, seeing that you've worked so hard to bring her back to life. While you're serving your time, it would end up on the market, and being the astute businessman that I am," he said, tugging his jacket closed and buttoning it, "I'll rescue her. Jewel Beach Resort will be mine no matter which way this goes." He paused to flash her an evil grin. "I'll give you thirty days to think about your options, Ms. Davenport. I hope you choose to become a Stamer. It's the best and easiest route for both families. You and Trevor would make a fine couple."

Xio wanted to say something, but her tongue was too heavy with anger and disgust. Realizing that she was actually about to hurl the chair at him, and not wishing to go to jail for murder, too, she released her hold on it, and stepped back.

Stamer cleared his throat. "You might not believe me, but I would hate to drag you to court and see you locked up for the next twenty years. It would be such a waste. I know that Jewel Beach and your family are the two most important things in the world to you. What will happen to Akilah and MJ if you are locked away? Have you thought of what their lives would be like growing up without you? I mean, Akilah already has issues, and—"

Xio had had enough. "Get the fuck out of my office, Samuel

Stamer!" She pointed to the door, her lips trembling as she fought to hold it together.

His nostrils flared in shock. "Xiomara Davenport! If Malik heard—"

"I. Said. Get. The. Fuck. Out."

Momentary fear flashed in his eyes as his gaze followed her hands reaching out to grab the chair's back. In that second, he knew that she knew, that *he* knew, he'd gone too far.

"Oh well. I'm through here, anyway. Weigh all your options and pick the best one, Ms. Davenport," he rattled off, speed-walking to the door.

When it closed behind him, Xio growled aloud. "Stupid. Stupid. Stupid. How the hell did you let that piece of crap get the upper hand of you, Xiomara!"

She stormed back and forth, pumping her fist and kicking the air as she thought of all the times in the past year that Trevor had told her how sorry he was to have hurt her. He'd been buttering her up, making her feel comfortable with him, getting her to trust him enough to turn her back on him. Give him the chance to switch out the contract.

Her skin burned with anger. She eyed the contract on the table. Snatching it up, she twisted it in her hands, as she began pacing again, refusing to look at her father's pictures. She couldn't bear the look of shame and disappointment she imagined would be in his eyes. She had failed him—worse than Fitzroy had done. At least he had the good sense to stay away from Stamer.

She growled at the silent room again. If she'd only listened to her mother.

"What now!" she barked at the knock on her office door. "You want my heart and soul, too?"

"Are they up for grabs?"

Chapter Four

BURN

Xio turned at the sound of the deep, baritone voice. Her heart nearly stopped when she saw the impossibly tall, sexy man standing in her doorway on Viking-like legs. Tight muscles rippled under his white V-neck shirt, and dark waves of hair brushed mile-wide shoulders. With an unyielding jawline, a classic Grecian nose, and firm, sensual lips, he was the sweetest piece of eye-candy she'd ever laid eyes on.

The tightening in her body put her on high alert as she stood motionless, captivated by his arresting good looks. Her breath caught in her throat, and her skin tingled, not from fear or alarm, but from something she hadn't felt for a long, long time.

Perhaps never.

"Um—I—I'm—um…" Her brain went numb as he stepped into her office and closed the door.

She felt the power that coiled within him as he walked toward her. When he came to a stop in front of her, she stared helplessly into a pair of green eyes that were even darker than emeralds.

Xio felt an involuntary contraction between her legs. She'd

never felt so alive and excited, yet so weak and vulnerable by the mere sight of a man.

"Did I catch you at a bad time?" he asked, taking a swift sweep of the office before his eyes came to rest on the crumpled wad of paper in her hand.

Xio trembled from his closeness and the faint smell of his sandalwood aftershave. Taking a quick, shallow breath, she shook the fog from her brain and dropped the contract on the desk behind her. "No… Well, yes… No… I'm sorry… I… I thought you were someone else." She sounded like a bumbling idiot, but there was nothing to do about it.

A smile cracked his lips. "Obviously. I hope I didn't disappoint you. I'm Rapheus Giannopoulos. I booked The Davenport for a week."

So, he was the guest who'd called from San Francisco yesterday to reserve the villa and a rental jeep, and ask that the twenty-four-hour staff that came with the villa only be in the house when he was not there. Privacy was his primary request, and he'd already included generous tips to compensate any inconveniences his request might cause.

Hot and decisive, he seemed to suck up all the air in the room. The AC was at full blast, but Xio suddenly felt a different kind of heat from what she'd been experiencing a few minutes ago. Her body felt flushed and heavy, like someone had taken control of her.

"I'm Xiomara Davenport. Welcome to Jewel Beach Resort." She offered him a wide smile. And why not put on the charm? Twenty thousand dollars a night for six nights was a lot of money. Whether or not Jewel Beach survives, she would need that money for expenses and payroll.

She glanced at his hands—his left curled around a copy of The Davenport brochure, and no ring, she noted. They were strong and broad, the kind of hands that would make a girl feel safe and wanted when placed on her body in just the right spot. Something warned Xio that touching him would be an open invitation for more… *More of what?* She had no idea.

Palpitating heart and clammy hands aside, her job was to be friendly with her guests, even the petty ones who always found something to complain about, just to have a few hundred dollars knocked off their bills. Her job was to be professional, too, she conceded, reluctantly offering her hand. "It's a pleasure to meet you, Mr. Giannopoulos."

The moment they touched, shock waves rolled through her body.

He sucked in his breath sharply, but when she tried to pull away, he tightened his grip. He brought her hand to his lips and kissed her wrist, ever so lightly, sending shivers up her arm, across her chest, and into her heart.

"The pleasure is all mine, Xiomara Davenport."

She liked the sound of her name on his tongue. His voice was thick and hypnotic and trickled through her like warm molasses soothing the aches inside her. Xio felt herself drifting, falling into him. After the bad luck she'd had with men, she was no longer the kind of girl who was prone to swooning, but the hint of a smile playing at the corners of his tempting mouth, told her that Rapheus was the kind of man who was used to women swooning over him.

Snap out of it. Be professional.

When she pulled her hand away this time, he did not object. She shook her hand as if to rid herself of his energy, but it was no use. His touch was branding. He was the second man today who had invaded her space and rattled her spirit, and it wasn't even noon, yet. She cleared her throat. "I'm sorry for barking at you. You caught me totally off guard."

He acknowledged her apology with a nod. "That's alright, Ms. Davenport. We all have bad days."

Xio was taken aback at his consideration. Another guest might have thought her rude and unprofessional, and might have been inclined to make her life difficult for the duration of their stay, if not outright cancel the reservation.

"I've had my share of bad days, at times, bad weeks," he continued, as if reading her thoughts. "But I do admire a woman with passion," he said with a subtle ease. "I imagine your mood had something to do with the man I encountered on my way up. He was grinning like the cat who caught the mouse."

Xio was impressed that he could read Stamer by just the look on his face. "Very good observation," she said. "He's a piece of work, a—" She clamped her mouth shut, amazed that she was about to disclose her personal problems to a perfect stranger.

But was Rapheus Giannopoulos really a stranger? He looked vaguely familiar—like a face from a buried memory.

"I wasn't expecting you until this afternoon. My assistant should have called to let me know you were coming upstairs. I'm sorry." She'd told her not to let anyone up at all—not while she had Stamer to deal with. She was going to wring Olivia's neck.

"Don't be too hard on her," he said, folding the brochure and sliding it into his back pocket. "She was on a phone call, and I kind of slid past her when I saw Mr. Piece of Work leaving." He gave her an amicable smile that was void of any hint of an apology.

He was charming. Xio would give him that. She walked to her chair, putting the large desk between them to give her the space she needed to rein in her confusion, her tension, or whatever the hell was going on inside her. His unexpected appearance had made her forget about her current predicament for a few short minutes, but the stark reality of her dire situation was back. She had decisions to make, things to do that did not involve chitchatting with her guests. If she didn't make the right decision, Mr. Giannopoulos would be one of the last guests she would have the pleasure of servicing. "How may I help you, Mr.

Giannopoulos?" she asked, in an attempt to extinguish the tantalizing thoughts that came to her mind at the idea of *servicing* him.

"Raph." He stepped closer to her desk as if indicating that nothing could stand between them. "My friends and family call me Raph."

"Raph." Xio wasn't about to tell him that her friends and family called her Xio. He wasn't her friend. Strangely, that fact caused a heaviness to center in her chest. *Did she want to be his friend?*

Xio licked her dry lips and pulled herself together. "Is the villa to your liking? As I said before, we weren't expecting you until this afternoon. I'd planned on doing a walk-through before your arrival to make sure everything was in order."

"I haven't been to the villa, yet, but if you have some time to spare, you could come with me. It might be a more appropriate place to explain why I'm here."

Xio glanced at her watch, then at her calendar. She would be running nonstop until eight tonight. The Davenport walk-through was scheduled for two thirty because Raph was not supposed to arrive until three thirty. If she moved it up now, she wouldn't have time to meet with her mom for lunch, nor with the housekeeping staff after that.

"I understand if it's an inconvenience," Raph said, as if he could see the clock with the out-of-control hand spinning in her head. "I'm sure you're on a schedule. I don't want to get in your way."

Xio couldn't imagine that anything he had to say could get in her way as much as Stamer and her own misplaced trust. *Hah!* If he only knew that the threat of losing both the hotel and her freedom loomed over her, he'd probably laugh.

"It's not..." *Wait a second.* She did not owe this man any kind of explanation about her life. She straightened her shoulders. "You said you had a specific reason to see me."

"Yes. Right. Well, um…"

Xio was relieved to hear him stumbling over his words. At least he was human, even if he looked like a Greek god.

"Ms. Davenport, my grandfather asked me to give you something."

Xio tilted her head on a frown. She didn't know anyone named Giannopoulos—well, not until just now. "I don't think I know your grandfather."

His brows arched. "Really? That's strange. He said he used to stay at The Davenport when he visited Akilina."

Xio's frown deepened. *Strange indeed.* When she took control of Jewel Beach, one of the first things she did after renovating The Davenport was contact the guests who'd stayed there over the years to let them know the resort was back in business. It was a short list, and she knew all the names by heart. "I don't recall the name Giannopoulos. Does he have a different last name?"

"He was my father's father, and his name was Andris Giannopoulos. I don't know the last time he visited. Could have been years ago. Maybe you're too young to remember him?" He gave her a strange stare as if he expected her to say something.

She had nothing.

"Anyway," he continued, his green eyes darkening with sadness, "he passed away three weeks ago."

"I'm sorry." Xio felt a sinking feeling in her belly. She understood the pain of grief. "Were you close?"

"Very. My father died when I was six, so he was more like my father than my pappoús—sorry, I mean grandfather."

Xio's eyes shifted to her father's portrait.

"Your father?" Raph asked, following her gaze.

She lifted her head and nodded.

"How old were you?"

"Twenty-one. He had a heart attack during my senior year at NYU." Xiomara ran a finger across the face of her watch and cleared the lump from her throat. "I didn't get a chance to say goodbye. I'm still not over his death. Foolish, huh?"

"Not at all," he said in a gentle voice. "You never get over losing someone you love."

"Are you an only child?" Xiomara asked, remembering how her siblings had helped her through the pain of losing their dad.

"I have two brothers. We're triplets, actually," he added on a faint smile. "Neo was born five minutes after me, and two minutes before Tele. Or, that's what we've been told."

"Oh, wow." Xio wondered if they were identical, and if she would be able to tell them apart.

"We aren't identical," he supplied, as if reading her mind again. "What about you? Do you have siblings?"

Xio nodded. "A younger sister and brother." She didn't bother mentioning her half brother since she'd long ago disowned him after what he'd done to her family and to JBR.

"How old were they?" Raph's eyes were bathed in curiosity.

Xio thought his question a bit too personal, seeing they had only met a few minutes ago. But then again, she didn't feel like he was a stranger, and oddly, she didn't mind answering his question. "My brother, Malik Junior, was only two, and my sister, Akilah, was six. Malik has no memory of our dad, but Akilah…" She stopped as she recalled the many sleepless nights when she'd had to rock her little sister to sleep as she cried. Their mother had been too absorbed in her own grief of losing her husband, the love of her life.

"What about Akilah?"

Xio felt powerless to ignore his questions. It was as if they were old friends who were simply catching up. She folded her arms on the back of her chair and leaned forward. But when his eyes lazily slid from her face to her breasts, sending a slow heat spreading through her, she straightened up.

He came closer to her desk, his eyes brimming as if he knew that his nearness made her uneasy. He was a man who was used to getting his way where women were concerned, Xio thought, even as she caved to his questions. "Akilah never got over losing Dad, you know. She didn't have enough time with him."

"I get that." His eyes had a faraway look. "I was also six when I lost my father."

"Right, so you would understand how she feels, like she was…" Xio glanced skyward looking for the right word.

"Cheated," he provided.

"Yes. Cheated." Xio was going to say abandoned, but cheated sounded more like how Akilah felt. "She was only just beginning to form lasting memories with him—the kind he and I had before she came along. She's fifteen now and acts out by hanging around men who are way too old for her."

"That's a dangerous game she's playing," he said, placing his hands on the edge of her desk. "She could get hurt."

"Believe me, we know. Last year, she fooled a twenty-eight-year-old guest into believing she was nineteen. She thinks it's funny to mislead men about her age. She doesn't understand the consequences."

"I doubt she fooled him," Raph stated in a cold tone, bordering on disgust. "I'm sure he knew she was a child."

Xio blinked at Raph's disdain for a likely pedophile, and concern for a young girl, neither of whom he knew. This was the kind of man Akilah and Malik would have benefited from having in their lives after their father died. It was one of the reasons Xio had wanted to marry Trevor. They looked up to him as a big brother—since their real older brother didn't care about them any more than he cared about her. After Stamer's visit this morning and learning of the father-and-son plot to steal her hotel, Xio wished she could scrub the "Trevor" chapter of her life from her memory.

"You're probably right. Anyway, thankfully, our mother found out and put a stop to it before it became an issue," she said. Her mother had been so desperate to keep her youngest daughter safe that she had sent Akilah across the river to their great-grandmother, Kaiah—Ynoa's Chieftess—where she had no access to a phone or social media for a couple months. "Akilah is no longer allowed to walk around Jewel Beach by herself."

He folded his arms across his chest, a smile on his lips and a twinkle in his eyes. "Well, if I see an unaccompanied Akilah roaming about, I'll ring the alarm bells."

Xio was about to point out that he didn't even know what Akilah looked like when she remembered she was speaking with a guest, not someone who was part of her life. Unlike Akilah, except for business, *she* tended to avoid relationships with men. She didn't trust them, and she'd gotten a brutal reminder as to why when Stamer came knocking earlier. She had a shitty bullshit detector when it came to men, and she was already getting way too comfortable with this one. "Um…"

Her office phone buzzed, saving her from having to gracefully change the subject without offending a guest. "Excuse me a minute," she said.

"Of course." He walked over to the sliders overlooking the sea to give her some privacy.

She picked up the receiver. "Yes, Olivia."

"I'm sorry about Mr. Giannopoulos coming up unannounced. I asked him to wait for me to buzz you. I was on the phone with Hazel, and—"

"It's okay." He was already here, taking up her time when she should be figuring out a way to keep her family's company out of Stamer's hands, and herself out of jail. She gave Raph's body a raking stare as he gazed out the sliders with his back to her. With his hands shoved into the pockets of his slacks, he stood tall and powerful with a commanding air of self-confidence about him. He wasn't the kind of man one kept waiting. Her eyes glided down to his legs, firm as tree trunks. Warmth seeped between her thighs.

She shifted her eyes to yesterday's report on her desk. "Is everything okay with Hazel? She wants to make more changes?"

she asked of the bride whose extravagant wedding JBR was hosting next month.

Olivia paused before answering, then said in a cautious voice, "Something like that. Let's talk after Mr. Giannopoulos leaves."

Which shouldn't be too long, she thought, even as a prickly feeling crawled into her belly as she wondered what could possibly go wrong with Hazel's wedding, an event that was bringing in half a million dollars. "Okay. I'll be down in a bit." She had a hotel to run, things to do, but before she could tend to her business, she had to get rid of this gorgeous creature who was tempting her to throw caution to the wind.

"Oh, Xio."

"Yeah."

"Should I send Mr. Giannopoulos' bags to The Davenport? He left them here."

Xio cast a quick glance at Raph. "Yeah, do that. Thanks. We'll talk soon," she said, then hung up.

Raph walked back over to her desk. "I'm obviously keeping you from your work, I apologize," he said in a courteous voice.

"Apology accepted." For the first time, Xio noticed the amber flecks in his eyes. *Sexy.* "You said your grandfather asked you to give me something."

"Ah, yes." He reached into his back pocket and pulled out a light-blue envelope. "He asked me to deliver this in person," he added, handing it to her, his eyes fixed on her face, as if he was studying her reaction.

"Oh, my God," Xio whispered, when she saw her name and the strange words scribbled across it. Her heart raced at a faint memory of sitting on a man's lap as he wrote her name on an envelope this same shade of blue. *What name had he called her?*"

"What is it? You look as if you've just seen a ghost." His expression was tight and strained.

"Not a ghost. Just a memory," she said, lifting her eyes to meet his.

His head tilted to one side. "I hope it wasn't an unpleasant one."

"No, it wasn't," she responded quickly to ease the growing anxiety in his eyes. She turned the envelope over in her hands and, moving from behind her desk, walked over to a small green leather couch.

"What did you remember? If you don't mind me asking," Raph said, following behind her.

She sat down and looked up at him as he towered over her, an intense burning in his eyes. "I remembered sitting on a man's lap while he wrote on a blue envelope. It was jarring to see my name and those words on the same envelope, just like all those years ago."

"Do you remember how old you were?"

Xio closed her eyes, and pressed her fingers to her temples. "Three or four," she answered, opening her eyes, and staring out the sliding door as another image of walking along the beach with the man and her father came into focus.

"Is there anything else?" Raph asked in a wistful whisper, as if he was afraid to disturb her focused trip down memory lane.

Xio gazed up at him warily. Now, she understood the faint sense of familiarity she'd felt when she first saw Raph. He had his grandfather's massive build, his square jawline, and his nose.

"No, I think that was the last time I saw him." Until she knew her relationship with this family, she would not share any more memories with his grandson. She placed the letter on the small, round table in front of her.

"If you think of anything else, I would love to know." He eased down on the other end of the couch.

Xio immediately felt the heat radiating from his body. Despite the lingering shock of faint memories circling in her mind, she found herself wanting to get close to him.

No! She shouldn't be craving him. He was a man, and she couldn't trust them. She shouldn't be feeling this comfortable with him. But, maybe she felt so at ease because she'd spent time with his grandfather and the nice lady who stayed with him at The Davenport when she was a child.

She turned her head slightly and the intensity of Raph's gaze sent waves of excitement through her. He smelled good. She wanted to taste him, feel his mouth moving over hers. On its own will, her body leaned toward his. She licked her lips, ignoring the buzzing of her office phone that seemed miles away.

It had been so long since she had allowed herself the simple pleasure of a kiss. She longed to recapture the ecstasy of a man's firm lips brushing against the softness of hers. She wanted this indulgence, just for a moment.

As if desperate to answer her call of intimacy, he slid across the seat and…

"Xiomara Jewel Davenport!"

At the sound of the door flying open, and the tone of voice she'd dreaded as a child, Xio snapped out of the hypnotic trance and jumped to her feet. She turned to see the mixture of anger and disappointment brimming in her mother's eyes as she stood at the door. But even in her rattled state of mind, Xio was also aware that Raph had shot to his feet and now stood between her and her fire-breathing mother.

"What in God's name is wrong with you?" her mom screamed.

"Who's that?" Raph whispered, turning to face her, worry in his eyes.

"My mother, Claudia," she hissed, tension climbing in her chest as her mother dropped her purse on the conference table and stormed across the floor, completely ignoring the six-foot-plus man standing between her and her daughter.

"Oh," Raph said, stepping aside.

"How can you even think about marrying that two-timing bastard again? Have you lost your mind, your dignity?"

"Mom!" Xio was appalled that her mother was airing her

dirty laundry in front of a guest. That call, a few seconds ago, was probably from Olivia to warn her that Claudia was on her way up. If she'd taken it, she would have known that her mother was pissed about something, and would have met her at the door, saving herself this embarrassment.

"I warned you, Xiomara. I told you not to get into bed with Stamer and—"

"Mom, just shut up! Please." It was the first time in her life that she had ever uttered those words to the woman who had given birth to her. The thought had never crossed her mind before. Claudia did not tolerate insolence from her children, no matter their age, but Xio had no choice. It was the only way she could think of to stop her.

Claudia dipped her head, and her brown eyes glittered with lethal calm as she pinned Xio with her *you have definitely lost your tired little mind* stare, followed by an indignant, "Excuse me?"

"Consider yourself excused, Mom." Claudia was the sweetest mother in the world, but God help the child who crossed her. Xio had crossed her mother repeatedly when it came to the Stamers. And Claudia was seeing red.

Xio seethed inwardly. She wasn't planning on telling her mother what Samuel had done until she'd had time to think and figure out a way to beat him at his own game. How the hell did he get to her mother already? And what did he tell her?

More than anything else, Xio was upset that her mother had embarrassed her in front of a guest—one she almost kissed. She could only imagine what was going on in Raph's head. He was probably wondering what kind of people his dear, deceased grandfather had gotten mixed up with.

Forcing down the humiliation in her throat, she faced Raph. "I'm sorry, but I have to take care of this little family matter." She pointed at the bar. "Please, help yourself to a drink or anything else you like. There's tea and coffee. And there are soft drinks in the fridge. I won't be long."

His gaze shifted curiously between her and her mother, but he said nothing. Probably too shocked to speak.

Xio picked up the letter, took her mother by the elbow, and walked over to her desk. She placed the letter upside down on her calendar, and tossed the crumpled contract into a drawer.

"What was that?" Claudia asked.

Ignoring her question, Xio pulled her across the room, down a corridor, past the kitchenette, and out to an enclosed verandah overlooking the two-hundred-foot pool, the white sands of Jewel Beach behind it.

Xio had looked out on this scene countless times with her father while he taught her what it took to run a successful resort. *"Make your guests feel relaxed and welcomed as soon as they arrive. Practice a 'Yes' culture. Before saying 'No', bend the rules as long as you don't compromise your integrity. Practice consistency, courtesy, and willingness to divert from the norm to make a guest comfortable and happy. That is what keeps them coming back year after year."*

She had followed her father's advice, and she was succeeding in every area. And now Stamer was threatening to take it all away from her. Her blood curdled. "I'm assuming you talked to Stamer," she said to her mother. "Did he call you? And please don't shout. He might still be able to hear us," she warned, rolling her eyes toward the front of the office where they'd left Raph.

As if it mattered, anyway. He'd already heard enough to mar his impression of the Davenport clan. She wouldn't be surprised if he canceled his reservation and hightailed it off the island by the end of the day. Between her barking at him, and her mother's raging entrance, she wouldn't be surprised if he'd already left.

Claudia's eyes followed hers, and her fury gave way to curiosity. "Who is he, and why were you cuddled up to him on the…?" Her brown eyes filled with hope. "Xiomara, are you dating again? Have you been keeping him a secret? He is so handsome."

Even though she felt like a teenager caught making out on the couch with her boyfriend, Xio was thankful her mother had stopped her from falling under Rapheus Giannopoulos' charm. "I'm not dating anybody, Mom." She pushed her hair away from her face. "Let's get back to why you barged into my office about to blow a gasket. When and where did you talk to Samuel, and what exactly did he say to you?" She wanted Claudia to go first to avoid revealing his whole ugly plot here and now if she didn't have to.

Claudia pressed her lips together in vexation before answering. "I came in early to check my inventory before our lunch date. I was in the boutique downstairs when he snuck up behind me." She shivered. "Just being near that man makes my skin crawl."

You and me both, and probably half the island's population.

"He said he'd just come from seeing you. I assumed it had something to do with the loan. Anyway, he started yapping about how proud Malik must be that you brought Jewel Beach back to life, and how he admires your good business acumen, yada-yada-yada. I knew he was buttering me up before he dropped his bomb, so I asked him what he wanted. That's when he gleefully told me that we were going to be family. That you and Trevor have been talking, and that you're giving him a second chance. He said an announcement could come any day now." Claudia's eyes grew dark and worrisome as she held Xio's hands. "Please tell me that you aren't marrying into that vile family. You barely escaped it the first time around."

Xio squeezed her fingers. "I'm not, Mom. Never in a million years." She shook her head vehemently.

"Then why is he spreading lies about you?"

Because he's a narcissistic asshole who assumed I would take the easiest way out of the corner he'd boxed me into, which only proves he doesn't know me at all.

"Did you default on your loan payments, Xiomara? Is that why he came to see you?"

Xio tugged free of her mother's grasp and pressed her hands into her stomach, trying to stop the panic threatening to overrun her.

"Xio, what is it, honey?" Concern spilled from her mother's eyes and voice as she placed a comforting hand over Xio's.

"I haven't defaulted on my payments."

"Then why did he come to see you? What did he want?"

Everything I have. Everything I've built. Xio inhaled deeply, and chose her words carefully. "Samuel didn't know about the loan Trevor gave me."

Claudia slowly pulled her hands away from Xio, her eyes flashing as she stared incredulously at her daughter. "What do you mean he didn't know? How could he not have known?"

"Well, it's a big bank," she said. "He probably isn't aware of every loan that is approved. Anyway, I should have known something was not right when Trevor said his father would not have agreed to the terms, and so it was best to keep him in the dark." Xio's disgust for Samuel multiplied by the second for upsetting her mother with his blatant lies.

"So now what? He's demanding you pay back the entire loan at once?"

"Something like that." She couldn't tell her mother that Samuel was blackmailing her into giving up Jewel Beach—the one company he'd always coveted. She couldn't burden her with the thought that her daughter could go to jail if she didn't cave to his demands.

"He knows you don't have eight million dollars sitting around. So, I'll assume he proposed that you marry Trevor to balance out your checkbook."

"That's one of his solutions."

"I don't see how that is your problem," Claudia stated. "That is between him and Trevor. Trevor is the one who lied to him. I don't see how he could hold you responsible. You should just tell him to go to hell, and that as long as you're making your payments, he can't touch you."

Xio faced her mother and her stomach heaved at deceiving her. "We both know that it's not that simple where Samuel Stamer is concerned."

"Can you get a loan from another bank to pay him off?"

The hope in her mom's eyes was like an icepick in Xio's stomach. "I tried three years ago, remember, and they all turned me down. The resort was in bad shape. No one had confidence in my ability to bring it back on track."

"But you did," Claudia insisted, touching a warm hand to Xio's cheek.

Yes, I did. Xio remembered the banker who had laughed in her face when she'd made her proposal. "Oh, Mom." Unable to pretend she was strong and capable any longer, Xio dropped her head wearily on her mother's shoulders. "I'm sorry, Mom."

Claudia folded her arms around her. "We'll find a way to work it out. Maybe you can ask your cousin, Tuolo, to co-sign on a loan. He runs a multi-million-dollar construction company. I know you didn't want to mix family and business, but the hotel is doing so well now, and—"

"Mom." Xio lifted her head from her mother's shoulder. "It's not that simple," she said, shaking her head from side to side.

"What is it, Xio?"

Taking a deep breath, Xio watched her mother's body stiffen, her mouth tighten, and her anger rise to fever pitch as she told her everything. "So," she concluded, "I'm definitely not going to prison and I'm not marrying Trevor, so the only solution I see at the moment is to—"

"Burn it down to the ground!"

"Mom!" Xio exclaimed at the hatred in Claudia's voice.

"That piece of crap has always wanted what your father had. Well, he's not going to have his hotel. Not while I'm living. If it's war that jackass wants, it's war he'll get. He has messed with the Davenports for the last time. I'd rather burn it all to the ground than see your father's—and your grandfather's life work in the hands of that bastard."

Xio appreciated her mother's enthusiasm and support, but destroying Jewel Beach was not something she was willing to do, even though, right now, she couldn't see any other way out.

Chapter Five

THE LIGHT

PERCHED on the edge of a bar stool, Raph sipped his ginger beer while looking out the window at hotel guests climbing into a small power boat docked on JBR's pier.

He brushed a lock of hair from his forehead and glanced at his Cartier watch. Why was he still here, anyway? He had delivered the letter. There was nothing keeping him from going on to the villa to settle in for the week, figure out where Aetós was, scatter his grandparents' ashes, and get back to his life in San Francisco.

Oh, you know why, his inner voice taunted. *She's hot and you want a go at her.*

It was clear to see from where Xiomara got her looks and her passion, he thought, remembering her outburst when he'd knocked on her door. Like mother, like daughter—strong and formidable—neither afraid to express her opinion or her anger. They had strong survival instincts, and he felt a strange affection growing inside him for the Davenport women.

Raph took a swig from the bottle as the image of Xiomara's slender, perfectly shaped body meandered across his mind. He loved the way her curves moved subtly beneath her dress. Visions of threading his fingers through her long black hair and trailing his hands slowly up and down her smooth skin made his mouth water.

He shifted on the stool as his shaft hardened. He was still mystified at his reaction when Xiomara's picture had popped up on his computer screen, a few days ago. So intense was her effect on him that that night he'd dreamed of them walking naked along a white-sand beach. He had no idea where the beach was, but the fact that they were naked didn't seem to bother them. It had felt like the most natural thing in the world. They'd been playing in the water and having so much fun that they hadn't noticed they'd been pushed away from the shore until a huge wave wrapped around them and pulled them farther into the deep. They'd clung to each other, screaming at the top of their lungs. Then the boom of a drum, or a bolt of thunder—he wasn't sure which—rumbled through the air.

Raph had jumped awake to a painfully stiff cock and the warm, sticky evidence that he'd had a wet dream. As he'd climbed out of bed and headed for his bathroom, he'd thought it strange that he couldn't remember the name and face of a woman he'd screwed the previous night, when the face of one he'd only seen on his laptop, and hadn't yet met, had made him come in his sleep. It wasn't even a sex dream. They were just fooling around like life was a breeze and they didn't have a care in the world.

He'd dreamed about her again the following night. In that one, they were children, around nine or ten years old. They were gathering seashells and digging for crabs in the wet sand. He remembered her smiling at him while she tugged strands of black wet hair out of her face. She was so pretty, he'd thought, watching her eyes shimmer in the afternoon sunlight. In his dream, he'd felt happy that they were together. And now that he'd met her, Xiomara was even more irresistible than in his dream.

Raph finished off his ginger beer, and set the empty bottle on the bar top. Sliding off the stool, he raked his hands through his hair and walked over to the window. People were strolling along the stretch of beach, and relaxing in hammocks suspended between palm trees on the lawn below. Some folks really knew how to let go and relax. A part of him wished he was one of them.

You were relaxed in your dreams.

There were two aspects about those dreams that had bothered him, and while in-flight to Akilina, he had called Gwen, a marketing specialist for a tech company in New York, who interpreted dreams on the side for her friends. Occasionally, when he flew to the east coast, they would hookup. She was a no-strings-attached woman. The kind he liked.

Gwen had said that being carried out to sea was a warning that he could be dragged into some kind of crisis and lose control of himself or his values. That had given him pause. With that interpretation alone, had he not been mid-flight, he might have canceled the trip altogether. Their nakedness indicated emotional vulnerability. Raph was less concerned about any chance of that happening. His emotions were under tight wraps.

You don't have any emotions.

Well then, nothing to worry about.

Digging for crabs with someone could be a sign of a problematic relationship, or it could mean that he needed to find some buried truths, she'd said. *No shit*, he'd thought. His grandfather had told him not to be afraid of the truth. But was Xiomara going to be a friend or foe in his search of that truth, and was he going to like what he found out?

Feeling restless, Raph slid his hands deep into the pockets of his slacks and began pacing.

Control—his one-word mantra bounced around in his head.

As a child, following his father and grandmother's tragic deaths, Raph had become particularly good at controlling his emotions, no matter what was going on in his small world. He could be so restrained, that at times, his mother had called him unfeeling. As he grew older and began thinking about the man he wanted to become, he'd developed a propensity to focus on what he needed, zero in on what was important, and discard the rest.

That skill served him well professionally and was instrumental in his and his brothers' successful launch of G3. However, it had not been beneficial to his personal life. The only woman Raph had ever loved had fallen in love with someone else. She needed someone more fun, she'd said. He'd tried to be 'more fun', but by then it was too late, and he'd been left with a broken heart.

The women he dated now, called him emotionally void and unavailable once they discovered that they couldn't get inside his head. He bore that label with honor, allowing nothing and no one to affect him to the point of distraction. His short-lived relationships ended the moment a woman began asking or expecting too much from him.

From the moment he'd seen her picture, Raph had known that Xiomara Davenport would be the biggest distraction of his life. When he'd touched her, his mind had exploded with images of them tangled up together in damp white sheets, weak, and satiated. It was sizzling, like nothing he'd ever felt before.

Raph needed to know a little bit more about her, to be certain that they were not related—that she was not his grandfather's child. But once that was out of the way, he wanted to lay her down on the couch, pull her dress up to her waist, and take her then and there—quench the lust, stop the burning, for the moment. And if they were good together, he would take Declan's advice to forget about business and enjoy himself in Akilina.

He would have his fill of Xiomara for the week, knowing that his emotions would be safe since he was heading back home after accomplishing the task he'd been sent here to do. But her mother had blown up his plans when she had barged in, questioning Xio's decision to "marry a two-timing bastard—*again.*"

Raph steered clear of women who weren't single beyond the shadow of a doubt. If Xiomara was engaged to be married, he would have to find someone else to warm his bed for the week, which shouldn't be hard to do. He'd caught the looks women were throwing his way when he'd walked through the lobby on his way to Xiomara's office. There were plenty of fish in the sea.

His pacing brought him to a map of Akilina on the wall near the door. Squinting his eyes, he studied it. The 251-square-mile, mountainous island was bordered on the east by the Atlantic Ocean and by the Caribbean Sea on the west. He counted twelve territories, three west of the long, snaking Caonabo River and the Nacanké Mountain Range. Mt. Cayacáo, with an elevation of 4,821 feet, was the highest of them all.

He trailed a finger against the glass, his eyes narrowing as he searched for Aetós where he was to scatter the ashes. It wasn't a territory, so it might be a village, or a town, but there were so many...

"Raph."

Xiomara's voice calling his name was like lightning zapping through his body. He turned, his breath catching in his throat as she walked toward him, her mother trailing behind her. As they met in the center of the office, the delicate scent of her perfume wrapped around him. He wrinkled his nose. He knew that scent—Diptyque Eau Rose. She had good taste. *And he had no doubt she tasted good.*

"I'm sorry you had to see that little outburst between my mother and me," she said, giving him an apologetic smile.

"I apologize, also," Claudia echoed. "I thought Xiomara was alone. I feel awful for my behavior. When I get upset, I tend to—well...show it."

"I've seen worse," Raph said, his eyes darting between the

two women who looked a lot alike, except for Xiomara's eyes. They were her father's.

"I don't want you to think that my family is—um—" Xio looked at her mother as if for backup. "We just—"

"No need to apologize." Their spat was a prayer meeting, compared to the ugly arguments between him and his cousins every time he visited Santorini. "As Tolstoy wrote, 'All happy families are alike…'"

"But every unhappy family is unhappy in its own way," Xiomara and Claudia said together, then laughed.

"Anna Karenina is one of my all-time favorite books," Xiomara said, folding her arms across her chest, and drawing his eyes to her breasts.

He swallowed his need to rid her of her dress. "See. We're all on the same page." He had no idea what was written on the next page, but the fact that he was on an island he'd never heard about until three weeks ago and delivering a letter to a strange, beautiful woman his grandfather obviously knew, meant they were part of the same story.

"My family has its own share of embarrassments to live down, Ms. Daven—"

She touched his arm. "No more Ms. Davenport. Please. After everything you've heard and seen this morning, you can call me Xio. That's what my friends and family call me."

Raph's heart somersaulted in his chest at the warmth from her touch. "Xio, it is then."

"Xiomara, you're forgetting your manners," her mother said.

"If your entrance hadn't been so grand, Mom, I wouldn't have, would I?"

Damn, she had guts. He liked her.

"Mom, this is Rapheus Giannopoulos. He's staying at The Davenport. Raph, my mother, Claudia."

"Mrs. Davenport, it's a pleasure to meet you." He shook her hand.

"It's nice to meet you, too. You can call me Claudia. I find the Mr., Mrs., and Ms. tiresome," she added, brushing her fingers across her forehead, pretending to swoon.

"Mom, stop being so dramatic." Xio scowled at her mother then raised her eyes to Raph. "I'm sorry, she can be a bit much at times."

Raph loved being in the presence of these two fascinating women. "Claudia, you can call me Raph," he said, giving her one of his charming smiles. "Do I recognize a New York accent?"

"You have good ears, Raph. Harlem, born and bred."

"You're a long way from home."

"Love will take you a long way from home, but you just make another one. If you're lucky, it will be more beautiful than the one you left behind."

Her words made him think of his parents, but before his mind had a chance to wander, Claudia tilted her face upward.

"Giannopoulos. Is that Greek?"

"Yes." Her question reminded him of why he had come here in the first place. He kept his eyes on her face, looking for a small hint that she recognized the name. "My grandfather used to stay at The Davenport when he visited the island. Do you remember him?"

She shook her head. "No. I don't think I've ever met anyone by that name."

"You must know him, Mom. I remember spending time with him when I was really little, and of him telling me bedtime stories in my bedroom. It must have been in Greek because I didn't understand what he was saying, but I liked the sound of his voice."

She might not remember exactly who he was, but the happiness in Xio's voice told Raph that she must have loved him, or at least had deep affection for him. The knowledge that his pappoús was adored by people beyond his immediate family made him feel good.

Xio went to her desk and brought back the letter. "Look." She held it out to her mother. "He asked Raph to bring this to me."

Claudia read the inscription. "Oh my gosh, yes. Yes... I... I remember them, now," she stammered, patting her chest as if to stop her heart from trembling. "Andris and Kerena. They used to come here every year. We spent so much time together." Claudia lifted her eyes from the letter and looked at Xiomara. "Xiomara, Andris and Kerena," she said softly, hoping to jog her daughter's memory. "They were your godparents."

Xio's mouth hung open. "Oh my God, of course," she said after a pause. "But mom, we haven't talked about them for years."

Raph took a step back. *Her godparents?* They were that close?

"Kerena was my maid of honor," Claudia continued. "My best friend in New York was unable to attend my wedding, so she stood in for her. Oh, my goodness. That was so long ago."

Raph felt a sense of quiet relief that they had remembered his grandparents. "I was beginning to worry that my grandfather had become senile when he told me about Akilina. It's good to know that he wasn't losing his mind."

"Of course. Of course. I could never forget Andris and Kerena Aetós. They were such a sweet couple. Kerena's death hit us very hard."

Aetós?

Raph's short-lived relief evaporated. It was obvious that Claudia knew his grandparents, but even as the puzzle pieces were sliding into place, the overall picture was still a mystery. His grandparents never went by Aetós, not as far as he knew. But then, he was beginning to realize there were a lot of things he didn't know.

He held Claudia's gaze. "Aetós? No, you must have them

confused with another couple," he said, massaging the crick in his neck as tension built inside him.

"No Raph, the Aetóses must have been your grandparents," Xio said, unshaken assurance in her eyes. "I remember him writing my name on this envelope." She ran her fingers slowly across her name. "And I remember playing on the beach with him and his wife. She had long white hair that stuck to her face when it got wet. We built sandcastles and collected shells on the beach. We would take the shells back to the house and she would let me brush her hair while she painted them."

Raph's entire body went numb. His dream—walking along the beach with Xio and collecting seashells… *You'll know her when you dream of her*, his pappoús had told him.

"My parents talked about them all the time when I was growing up. The name Giannopoulos threw me off. But I remember them now." Xio pressed the letter to her chest, as if cherishing the connection she'd had with her godparents.

"Oh my," Claudia touched her cheek with one hand, and placed the other on Raph's arm. "I just remembered that your father died with Kerena. I'm sorry. I can't imagine losing two people you love at the same time."

Claudia's caring touched Raph deeply. He gave a nod of appreciation. "Thank you, Claudia. Even after all these years, that means a lot."

"It will always hurt," she said, knowingly. "But we learn to live with the memories, instead of with them."

"Your grandparents were always nice to me." Xio broke the silence of grief that had settled over them. "We have pictures of your grandfather and dad smoking cigars on the patio of The Davenport, while your grandmother played with me in the pool."

"Those were good times," Claudia said with a tremor in her voice.

Xio rubbed her palms against her bare arms slowly. "I just wish I could have seen your pappoús again before he died."

Claudia drew her head back quickly and stared at Raph. "Andris died? When?" Alarm siphoned her voice.

"Three weeks ago," he said, shifting his weight from one foot to the other. The information he'd gotten so far was already weighing him down, and he was sure there was more to come.

"Oh…" Claudia placed her hands to her throat. "Oh no…" Her eyes closed and her chest heaved on a deep sigh, and when she opened her eyes again, they were misty with tears.

Raph tightened his jaw and forced composure into his system. He did not break down in front of people. And he wasn't going to start now.

Claudia laid a comforting hand on his arm. "I'm so sorry. He was up there in age, but the Andris I knew was so full of life, we thought he would live forever."

"Ninety-three was his forever." Raph cleared his throat. "His passing was a blessing, though. He suffered a stroke two years back and hadn't been able to speak or move much."

"Goodness. Poor Andris to suffer like that in his last years, and then not be able to say goodbye to his family."

"Actually," he said cautiously, "Pappoús was able to speak at the end. It was somewhat of a miracle. For his last week, we were all able to talk with him."

"That was a miracle," Claudia agreed.

"We thought he would make a full recovery, even at his age. I know it sounds crazy, but it seems he came back just to say good-bye… and I guess to tell me about Akilina. He'd never told me about the island until the night he died."

Xio flipped her hair behind her back and her forehead puckered. "Wait a minute, he never told you about us?"

"Why did he wait that long to tell you?" Claudia asked.

"That is the question of the century." Raph said. "Claudia, I would love to hear more about my grandparents' visits to Akilina if you have the time. What they did when they were here. Their relationship with your family. Whatever you can tell me would be deeply appreciated."

"Of course," she said eagerly. "It's nice having someone to share memories of them with."

"We should sit." Xio led them toward the sitting area on the other side of the office.

Once Xio was settled on the club chair and Claudia on one end of the sofa, Raph sat down on the other end. The faint sound of children's laughter drifted up from the playground beneath the window, making him wonder if his pappoús had ever played with Xio on that same playground."

"Remind me, Mom, how did they become my godparents?" Xio asked, examining the envelope on her lap.

"I'm wondering the same thing." Raph leaned toward Claudia.

Claudia's face brightened as she laid back into the cushions. "When I told them I was pregnant with you, it was Andris who asked me if they could be your godparents. Honestly, I was so thrilled. Your father had known them for years before we were married, and I had come to love them, too. We were so close and I wanted them to be part of your life.

"The day she was born," she continued, turning to Raph, "Andris and Kaiah—Xio's great-grandmother on her father's side—came to see her in the hospital, and while they stood over her basinet, Kaiah asked if I would name her Xiomara Jewel. She said it was an old family name and that it was fitting for her. I already had a name picked out, but— well, Xiomara, you know how your botoá is," she said, giving Xio a wary look. "She usually gets what she wants in the end, so there was no use arguing. Besides, Xiomara Jewel sounded so much sweeter than the name I had settled on."

It was sweet, Raph thought, giving Xio a quick smile.

"Kaiah said Xio was the light that would bring hope and truth to us all," Claudia said.

Follow the light that leads you to truth…

A cold chill crawled through Raph's veins when Claudia echoed the words his pappoús had written to him. His eyes caught Xio's, and she seemed as uneasy and confused as he was. Was she the light Andris had told him to follow to find the truth? And what truth was he talking about? Truth about whom, about what?

Raph felt like he had been dropped into the middle of an episode of the *The Twilight Zone* with no script or instruction about what to do or expect as the story played out around him. He glanced over at the bar, tempted to go pour himself a strong one. His gaze inevitably searched out Xio's and, as their eyes locked, a bewitching feeling sizzled between them. That tug he'd felt before intensified, causing his stomach to tie up in knots.

"I still have no idea what she meant by that," Claudia said, seemingly unaware of the spell coiling between her daughter and him. "He used to call Xio by that name written on the envelope, *I miki*—"

"*I mikrí mou kóri.* It means 'my little daughter'," Raph said in a shaky whisper. His body grew colder, even as his skin felt as if it was on fire.

Claudia gave him the same look of concern that he still got from his mother when she knew there was something wrong. "I could imagine this is a lot to take in all at once."

She had no idea. It wasn't the information that had him in jitters. It was the secrecy behind it. There were so many questions, Raph didn't know which one to ask first. But he knew that the best way to solve a problem was to begin at the beginning, so he turned to the only person who could give him answers. "Claudia, you said that your husband was friends with my grandparents before you met him. But do you know how they met, or when my grandparents first visited Akilina?"

"Oh yes, I've heard stories."

Xio leaned forward, staring at her mother with curious anticipation.

Chapter Six

FRIENDSHIP

CLAUDIA CROSSED her ankles and folded her hands on her lap, contemplation etched into her face. "Well, Malik told me that his mother, Sanaa, told him that Andris first visited Akilina in nineteen-fifty-eight, the same year he was born. Max, Malik's father, was running Jewel Beach at the time. That's where Andris stayed."

"At The Davenport?"

"The Davenport wasn't built until eighty-three," Xio said.

"That's right," Claudia confirmed. "Your grandparents booked it in advance every year after that. Anyway, Andris asked a lot of questions about the history of the island. Max and Sanaa thought he was just a curious tourist, but at some point he told them he was born here, and asked if they knew anything about a Greek couple who lived on the island around nineteen-twenty-seven to nineteen-twenty-eight. They didn't, and when they asked why he couldn't get answers from his parents, he told them he hadn't known he was born here until after they had passed. Sanaa told him that her mother, Kaiah, might have answers, so she took them to meet her. And just like that—" She snapped her fingers. "Andris and Kaiah became friends. By the time I came along, they were two peas in a pod."

"Is she still alive?" he asked eagerly at the prospect of meeting and talking to her.

"Very much so, although she's…" Claudia pressed a finger to the corner of her mouth and turned an enquiring face to Xio. "How old is Kaiah, ninety?"

"Ninety-four," Xio answered, shifting nervously in the chair as if she didn't want to talk about her great-grandmother.

"Ninety-four and as sharp as a knife. Maybe Xio can take you to see her."

Xio cleared her throat and pinned her mother with a censuring look. "Mom, you know I can't just take him to see Botoá." Her fingers fidgeted around the edges of the envelope.

"I'm sure she'll bend the rules for Andris' grandson." Claudia flipped her wrist dismissively.

Xio shook her head, and rolled her eyes, clearly annoyed with what her mother had suggested. "Were my godparents also friends with Sherylyn?" she asked.

Raph admired her tact for changing the subject, or in this case, bringing it back on course. "Who is Sherylyn?" he asked.

"My father's first wife."

Bad blood? he wondered, at the disdain in her voice.

Claudia gave her daughter a stern-faced look before saying to Raph, "I asked Malik the same thing, and he said they never took to her, or to Fitzroy, Xiomara's half brother."

"I can understand that," Xio murmured with a jerk of her head.

Definitely bad blood. No wonder she hadn't mentioned her half brother when he'd asked if she had siblings. "My grandparents obviously liked you, Claudia." He gave the older woman a warm, friendly smile, hoping to offset whatever silent battle was going on between her and her daughter. "I can see why you got along."

"Andris and Kerena were easy to like, too." Claudia said, returning the warm compliment.

"*You* are easy to like."

"You are too sweet, Raph, especially after my hysterical entrance."

"I'll admit I was a little scared." He grinned.

"I doubt that. You don't look like the scare-easy type," she threw back at him.

They all laughed.

Raph was eager to move the conversation along. "I wonder how Pappoús knew he was born on Akilina if his parents never told him. And how did they end up here in the first place?"

"What makes anyone want to travel anywhere? Curiosity. Interest in learning about a new place. Chance, as in your case, Mom."

Raph cocked his head. "Chance?"

"Yes. I wanted a Caribbean vacation, but I didn't know which island to visit. I wrote some names on pieces of paper and put them in a cup. Akilina was the lucky winner. Or I should say, *I* was the lucky winner." Her eyes misted as she looked at her daughter. "I met the love of my life here. He gave me twenty-two wonderful years and three beautiful children. I can't imagine my life without any of you," she added, smiling affectionately at Xio. "I have to believe that it was destiny, not chance."

"That's quite a lovely story, Claudia."

"Raph, I could fill a book with all the lovely stories I've collected since coming to this island."

"That is a book I would most definitely read." Her visit to Akilina might have been destiny, but neither destiny nor chance had sent his pappoús here. He had been looking for something.

"Well, whatever it was that brought Andris and Kerena here —destiny, chance, curiosity—they loved Akilina. They always said they were happiest when they were here. Andris cried every time he left, as if he was leaving his home."

He was. The information caused Raph's throat to tighten up. Claudia had answered some of his questions, but several more mysterious ones had taken their place. As he came to understand the depth of secrets he had to uncover, his dream of digging in the sand with Xio began to make a lot more sense. It was about discovering his own family's buried secrets.

"Claudia, did my parents ever visit Akilina?"

"Your father did."

So he'd been keeping secrets, too. "So you met him?"

"No. Malik said he came down a few times when he was little and once when he was a teenager, long before I even knew Akilina existed. They were about the same age. Malik said Xander was miserable the whole time he was here." She chortled. "He hated the heat, the flies, the mosquitoes, the food… He just hated it."

Raph laughed. "I could imagine. My mom says he preferred city life."

"The tropics aren't for everyone."

"They certainly aren't. Did Andris come here after my dad and grandmother died?"

"Yes. He did. Only once, and it was the last time we saw him."

"He came to say goodbye." Raph leaned back and draped his arm over the back of the sofa and stretched his legs out beneath the coffee table.

"It would appear so. He was here for about three weeks, I think." Claudia looked to Xio. "Xiomara, that was the same year Papa died." She turned back to Raph. "That's Malik's father, Max. Anyway," she continued, "Andris kept to himself a lot that year, and when we did see him, mostly to make sure he was eating, he didn't talk much." Her eyes brightened. "Although, he spent a lot of time with Xio. He took her to the beach, and for a couple of drives around the island. Sometimes, he would just sit and talk to her in Greek, and she would listen as if she understood what he was saying."

Raph noticed the concentration growing on Xio's face as she bit into her bottom lip, as if she were trying to pull more memories from her mind and string them together.

"The day before he left," Claudia continued, "Andris asked if Xio could spend the night with him at The Davenport. Of course, I had no hesitation. I trusted him with my child."

"That was the night he wrote my name on this envelope," Xio said, rubbing her thumb over her name. "He was crying. I remember his tears falling on my hand."

"You brought him a lot of joy and comfort in those few weeks, Xio. It was such a terrible time. Malik and I were numb with shock. We didn't know what to say to him, so— I'm sorry to say it now… We were kind of glad that he didn't want to talk. Sometimes we just sat for hours and said nothing." She let out a heavy sigh. "At least he's with them, now."

"And Dad, too," Xio whispered, staring at Raph through blurry eyes.

A hush fell over the room as they paid silent respect to the dead.

Raph swallowed hard and held himself in check, but when Claudia sniffled, he rose and walked over to a small wooden table next to Xio's desk. He picked up a box of tissues, and a small wicker waste basket, and carried them back to the sofa. The moment he placed the box on the coffee table, Claudia and Xio grabbed tissues, and began dabbing their eyes.

"I'm a mess." Claudia dropped a used tissue into the waste basket, and reaching for another.

A tear unexpectedly fell on Raph's shirt. Astonished that he had let his guard down in front of two women he just met a little over an hour ago, he walked over to the bar to give himself time to regain his composure. He filled three glasses with water from the pitcher, drank one down, and took the other two over to the grieving women.

"Thanks," Xio said, immediately placing the glass to her lips.

He offered the other glass to Claudia.

"Your mother raised a true gentleman," she said.

"She certainly tried to. I can't say we made it easy for her. I don't think I would wish triplets on my worst enemy. We were all so stubborn and wild."

"My hats off to her." She laughed while saluting mockingly. "I have one boy and he's a handful."

"Malik Junior." Raph returned to his seat, thankful that the mood had lightened.

"We used to call him Junior, but when he turned eight, he insisted we call him MJ," Xio said, leaning forward to set her glass on the table.

"No boy wants to be called Junior. My mother tried calling me Junior because my middle name is Xander, but I nipped that in the bud."

The women laughed, and he smiled. Something about his ability to make Xio laugh made him feel good. He turned to Claudia. "By the way, do you have any idea why my grandparents would have used a different name while they were here? You knew them for all those years, but didn't know that their real name was Giannopoulos?"

Claudia shrugged, at a loss for words.

"Privacy, maybe," Xio offered. "Many of our guests use aliases, especially celebrities who want to be normal—hide away for a while. Sometimes it's that simple."

The Giannopoulos name was well-known because of the family's wine business, Giannport, and more recently because of G3, so he could understand the need for privacy. But normal? There was nothing normal about his grandfather's secrets, nor his waiting until his last moments to spin a web of confusion, then asking him to travel to an island he had never heard of, to deliver a letter to a stranger, and scatter his ashes.

His gaze switched from daughter to mother. "As well as bringing this letter to Xio, Pappoús asked me to scatter his and Yaya's ashes at a place called Aetós. I don't know if it's a town, a village, or…" He spread his hands in irritation that he had to rely on others for the simplest pieces of information. "I was looking for it on your map." He pointed to the wall. "But I couldn't find it."

Xio shifted. "Like most remote Megiri villages, you wouldn't find Aetós on that map."

He cleared his throat. "I don't mean to seem ignorant, but what is a Megiri?"

Claudia snorted and pushed to her feet. She gave him a sympathetic smile. "I know exactly how you feel, Raph. When I came to Akilina, thirty-five years ago, the only thing I knew about the island was that it was beautiful and warm. Most people come here and leave without ever knowing."

"Knowing what?"

Claudia turned to her daughter. "I'm going to freshen up in the ladies' room while you give Raph a little history lesson."

After Claudia left, Raph turned his questioning eyes on Xio. "What do I need to know?"

She placed the envelope on the end of the coffee table. "To answer your first questions, the Megiri are an indigenous group, one of the first to come to the Caribbean from South America."

"Oh. I've never heard of them," he said, with a tilt of his head. "I've heard of the Caribs. I think I read about them in school, but we know from whose perspective those books were written," he quipped, leaning forward, and placing his arms across his knees.

A flash of innocuous humor crossed her face. "There were several tribes living on the islands. The Kalinago, Ciboney, Taíno, Macorix, to name a few," she said, toying with the lace at the neck of her dress. "And, of course, the Megiri. On our island, they mostly live in the territories east of the Caonabo River. That side of the island is called Ynoa—well, really the island itself is called Ynoa even though it's known as Akilina, especially in the west, but anyway, that side of Ynoa is protected."

"Protected from what?"

She brandished her hands in the air. "Foreigners. Outsiders. Anyone who isn't Megiri or *Guaitiari*."

"Is the Guaitiari another tribe?"

"No, not really. It's more of a culture. The Guaitiari are the descendants of former enslaved people who escaped to Ynoa from other islands. Since they came from so many different tribes in Africa, when they came here, their cultures blended into something entirely of its own. The Megiri called them Guaitiari. It means good friends in Megiri. It's a similar idea to the Creoles, or the Gullah and Geechee in the southern U.S. We are not black, and even though we came out of Africa, we're not Africans. We're Guaitiari."

Raph knew about the Creoles. He'd never heard of the Gullah or Geechee. But he wasn't about to put anymore of his ignorance on display, so he nodded as if he knew what the hell she was talking about and made a mental note to look them up later.

Her lips twisted thoughtfully as she turned her head and stared across the room at the portraits on the wall next to her desk.

"Your ancestors?" he asked.

She nodded as she zeroed in on the portrait of her father. "They were all former CEOs of Jewel Beach," she said, before turning her attention back to him. "If you really want to learn about our culture and history, you should check out our public library in Anacaona."

"I'll be sure to do that." Raph straightened his back and pushed the sleeves of his shirt up to his elbows. It was cool in the room, but he was getting hot under the skin. He knew it had everything to do with the fact that he was alone with Xio, and even though their conversation was far removed from anything sexual, thoughts of making love to her flooded his mind. He stretched one arm across the back of the sofa and rested the other on the side. "So where exactly in Ynoa is Aetós?"

"Aetós is in the Nacanké Mountains. It's a four-hour hike into the village on the shortest trail, but it can be dangerous if you're not familiar with the terrain, especially in the rainy season. Or, it's six to eight hours along the switchback trail, depending on what kind of shape you're in," she added, her gaze sliding appreciatively down his body.

"That's some climb," Raph murmured, forcing his heart to be still and his cock not to react to the warm promises in her gaze. "I guess I'll need a guide?"

"You will, but first you'll need a visitor's permit to travel that far into Ynoa. Visitors are only allowed in Arijua, the first territory east of the river, but they still need permission to go there."

"Okay…and where would I get this visitor's permit?"

"You must apply at the Department of Megiri Affairs. It's located at the Bureau of Tourism in Anacaona. But I have to warn you. About ninety percent of applicants who want to travel beyond Arijua are denied."

"That's a lot of denials," he said on a shaky laugh.

"Well, the Megiri value their privacy and protection."

"Do you know if my grandfather was allowed into Ynoa without a permit?" he asked.

"Of course, he was," Claudia said, walking back into the room.

Although her voice sounded bright, the puffiness around her eyes told Raph that she had been crying in the bathroom.

"Andris was born here. He could go anywhere on the island he pleased," she added.

"What about my grandmother. She wasn't born here, so is there some kind of spousal privilege to travel freely?"

Claudia sat in the chair next to Xio. "Spouses can travel freely into Ynoa after they've been married for twelve years. Before that time, they have to apply like everyone else, although those application are rarely denied. But I know what you're thinking, Raph. it doesn't work that way for descendants. There's no special progeny privilege. Since you weren't born here, you'll have to apply like everyone else."

There went his hope that his relationship to Andris would get him a free pass. He hoped he was one of the ten percent who was approved.

"Kerena was never denied, though," Claudia continued in an animated voice. "Mainly because Andris was friends with the *dacica*, who eventually granted her a special travel permit, so she didn't have to do the paperwork every year. She just had to present her ID at the Department of Megiri Affairs and they handed her the pass."

"Here's my ignorance at play again, but what is a dacica?" Raph asked.

"A *dacica* is a chief. She's the head chief of the entire island. Now, a male chief is called a *dacique*." She threw her daughter a sideways glance. "Didn't you explain all this to Raph?"

"There's only so much information you can cram into five minutes, Mom. The important thing is that Raph now knows what he needs to do to get to Aetós to scatter his grandparents' ashes."

"It's a pity Andris didn't tell you anything about Akilina, or give you any answers until just before he passed," Claudia said.

"He didn't give me any answers at all," Raph stated. Not even in that letter he got after his death. "And if he'd died just ten minutes earlier than he did, he would have taken all of his secrets to the grave. It would all still be a mystery, and we wouldn't be having this conversation."

Claudia became rigid, her eyes wide. "Oh my gosh, I'd forgotten about…"

"Forgotten about what?" both he and Xio asked at the same time.

"We invited Andris to dinner one night when he was last here. It was his first visit to Eagle's Nest on that trip."

"I'm sorry Claudia, but what's Eagle's Nest?" Raph asked.

"Eagle's Nest is our home," Xio said with pride. "It's on Mt. Aymaco, about a twenty-five-minute drive from here."

"Right," Claudia continued. "We talked about Kerena and Xander, and even though he cried through most of it, I know it did him good to talk about them with someone who knew them in this place." She sighed and boxed her lips before continuing. "After dinner, he and Malik went to Malik's office for cigars, as they usually did. But just a few minutes later, Andris ran out of there, almost knocking me over in the hall-way. I called after him, but he just raced out of the house like he'd seen a ghost."

"What happened?" Raph asked, leaning into her, as Xio was also doing.

She shook her head. "I don't know. Malik came out of the library a few minutes later. Neither of us had any idea what happened. Malik said he had left him at the door of his office while he went to get some old photos of the four of us, thinking it could lift his spirits… But he just left."

"That's very strange."

"I'd say. The next day, he went into Ynoa, spent a few days with Kaiah, and…" She paused and looked up at the ceiling, her face puckered in concentration, then she looked at him. "Malik said that just before Andris boarded the plane, he told him the weirdest thing."

"What?" Xio asked softly.

Raph was silent. He was hanging onto Claudia's every word.

"He said Andris told him that his family had a disturbing

connection to Akilina that went back hundreds of years, and that he would tell him about it the next time he visited."

Raph sat back, and forced himself to breathe through the knots in his stomach. He could feel his Adam's apple vibrating as he swallowed. Was that disturbing connection the thing that his pappoús had said he was sorry for not telling him on his deathbed? Finally, he asked Claudia, "Do you have any idea what he could have found out?"

She shook her head. "No." She reached across the coffee table and gave his knee a comforting tap. "Malik said Andris had looked scared when he'd told him. Over the years, we talked about it and speculated about what it could be." She sank back into the cushioned chair. "I just don't understand why he never told you or your brothers anything about it, either. I mean, you were the only family he had left. Was the thing so bad that he felt he had to take it to his grave?"

Raph was beginning to wonder the same thing. If what his grandfather had found had scared him, did *he* even want to know? Of course he did. "What about Kaiah? Does she know anything about it?" he asked,

"I asked her many times. She was just as confused as we were."

Raph rubbed his hands up and down his thighs as shock gave way to frustration. "Did you talk or write to him at all over the last twenty-seven years? He might have given clues in a phone call or a letter?"

"We called him. And we wrote. But he never responded. And he never came back to see us. I thought he would call me back after Malik died, but nothing. Maybe the memories were just too much for him," she added in her friend's defense. "People grieve in different ways, and we can't judge them for it."

Raph's chest tightened at the image of his grandfather rocking and groaning on the floor after hearing that his wife and only child had been killed in a car crash. "I'm sure it wasn't personal, Claudia. He was a changed man after Yaya and Baba died. He never talked about them with me and my brothers, either. He became a recluse, even toward us, in the first few years following the accident."

"It's the kind of pain that stays with you until you draw your last breath." She toyed with the diamond and platinum wedding band on her finger.

Raph saw in her, the same sorrow his mother still carried after all these years. Torment twisted in his belly. He breathed in deeply, forcing the raw emotions back into the closet he'd locked them inside years ago. He didn't do well in these kinds of situations. He avoided them. He pulled at the collar of his shirt as he felt the walls closing in on him. He needed to get out. He...

"Well, he obviously didn't forget about us."

He let out his breath as Xio's voice broke through the morbid silence, yanking him back from tumbling into despair.

"He sent you down here to deliver this to me," she said. "Maybe it's an apology for his silence."

"Why don't you open it... It might have some of the answers Raph is looking for," Claudia said, reaching over as if to take the envelope from Xio.

Xio stood up and stepped away from her mother.

Raph pushed to his feet, eyeing the envelope clutched to her chest. "I'm with Claudia, Xio. We're all sitting here guessing at answers, when you could be holding them in your hands."

"Maybe, but... I'm sorry, Raph. I'd like to read it for the first time when I'm alone. And I'm not ready to open it right now."

Xio's cellphone began ringing. "Excuse me," she said, hurrying over to her desk like a pack of wolves was chasing her.

Raph looked at his watch, then at Xio with her phone clipped to her ear. "I've taken up enough of both of your time," he said to Claudia. "I should probably leave and get settled into The Davenport."

Claudia looked at a clock hanging on the wall above Raph's

head. "It's fine, Raph. The only thing she has right now is a lunch meeting with her mother, and I'm already here."

Xio was the CEO of Jewel Beach, but since it was a family business he shouldn't be surprised if her mother worked beside her. "You're involved with the hotel, too?" he asked.

"Oh God, no. I'm a fashion designer. Have been all my life. Jewel Beach carries my children's line, Bluewaves. That's what our meeting was about."

"Oh, that's impressive."

"Thank you, but Bluewaves is more of a hobby. I have a line of women's clothing, and boutiques here on island and in New York. I love what I do." She smiled with pride.

"As you should."

"She mostly does evening and formal wear, but she designed these dresses we're wearing," Xio said, returning to the circle. "She's always in high demand."

"I can see why," he said, admiring Claudia's gold sleeveless dress. "Your work is beautiful, Claudia. I should stop by your store to get something for my mother."

"Thank you, Raph. Stop by anytime. Now, what do you do?"

"My brothers and I started a real estate development company when we were still in college. It's called G3, for Giannopoulos three."

"Now, that's impressive. I'm sure it's very successful."

"We do our best." He felt his face flush. He always felt uncomfortable talking about his and his brothers' accomplishments. He preferred to let people draw their own conclusions about G3's success.

"That's wonderful. It must be a lot of hard work," Xio said.

"It is. We got our hard work ethics from our grandfather."

"Andris worked?" Claudia asked, flabbergasted.

Raph thought the question strange coming from someone who'd known him so intimately, that he'd been the godfather of her child. "Yes, of course. He ran our family's wine business. We were the most productive in all of Europe for a hundred and fifty years, but even before that, Giannport was a successful ship-building company for more than six centuries."

An awkward silence hung between them, and although Raph knew the answer, he asked, anyway. "He never told you?" It came out more like a statement than a question.

Claudia shook her head. "No. He said he was independently wealthy. We just assumed he belonged to one of those old elite European families with generational wealth."

Well, that was *the case.*

Claudia folded her arms and shook her head. "I guess we didn't really know Andris as well as we thought." She stared out a window where coconut trees swayed. "I would say, we didn't know him at all."

"That's not entirely true, Mom." Xio said. "Just because you don't know what someone does for a living, it doesn't mean you don't know them. And on the flip side, knowing someone's profession doesn't equate to knowing them, either." Her eyes settled on her mother's face. "Akilah and MJ knew what Dad did, but they never had the chance to know him as their father, as their dad, as a man. You knew Andris, Mom. You knew his personality and his character, which are the most important parts of a person. You just didn't know his line of work. That's all. That shouldn't change the way you feel about him."

"That's so true, Xiomara." Claudia touched Xio on the shoulder. "Thank you for pointing that out. Very insightful."

Xio smiled as she turned to Raph. "I'm sure he had his reasons for not saying anything to you, too, Raph. Maybe he sent you down here to learn about what he couldn't tell you."

I know he did. He wrote it out in black and white. But Raph still felt betrayed. He'd been closer to his grandfather than his brothers were, yet, for twenty-seven years, Andris never trusted him enough to tell him about Akilina. After what he'd learned this morning, he felt as if he knew him less.

Claudia squinted up at him. "You look a lot like him, you know. Has anyone ever told you that."

"All the time."

"Yes, indeed." Xio smiled sweetly at him.

It's all he, Neo, and Tele had been hearing since they were little boys. Before the accident, people used to say that he and his brothers looked like their father, who, in turn, resembled their grandfather.

"How long will you be staying on Akilina?" Claudia asked.

"Well, I planned for a week, but since getting into Ynoa and up and down the mountain into Aetós might be a hassle, I think I might have to extend my stay." His eyes unconsciously met Xio's. The thought of staying longer to get to know her better didn't bother him at all.

But, she's marrying a bastard, remember?

"That wouldn't be such a bad thing. The longer you stay, the more chances you'll have to get answers."

"I couldn't agree more, Claudia." His eyes wandered back to Xio, and through long, black lashes fanning her high cheekbones, her eyes glazed with a hint of desire.

She stepped back from him and said, "Mom, you have to pick up Akilah from school."

Claudia's face went flat. "What did she do now?"

"Nothing. She isn't feeling well."

"Why didn't she call me instead of bothering you? She knows how busy you are." Her frown deepened.

"She's been trying, but your phone is off."

"Oh gosh! I turned it off after that bastard——"

"Mom, I have a hotel to run. I'm sure Raph has things to do, and you need to pick up Akilah." She pressed her lips in a firm line and tapped the face of her watch.

Well done, Raph thought, as she walked over to her desk, picked up a folder, and opened it. Sexy, sophisticated, and not afraid to take control. After all that was said and done this morning, he could finally admit that he wouldn't mind one bit if she became the distraction he was so desperately trying to avoid. That is, if she wasn't about to marry a two-timing bastard.

Claudia walked over to the conference table, pulled her phone from her purse, and turned it on. "Oh boy, so many missed calls." She dropped it back into her purse and turned to Raph. "It was nice talking with you, Raph. I hope we see each other again before you leave."

"I hope so, too. I'd love to hear more about my grandparents. Let me give you my number."

Claudia fished out her phone again, created a new contact, and added his number as he called it out.

"Call, or text. Either is fine," he said.

"I will." She picked up her purse and looped the straps over her shoulder. "This might be the beginning of a great friendship between us," she said.

"Or the continuation of one that began years ago," he replied.

"I like the sound of that." Claudia turned to her daughter. "Xio, I'll see you at home. We can have our meeting tonight. I'll set time aside for it."

"If I get home early enough," Xio replied, then caught Raph's eyes. "Um— Raph, Olivia had your luggage sent on to The Davenport. I hope that's alright."

"Of course it's alright. I'd rather it be at the villa, than sitting in her waiting room where I left it. I'll thank her on my way out."

Raph opened the door, and once Claudia stepped out into the corridor, he turned and gave Xio his most charming smile, and said in a voice laced with promise and warning, "We will pick up where we left off before your mother interrupted us, Ms. Davenport."

Chapter Seven

HOME

The moment Raph drove through the automatic black steel gates leading to The Davenport, he felt like he had arrived in the Garden of Eden. Slowing to a cruise on the paved road, he rolled down the windows of the Jeep and was immediately serenaded by singing birds and the distant screeches of parrots in the forest on either side of the driveway.

About a quarter mile past the main gate, he slowed down when he came to a sign pointing to The Davenport's stables. Raph wasn't a horse lover, but he couldn't resist the vision of Xio seated in a saddle in front of him while they galloped along a moonlit beach, his cock rubbing against her backside as they moved in time with the horse's gait.

Raph eased off the brakes and continued cruising past fruit trees and manicured tropical gardens. The road ended in front of a wide green lawn, with flowering trees, their blossoms drifting in the breeze and blanketing the grass. Small white butterflies fluttered around the flower beds near a stone fountain that fed into a brook winding its way between the trees.

Beautiful, Raph thought as he came to a stop in front of the white-stone villa. A cool, ocean-scented breeze immediately wrapped around him like an inviting wave, reminding him of the breezes off the Aegean Sea. He hadn't explored Akilina yet, but just being at The Davenport, he could understand why his grandparents had loved it here so much.

Following a narrow gravel driveway around the lawn, Raph parked the Jeep in one of the two carports.

Warily, he eyed the door that led from the carport into the villa, and a sudden tightness in his throat warned him that he wasn't ready to go inside the house where his grandparents had spent so much time. He needed a moment to clear his mind and grapple with his feelings about everything he'd learned this morning. With a sigh, he reached for his cell from the center console, and exited the jeep.

The gravel crunched under his shoes as he followed the path to the back of the house. Ynoa's national flag flapped noisily on a pole at the bottom of the stone steps that led up to the patio. His cellphone rang, diverting his attention. He glanced at the screen and answered the call. "Hey, Declan."

"Raph, I was beginning to think you were too preoccupied for me. You don't decline my calls."

Declan had called while Raph was waiting in Olivia's office to see Xio. "I'm sorry about that. I had another meeting. What did you find out about Cleon?" he asked, his eye following a purple hummingbird hovering over a bush of yellow flowers before speeding off toward the forest.

"A lot of things." Declan replied with unchecked glee. "Your cousin is on the brink of bankruptcy. He owes taxes and other fees going back a decade, and he lost three of Giannport's major accounts a couple years ago."

Raph had known about Cleon losing the accounts shortly after his grandfather's stroke.

"Cleon has dug himself into a hole and can't seem to find a shovel," Declan continued. "It's amazing that he's been able to keep all of this under wraps. I'm not even sure if I've gotten to the bottom of his failures."

Raph climbed the steps to the patio and took a quick glimpse at the amenities: a bar, full outdoor kitchen, dining and seating area, a hot tub, and a seventy-foot-long infinity pool. Relaxing, and private—the way he liked it. The sunlight bounced off the inviting waters of the pool, and Raph couldn't help but wonder if Xio was a one-piece or a two-piece kind of woman.

"Cleon is sitting in his own shit, man," Declan said, with a resounding laugh, reining in Raph's thoughts.

"Are you sure about all this?" he asked. "His lifestyle says otherwise."

"I most certainly am. It's all in the email I sent you. I guess you haven't read it yet?"

"I haven't." He'd had no time for anything this morning after he'd pushed his way into Xio's office.

"Do I detect a lack of interest, Raph? I thought you'd be thrilled to have the dirt on Cleon so you can stick it to that bastard. What's going on with you?"

A lot. The avalanche of information about his grandfather's life on Akilina had taken precedence. But he couldn't share any of it with Declan, his most trusted friend—not until he got some answers to his ever-growing list of questions.

It was a little after twelve noon, and he was missing his daily swim. Early morning laps in his rooftop pool in San Francisco were what prepared him for the day.

He wondered about Xio's coping routine. Did she swim? How would she look in a skimpy bikini with her breasts spilling over the top, and the cheeks of her firm ass peeking from beneath her bottom? He fantasized about her walking out of the villa while he waited in the pool. She was wrapped in a white towel, and as their eyes met, she dropped it and...

"Raph, are you still with me?"

Raph shook the vision of Xiomara from his mind—of

untying the strings of her black bikini bottom with his teeth and watching it fall to her ankles. He walked over to the bar. The mere thought of having his mouth on her made him hot.

"I'm here, Declan. Just need something to drink," he said, scanning the bar. Choosing to keep a clear head over losing himself in a bottle of Balvenie or Belvedere, he opened the fridge and found it stocked with Caribbean beers, sparkling waters, and soft drinks. He chose a bottle with a guava, a slice of lime, and the word *Magua* printed on the label. Popping the lid, he took a long satisfying swallow of the tangy pink drink.

"Must be hot down there, huh?"

"As one might expect on a tropical island." He tried to peer through the retracting glass doors of the villa into the interior, but the glass was tinted. Just as well since he still wasn't ready to go inside. He wondered if he would ever be ready. He sighed heavily and undid the buttons of his shirt as he edged toward an umbrella-shaded chaise lounge. He eased down on one side of it and placed his drink on a low, black top table.

"Are we going to talk about this now, or should I call back when you can give me your attention?" Declan asked with a thread of frustration in his voice. "I'm on my way to the airport. The Portland meeting is in a few hours."

After years of friendship and working side-by-side, Raph understood Declan's impatience. He was a man who took his work seriously and didn't like to have his time wasted. He took another sip of Magua, then asked, "What's Cleon's plan? Is he looking to borrow money?"

"He's trying to sell."

"What? His house? His boats?"

"The Aetós vineyard. He's gotten two offers already. One from one of those up-and-coming craft wineries here in California, and one from the Leroux family in France.

The Leroux family, Raph thought, tapping the mouth of the cold glass bottle to his lips. *How do I know that name?*

"Remember they bought the first vineyards Cleon sold off in the Loire Valley?" Declan explained, apparently reading Raph's silence.

"Mmm. That's it." Raph remembered how crushed he had been by the sale of two of his grandfather's most prized vineyards. "Some of our best bottles came from those vines. The Leroux must be doing well."

"Right, but, Raph, this last remaining vineyard in Aetós is a different story."

"Meaning?" Raph placed his phone on the table, pressed the speaker button, and stretched his legs out in front of him.

"It's the land the buyers are after. As you know, the vineyard has depreciated in value over the years. The grapes aren't worth much of anything anymore and the place has been bleeding workers since Cleon took it over."

Yes, he knew all that. His grandfather had told him that even though the Aetós vineyard was never as profitable as the others, he'd held on to it because of its sentimental value. It had launched the family's successful wine making business. And now Cleon was trying to sell it. He folded his hands behind his head and stared at the green rugged outline of the Nacanké Mountains in the distance, a wicked thought forming in his head.

"Raph," Declan continued, "Cleon called looking for you this morning. He didn't say what he wanted, but I have a damn good idea why he called. The offers are much lower than his asking price."

"He waited until my grandfather was dead to see if I was interested in purchasing the vineyard that had held so much sentimental value for him." Raph's body shook as he chuckled at the absurdity of Cleon coming to him for a favor.

"Sounds about right." Declan replied. "The little shit!"

Raph took another sip of Magua. "What's he asking?"

"Five mil."

"He's more delusional than I thought." *Leave it alone.* Raph's grandfather's words echoed in his head. If Raph's father had lived, that vineyard would not have fallen into disarray and it would still be producing wine. Raph could not leave it alone. It was prime real estate and it should remain in the family. "What's the highest offer?"

"Two mil."

"Add another twenty thousand and do whatever you have to do to get rid of the other buyers."

"Consider it done."

He did not miss the excitement in Declan's voice at the challenge set before him. Raph finished off his Magua and placed the empty bottle on the table.

"What are you going to do with it once you have it?" Declan asked.

His eyes followed a sea bird gliding across the cloudless sky. He shifted on the lounge. "Don't know. When I figure it out, you will be the first to know."

"Can't wait." Declan paused then added cautiously, "But Raph, there's more to it."

"What?" Raph asked, just as cautiously.

"It looks like your grandfather had been bankrolling Cleon for the past eight years. We're talking tens of millions of euros."

He sat up straight. "What the hell for?"

"I don't know, man. All I know is that Andris had an account with an Italian bank, and Cleon had been withdrawing just shy of a million euros every month."

"Fuck!" He'd always wondered how Cleon could afford his cars, boats, and houses when the vineyard in Aetós, his only source of income as far as Raph knew, had been failing for years. Raph had suspected that he might have been mixed up in some shady business dealings, but it wasn't his business, so he'd never poked his nose into it. Now, he wished he had. What did Cleon have on his grandfather?

"Which bank?" he asked Declan.

"La Banca di Bianchi."

La Banca di Bianchi was a fairly new international bank that was already giving the older, more established banks a run for their money. Raph had been impressed by the shark-like business savvy of the Italian-American founder, Massimo Andretti, whom he'd met at a bar in London some years ago. Raph was in the UK to see a British Airways flight attendant he'd been dating at the time, and Massimo was there on family business—something to do with his younger brother who'd gotten mixed up with some crooked people. He hadn't elaborated. Raph remembered how tired and haggard Massimo had looked—kind of the way he himself had looked in the two weeks immediately following his grandfather's death. They had struck up a conversation and exchanged contacts, promising to stay in touch.

"What I can't understand, Dec, is why I didn't know about any of this. I'm the executor of the damn will."

"I'm sorry, Raph. I know it's a lot to take in. Your grandfather was keeping a whole lot from you."

You have no idea. His pappoús had more secrets than Superman.

Declan cleared his throat. "There's one more thing. There was a second account at the same bank, and as of two weeks ago, it had a balance of just over four-hundred million euros."

"And now?"

"And now, the account is closed."

Raph's stomach clenched and his heart pounded in his ears. "What do you mean it was closed? Where's the money, now?"

"I don't know. I hit a brick wall. Raph, I'm sorry to be the one giving you this news."

The knots in Raph's stomach grew tighter. He pushed to his feet and marched agitatedly back and forth along the width of the pool, raking his hands through his hair as he tried to contain his anger. Why, of all the banks in Europe, had his grandfather chosen that one for his clandestine dealings with Cleon? And how the hell does four-hundred million euros just disappear? There was only one way to find out.

He marched back to the table and picked up his phone. "Declan, I need to know where that money went. Set up a call with Massimo Andretti at his earliest convenience."

"Okay, boss. Um—does he know who you are?"

"Just tell him Pumpkin Pie."

"Pumpkin Pie? What the hell does that mean?"

Raph chuckled in spite of the seriousness of the situation. "I met him in London a few years ago. I'll give you the details later. Just tell him Pumpkin Pie needs to talk to him."

"You got it. I just got to the airport. I'll hit you up later."

"Thanks, Declan. And good luck in Portland."

Raph tossed his phone on the table, half hoping it would break in two, making it impossible for Declan to call him with more bad news.

Frustrated and angry, he stripped off his clothes, walked to the deep end of the pool and dove in, slicing through the surface like a hot knife through butter. He effortlessly propelled his way to the other side, creating such little turbulence and noise that a bat would not have known he was there.

Raph had no idea how many laps he'd done, but once he felt his strength waning, he pulled himself out of the pool, shook the water from his shoulder-length hair, and stood facing the beach at the far edge of the lawn. With his arms outstretched and his eyes closed, for a few moments, Raph relished the cool breeze brushing over his naked body and the sound of the wind rustling through the trees.

Feeling more in control, he opened his eyes and turned around, only to have the wind knocked out of him when he saw the glass doors. He still wasn't ready to face the influx of emotions awaiting him inside. He snatched a towel from a stack on a table and laid it over the chaise lounge he'd occupied earlier, then walked over to the bar. Still naked and wet, the water dripped down his legs, leaving a silvery trail on the tiles behind him.

Magua wasn't going to do it for him this time. It was early in the day, but, *shit*, he needed something to take the edge off the clenching in his gut. Grabbing a glass, a bottle of water, and the bottle of Balvenie, he made his way back to the chaise, dropped his weight onto it and poured himself a drink. The notes of sweet, creamy toffee gave way to vanilla and honey as the Scotch slid down his throat. He gritted his teeth and took another sip, then laid his head against the cushion as the stories he'd heard from Claudia this morning barreled through his mind like a bumpy, noisy freight train.

His mind jumped from one revelation to the next as he tried to latch on to bits and pieces of the conversation. For thirty-four years—six of which he'd been alive—his grandparents had been living a double life, visiting this island, and building a lasting friendship with Malik and Claudia—even standing as godparents for their first child. Why? What was so special about the Davenport family that he couldn't—or wouldn't share them with his own?

Raph remembered the instant and inexplicable connection he'd felt with Xio when he first walked into her office. He had never felt that kind of magnetic pull toward another person before, and he knew without a doubt that it would not have happened with any other woman.

The Davenports were special, for some unfathomable reason, which brought him to Claudia's claim that his pappoús had promised to tell Malik about some disturbing family link to Akilina that was centuries old. What on earth could that be? What secret about his family was buried on this island?

His father had been in on the secret, too, Raph realized, as a pang of betrayal coursed through him. Why, during the times his father had sat with him and his brothers, teaching them about their family history, did he never once mention Akilina, that he'd been here, never liked it, and that his parents still visited on a regular basis?

And if he was denied entrance into Ynoa, and a chance to meet Xio's great-grandmother to ask her for some insight, he would probably never know the answers to his growing list of questions. But then again, would his pappoús have asked him to go to Aetós if he didn't think he would be granted a permit? That thought gave Raph a tiny bit of hope that his application would be granted.

His mouth felt like dry, old paper. He tabled his drink and opened the small bottle of water, drinking it down quickly. It quenched his thirst, but did nothing for the sinking feelings of confusion and melancholy that now crawled through him.

Raph glanced at his watch. It was a quarter past one. Xio had told him to go to the library if he wanted to learn more about the island's history. He wondered if he looked hard enough, if he might discover a clue to his family's connection to the island—a newspaper article, or something buried deep in the archives that his grandfather had found, but never revealed.

He reached for his phone, Googled Akilina Public Library, and then looked up the hours of the Bureau of Tourism. The library was opened until four-thirty and the tourism office until two. It was too late to file his application, but he still had enough time to take a quick shower and head out to the library.

He swung his feet over the side of the chaise and stood. His thoughts immediately went to Xio and his mind reeled with every little detail of their morning together—from the moment he stepped into her office to the moment he left her with promises of taking up where they had left off before her mother interrupted them.

With his cock growing with anticipation, he let out a mournful sigh at thoughts of him and Xio in bed. He collected his clothes, took the empty bottles over to the outdoor kitchen, dropped them into the recycling container, and returned the whiskey to the bar.

All thoughts of Xio disappeared like lightening when he stood in front of the door. Raph could no longer avoid the inevitable. He slid open the slider on the far right of the villa and stepped inside.

But instead of the rush of sadness he'd expected, an overwhelming atmosphere of familiarity spiraled through him. It was the same feeling of warmth and sense of belonging he used to get whenever he visited his grandfather in Santorini, the place where he and his brothers were born and lived for the first six years of their lives.

"Okay, it's not so bad," he said to the cordial silence, sliding the door back into place. He dropped his phone and clothes on a chair near the door, walked around the beige leather sectional and across the terra cotta floor.

Remembering that he was butt naked, he killed the temptation to walk out onto the verandah off the dining room when he spotted people jogging along the beach. He went into the gourmet kitchen and checked the double refrigerator. It was fully stocked with drinks, fruits and vegetables, and a platter of cold-cuts and cheeses. Before closing the fridge, he took a piece of cheese from beneath the cellophane, and popped it into his mouth.

An affectionate smile curved his lips as he imagined his yaya baking *tsoureki*, the sweet Easter bread that he and his brothers used to love so much. Sometimes she would take them into the kitchen in Santorini and let them help her mix the ingredients and roll and twist the dough with the smell of vanilla, anise, and orange in the air.

"Oh, Yaya, I miss you," Raph whispered, then left the kitchen before he lost it altogether.

Back in the living room, he collected his phone and climbed the stairs leading to the second floor. He walked along a short corridor and opened the door of the primary suite. He passed through a sitting area overlooking the pool, and into the bedroom with warm, earth tones that immediately soothed him.

But when he spotted the blue velvet case that held the urn with his grandparents' remains on the white marble-topped dresser, the short-lived peace dissipated into sadness. He was reminded of why he had come to this island paradise. It wasn't for fun and pleasure, but to fulfill a dying request. It was because the person who had raised him into the man he was had died.

Raph felt a heavy pressure in his chest cutting off his breath as he walked on unsteady legs over to the dresser. With equally unsteady fingers, he opened the case, removed the urn, and clasped his hands round it. He was suddenly overwhelmed with feelings of isolation and abandonment. They weighed him down as the realization that his grandfather was really gone sank into his bones. This trip to Akilina would be Andris' last. When Raph left for San Francisco next week, he would be going home alone.

Anguish centered in Raph's chest like steel at the thought of never seeing his grandfather, never hearing his voice, or feeling his cool hand brush his brow ever again. He closed his eyes, and as weeks of suppressed tears streamed down his cheeks, Raph forced everything and everyone else from his mind, and opened himself to the flood of precious moments he'd amassed over the years with his beloved pappoús.

"Pappoús, you're home. You're finally home," Raph whispered in a choked voice.

Grief cut through his stomach and welled up into his throat, and this time, Raph didn't have the strength to suppress it.

Overwhelmed with the bottled-up pain he'd been carrying around for three long weeks, he placed the urn on the dresser and, staggering over to the bed, Raph collapsed into the cool comfort of the mattress, and yielded to the waves of sorrow tearing mercilessly at his heart.

Chapter Eight

FALLING APART

Pepper-water, lime, and salt…and a bottle of wine

AFTER RAPH and her mother left, Xio had tried to get some work done. But after an hour of failed attempts, she closed her laptop and slipped it into her tote. She locked up her office and took the stairs down to Olivia's.

Her mind was in disarray, not just from her run-in with Stamer, and the interesting stories her mom had revealed about her godparents, but also from the way her body had been reacting to Raph from the moment he'd come through the door of her office.

During the hour they'd spent with her mother, all she'd been thinking about was taking her clothes off slowly and provocatively while he watched from a chair, stroking his cock.

"Excuse me."

Xio jumped, thankful she was already on the bottom step of the stairs. "Hello," she said to the girl who looked about Akilah's age, squinting at the hotel map in her hand. "Are you lost?"

The girl nodded. "I'm looking for the Yellowtail Grill. I thought it was down here."

Xio smiled. "You've come too far down the hallway. It's…" She glanced through the glass wall of Olivia's office. She was sitting behind her desk with her phone clipped to her ear while she typed rapidly on her laptop keyboard. "Come, I'll walk you back," she said, beckoning for the girl to follow her.

"Okay, thanks. Sorry to bother you."

"It's no bother at all. Is this your first time on Akilina?" she asked as they hurried along the crowded breezeway.

"Mm-hm. Winter vacation. It's really nice here though. I wish we didn't have to leave."

"I know what you mean. I don't want to leave either," she said with a wink, masking the inner crisis that she might have to leave JBR sooner than she ever thought she would. "Ah, here we are. "The Yellowtail Grill is down there." She pointed to her right. "It's just at the end of this walkway. You can't miss it."

"Oh, awesome. Thanks!"

"You're very welcome."

The girl set off speed-walking.

As Xio turned around to retrace her steps, her phone pinged. She pulled it out of her bag to see a text from her mother. Akilah was asleep in her room. Mrs. Nnadi, their housekeeper, was staying late to keep an eye on her so Xio didn't have to. MJ was going to a friend's house after school and would stay there for dinner. Claudia would pick him up this evening when she left the boutique.

Perfect, she thought as she made her way back to Olivia's office. Olivia was still on her phone, so Xio quietly let herself in.

"No, we can't do that, Sita," Olivia said into the phone, while giving her boss an acknowledging nod.

Xio placed her brown Louis Vuitton tote on the chair in front of Olivia's desk and perched on the arm, her body tense and erect as she waited for Olivia to finish her conversation with the General Manager.

"No way. We've upgraded them twice already," Olivia said.

"Do they— Right. No. No. Offer them dinner on the house tonight. That's it. Yes. Sure. Why not? And get Jacey on it. We don't want them leaving a bad review. Okay. You, too. Thanks, Sita." Olivia hung up and rolled her brown eyes skyward on a growl.

"You handled that well," Xio said in appreciation.

"It's the Whitlocks. The guests from hell."

Xio had heard that name mentioned during the reading of the disgruntled-guest list in a meeting with her staff a few days ago.

Olivia came around her desk to stand in front of Xio. "They're only here for six days, and we've upgraded them twice, yet they keep finding things to complain about. Now they want a villa for the couple nights they have left, and…"

Xio covered her face with her hands and groaned.

"Sorry," Olivia said, instantly catching the drift. "I know you have bigger fish to fry."

"Or gut." She dropped her hands.

"What did Stamer want?"

Xio pressed her lips together before answering. "It was a set-up from the beginning, Liv."

"A set up? What kind of set-up?"

Xio gave her a summary of the scheme, watching her eyes and mouth widen with shock and disgust as she got deeper into the plot.

"What a slimy piece of shit!" Olivia cried out, when Xio told her that Stamer was threatening to have her thrown in jail.

"Yep. I got into bed with the slimiest piece of shit on the island," she said, the emotions she'd had to bottle in order to deal with Raph, and then her mother, rising to the surface now.

Olivia shook her head in dismay. "I can see Stamer pulling something like this. It's how he rolls. But Trevor? That shocks the hell out of me. He loved you."

"Ha! You call this love?" Xio said on a snicker. "Bottom line,

I should have seen it." She shot to her feet, too anxious to sit still. "I should have seen it!" she yelled through clenched teeth, while she curled her hands into fists at her sides to keep from throwing something across the room.

Olivia stood in front of her. "You couldn't have. Don't beat yourself up, Xio. You were desperate to save the resort, and you did. But Xio, your father would be the first to tell you that nothing is worth sacrificing your happiness. If you marry Trevor, you will be miserable for the rest of your life."

"I never considered that option for one second. After what he did to me… My skin crawls whenever I think of… Augh!"

"Good. I'm glad to hear that. I want to punch that fucking loser in his face every time I see him," Olivia said, taking Xio's clenched fists in her hands and rubbing her fingers across her knuckles. "And you're not going to jail either."

Xio closed her eyes and breathed in and out deeply and slowly, and soon she felt the tension leaving her body and her fists uncurling from her friend's gentle massage. She opened her eyes and gave Olivia's hands an appreciative squeeze.

Olivia nodded, then said in a calm but deadly voice, "Somebody needs to put a stop to Stamer. He has ruined enough lives on this island because of his fucking greed. So whatever you're planning, Xio, you can count me in. I'll hold the bastard down while you gut him like a fish. Just tell me what you want me to do." She jammed her hands on her hips.

Despite the heaviness in her chest, Xio smiled at Olivia's stand of solidarity. She and Olivia had been friends since they were kids, and she knew that if she ever had to hide a body, Olivia would be the friend to call.

"What do you want me to do, Xio?" Olivia reiterated, a mixture of anger and worry in her voice. "How can I help you?"

Xio picked up her bag and draped the straps over her shoulder. "Right now, I want you to clear my calendar for the day. Call my therapist and try to get me an appointment. I don't care if she only has ten minutes to spare. I need to see her. Then I'm going home."

Olivia grabbed her tablet from her desk. She opened the calendar app, and her fingers flew across the screen with lighting speed, then she looked up at Xio. "I'll make the calls and reschedule for tomorrow, and I'll do the rounds with the dinner guests tonight.

"Oh, damn." Xio had forgotten that it was her night to mingle with the guests at Choréta, JBR's fine dining restaurant.

"Xio, don't worry about it. Seriously, get out of here. I'll text you if I can get you an appointment."

"Thanks, Liv. You're the best." She turned and walked to the door.

"See you tomorrow," Olivia called after her.

THE SUN WAS EDGING toward the horizon when Xio pulled her red Lexus into the family garage and parked next to her father's Range Rover.

She leaned back and closed her eyes as she was flooded with memories of driving through the island with her dad, just the two of them, belting out the latest songs at the top of their voices, not caring that they were off key. He always knew how to make his children smile through their pain and their sadness. She missed him every day, but especially today. "I'm sorry, Daddy. I've been so stupid," Xio whispered on a ragged breath, tears stinging her eyes.

She brushed them angrily away, picked up her tote from the passenger seat and exited the car. She hurried up the steps from the garage to the main floor, walked into the *iabora*—the small shoe room that was in every house on the island—removed her heels, and bolted up the stairs. The marble tiles were smooth and cool under her bare feet.

She took a quick shower, then headed back downstairs, ate some of yesterday's pasta salad, poured herself a glass of wine, grabbed the bottle, then made her way outside to her favorite spot.

Xio took a sip of wine, then placed her glass and the bottle on a stone table before climbing into the hammock hanging between two palm trees. Her stomach was in knots; her head was pounding and every breath she took caught in her throat.

The half hour she'd spent with Ola had been so exhausting that instead of coming home, she'd driven out to Calli Beach on the northwestern tip of the island. The beach was secluded between two hills and, because of its isolated location and rough waters, was never crowded. Xio had discovered it on a drive soon after she'd gotten her license, and since then, Calli Beach had become her go-to place when she needed alone time.

She'd needed to be alone so she could scream at the ocean and rage where no one could see or hear her. She'd stayed there a few hours, sitting and thinking, then pacing and shouting, until hunger had forced her to leave.

Xio finished off the wine in her glass, then set it on the table. Knowing that the bottle would be empty by the time she went back inside, she decided that there was no need to measure her portions. She reached for the bottle, and took a long swig, red drops dripping down her chin.

Screw it.

Ola, her therapist, had reminded her that she had a pattern of ignoring red flags, and the conversation had eventually circled around to Toby Warner, her first boyfriend, and first heartbreak, and the nightmare he had put her through in the months after her father's death. She'd met Toby as a freshman at NYU, and with all the naivety of an eighteen-year-old, she had thought that after college, they would get married and start a family. She'd given up her virginity, believing that he felt the same way.

Three years later, shortly after returning to campus from her father's funeral, the ugly truths about Toby's interest in dating her had come to light. He had manipulated and used her, and had made their relationship and sex life the butt of jokes all over campus. Some of the people she had called her friends were in on the disgusting trick. She'd felt so stupid, humiliated, and devastated that she'd almost dropped out of college to get away from the people who knew the truth.

Xio tipped her head back, and, raising the bottle to her lips, she let the cool, tarty wine slide down her throat, willing it to numb the aches inside her, before laying it next to her in the hammock.

Her skin felt clammy, and sweat broke out on her forehead at the memory of the emotional trauma she'd suffered at the end of that year. Xio forced the bile back down her throat. As the hammock swayed, she closed her eyes and took deep long breaths while she envisioned herself drifting on a white fluffy cloud with only a clear blue sky above her.

After a minute or two, when she felt the tension easing, she opened her eyes and looked up at the patches of sunlight filtering through the palm tree fronds. But then her thoughts transitioned to Trevor, and she took another drink.

She'd thought Trevor was different because they'd grown up together. Even though there was animosity between their families, they still ran in the same circles. Because she had an abhorrent half brother, who was nothing like their father, she had never judged or condemned Trevor for his father's character. She had trusted him with her broken heart after she'd come home from the States with her damaged self-esteem, only to have him fuck her over, not once, but twice now. And the second time, she had practically asked for it.

Men were never sorry for anything. They weren't sorry for

hurting you, no matter how many times they said they were. They were only ever sorry for getting caught. She could at least give Toby credit for not apologizing for what he'd done to her. He wasn't sorry, and he hadn't pretended to be. That was the only honest thing about him. But Trevor...

Xio took a swallow from the bottle, then another. She wanted to numb her brain so she didn't have to think about the hot water she was in.

She was too trusting, always looking for a hint of goodness in people, and look where it had landed her. She was about to lose the company that has been in her family for generations. More than three-hundred years ago, her forefathers had toiled to build a successful hotel that started out as a boarding house and safe haven for newly arrived escaped slaves who came to Ynoa. And because of her inexperience and stupidity, she was about to lose it. All because of a man.

"Fuck!" Xio covered her face with her hands as if trying to hide her embarrassment from the world. She felt like such a loser. Her father and all her ancestors must be turning over in their graves. She should have listened to her mother. She should have taken heed of everything her father has warned her about the Stamers. She should have known better.

Xio gulped hard, hot tears slipping down her cheeks, dripping off her chin, and soaking her chest. Harsh sobs rocked her body as the reality of losing Jewel Beach to Stamer made her heart ache with defeat. Her stomach knotted at the thought of people whispering behind her back, calling her stupid for trusting the man who had broken her heart, and careless for getting into bed with a crook whose bank was known for destroying people's lives.

She swallowed hard, the knowledge that she was a failure twisting inside her like a knife, ripping to shreds the pride and happiness she'd felt this morning at the rewarding knowledge that all the hard work she'd done and the long days and sleepless nights she'd endured for the past four years was finally paying off. All of it was in vain. And these mother…

Xio grabbed her hair at the roots and tugged. "Fuck you, Trevor!" she screamed at the wind. "Fuck you, Samuel Stamer! Fuck your whole fucking family! I hope you all rot in hell! All of you can kiss my ass…"

Xio beat her fists into the sides of the hammock so furiously, she tipped herself out and fell flat on her face. "Ahh, fuck you, too!" She kicked the hammock, then scrambled to get her bottle of wine before its content spilled out.

She sat up, hung her head between her knees, and cradled the bottle on her lap, wondering what the hell she was going to do.

Everything had fallen so horribly apart…

Chapter Nine

REST

THE SUDDEN SOUND of raindrops pelting the roof pulled Raph from sleep. He opened one eye and peeked through the semi-darkness, confused as to where he was until he spotted the two potted palms near the verandah door. He'd finally fallen asleep staring at them through blurry, tear-filled eyes.

Holding his arm up to his face, he checked his watch. It was 9:13 PM. Groaning, he rolled over onto his back and stared out the glass into blackness, annoyed that he had slept all day instead of going to the library. But given the circumstances, he hadn't been in any shape to face the public.

It had been at least eleven hours since he'd arrived at The Davenport with his head spinning from what he'd learned about his grandfather from Claudia Davenport. And just when he thought he'd heard it all, Declan had dropped another bomb on him.

His mind had been stretched beyond its limit, so it was no wonder he'd given in to the desire to lie down and rest for a while. What he couldn't believe was that he'd fallen into a deep sleep in the middle of the day. Declan had warned him that it was only a matter of time before he crashed and burned after going nonstop for weeks. He was dead right about that. He was jet-lagged, fatigued, and emotionally burned out.

He'd needed that rest.

Raph's stomach growled, reminding him that he hadn't eaten in more than twelve hours either. How could he have even thought about food when his stomach had been tied up in knots since he set foot on the island, and his heart had been doing flips since he met Xiomara Davenport?

"Not tonight," he mumbled, as lust stirred at the thought of Xiomara.

Raph tossed the white cotton sheet off his body, swung his legs over the side of the bed, and shot to his feet, but a bout of vertigo forced him back onto the bed. With his feet planted on the floor, he put his hands out in front of him until the spinning stopped. His stomach growled again, louder and longer than before. It was raining, and too late to drive anywhere for dinner, so a sandwich would have to do for tonight.

He waited a few more minutes to make sure he'd regained his equilibrium before he attempted to stand again. Satisfied he would not collapse on the floor, he turned on the bedside lamp, and headed for the bathroom.

For a split second, Raph wished he hadn't put the staff on an as-needed basis. He was certain they would have had a hot, delicious meal to appease his hunger. The savory flavors would have drifted up the stairs and enticed him out of bed hours sooner.

Then you wouldn't be able to swim and walk around the house naked with a hard-on, would you?

He glanced down, and sure enough his cock was standing at attention.

So, no, he didn't regret putting the staff on an as-needed basis.

Chapter Ten

ROCOTIÉRI

Xio bolted up in her bed, gasping for air, her hands clutched to her breasts as a series of sharp pains ripped through her chest and spiraled downward into her belly. She took deep, steady breaths until she could finally breathe comfortably again.

It was 4:10 AM. She picked up the AC remote from her nightstand, adjusted the temperature, then, laying back against a wall of pillows, she pulled the cotton sheet up to her chin and closed her eyes.

It had been years since she'd had that dream. In it, she was a teenager walking through a Megiri village, waving at everyone she met. Her heart was pounding with excitement as she hurried home, but when she reached her hut, an eagle flew in front of her. Then the excitement in her heart turned to wrenching pain as she stared at the eagle thrashing around on the ground with an arrow embedded in its breast.

She always awakened with an excruciating pain in her chest. She could never understand why she felt as if the arrow had pierced her own heart.

Xio sucked in air sharply as she recalled the first time she'd had that dream. She was thirteen, and had returned home from the monthly *Rocotiéri*—a ceremony that was held in every territory every full moon in Ynoa. During the ceremonies, the priests communicated with the dead, and the memory keepers recounted the history of the villages.

Since she was an infant, Xio had been attending Rocotiéri with her grandmother, Sanaa, the only child of Dacica Kaiah, Xio's great-grandmother, and ruler of Ynoa for sixty-four years.

That particular night, after Rocotiéri was over and the adults sat around the bonfire in the *batey*—the village ceremonial park where all important events were held—smoking and talking under the full moon, Xio's friends and cousins had persuaded her to explore some nearby burial caves with them. It was forbidden to enter a burial cave on the full moon when the spirits of the dead had come out to communicate with the priests during the ceremony, and roam the village, reflecting on their time among the living. If their paths were blocked on their return to their resting places, they could end up roaming the earth indefinitely by shadowing a descendant, whether or not it was that descendant who had blocked their path.

When she'd awaken with the pain in her heart that first morning, Xio had known that she had been shadowed. Not wishing to get herself or her friends and cousins in trouble, she had never told anyone, nor had she ever entered another burial cave during Rocotiéri again.

Xio rolled over and stared at the Ashanti mask hanging on her wall, a piece she'd bought during a trip to Ghana and a constant reminder of her African roots. But she was also steeped in Megiri traditions.

She closed her eyes and saw herself as a little girl, sitting on a mat in the batey, watching the *rahami*, the village medicine men and women, placing *cohiba*, or tobacco, mixed with other herbs into the shallow heads of the stone *zemis* at the front of the batey, and lighting them on fire. The priest and the chief would inhale the smoke through curved wooden pipes, then they would lean forward with their elbows on their knees and, with their heads bent and their eyes closed, they would communicate with the dead.

Xio loved the beat of the drums, signaling the village to the batey, and the blowing of the conch shell, indicating the time for storytelling. She smiled as she thought of her favorite part of the night—playing with the other children, the laughter and chatter of the villagers, and the clinking of seashells worn around the women's ankles—some of them her aunts and cousins—as they circled the reveling crowd with baskets of barbecued meats and fish, vegetables, and cassava bread.

She could almost hear the beating drums and the music from the flutes, the *guiros*, and the *maracas*, and of being caught up in the trance and joining the circle of dancers around the bonfire— her painted body twisting and writhing, her feet skipping off the ground, the tips of her long hair swinging across her hips, and her arms circling her head as the magic echoed deep inside her, and then…

Xio's smile withered, and her hands curled around the edge of the sheet as the door to the room where her very first heart-break was stored cracked open, just a tad. She was fourteen and was finally beginning to make sense of the customs of her Megiri ancestry, when her monthly trips across the Caonabo River ended with the sudden dead of her toá.

Xio recalled her great-grandmother on her knees in front of her daughter's burial cave, her face painted black, sobbing hyster-ically, tugging at her long, gray hair, and bowing her head to the ground while mourners formed a circle around her and chanted in chorus. After losing their mother, Xio's father and his two sisters, Neha, and Zola, spent a lot of time at BÓ-Caneye—the Great House in Xiobayo where the chief lived—trying to console their grandmother as she grieved the loss of her only child.

Xio had visited her botoá with her father, but that too came to an end when Xio's mother landed a three-year contract as a fashion consultant at Alexander McQueen in New York, and enrolled Xio into a boarding school in the city. Xio had protested because she didn't want to leave her friends and her family, especially her botoá. But Kaiah had told her that it was a good thing for her to explore the world outside of Ynoa, and promised that she would be here when she returned home.

Returning home had taken ten years, and when she finally did come home, fighting Fitzroy for control of Jewel Beach, and then working around the clock for four years to make it a success again had left her with little time to visit her botoá.

Her chest swelled as tears damped her eyes. Rocotiéri wasn't the only reason she used to look forward to crossing the river as a child with her grandmother, and then her dad. She loved being with her botoá, sitting and talking with her, or just sitting and saying nothing at all, feeling happy and content to be near her, and feel her arms around her.

Those times Kaiah wasn't the dacica of Ynoa. She was simply Xio's great-grandmother who doted on her and treated her like a little princess. Although Kaiah had three other great-granddaughters through Xio's aunts, Neha and Zola, Xio felt as if she was her favorite. And maybe she was because she was Kaiah's first great-granddaughter.

Xio turned her face to the verandah doors as a shaft of early morning light cut through the darkness. Knowing she would not go back to sleep, she got out of bed and pulled on a robe. She might as well get her yoga and meditation in, she thought, walking into her sitting room, and turning on the lights.

When she spotted her bag on the ottoman where she had left it yesterday afternoon, she remembered Andris' letter. Certain that she would not be able to focus her mind without knowing what was in that letter, Xio walked to the ottoman, sat down on the matching couch, then pulled the envelope from her tote and opened it. She frowned when she noticed that it was written two years ago.

. . .

March 15, 2018

My Dearest Xiomara,

First, let me introduce myself in case you don't remember me, or your parents never told you about me. My name is Andris Giannopoulos, but I used the surname, Aetós, when I visited Ynoa, long before you were born. My wife, Kerena, and I were close friends with your parents, your grandparents, and your great-grandmother—Dacica Kaiah. The last time I visited Ynoa was in 1993, when you were three years old. Xiomara, I am your godfather and Kerena was your godmother. But sadly, she left us twenty-five years ago, which is the sole reason I stopped coming to Ynoa.

The beautiful memories we made there together over the years were just too painful to relive. Our times in Ynoa were our happiest, and every year we looked forward to coming down and spending time with your family, but especially after you were born. You were the most beautiful baby girl we had ever seen. We loved you so much.

Although I was not there to watch you grow up, Xiomara, I want you to know that I think about you often, i mikrí mou kóri. From time to time, I check the online version of Akilina News to read about your accomplishments, graduating from NYU and Princeton with the highest honors. You were a curious and highly intelligent child, and you have grown up into an independent, beautiful young woman. Your parents did an exceptional job raising and directing you.

Unfortunately, I am also aware of the struggles you've had to face since your father's passing. It broke me to watch JBR deteriorate under your brother's management. But, Xiomara, I'm so proud of you for taking on the challenge of trying to restore your family's legacy to its former glory. I have every confidence that you will succeed and make your father very proud of you.

Xiomara, my dear, my apologies and regrets are too numerous to mention, and time isn't on my side to list them now. I know I failed you and your parents by disappearing from your lives, but I also failed my own family in much bigger ways.

Most specifically, I failed my grandson, Rapheus. There were so many things I should have told him when I had the chance and even now as I write this letter, I'm still trying to figure out how to tell him the truth about our family's history. I'm not sure that I will ever have the courage to do it.

If you're reading this letter, I hope it means you have met Raph and that he has finally made it to Akilina. I know I don't have any rights to ask you for any favors, but when you live to be 91 years old, you do it anyway.

Running a successful hotel is a huge responsibility and demands a lot of time. But I'm asking if you could find it in your heart to put aside some time to take Raph to see your great-grandmother if she's still alive when he gets there. I know Kaiah will help him find his way to Aetós. I put a large burden on his shoulders in sending him to Ynoa, and I know he'll need help and support finding his way around and dealing with his emotions. But please, do not let him know that I have asked you to help him.

I mikrí mou kóri, again, I wish I had been there to watch you grow. I have never forgotten you and I've always remembered the three years we had together. Please give your mother my love.

Your godfather, always,
Andris

Xio's throat was tight with emotions as she stared at the sheets of paper in her hands. Her heart swelled with pity for him, even as she wondered about the disturbing story he'd promised to tell her father and still, obviously, hadn't been able to tell Raph.

But, hell, she had her own shit to deal with. A fucking dragon was about to burn down her castle, and Andris wanted her to turn her back on the dragon, and take a field trip into the rainforest with his grandson? He himself said that running a successful hotel was a huge responsibility and demanded a lot of time, so where in heaven's name does he think she would have time for Raph?

A cock crowed in the distance.

Xio placed the letter back into its envelope, set it on the ottoman, and walked out onto her verandah. She pulled her robe tighter against the cool mountain air seeping through the thin cotton fabric. The pre-drawn sky was a canvas of gray and blue hues.

This was the time of the day that Xio always enjoyed most. She coveted the peace and quiet before the world awoke and began making demands on her. But there was no peace and quiet in her soul this morning. Her world was about to topple off its axis, and there was not a dam thing she could do about it.

Biting her lips, Xio leaned against the railing and eyed the blue envelope sitting on the ottoman. Maybe she should go to Ynoa. She hadn't seen her botoá in a while. She used to find peace and quiet there when she was a child. Maybe there was some left over for her tired battered adult soul this weekend. If she was going to lose the hotel, she was going to lose it. Stamer had given her thirty days. She was down to twenty-nine, so what was another three?

Being with her great-grandmother always calmed her and made her feel better about herself, and right now that was exactly what she needed. She needed to hear tales of her brave ancestors to let her know that she was not a failure, that she came from long lines of kings, queens, daciques, and dacicas, and that a piece of dried shit like Samuel Stamer, who probably didn't even know the name of his great-great-grandfather, could go fuck himself.

She needed her botoá. She needed calm.

Chapter Eleven

THE INVITATION

RAPH LEANED against the railing of the bedroom verandah, sipping his coffee. From his perch, he could see cars and jeeps driving along narrow roads winding their way up the steep hills of Akilina. A mosaic of different colored houses—purple, yellow, white, and blue—dotted the lush green landscape, and the shrieks of laughing gulls, gliding above the morning's calm sea, echoed in the distance.

He was still frustrated that he had slept through yesterday afternoon and evening, putting him one day behind with his application to visit Ynoa, and his research at the library for anything he might find on his family's connection to Akilina. He had no idea how many centuries his grandfather had been talking about when he'd mentioned it to Malik. It could have been one, two, three, or a thousand, for all he knew. What he did know was that if the Giannopoulos family had roots on Akilina, he needed to find them.

Raph stiffened as a chill worked its way up his spine.

Throughout the night, he'd dreamed of being pushed off a steep cliff into dark, cold waters, before being dragged down to the bottom by gnarled tree roots winding and twisting around his arms and leg, forcing the air out of his lungs as it tightened around his neck like a boa constrictor. Pain shot through every nerve in his body as he fought to free himself, and just when he thought he would surely drown, he was catapulted back to the surface. He'd awakened thrashing around on the bed and coughing as he tried to expel sea water from his lungs.

Finally realizing that it was only a dream—the same one he'd had for the first time after cleaning the clock with his pappoús when he was thirteen—Raph had tried to get out of bed to change the sheets, drenched with his sweat, but he'd had no strength to move. All he could do was lie there helplessly, trying not to fall asleep again.

But he had. And the nightmare had returned, two more times.

When dawn finally broke, Raph was so exhausted, he'd just wanted to stay in bed, but he'd found the strength to drag himself down to the kitchen to make a strong pot of coffee.

It was still too early to call Gwen to ask her for some insight. Yet, without understanding the meaning behind his nightmare, he knew in his gut that if he left Akilina before he got to the heart of the matter concerning his family's link to the island, that dream would haunt him for the rest of his life.

Raph finished his coffee and watched a laughing gull and a pelican fight over the pelican's catch. The battle was over in a matter of seconds. The gull flew away with a piercing screech of victory, and the defeated pelican dived into the water again.

Raph went back into the bedroom suite, his determination to find answers as strong and urgent as that of the pelican to find and keep its next catch.

As he set his mug on the bureau, his phone pinged from the nightstand. He walked over and picked it up to find a text message from Claudia.

> GM, Raph! If you haven't yet made plans for this evening, and are free, we would love to have you over for dinner. We'll be eating around sunset, but feel free to come any time you want. I'll be working from home today. I'm planning to make lamb. Let me know if you have any food allergies or if you're a vegetarian and I'll make the necessary changes. Looking forward to seeing you!!!

Raph couldn't help but smile at the prospect of seeing Xiomara tonight, of hearing her sexy voice, and breathing in her scent. He knew his thoughts should be focused on learning more about his pappoús' time with the Davenports, but all he could think about was getting a chance to feel the smooth silkiness of Xio's skin under his palm at some point during the night.

He sat on the bed and typed his response:

> Hey, Claudia! Thank you for the dinner invitation. I'm free and would love to join you. Looking forward to seeing you and meeting the rest of your family. Lamb sounds delicious. No food allergies and I'm not a vegetarian.

> Great!

> Can I bring anything?

> Just yourself. I'll drop a pin later with instructions on where to park. Let yourself into the house through the carport door.

> Copy that. And thanks again, Claudia.

> You're very welcome. See you then.

He waited a few seconds before he dropped his phone on the bed, then laid back, his mind reeling with visions of Xiomara.

THE LIBRARY WAS as quiet as a graveyard, with only a handful of patrons trickling in and out of the modern two-story building. From his table, covered with books and open newspapers, Raph had been able to watch the light buzz of activity outside in the square—a poet, wearing a headband dripping with long strands of shells reciting lines from atop a painted wooden crate, farmers calling out their goods to passersby, and the friendly beeps of car horns as drivers waved to friends on the street were all muffled by the thick, floor-to-ceiling windows.

Inside, the peaceful silence he had enjoyed for the last four hours was broken when the library's double doors swung open to a small group of high school students. A girl with long braids falling to her waist chased a boy holding a three-ring binder above his head. His mischievous look of satisfaction when she caught him and wrestled her binder from his hands was quickly diminished by the gentle scolding of the librarian from behind her desk. The boy whispered his apology, and the group disappeared into the stacks.

After his morning swim at The Davenport, he'd driven into Anacaona and filed his application to enter Ynoa with the Department of Megiri Affairs. Mr. Tridoux, the agent he'd seen, had assured him that scattering the ashes of a citizen in his Ra wasn't unusual. But he needed permission from *Mitayna* Luyaron, the sub-chief of the territory of Yacao where the village of Aetós was situated—something Xiomara and Claudia hadn't mentioned yesterday. Mr. Tridoux had assured Raph that it was just routine and nothing to worry about. He hoped so.

Raph had spent the rest of the morning and early afternoon at the library, combing through reference books and archived journals from the 18th and 19th centuries. But he couldn't find a single mention of anyone named Aetós or Giannopoulos. He'd learned that the Taíno and Megiri living on Hispaniola had massacred a band of Spaniards in retaliation for the enslavement, kidnapping, and raping of their women in 1493, and about a boat from Barbados with twenty-seven escaped slaves, fifteen Megiri tribesmen who had been previously kidnapped from other islands, and four *guayanki*, or "pale men", that had landed on the island in the mid 1600s. The only person named in the account of the party from Barbados was Eagle Davenport, one of the escaped slaves who went on to help the Megiri fight European invaders.

He wasn't sure if Eagle Davenport was related to Xio, but he added it to the list of questions he wanted to ask her tonight.

Part of him wanted to spend the rest of the day reading in solitude. Some of the records he came across about warriors and Megiri raiders were as captivating as the adventure books he had read with his brothers when they were kids. But frustration set in as he accepted that he wasn't going to find any of the answers to his questions in a book. He couldn't find any mention of Greek influence or a clue that might have caught his grandfather's attention, almost thirty years ago.

Raph checked the time. It was still early—still hours before sunset, but Claudia had said to come at any time, and he knew he would learn more about his family from her than he would at the library by himself. Besides, he had no idea what he was supposed to be looking for, anyway.

Stacking the books he'd used onto an empty cart next to the librarian's desk, Raph thanked her for her help, and bounced down the stone steps into the square. His jeep was parked half a mile away along the bay front road. After walking through town under an unrelenting tropical sun, Raph caught a whiff of himself, and decided to drive back to The Davenport to freshen up before dinner.

<hr>

Forty-five minutes later, Raph navigated his way through the narrow roads of Anacaona, away from the busy town center, turned left off Kati Road, and into the residential area of Cedar Grove. He drove past houses with sheer lace curtains swaying in the afternoon breeze behind louvered glass windows, and low, cinderblock and iron fences.

Weathered trees flanked the road on either side, some with their twisted roots above ground, reminding Raph of his reoccurring nightmare last night. He shook off the ominous feeling and slowed to a stop as he glimpsed a herd of donkeys leisurely crossing the road a few yards ahead.

The car rental agent at Jewel Beach had warned him to watch out for donkeys and goats that were notorious for wandering out into oncoming traffic. Raph had assured the agent that he was used to sheep wandering out into the roads in Greece. He didn't expect donkeys and goats were any different, and they weren't. Patience was the key.

Once the last small brown donkey made it to the other side and joined those already grazing on the grass between the road and the fences surrounding the houses, Raph eased off the brakes, feeling an even greater sense of home in Akilina.

He drove for a few minutes until he spotted a road sign that read *Mt. Aymaco Estate.* Turning up a winding road, he passed several driveways leading to what he could only imagine were private properties tucked away behind dense forest. A wide canopy of flamboyant tree branches covered the narrow road, their red flowers carpeting the ground. Raph felt as though he were driving into another realm, far removed from the daily grind and chaos that seem to infect the world.

A quarter mile further up the mountain, he came to the end of the road and the last private entrance. A white stone slab with *Eagle's Nest* engraved on it swung lazily in the breeze from its wooden post. Tension and excitement about what he might learn from Claudia, and the thought of seeing Xiomara again, knotted in Raph's stomach as he took the turn and climbed higher and deeper into the rainforest.

His trepidation soon gave way to awe when the thick brush opened into a field of long grass and wildflowers, and he first caught sight of the palatial three-story home looming against the lush greenery of the mountainside, and the unobstructed view of the Caribbean below. From this height, the ocean seemed to shimmer like glitter in the afternoon sun.

The driveway forked into two lanes that looped around a courtyard of pretty flower beds and a fountain with a bronze eagle, a continuous stream of water gushing from its wide-open mouth into the stone cauldron beneath its feet. Raph wondered if the fountain, and the name of the estate pointed to a connection between Eagle Davenport and *his* Davenports. As he was beginning to understand the prominence of Xio's family, a sense of intimidation seized him—something Raph did not often feel. *Who were these people?*

Just past the courtyard, he found the carport where Claudia had told him to park. He pulled his Jeep into an empty spot, and killed the engine. He was almost three hours early—too early, he thought, to go into the house. Claudia could still be working. As gracious as she was, he didn't want to push her hospitality, so he exited the Jeep and walked out to a green lawn with dozens of palm trees in neat rows. Noticing a stone path leading toward a walled garden behind the house, he pushed his hands into the pockets of his tan cotton slacks and headed toward it.

The path was winding and shaded from the sun, and after a few minutes he opened the top two buttons of his forest green button-down shirt for the mountain air to cool his skin. He couldn't believe how much cooler it was up here compared to the unrelenting heat in town. A sheep bleated in the distance. He laughed to himself, wondering if Claudia was butchering her own sheep for dinner tonight.

As he rounded a high hedge, the sound of a woman's voice made him stop in his tracks.

He peered around the corner and spotted a teenager sitting

on a lounge chair at the edge of a swimming pool, the pool house casting a long shadow over her.

"I already told you. I'll sneak out and meet up with you later, so why you asking me again?" She sucked her teeth in annoyance.

Shit. This must be Akilah. What should he do? Let her know he was here or try to ease back toward the house? Deciding he would sneak away, he turned slowly on his heels, but as he took his eyes off Akilah and looked behind him, he froze. Two brown lizards, about a foot and a half long, sat in his path like guardians of the estate, eying him with what he hoped was only curiosity. Without knowing how to read the body language of the biggest lizards he'd ever seen, and with no way of knowing if they would become aggressive, Raph stayed put, his eyes trained on the reptiles, waiting until they gave way so he could make his escape.

"I can't sneak out that early," he heard Akilah say. "Mom's having some guy over for dinner…"

Oh, so the conversation was about him. He wondered who she was talking to.

"No. I can't get out of it. She said I have to be there, and that I be on my best behavior." She giggled. "Like I know what that is."

A long silence followed before she spoke again. "I don't know. It's someone from the resort. Some rich guest. You know how she likes to entertain… Cause he's staying at The Davenport, that's how I know. Anyway, Mom says his grandfather used to know my dad, or something like that. Why, you jealous I would dump you for him?"

Raph waited, trying desperately not to make a sound while keeping an eye on his reptilian captors.

She laughed. "Xio? A boyfriend? *Pleeeeeease…*" A short silence ensued and then she said in a clear, adamant voice. "No—why would you even say… No. My sister isn't cold. She's just being careful after—you know—I mean everyone knows what happened between her and Trevor…"

Wait. Who the hell was Trevor? Raph slowly peeked around the hedge, now fully immersed in Akilah's conversation.

"Well, he had his chance and he screwed it up," Akilah said. "She wouldn't go there again, trust me. I don't care what he told you… I know my sister and it isn't happening."

Was Trevor the two-timing bastard Xio was about to marry? Raph's pulse sped up as he waited with bated breath.

"Yeah, I get it, but I'm still vexed with him. I used to like him, but now every time I see him, I just want to kick him in the balls…"

Damn. What did this guy do?

"Exactly," Akilah said. "I mean, I get that it was embarrassing, and everybody was feeling sorry for her, and all. But seriously, get over it already. I'm sorry, but he's not even worth it. It's been like five years. I don't even think she's gotten laid since then. That's probably why she's so uptight and on my ass about everything. A girl's gotta get her little 'somethin-somethin', you know…"

Shit! Five years was a long time for anyone to go without sex. Five days was bad. It had been four days for him, and he was already feeling jumpy. Maybe Xiomara was the perfect scratch to his itch. How much convincing could she possibly need after a five-year dry spell?

An image of him and Xio locked together under a rushing waterfall in the middle of a rainforest suddenly flashed across his vision like an old forgotten memory. His shaft throbbed against his thigh as he pictured their naked bodies rolling against each other while the water pounded the rocks around them. He could taste her, smell her, feel her, tight and wet. *Where was this fantasy coming from?*

"You got that right," Akilah said. "I'll cut your balls off, roast them over a fire while you watch, and then make you eat them if you ever do some crap like that to me, Jamon. I'm not kidding."

A threat like that would have had Raph shaking in his boots when he was a teenager.

"What time can you be here? I'll slip out when Mom and Xio are busy with their after-dinner production… You know it's gonna be a whole song and dance. They can't help themselves…"

Well, fuck me very much. Raph needed to leave. He wished he hadn't happened upon her. Carefully, he turned, relieved to find the lizards had left as quietly as they had appeared. Or maybe he'd just been too engrossed in Akilah's conversation to have heard them scurry away.

Raph breathed easily when he made it back to the carport. Feeling like he'd encroached on the Davenports more than if he'd just gone inside when he first arrived, he headed straight to the door that led from the carport. He eased it open and stepped into a small room with cubicles, shelves, and a closet. He closed the door quietly behind him and found the pair of brown slippers that Claudia had left under a built-in wooden bench for him.

As he sat down to remove his shoes, the warm smell of curry drifted his way, teasing his taste buds. It had been a while since he'd had a home-cooked meal. He missed the intimacy of sitting down at a table surrounded by people he cared about. Yes, he had that occasionally when he visited with his mother, his brothers, and little Petra, but those visits were few and far between since they all led busy lives far apart from each other—he and his mother in California, Neo in New York, and Tele in Colorado.

Raph placed his shoes into an empty cubicle and slid his feet into the slippers. They were a perfect fit. He couldn't wait to see Xiomara, to be close to her, sit next to her at dinner, and get lost in her mesmerizing brown eyes.

Lost in her eyes? Who are you, and what have you done with Raph?

Raph didn't get lost in anything, least of all a woman's eyes. Her body? Definitely.

Shaking the lovey-dovey visions from his head, he stood and walked down a short hallway with white marble floors and a glass wall that opened up to a small garden with a birdbath and an Adirondack chair. The opposite wall was lined with crystal sconces between landscape paintings of tropical scenes from every corner of the world—beautiful oil paintings of Bengal tigers, jungle leopards, and toucans, black sand beaches with towering Royal palm trees, and lush green forests.

"They sure know how to live," Raph murmured, following the hallway as it veered to the right. "Hello?" he said, sticking his head briefly into an open doorway and finding what he assumed was a guest bedroom that looked out onto the main courtyard.

Moving a few steps beyond the bedroom, he reached the beginning of a longer hallway with a staircase at the end. "Hello?" he called down the hall, again only to be met by silence. He turned around, deciding to follow his nose to the kitchen through what looked like the main foyer. At least that would be a safe, non-intrusive part of the house to wander about in.

But as he stepped into the grand entry hall, Raph came face-to-face with the youngest member of the Davenport family. Malik Junior—MJ—was tall for his age, and from the thick head of curly black hair and his square face, Raph thought he might mature into a devilishly handsome young man in a few years. Girls would be going wild over him, if they weren't already.

MJ was barefoot, and wearing white loose-fitting pants with a red waistband, embroidered cuffs at his ankles, and a black vest.

"Who are you, and what are you doing in my house?" MJ's striking brown eyes glowed like an autumn fire, and his lips drew back into a scowl as he assumed a position similar to the half-front stance that Raph remembered from his karate days.

Amused, he stepped toward the boy, a wide grin on his face. "Hi, MJ, I'm—"

"Mom! There's a guayanki burglar in the house!" MJ screamed at the top of his lungs.

"MJ, I'm not—"

Like a wave rolling across the ocean, the kid twirled his lean frame in one fluid motion, and in the blink of an eye, Raph felt MJ's left heel connect to his stomach, knocking the wind out of him and sending him hurtling into the wall. *Damn,* he thought holding his stomach while his breath tried to catch up with him, the boy was strong, and he delivered with precision.

As he struggled to regain his composure, Raph caught a glimpse of Xio coming through the opened double doors. His breath solidified in his throat as their eyes caught and held for a split second—a mistake to have taken his eyes off MJ, he realized, when MJ's right heel slammed into his stomach.

As he went down, Raph heard Xiomara yell, "MJ, noooo!"

Chapter Twelve

THE TAKEDOWN

"Oh Lord!" Xiomara dropped her bag and flew across the floor.

MJ hovered over Raph, ready to attack again if he moved a muscle.

"MJ, relax," she said, pushing him out of the way. She dropped to the floor and leaned over Raph, her heart pumping. "Raph, did you break anything?" she asked, watching him clutch his stomach as he curled into a ball.

But all Raph could do was gasp for air, his breath coming out loud, hard, and sharp.

Having the wind knocked out of her in kickboxing, Xio knew his pain, and that there was nothing to do but wait until he caught his breath. She turned to her brother. "MJ, why did you kick him? You know the rules. You're never to attack someone without reason or provocation."

"But I had a reason, Xio. I asked him what he was doing in my house, and he didn't answer. I thought he was a burglar. You and Mom are always saying I'm the man of the house." He crossed his arms and stood with his legs apart, still ready to pounce into action despite her admonishment.

"Not everyone who walks into the house is a burglar, MJ," she said in a softer tone. She admired his bravery, but, she couldn't ignore the possibility that her little brother could have gotten hurt if Raph had indeed been a burglar with malicious intent. The man was three times MJ's size and could throw him across the room with little effort.

Two of their neighbors' houses had been broken into a few months ago, so Xio understood MJ's knee-jerk reaction after coming face-to-face with a stranger in his home. Xio shifted her focus to Raph, who had stopped gasping and was now lying motionless on the floor, his face askew with pain.

She didn't know what part of his body had collided with the wall or the hard marble floor. She leaned over him and inspected his head and shoulders, his warm unsteady breath fanning her face and neck, making her body flush. She drew back on a ragged breath. At least he wasn't bleeding. "Raph."

"I'm… I'm alive," he said, swallowing and winching as he tried to get up.

MJ knelt beside her. "You know him?"

She really did not know him. At least not well enough to know if he was going to be trouble or not. "Go get me a cold pack from the freezer and get my phone from my bag." She didn't know if she needed to call a doctor.

"I'm sorry, Xio. I didn't mean to hurt your boyfriend," MJ said in a despondent voice.

"He's not my boyfriend." She shooed him off to do her bidding, smoothed her hair behind her shoulders, and cupped Raph's chin, turning his head to face her. His eyes were closed, his long dark eyelashes brushing the tops of his cheekbones. Her heart drummed with worry. "Raph, can you hear me? Are you okay?"

"Yes, I can hear you, Xiomara," he said in a throaty voice, opening his eyes to meet hers. They had a hint of a smile as he held her stare.

She let out an audible sigh of relief. "Are you alright?" she asked, in a choked voice.

"Yes, I'm alright." His sexy smile made her heart turn over.

God, he was gorgeous. She lowered her gaze to his slightly parted rosy lips—the bottom one a little fuller than the top—with a perfectly shaped cupid's bow. She salivated at the thought of running the tip of her tongue along the perimeter of his sensual mouth.

"Did you hit your head?" she asked, forcing her thoughts back to his well-being.

"No. I didn't hit my head. My shoulder took the brunt of the fall, and my gut feels like it's been trampled by a herd of elephants. It hurts to breathe."

"I'm sorry. MJ's teacher told us about his mean heel kick."

"It is mean, and that's why I stayed down. Two kicks in the gut were more than enough. Don't be too hard on him, though. He saw a strange man in his home and he reacted. I might have done the same thing when I was his age." He tried to get up, but slumped back with a grunt.

"Lemme see." The top two buttons of his shirt were undone, but the opening didn't give her enough space to get a good look at his shoulder. Unbuttoning two more, she gently pulled his sleeve down. It was only after she saw his bulging biceps rippling beneath his smooth olive skin that she realized she'd made a terrible mistake in undressing him.

Her breath caught in her throat when his long warm fingers curled around her wrist and, ever so gently, he brought her hand against his chest. Her fingers instinctively burrowed into the thin mat of dark, silky hair beneath her palm. Her breathing became shallow and her eyes shifted from the tempting hardness of his shoulder and arm to his face.

Their gazes locked and held.

Fire spread through Xio's veins, and a series of powerful contractions rippled deep between her thighs and ricocheted throughout the rest of her body. She tried to pull her hand away, to disconnect herself from him, but he held it fast where his heart drummed beneath her palm.

Time ground to a halt, and as they stared, seemingly help-lessly, into each other's eyes, a raw, sensuous energy wrapped around them, twisting tighter and tighter like two ghosts coiling slowly around each other in an intimate dance. Again, like yesterday in her office, Xio sensed that undeniable, unrelenting attraction to him. Her heart felt as if it would jump right out of her chest. She licked her bottom lip as her head began a lazy gravitation toward his.

"How is it?"

His eyes glowed with a savage inner fire and burned with the same ferocity as the one raging inside her. She cleared her throat. "How is what?"

His gaze slid to the spot at her throat that pulsed in time to the heavy beating of her heart. "How's my shoulder?"

She looked again, this time with more scrutiny. "It—um—it's a little bruised. A little red and swollen. But the skin isn't broken." That sounded so naughty, Xiomara thought, but it didn't bother her. It had been a while since anyone had evoked that kind of salacious thought in her mind.

"Then I guess I'll live."

"I guess." She offered him a timid smile. "We should get you off the floor."

"Here, Xio."

She pulled free from Raph and looked up as MJ returned with an ice pack with a Velcro strap in one hand, her phone in the other, and his iPad tucked under his arm. She rolled her eyes at the fact that he'd taken the time to get the iPad from the family room. However, she was thankful that he was still too young to sense the sexual energy lingering in the air.

She took the ice pack from MJ, helped Raph sit up against the wall, then wrapped it around his shoulder. He winced when she secured it into place, sending pain cascading through her as if she, too, had suffered the injury. She beckoned for MJ to stay beside him as they helped him into the sitting room and onto the white leather sofa.

She stared at MJ. "You're lucky Raph isn't seriously hurt. He could have hit his head and gotten a concussion."

"I'm sorry, Raph, I—"

"Mr. Giannopoulos."

"What?" he asked, one corner of his mouth lifted in skepticism at his sister. "Mr. Gi…Gino…los…polos."

"He can just call me Raph," Raph said with scarcely contained humor at MJ's butchery of his name.

Xio boxed in her lips to keep from laughing out loud.

"I'm sorry, Raph," MJ said. "I didn't know you were Xio's boyfriend."

"He's not my boyfriend," she hissed through clenched teeth. *How many times did she have to say it?*

"Not yet, anyway." Raph winked at MJ.

"You sure you didn't hit your head?" Xio asked teasingly, at his attempt to put her little brother at ease.

MJ sat down next to him. "I'm really sorry I kicked you."

Raph squeezed his knee. "Apology accepted, MJ. I feel sorry for any burglar who comes up against you."

"Yes, we girls feel very safe with him around," Xio winked at her little brother who grinned at the praise he was getting. He looked so much like their father.

"Raph, oh good, you made it."

Xio raised her head to see her mother walking down the last few steps of the staircase, and crossing the spacious foyer. Claudia was wearing a red and white polka-dot apron over her peach dress. When her mother wore an apron, it meant she was in for some serious cooking.

Her mother had texted to let her know that Raph was coming for dinner, but Xio hadn't expected him to show up almost three hours early. She'd skipped her kickboxing lesson to get home in time to take a shower and put on something comfortable, even sexy, she was thinking, not greet him in clothes she'd been running around in all day long.

"My God! What happened to you?" Claudia gasped when she saw the ice pack under his shirt. "Did you get into an accident on the way here?"

"He fell," Xio said, when Raph hesitated and glanced uncertainly at her and then at MJ. There was no need to throw her little brother under the bus, just yet.

"What?" Claudia edged MJ out of the way and sat down next to Raph. She undid the Velcro strap and removed the pack from his shoulder. "Goodness! That was a nasty fall," she said in a flushed voice. She replaced the pack and pulled his shirt back into place.

Xio walked around the coffee table and sat down in a loveseat across from the sofa.

Malik came and sat next to her. He put his iPad next to the crystal vase of roses on the table, slid his hands under his thighs, and stared at Raph and Claudia. Xio knew her little brother must be dreading his fate once their mother found out that he had kicked Raph. She ruffled his curly hair affectionately.

MJ relaxed and leaned back against the cushion.

"How did it happen?" Claudia asked impatiently while she ran her hand through Raph's hair, apparently feeling for bumps on his head.

Xio peered at MJ out of the corner of her eye. His head was bent, his toes curling and uncurling on the Persian carpet, and his eyes fastened to the front cover of *Benin Bronzes: A Stolen History* lying on the table. MJ loved pouring over the worn pages of the coffee table book that was their father's favorite, tracing his little fingers over the photographs of the exquisite metal sculptures and plaques.

Xiomara didn't want to get him into trouble, and while she

might avoid telling the truth, she wouldn't lie outright for him—bad precedent to set, she thought, recalling how Fitzroy had relentlessly used her to lie for him when they were children. "It was MJ, Mom," she said. "He kicked Raph. That's why he fell."

"MJ!" Claudia shot her son a withering look. "Why would you do something like that?"

MJ's head shot up. His lower lip hung low, and his eyes filled with fear. "But, Mom, I—"

"He thought Raph was—" Xio began.

"It wasn't his fault." Raph spoke up on behalf of his attacker. "He thought I was a burglar."

"Well… There were some recent break-ins down the hill…" Claudia turned to MJ. "But MJ, you could have seriously hurt Raph. Or gotten hurt yourself! My God, imagine if he really was someone dangerous. Oh, MJ… Have you apologized to Raph?"

"He did. Profusely." Raph spoke up for MJ again.

His concern for and defense of her little brother were not lost on Xio.

"Really, it's okay, Claudia. I'm alright." He placed a reassuring hand on her arm. "It's just a little bruise. Trust me, I've had worse from my brothers. And at least no one can accuse MJ of cowardice," he added, smiling at the little man of the house.

Claudia shook her head in disappointment at her youngest child, while MJ sat back, relief spreading over his face.

Xio knew that both she and her mother were at fault for not telling MJ that they were having company. But she understood how it had slipped their minds. Claudia had been busy all day with her clients, and preparing the menu and the house, and Xio…well, she had more important things on her mind.

"You're sure you're okay?" Claudia asked, again, searching Raph's face for signs that he might be masking pain to protect MJ from being punished.

"I'm sure. I'm just sorry I caused so much commotion."

Claudia's face softened. "Not at all, Raph. I'm just so sorry you were hurt. Promise you'll let me know if you need something for the pain? Actually, you know what would be good for that?" she asked, poking tenderly at the icepack, her intelligent eyes dancing mischievously as she peered at Xio. "Maybe after dinner, Xiomara, you could take him for a soak in—"

"So, what are we having for dinner, anyway, Mom?" Xio cut her mother off. "It smells delicious in here?" She glanced at Raph, and was sure she detected a hint of amusement on his face.

"That's just the curried rice. And you know what we're having," Claudia added pointedly. "I sent you the menu." She turned to Raph. "Lamb, with my mint chimichurri, salad, squash, potatoes—I hope you like garlic."

"Sounds delicious," Raph said, grinning at Claudia. "I can't wait."

"Do you need help?" Xio wasn't quite sure if she wanted to be left alone with Raph after their *moment* on the floor.

"Cora and Meka did most of the prep work with the vegetables before they left," Claudia replied. "But I do need to get the sauces started. Excuse me, Raph." She stood to her feet. "I'll bring out something for you to snack on."

As her mother walked out of the sitting room, Xiomara shook her head in disbelief that she had actually tried to talk her into taking Raph to the hot springs after dinner. Sitting half-naked next to Raph was the absolute last place Xiomara wanted to be tonight. The way she was feeling about Raph would only lead to one thing—something she wasn't ready for. She couldn't afford another heartbreak.

"So, MJ, what type of martial art do you practice? I did karate when I was a kid," Raph said, ending the awkward silence in the wake of Claudia's departure.

"It's called *mdambé*," MJ said. "It's like karate, but better and harder 'cause you have to keep your balance while you kinda dance, like on a wave that's moving while you attack your challenger."

"Sounds cool, I've never heard of it. And you're so fluid. It did look like you were dancing on a wave."

"It started in Akilina," MJ said, excitedly. "It's from the Guaitiari who used to be slaves on other islands, and when they came to Akilina, they made it up. They brought it from Africa. Well, not all of it. It's similar to how the tribes used to fight in Africa, but they made new rules for it here."

"How long have you been practicing m…mdam…bé?"

"Since I was four. I got my red strip early." He rubbed his hands over the embroidered red cloth around his waist. "*Yanchi Nyoka*… Yanchi means teacher in mdambé. She says that I have the meanest *dapeo* and that I'm way ahead of everybody else."

"What's a dapeo?"

He gave Raph a sheepish grin. "Well, it's the kicks I gave you. It's a standing sweep kick with the heel."

"Ouch. It is mean," Raph said with a chuckle. "I hope never to be at the receiving end of another dapeo in my life."

"I'm sorry," MJ said again.

As Xio watched MJ, warmth bubbled up inside her. She loved that kid so much and would do anything to make sure he was happy.

Two years after their father died, Xio had thought that MJ needed some form of structure in his life, so she had encouraged their mother to enroll him in mdambé. At the very least, mdambé would provide a happy distraction from the chaos Fitzroy had been creating in their lives at the time. While vetting a couple schools, one of Xio's friends told her that Yanchi Nyoka had been a wonderful mentor and role model for his daughter after her mother passed away.

Even though MJ thrived under Yanchi Nyoka's instruction, Xio had sometimes wondered if he was still lacking a positive male influence, since he didn't have his father to guide him. She'd thought about transferring him to a different school with a male yanchi, but in the end, she had decided that perhaps gender wasn't important. What was important, though, was the fact that her little brother was happy, and she would do anything to keep it that way.

"You want me to teach you mdambé after dinner?" MJ asked in an excited voice. "You can teach me some karate moves."

As he scurried over to sit beside Raph, Xio could not deny the bond that was already forming between them.

"I haven't practiced karate for a long time," Raph answered, "but if you promise not to take me down again…" He pointed to his shoulder. "Sure. You can show me some of your moves and I'll show you some of mine."

"I promise not to hurt you again." MJ held out his fist.

"Okay. Let's do it." Raph said, fist bumping him.

Claudia returned, carrying a tray with chips, a bowl of fresh guacamole, her famous cauliflower parmesan bites, mini cassava toasts topped with diced tomatoes and basil, and a stack of plates.

"Can I help?" Raph stood up at the same time Xio did.

"No, you're the guest. Just sit back and relax. And I want no arguments from you," she added, as he was about to protest.

"Yes, Ma'am." He mimed zipping his lips and tossed an imaginary key over his shoulder, a playful grin on his face.

God, he was so sexy, even when he was being funny, Xio thought. And he was making her hotter and hotter by the second. "Mom, why don't we sit in the atrium. It's much cooler out there," she suggested, hoping the lush oasis of greenery, natural light, and mountain air would distract her from the thoughts swirling in her head about engaging in intimate combat with Rapheus Giannopoulos.

"Sure, honey. That's a good idea." Claudia walked toward the wall of folding glass doors that led to the screened outdoor room.

Xio stepped around the coffee table to open the door for her mother, but Raph beat her to it, his arm brushing against her stomach as he reached for the door latch. She stepped back as heat generated in her belly. *Not in front of my mother and my brother*, she told herself.

"If it's one thing my mother taught me, it's that I should always get a door for a lady. And I will accept no arguments," Raph stated, echoing Claudia's insistent that as her guest, he had no grounds for debate about helping.

Claudia chuckled, heartily. "Well, aren't you the perfect gentleman. Thank you, Raph. It's always nice to see chivalry in action."

"You are very welcome, Claudia." Raph pulled open the first frame of the door, and then the entire wall, letting the breeze flow through the house.

Needing something to do, Xio took one half of the tray and helped her mother down the two steps onto the polished marble floor. They placed the tray in the center of a square table made of rich, dark mahogany. Its surface, intricately carved with palm leaves and bougainvillea flowers, gleamed under the dappled sunlight filtering through the open retractable ceiling.

"Wow."

At the sound of Raph's voice, Xio turned around to catch a look of pure awe on his face as he descended the steps. He looked like a forest god, effortlessly blending in with the giant clay pots of palms trees, blooming orchids, and hibiscus strategically situated about the room.

"This is stunning," he exclaimed, leisurely strolling over to a section of a wall covered with lush ferns and a colorful array of wildflowers. "It's like being in the middle of a dense jungle."

"Thank you, Raph." Claudia's smile was bright and wide, reminding Xio of the lengths her father had gone to in order to create this captivating illusion of an inside jungle for his New

York City wife, who wasn't too keen on the real thing. "We like to spend a lot of time out here as a family."

"Or when one of us simply wants to relax alone," Xio added, pointing to the chaise lounges positioned around a stone fountain burbling gently in a corner. "That's my spot when it's raining cats and dogs outside and I have the house to myself."

"Maybe if it rains while I'm here, I'll come up and join you," he said, winking teasingly at her.

"You know, that sounds like a great idea, Raph." Claudia chuckled, then abruptly began to dole out orders. "MJ," she called to her son who was still inside on the sofa, his eyes glued to his iPad. "Go get the basket with the napkins and utensils from the counter. And wash your hands before you touch anything. Xiomara, bring out the pitcher of fruit punch. It's in the fridge. I had Meka make it with fresh passion fruit before she left. Rapheus, you sit down." She nudged her chin at four cushioned chairs with botanical print upholstery around the table.

"Where are Meka and Cora, anyway?" Xio asked, as her mother began setting out the plates.

"Cora's grandson is singing at a concert tonight, and Meka has a date. You know she hasn't been out much since her divorce. That bastard," she added under her breath. "Far be it from me to stand in the way of love. I mean—"

Xio clapped her hands, swiftly interrupting her mother before she went on a tangent about the pursuit of true love. "Who else wants something to drink?" She pointed to Raph. "Wine? Beer? Water? Or are you sticking to kiddie punch?"

He grinned. "I'll have whatever you're having, thanks."

"Xio, I put a bottle of Montrachet Grand Cru to chill. Is that okay with you, Raph?" Claudia asked.

"Yeah—yes, absolutely. That's one of my mom's favorite Chardonnays."

"It was your grandmother's, too," Claudia said, a hint of nostalgia in her voice.

"Then, that's what we'll have." Xio turned on her heels and walked toward the side door leading to the kitchen, almost colliding with MJ on his way back with the basket. "MJ, come back and help me with the drinks," she told him.

"Okay, Xio," he said in easy agreement, always eager to please his big sister.

Xio returned to the atrium with the punch in one hand, a corkscrew in the other, and a silver wine chiller bucket filled with ice and the Chardonnay under her arm. MJ trailed behind her with four wine glasses balanced precariously in his hands. Her mother was busy fixing Raph a plate while he sat on the edge of his seat watching, the corners of her lips curled. Xio realized that she liked seeing him squirm, knowing he wanted to help, but didn't dare.

MJ carefully set the four glasses next to the plates, then ran back inside.

Xio put the bucket on the end of the table farthest away from Raph, lifted the bottle, and deftly maneuvered the corkscrew between her fingers. With three twists and three quick moves, she opened the wine with a *pop!*

"Wow, you do that like a pro," Raph said.

"I'm a hotelier," she replied, pouring his glass first. "I hope I know how to at least open a bottle of wine by now," she added, while pouring a glass for her mother and herself.

"You've proven that you can," Raph said with a grin, as MJ returned with his iPad and sat in the chair next to him.

Warming inside to his compliment, Xio put the bottle back on ice. She then filled MJ's wine glass to the rim with passion fruit punch, while her mother finished filling the plates with appetizers.

She was about to sit in the chair in front of Mj when Claudia snatched it, leaving her with no other choice but to walk around the table and sit directly across from Raph. Her mother kept a straight face, but Xio knew it was a deliberate move to force her to face her insecurities about men.

Claudia raised her glass. "Let's toast to new friendships, and to those who brought us together."

"To friendships," Raph agreed, his gaze lingering on Xio's face.

The intensity in his eyes warned her that he wouldn't settle for just friendship. He wanted more. How much more, though? "Cheers," she said, clinking her glass to her mother's and Raph's, making sure to avoid physical contact with him.

"Mom, I can't lift my glass to toast. Xio gave me too much punch."

"No worries, buddy." Raph lowered his glass to MJ's and gently clinked it where it lay on the table.

Xio and Claudia followed suit.

"Oh, that's really good." Raph said, after they had taken their first sips of wine.

"Delicious," Claudia added on a second sip.

MJ put his mouth to the rim of his glass and slurped loudly before Claudia gave him a warning look. "Sorry, mom." He sat back, ran the back of his hand over his juice sainted lips, and opened the iPad resting on his lap.

Claudia directed a smile at Raph. "I sensed your anxiety because I won't let you help," she said. "In that, you remind me of my husband. He wasn't the kind of man who sat around and let women wait on him. He did the waiting in this house. Didn't he, Xio?"

"Yes, Mommy." Xio was always happy to talk about her father. "Daddy was an anomaly." She took a sip from her glass before maneuvering a chip loaded with guacamole into her mouth.

"I'll take the comparison as a compliment, then," Raph said, forking a cauliflower bite.

"It is of the highest level. Malik was a real gentleman."

Yes, her father was a gentleman, Xio silently acquiesced. He was the antithesis of her half brother, who was always contented to sit around while the women in his life waited on him.

"I have my mom to thank for my gentlemanly qualities," Raph said. "My brothers and I learned at an early age that if we wanted things done, we had to do them ourselves. With three boys to raise, she would have had to do a whole lot of waiting on, and she was not having it. She made sure we knew how to make a bed, cook, clean, and use the washing machine. She told us, point-blank, that she was not raising any spoiled brats."

"That's exactly how I raise my children," Claudia stated. "Did your mother ever remarry after your father passed?"

"Yes, but it didn't work out. They divorced after a few years." He fisted his hand resting on the table, and his eyes grew cold for a second.

"I'm sorry to hear that. Few people are lucky enough to find true love once in their lives, and even fewer the second time around." Claudia placed a cassava toast into her mouth and chased it down with a sip of wine.

"And far too many never find it at all," he said, a guarded look on his face as he placed a piece of tomato and basil toast into his mouth and chewed on it slowly.

"Which is a pity," Claudia murmured. "Everyone should experience true love at least once in their lifetime. I just hope that my daughters find men to love them as much as their father loved me, and that my son finds a woman who loves him as much as I loved his father."

"I think that's every parent's wish, Mom," Xio remarked, setting down her knife and fork and reaching for her wine glass. This talk of love was making her uneasy. She'd failed at it twice and she didn't need to be reminded of that. Xio still wanted the kind of love her parents had. The kind that reached beyond the grave, but she feared she would never have it.

Claudia glanced around. "Speaking of my daughters, where

is Akilah? Has anyone seen her? She told me she was going to the library to work on a project. MJ, go see if she's still there. Tell her to take a break and come and meet Raph."

"Okay, Mommy." MJ shoved a handful of chips into his mouth, got up, and walked into the sitting room.

"I don't like to bother them when they're doing schoolwork, but it's been two hours," Claudia said over the rim of her glass.

Xio thought she saw a shadow of unease flash across Raph's face. Before she could evaluate it, he stood, walked to the other end of the table where the bucket was, and refilled their wine glasses before reclaiming his seat. His lips were pressed firmly together, and there was a deftness in his movements as if talk of love made him uneasy, too.

MJ came running back to the table. "Akilah's not in the library," he said, settling into his chair.

Claudia shook her head. "That girl is going to be the death of me."

"Can me and Raph do mdambé after dinner, Mom?" MJ asked. "I want to teach him, and he's gonna teach me karate."

"I think we should leave mdambé and karate for another time. We don't want to exacerbate the injury to his shoulder."

"I'm fine, Claudia, really. As a matter of fact—" Raph set his glass down, reached beneath his shirt, and removed the icepack. "I think I've had enough icing."

"Are you sure?" Claudia took the icepack from him.

He rolled his shoulder back and forth and up and down a few times. "I'm very sure. I can hardly feel anything now."

"So… This means I can teach Raph mdambé then?" MJ asked.

"Well, I guess if Raph is still up for it later. He reserves the right to change him mind, though. Remember that."

MJ grinned at Raph. "Don't worry, I'll go easy on you," he said, popping a piece of cauliflower into his mouth and taking a sip of punch before curling his feet beneath him and returning to his game.

"This is so nice visiting with you," Claudia said to Raph. "You remind me so much of your grandfather. He loved my lamb and mint chimichurri. Every time he visited the island, I made sure to prepare it for him, at least once. While he and Malik entertained Xio, Kerena and I would sip this wine while we cooked."

"That's a really sweet memory, Mom," Xio murmured, reminiscing about her own faint memories of playing in the pool with her father and godfather.

"Thank you for sharing that memory, Claudia," Raph said with a catch in his voice, while reaching out to gently squeeze her hand lying on the table.

She chuckled. "Boy, could Andris eat. I was never confident I'd made enough food! I hope your appetite is as big as his was, Raph. This time around, I may have gone overboard."

"That's fine with me. I do have a big appetite." Raph eyed Xio over the rim of his glass as if to warn her that his large appetite wasn't limited to food.

Exactly what she didn't want to know. God help her.

Claudia glanced up at the sky. "Oh, my goodness. The sun is really going down. I had better finish dinner so we can still enjoy the sunset while we eat." Rising to her feet, she walked around the table and pulled the iPad from MJ's unsuspecting hands.

"Mom. I was just about to beat that level. Now I have to start all over again!" He crossed his arms in anger.

"Do you have homework, my boy?" Claudia asked in a calm voice as if she hadn't even heard him.

"I did it when I was waiting for Xio to pick me up." His mouth tightened with barely contained irritation.

"All of it?"

"I only had math." He held his hand out for the iPad.

"It's time for you to go upstairs and shower."

"But Mom—"

"MJ, now," she ordered in a firm but caring voice as she placed the iPad on the table.

MJ took a swift glance at Raph, jumped up, and stomped into the sitting room.

"You'd better lose that attitude, or I'll send you to bed right now. That means no mdambé with Raph later."

MJ halted in his tracks, then ran back and wrapped his arms around her waist. "I'm sorry, Mommy. I'll be good. I promise."

"I know, baby." Claudia brushed her palms over his dark curls then, bending over, she kissed his forehead. "Now, take your dirty dishes to the sink, and get upstairs."

MJ quietly did as he was told and slinked back inside.

"And while you're up there," Claudia called after him, "poke your head into your sister's bedroom, and if she's in there, tell her to come down and meet our guest."

"Okay."

Sighing, Claudia looked from Xio to Raph. "Dinner will be ready in an hour and a half. Xiomara, make Raph feel at home until then." She picked up her plate and glass from the table and made her exit.

Xio wished she had the guts to tell Raph she needed to shower and change before dinner, but her mother had asked her to entertain him.

He looked sexy in his loose tan slacks and green shirt, smelling fresh and clean like he just stepped out of the shower, while she was stuck in the clothes she'd been wearing all day.

"Come on. Let me show you the views." She picked up her glass and stood up.

"Sure." He grabbed his glass and immediately followed her to the screen door leading to a wide, tiled verandah.

She opened the door and let him walk out ahead of her, so she could admire his tight ass under his pants. She wondered how those perfectly shaped globes would feel in her hands.

Hmm. It's a moment of weakness, Xio. It's just a moment of weakness.

Chapter Thirteen

WILD GOOSE

"I thought the view from The Davenport was nice, but this is seriously amazing."

"It sure is." Xio was standing with Raph at the edge of the verandah. "That's the Caonabo River, and that's the Euka River," she said, pointing to where mountains dipped into a valley. "Those mountains over there are in Ynoa."

"Damn. With a view like this, I would sit out here all day. I'd set up my home office right here."

Xio smiled. Eagle's Nest was the most coveted home on Akilina and Xio was so grateful that her family didn't need the income from Jewel Beach to sustain it. Her father had made sure of that by paying off the mortgage he'd taken out for the latest renovations, and by leaving her mother with more than enough to take care of the twenty-five-acre estate for the next hundred years and beyond.

"My dad built this home in 1978," she told Raph. "Well, he pulled down the old shack that was here, and built this more modern home. He and mom have done renovations here and there over the years."

"It's lovely," he murmured, then added, "Perfect," as he gazed into the distance, taking in the view.

Xio placed her glass on the railing and rubbed her hands up and down her arms. She'd brought Raph outside because she didn't want anyone overhearing their conversation.

"What is it?" He cocked his head. "Something bothering you?"

Crap. He could read her that easily? She dropped her gaze to the floor and leaned against the railing, trying to figure out how to broach the subject. She raised her lids to find a fixed expression in his emerald-green eyes. "MJ likes you, Raph." She forced restraint and curtesy into her tone. "Which is why..." She paused, searching for the right words to continue.

"Which is why?" He spread his hand in question.

She shook her head and shifted her weight. "No, never mind."

"What were you going to say, Xio?" Raph asked in an uncompromising, yet oddly gentle voice.

She straightened her back and raised her head. "I don't want MJ to get hurt."

His jaw twitched. "How would he get hurt?"

"Because...." Xio picked up her glass and twirled the stem between her fingers while she thought of the best way to explain what she meant.

"What makes you think I would hurt him, Xiomara?"

"You wouldn't, intentionally, Rapheus." She took a deep breath. "MJ is already getting very attached to you."

He stood still with one hand thrust deep inside his pocket, the other tight around his wine glass. "Is that a bad thing?"

He sounded annoyed, she thought. "MJ is starved for masculine interaction. He's soaking up everything you throw his way. What do you think is going to happen when you go home and forget about him?"

His laugh resounded around the verandah. "You think I

could ever forget about an eleven-year-old kid who kicked my ass?"

Xio couldn't help the smile that parted her lips. "Okay, well, you have a point there," she said.

"All jokes aside, trust me, I know how MJ feels. I was six when my father died. My mother remarried four years later because she thought my brothers and I needed a father figure. Her husband turned out to be anything but fatherly."

He paused, his eyes hardening as they'd done when Claudia had asked him if his mother had ever remarried.

He sucked air into his lungs. "Bob was more interested in tunneling his way through the money my father left us. Anyway, I meant what I said. I won't forget about MJ."

"That's very sweet of you to say. But why?"

"Why?" he reiterated her question. "Why do I like your family when I've only just met you? I don't know, Xiomara." He chuckled warily. "Maybe it has something to do with my family's connection to the island that my pappoús was supposed to tell your dad about. Maybe it involves your family, too."

"If only he had told him what it was—or told you. But we may never know what that was about." She didn't like the thought of her family having anything to do with his family's disturbing secret, but she kept that to herself.

He leaned against the support beam. "Maybe not, but I haven't been able to take my mind off it—of all the things your mom told me yesterday."

"I can understand that." Xio hadn't been able to take hers off what she'd read in her godfather's letter. She was still trying to figure out a way to let Raph know she would take him to Ynoa and to Kaiah without telling him that it was what his grandfather wanted. She couldn't imagine what truths Andris had been hiding from his grandson, or why she'd been roped into all of it.

She winced at the sharp pangs of hunger in her stomach.

"Do you mind if we go back inside? I haven't eaten since breakfast and I don't think I can wait until dinner."

BACK IN THE ATRIUM, Xio finished off the bowl of guacamole with the rest of the chips between sips of wine. When she looked up, Raph was standing behind a chair, his eyes dusted with the same kind of desire as when he was lying flat on his back after MJ had taken him down. "I told you I was hungry," she said, defensively.

He leaned on the back of the chair, his fingers curling around the polished wood. "You know, you're very sexy when you eat."

What, does he have a food fetish? And yet his words sent a flash of lust through her core. She licked her lips and shifted to stop the quivering in her sex. This man was dangerously sexy, and he was making her want things she hadn't wanted in a long time. Or maybe she'd wanted them, but was too afraid to go after them. "You shouldn't say things like that," Xio said, looking around. "Someone could hear you."

Raph pulled the chair out and sat down. "There's no one here but the potted plants, and who's going to care anyway." He held her gaze. "I just wanted to let you know that, in case you were wondering. You're very sexy."

As much as her body wanted what his eyes and words were suggesting, Xio wasn't ready. She didn't know if she would ever be ready. "I wasn't wondering," she said with an arched brow. That was all she was going to say, and it was time to change the subject. "I know I don't remember a lot about him, but it's strange to think that your grandfather never told anyone about us. Never talked to you about my parents. Were you two close?"

"Very close. He was my best friend when I was growing up." He lowered his gaze to the table and traced a finger along the outline of a bougainvillea flower carved in the wood. Finally, he raised his head, and Xio detected a mistiness in his eyes. "But like

I said yesterday, everything I know about Akilina…he waited until minutes before his death to tell me. We were with him for almost two weeks before he died, and he never hinted that there was something he needed to get off his chest."

His sadness seeped into Xio's pores. "Oh, Raph. I'm so sorry. I didn't realize it happened like that."

"It was so out of the blue, and he was so vague. I mean—" Raph leaned back and tilted his head to the sky before bringing his attention back to Xio. "In fairness, he wasn't able to say much in those last moments. But if I'd only had ten more minutes with him, I could have gotten some of the answers I need. Now, I can only guess at why he did what he did." He sighed wearily. "He took my dad and grandmother's deaths really hard."

Xio crossed her ankles and stared at the row of cacti along the inside wall of the atrium. She wished she could share the contents of Andris' letter with him, let him know how much his grandfather regretted not telling him what he wanted to. "Well, naturally, I'm sure he did. That had to have been such a traumatic event for your family. My mom told me what happened this morning. She'd been sparing me all these years. How terrible…"

"Yes, but…you see, he was never really able to talk about them again. He didn't erase them from his life… He still kept their personal items around the house, and he kept some of my grandmother's dresses in her closet right where she'd left them. But he could never talk about them or their deaths. He became fragile, in a way. Almost reclusive, except with us—me, my brothers, and my mom, I mean. I just wish he'd been able to open up to me more. I wish he had trusted me."

Xiomara remembered Andris' words in his letter. The pain had been too great for him to maintain his relationship with her own parents after his devastating loss. "I'm sure he did trust you, Raph. After all, it was you he asked to carry out his last request."

He reached across the table and emptied the rest of the wine from the bottle into their glasses, then took a long sip from his before placing the glass back on the table.

Remembering how she had finished off a whole bottle by herself yesterday, Xio was tempted to offer him something stronger to numb his pain. "So, what did you do today?" she asked, sensing that he'd reached his limit and didn't want to talk about his grandfather's last moments, anymore. "Did you get a chance to explore Akilina?"

"A little bit. I went to the library in town."

"Oh. Did you find out anything about your family?" She folded her arms across the edge of the table.

"No, but I read about an Eagle Davenport, an escaped slave who came here from Barbados in a boat with some other people. It was intriguing to read about the major role he played in the wars against the colonists. I wasn't sure if he was the same Davenport…if you are related to him."

Xio smiled. "He is. I am."

"Wow, the Davenports have been here a long time."

"Yes, he was actually the first escaped slave to come here. It was because of him that so many others found freedom here, too."

"Your family must be very proud to be related to him."

"We are." Xio felt the familiar smile playing on her lips every time she spoke of Eagle. "Actually, in appreciation for leading multiple attacks on the French and British, the chief gifted Eagle this land and offered him the hand of his daughter, Princess Ismé. He built his first home here and called it Eagle's Nest." She waved her hand around. "Generations of Davenports have always lived here."

"Your family is steeped in history and royalty. I'm… Wow." He sat back and spread his hands, his eyes and voice lathered with admiration and reverence.

Xio wondered what he would say when she told him that, not only was she a descendent of Eagle, and about his family history, but that she was also the great-granddaughter of Dacica Kaiah, the most powerful person on the island, and that she was the Princess Xiomara of Ynoa. "Anyway, did you fill out your application to travel to Ynoa?" she asked, deciding he'd been awed enough for now.

"Yeah."

"That's good. How did it go?"

"The agent said he didn't see any reason for my application to be denied. But he also had me fill out a form for the sub-chief of Yacao. He said I needed her permission to scatter their ashes in her village."

"Oh, sorry. I forgot to mention that."

"If I'm denied, what's the worst that could happen?" he uttered a shaky laugh. "I take their ashes back to San Francisco with me? It's not the end of the world, or the least of my problems." He leaned forward and, dropping his elbows on the table, he buried his face in his hands and growled.

Xio felt his annoyance. Maybe this would be the time to tell him that she would take him to Ynoa. Tell him who Kaiah was and that she might be able to answer some of his questions. She'd been looking for a way to bring it up without being too obvious, and without alerting him to the letter and the motivation behind her offer.

He suddenly sat up straight. "There's something in my gut telling me that this wild goose chase to Aetós has something to do with my family's connection to the island. I don't know why. It's just there." He pressed his fists into his stomach, then leaned toward her. "Maybe there are answers in the letter my pappoús wrote to you. Have you read it yet?"

"Whoa, whoa, whoa. Be still my beating heart."

At the sound of her sister's voice, Xiomara turned her head to see her standing in the doorway between the atrium and the sitting room.

She could kiss Akilah.

Chapter Fourteen

GOSSIP GIRL

Tall and pretty with a moon-shaped face, Akilah did look at least twenty years old.

"Hi," Raph said, standing, and instantly regretting his overly exuberant tone.

"You must be Raph."

"I am. And you are Akilah, I suppose."

Her hand went dramatically to her chest, and she fluttered her eyelashes. "You know my name? How sweet."

"Well, it's not that hard to figure out, Akilah," Xio said, rising to her feet and pinning her sister with a cautionary glare.

Akilah sucked her teeth and sent her a dismissive flash of the eye.

"You're the only one in the family he hasn't met yet," Xio noted. "So don't go reading anything into it."

Raph folded his arms. From what Xio had told him about Akilah, he knew she was trying to rein in the girl's callow and misplaced advances. "Xiomara is right," he said, in a deliberately silvery tone, as he took a step back from her. "I met your mom and sister yesterday, and I just met MJ. You were the missing Davenport, Akilah."

"Well, I'm not missing anymore. Am I?" She giggled, exposing her naivety. "It's nice to meet you," she said, offering him her hand.

He took her hand, but before he could return the pleasantries, MJ, still in his mdambé uniform, appeared beside his sister, looking as formidable as Raph remembered.

MJ deftly untangled Akilah's hand from his. "He's Xio's boyfriend. So back off, Akilah!" he said with reproach.

Akilah rolled her head toward Xio. "Why didn't you just tell me, then? Finally! You have a boyfriend! And he is hot!" She gave Raph an approving once-over. "Way hotter than Trevor, if you ask me. Owww, sisterrrr!" She raised her hand for a high five.

Xio ignored her on a groan and threw her hands into the air. "Raph is not my boyfriend. MJ, stop saying he's my boyfriend!"

"Well, you were looking at each other like boyfriend and girlfriend when I brought you the ice."

"What are you talking about, MJ?" Xio sighed.

"With goggly eyes. Like they do on TV when they're in looove," he said in a comical tone before pulling his iPad from the table, and running back inside.

Xio stiffened, and as her hands clenched at her sides, Raph couldn't help but relish the memory of making googly eyes with her.

"Well, if you're not claiming him, I guess he's fair game." Akilah's voice was silky and laced with the kind of danger Raph was sure she was still too young to understand.

He pinned Akilah with a measured stare. "I don't play games, Akilah. And I definitely don't play them with kids."

She was visibly taken aback and embarrassment shadowed her face, but she quickly regained her countenance and lifted her chin. "I don't play games either, man. I was just saying…"

"That I'm hot. I get it," he appended, to set her at ease.

"Right." She gave him a smile that made him feel like he'd passed her test and somehow gained her respect. "You get it."

I do. It wasn't unusual for girls her age to swoon over him. In Akilah's case, Raph was beginning to suspect that her come-ons were, in fact, just a game to her. But even if she didn't have any intentions of following through, she was playing with fire.

"So, Raph, my mom says your grandpa used to know my dad."

"That's what I was told."

"Did you know him? My dad, I mean?" Her voice underlined the need to build any connection she could with her dad, no matter how distant.

"Unfortunately, not." He glanced at Xio, who seemed contented to stay out of the conversation. He hadn't missed the relief on her face when Akilah's interruption had spared her from answering his question about his grandfather's letter. He wondered if she would have answered him truthfully. Had she read it or not? That was the burning question.

"You're staying at The Davenport, so that means you have money, right?" Akilah asked.

"You could say that." He shrugged.

"Like, how much would you say?" she asked tongue-in-cheek, daring him to answer.

"Akilah, you shouldn't ask people questions about their money. Especially someone you don't know."

"Of course she should. How else are you supposed to get to know someone if you don't ask questions?" He flashed a meaningful grin at Xio. "I've got a few billions, Akilah."

Akilah balked "You're a billionaire?"

"Yep."

"I think you're the first billionaire I've met. But you seem cool. I could lime with you."

Raph chortled. "Well, thank you, Akilah. I try to be cool, and I'm glad you think you can lime with me, whatever that means."

"It means…" She rolled her eyes. "You Americans call it hanging out."

"Oh. Then sure, we can lime."

"It seems you and Akilah are getting along quite well," Xio said.

"Yeah, I think we are. Right, Akilah?"

"Mhm." She nodded eagerly.

"Perfect. So, you won't mind if I excused myself. I have some things to take care of before dinner."

The fact that Xio felt comfortable leaving him alone with Akilah, told him that she trusted him not to get tangled up in her little sister's web. He was glad for that. But that he *wanted* her trust in the first place, had him scratching his head.

"I'll see you in a bit, then. Akilah, why don't you give Raph a tour of the house."

"Ooo, aren't you lucky. Only special guests get a tour of Eagle's Nest."

"I guess I'm a special guest, then."

"Behave yourself, Akilah," Xio said before leaving them.

Raph watched her until she disappeared from view, loving the subtle sway of her hips. When he turned around, Akilah was sitting in MJ's chair with her feet drawn up under her and a plateful of cauliflower balanced on her thighs.

"You mind if I have a snack before I give you the *tour*?"

She said *tour* like it was a dreaded task she had been forced to perform a million times.

"We don't have to, you know." After all, he hadn't come to see the house. He'd come to see Claudia and Xio and… He eased down into the chair that Xio had occupied. The faint lingering smell of her perfume teased his nose.

Akilah observed him dubiously through narrowed eyes as she nibbled on the parmesan bites. "You sure there's nothing going on between you and my sister? 'Cause she sure is acting like she likes you, and you're acting like you like her. The way you look at her, man…"

"I do like her." That much was easy to admit. As for the "something" going on between them… Well, he couldn't talk about what he did not yet understand. He wanted to believe that had he and Xio met under normal circumstances—running into each other at a party, catching each other's eyes as they passed on the street, or introduced by a mutual friend—they would have already found themselves together in bed. "How do you know your sister likes me?"

"Duh." Akilah smirked as if he should know the signs. "By acting like she *doesn't* in front of people. As soon as I showed up, she was cutting her eyes at you behind your back."

"She was?"

"Mm-hm. And she got all weird when MJ said you were her boyfriend." She poured some fruit punch into Xio's empty wine glass.

Raph waited while she drank, deliberately taking her time, and then refilled the glass.

"She's been weird around guys ever since—" Akilah paused to take another sip of punch. "She was screwed over twice, you know."

"Twice?" He knew he shouldn't indulge Akilah, but he couldn't help himself. He was anxious to get his fill of the gossip dripping from her tongue.

"Mm-hm. Some college boyfriend broke her heart. I think he was her first. And then, like five years ago, this assho—"

She stopped and eyed him warily, apparently waiting for him to chastise her for using inappropriate language. Raph had no idea what the man had done, but if he'd hurt Xio, he was an asshole, so in this case, he had no intentions to criticize Akilah for speaking her mind. "Go on," he prompted, with a swipe of his wrist.

She sucked her teeth in disgust. "This guy, Trevor, he cheated on her. He got another girl pregnant while they were engaged. I mean, that's just…nasty. And then he went and married the baby's mom."

"How did the first guy break her heart?" he asked, holding his breath.

Akilah set her plate down on the table, finished her drink, and sat back. "I don't know," she said on a shrug. "I was like five or six at the time. I think I remember him coming down here a few times. Anyway, a few years ago, I heard Xio talking about it on the phone with her high school friend in New York."

"Were they high school sweethearts?"

"Uh-uh. She went to an all-girls boarding school in New York that Mom went to." She rolled her eyes. "Boring. Last year, Mom tried to ship me off to that same nunnery, but she backed off when I threatened to run away."

Raph had no doubt that Akilah would have held her promise if she was forced to do something she didn't want to. Maybe she didn't want to leave Jamon behind.

"Anyway, she met this boy in college and they were together for a couple years. I don't know why they broke up, but it messed her up real bad. And it was right after Daddy died, too." Akilah's voice spewed anger. "I mean, couldn't he have waited until she'd healed a little?"

As detached as he was from the women he dated, Raph couldn't imagine doing something that heartless.

"So," Akilah continued, "between him and Trevor, my sister's all messed up when it comes to guys. Trust issues, you know? And I can't say I blame her. Men are toads." She made a gurgling sound of disgust in her throat, then grimaced. "Well, most of them."

"There are a lot of two-legged toads walking around." He wanted to crush the two who had hurt Xio. Ice inched through his veins even as he mulled over Akilah's brief account of Xio's heartbreaks.

He had to tread lightly with Xiomara from here on out. The last thing he wanted was to disappoint her or cause her any more pain. Once he scattered his grandparents' ashes, he was leaving Akilina. And once he left, he planned to forget that he'd ever met Xiomara Jewel Davenport.

Like that could ever happen.

His and Akilah's phones went off at the same time. They both fished them from their pockets. It was a group text message from Claudia. Despite his impulse to leave them and forget them, he smiled, feeling like a member of the Davenport family.

"Dinner's—" They both started to say, and then laughed together.

Chapter Fifteen

ALLIANCE

"Dinner will be ready in forty-five minutes," Akilah said, her eyes glued to her phone as she scrolled through it.

Raph was disappointed that their conversation about Xio had been interrupted, but at least now he would understand any hesitations she might have about sleeping with him.

They stood, and Akilah slid her phone into the side pocket of her denim shorts. "We have plenty of time for a tour before dinner," she said, smiling up at him.

It was a big house, but he hoped the tour wouldn't take that long. He was hoping to spend some more alone time with Xio.

"Well, you've seen the atrium. It's nice out here when you want to be outside, but not outside-outside."

"Indoor-outdoor living. I get it."

"Right." She stepped into the sitting room. "This is where Mom entertains," Akilah said, rolling her eyes and making a flourishing sweep with her hands. "It's all very posh and elegant."

She pointed to her right. "That side door takes you to the kitchen and the family room. But Mom doesn't like anyone in there when she's cooking. Come on," she added, hooking a finger, and pretending to drag him along with her.

"So, what kind of work do you do? You look kind of young to be a billionaire. Did you inherit money from your dad or something?"

He was beginning to love Akilah's candidness. She asked the questions adults were too afraid to ask. "Eventually, I got some money from my dad, yeah, but by then, the company my brothers and I started was already successful. We didn't need our dad's money, so we gave most of it away to charity, and set up some scholarship funds for kids in the cities where we live."

"That's cool. I want to do stuff like that, helping people, you know, like my dad used to do. He gave money to our schools and helped people start their own businesses. He even started an intern program so people could train to be chefs and open their own restaurants. I want to help people, too," she repeated with passion this time.

"And I'm sure you will."

She stopped in the foyer at the bottom of the marble staircase.

"I can't take you upstairs," she said, "but there are four bedrooms up there, and each with its own bathroom, sitting area, and verandah. Mom's room is on this side." She pointed up to her left. "Xio's is over there on the right, and me and Malik are over this way. They get a view of the ocean and part of the mountains, but we just get mountain views. I think I like the mountain better anyway, except the sun shines right into my bedroom in the morning, which sucks. I am so not a morning person." Akilah groaned.

"That's the powder room." She pointed to the back of the stairwell as they left the foyer and took a right turn down a hall, similar to the one through which Raph had entered the house. "And these stairs go down to the game room and TV room. That's where me and MJ hang out when we have friends over. You into video games?" she asked.

"My brothers and I used to be when we were kids."

"How many brothers do you have?"

"Two. We're triplets."

"Triplets. Dang. In there is the library." She waved her hand dismissively as she passed the opened door.

Raph followed her, catching only a glimpse of an overly crowded bookcase, a blue armchair, and a round polished wooden table in the center of the room.

"Mom makes me study in there. MJ can do his homework in his room, but she says I get too easily distracted. I don't really. I just think most of my classes are so easy. I'd rather be doing anything else."

"I'm sure you would."

"Anyway, I can't imagine two more of me. Are you and your brothers identical?"

"No, but we do look a lot like each other. You can tell we are brothers." He pulled his phone from his back pocket and scrolled through his photos, turning the screen so Akilah could see. "This is Tele, the youngest, and this is Neo," he said, pointing.

She scrunched up her face. "Mmm. Rich and cute. You guys must get a lot of girlfriends, huh." She tilted her head and looked at Raph with speculation. "Is that why you and Xio aren't... Do you have a girlfriend?"

"No," he said, way too quickly. "I'm not seeing anyone. But Xio and I just met, and I'm only here for a week."

She folded her arms. "So you're saying that all you need is a little more time?"

"Oh, Akilah." He met her challenging stare. "You are good. And I'm not saying anything." He tapped his finger to his nose, just like he did when his seventeen-year-old cousin, Sebastian, tried to psychoanalyze him.

"Whatever you say, Raph. Anyway, here's the dining room. Mom had the table laid since before I left for school this morning. She's such an overachiever," she added with a playful eye roll. "I definitely didn't get that from her."

Raph was in awe of the crystal chandelier suspended over the table set with gold leaf porcelain and crystal. He was beginning to think he'd underdressed, and the aromas coming from the kitchen made him hungrier.

They headed back toward the foyer and Akilah pointed off to her left. "There are two guest rooms down there, but they're being renovated, so I can't go down that way."

"No problem. I know what guest rooms look like."

"Right. So, how did you and your brother's start your company? Where'd you get the capital if you didn't yet have your dad's money?" she asked, as they entered the foyer.

Raph was beginning to think that Akilah was gravely misunderstood. She was a breath of fresh air, and sharp. He imagined G3 could use someone with her tactics. "You can accomplish anything you put your mind to," he said, his voice portraying his growing fondness for her. "But I won't lie to you. Our name didn't hurt us. And the fact that we didn't have to worry about student loans or work our way through college made things a lot easier. We had a very privileged life, just like you. But after we pooled our money, bought, and flipped our first property, it didn't take long before we were able to convince an investor that we had what it took to build something great."

"Maybe you can teach me the basics of starting my own company, then."

"What kind of company are you thinking of?" They stopped at the alcove under the stairs.

"Marketing and advertising. Global Horizons Marketing," she stated, moving her palms through the air as if reading the sign. "It's going to be the biggest marketing company on the planet."

Raph weighed her with a meritorious squint, awed that she already knew what she wanted to do with her life, and had the name of her company picked out. Her sense of self-determination mirrored his, Neo's, and Tele's, who started paying attention to real estate when they were in high school. "That's pretty impressive, Akilah. Do your mom and sister know about your ambitions?"

"Hardly. Xio is so busy with JBR, and Mom with her business." She shrugged nonchalantly as they continued walking past the sitting room toward the hallway where Raph had first entered the house. "They don't think much of me, anyway. They're more worried that I'm going to end up a teen mom or do something to mess up my life. They think I'm a total wreck. One of these days, I'll surprise them," she added, with an obstinate ring to her tone. Her eyes were filled with determination. "Maybe we can work together in the future. That is if you ever decide to do business on the island." She halted in mid-step. "Oh, but wait, you can't."

"Why not? Hey, I'd get into business with you. I'm always looking for fresh ideas."

"Because of the land ownership laws."

"What are those?" he asked, his gut tightening as they passed the spot where he had come face-to-face with MJ.

"Only people born on the island can buy land," Akilah, said as they walked down the corridor he'd passed on his way into the house.

"Really?" He wondered if his grandfather ever bought land here. And if he did, who owned it now that he was dead?

"Stupid law if you ask me." She stopped at a door on the left and opened it. "This is my mom's office. She calls it her creative pad. You know she's a fashion designer, right?" Akilah asked.

"She told me." Raph took a swift glance inside the meticulously organized room. It was filled with racks of clothes, three sewing machines, bolts of fabric stacked high on tables and against the walls, and cork boards covered with sketches and fabric samples.

"About the property-owning laws," he said, as they moved on, "I have to disagree with you. They keep money and power-hungry people like me from ruining your beautiful island."

"Yeah, but it's not everybody who's out to exploit us. They could still let people like my mom buy land. She's been married and living here for more than thirty years, and the only way she was able to even own our house was because my dad left it to her in his will. So the person they love has to die first. I don't think it's right or fair. One of my friends in school wants to be a politician and get our government to amend the laws, and maybe allow people to buy property if they've been married and living here for like ten years or something."

"Well," Raph said, impressed, "that's progress in the making. Just tell your friend to make sure the law still protects you and future generations."

"Yeah, yeah, yeah, I'll tell her."

They stopped at the last room. "Hey, Raph." Akilah placed her hand on his arm. "Would you want to come to my school as a guest speaker? I'm the president of Career Club and we're always looking for people to come talk to us. Could you come to our next meeting? It's next Friday."

"I'm sorry, Akilah, but I'm leaving on Friday."

"Can't you leave on Saturday instead?" She stared at him like she was pleading with her father to let her go to the school dance.

"I can't, Akilah, I have a meeting on Saturday."

"A meeting on a Saturday? What's the point of being your own boss if you can't slide a meeting here and there?"

Raph grinned. "You don't get to be the boss by slacking off. I'm sure Xio and your mom would tell you that. My company's reputation is only as good as my own. Rescheduling meetings whenever I feel like it is a sure way to cause others to lose trust in my company."

"I'm sure whoever you're meeting with won't mind getting their Saturday off," she insisted, batting her thick lashes at him.

What was it about the Davenports that touched him so deeply? Yesterday, he had stood between Xio and her fire-breathing mother. This afternoon he had earnestly defended MJ after the boy attacked him. And now, here he was thinking of changing his flight to speak at Akilah's school. "All right, you win. I'll be there."

"Thank you!" She threw her arms around his waist and hugged him tightly.

Raph squeezed her gently. She was a sweet kid. He put some space between them. "I'll cancel my meeting, but I want you to do something for me in return."

Her eyes narrowed, and her lips twisted dubiously.

"When I…" He paused. He had to choose his words carefully. Akilah had just shared her aspirations with him—something she hadn't shared with her own family, and he had promised to speak at her school. He wanted to create a level of trust between them, and that could only happen if he admitted that he'd heard her conversation earlier. He cleared his throat. "Earlier, when I—"

Her phone buzzed. She pulled it from her pocket and frowned as she glanced at the screen. "Hold on a minute." She placed it to her ear and walked a few feet away with her back to him, but stayed close enough for him to hear her.

"Hey… No… That's fine… I— um… I can't see you tonight. 'Cause I can't. Trust me, if I could get away, I would."

Raph grinned as her little lie confirmed his suspicions that Jamon was on the other end of the call. He still didn't know if Jamon was a boy her age, or a man too old to be messing with her.

"I'm sorry you already swiped them… I know… I've stolen liquor before… Just put them back or…or just hide them in your room or something… I'll try to sneak out tomorrow night."

Raph didn't know what the drinking age was here, but as a teenager growing up in the States, the only way to get liquor was to steal it from your parents' stash or get someone older to buy it for you. If Jamon had stolen his, he hoped that meant he was Akilah's age.

"Excuse me?" she exploded, holding up her hand and sticking a finger in the air. "Listen, I can change my mind anytime I want." She gasped. "What was that? You are giving *me* an ultimatum? So, you think you own me because we— Uh-uh." She stomped her bare foot. "No, you be quiet. Nobody gives me ultimatums, and if you want to go be with Keya, be my damn guest. Boy, bye!" She ended her call and let out a growl before turning around.

Raph was grateful for the miraculous timing of Jamon's call, and as she walked back to him, he applauded the way Akilah had handled him. "Boy trouble?" he asked, tongue in cheek.

Akilah rolled her eyes in apparent irritation. "Just some stupid boy who thinks he owns me because we made out a couple times. I was going to sneak out after dinner and meet up with him, but now..." She sucked her teeth. "I don't even know if I want to—" Her hand flew to her mouth. "You're not going to tell my mom or Xio, are you?"

"Tell me and Mom what?"

Raph's head shot up as Akilah spun around.

His eyes hungrily swept down Xio's body as she approached them from the back stairs. She looked delicious in a floor-length floral-print dress, the thin straps and low cut neckline making him twitch. Her hair was pulled back from her face and twisted into a thick, long braid that rested across one shoulder.

As she came closer, he fought the urge to tell Akilah to get lost so he could do adult things with her sister. A round pendant on a beaded gold chain lay cozily between her breasts. He was jealous of that little gem glowing against her brown skin. It was as if his heart had suddenly developed a life force of its own and wanted more than physical gratification—the only thing he has ever wanted from a woman.

"Ahem." Xio cleared her throat.

He pulled his eyes away from her chest to find her face shrouded in expectation.

"What don't you want Raph to tell me and Mom?" she asked her little sister.

"It's a surprise," Akilah said.

"What kind of surprise?"

Akilah glanced up at him with uncertainty.

He placed his hands on her shoulders and gave her a reassuring squeeze. "If we tell you, then it would no longer be a surprise. Would it?"

Xio smirked. "Really, Raph? That old, tired line is the best you can come up with?"

"It may be old and tired, but it's the truth," Raph said.

"Whatever. Anyway, I really do hate to break up your little covert alliance, but Akilah, Mom needs your help in the kitchen."

"Argh… Can't you help her? I'm still showing Raph around."

"I'll show him the rest of the house. Go on," she coaxed when Akilah glared at her. "Mom's waiting, and we're all starving."

Akilah sucked her teeth. "See you at dinner, Raph."

"Of course."

Watching her walk away, Raph got the feeling that more than anything, Akilah was just plain bored out of her mind. With her intelligence and ambition, she probably felt as trapped on this little island as he used to feel on Santorini.

"She really likes you," Xio said, tilting her head back to study him. "She doesn't like a lot of people, and not a lot of people seem to take to her so quickly."

"Maybe a lot of people are reading her the wrong way." A smile tickled the corners of his mouth. "I find her very easy to like."

"As opposed to me?" she quipped. "You said the same thing about my mother yesterday." Her perfectly arched eyebrows raised a fraction. "What do you think about me?"

"I'm thinking… You look lovely in that dress." It was the first compliment he'd given on her looks, and he liked seeing her blush. "The thing is, you're stunning in everything I've seen you in so far, Xiomara."

"Wow, Rapheus." Her blush grow brighter. "That's unexpected. Thank you." She placed her hand on the gold handle of the door they were standing in front of, and turned her head as if to hide her feelings—whatever they were—from him.

What he really wanted to say was that his head had been spinning with fantasies about her, that even though she looked good in everything she wore, it would blow his mind to see her wearing absolutely nothing at all, shivering as his fingertips trailed across her breasts then circled her nipples. He'd said as much, and more, to other women, just to help them make up their minds about joining him in bed.

But Xiomara was different, and after spending more time with Akilah, he'd decided that sex with Xiomara was no longer on the table. He was getting too close with her family, and he respected and liked her too much to play with her emotions. And the thought of Akilah adding him to her list of toads was distressing.

Although he'd only known Xio for a short time, he couldn't imagine what could have possessed both of her exes to break her heart.

"This was my father's office." Xio pushed down on the handle and opened the door.

Chapter Sixteen

NOSTALGIA

The moment Raph stepped into Malik Davenport Sr.'s office, he felt his grandfather's presence wrapping around him like an old cloak, and the memories Claudia had shared began playing out in his mind like a movie scene: the two men sitting at the mahogany desk in the center of the room, relaxing on the patio that overlooked a sloped forest of trees, joking around as they sipped cognac, or rum, or whatever Malik poured from the black marble-topped bar in a corner of the room, while talking about their families, businesses, and future endeavors.

Raph was a master at camouflaging his feelings and shading what was really going on in his head. He'd played the role well with the Davenports, so far. But here, in this private room filled with memories, and in the presence of Xiomara, a woman who rocked his heart off rhythm every time he thought of her, he felt his façade melting away, and he made no attempt to maintain it.

He blinked back the stinging tears blurring his vision. "My pappoús did spend a lot of time in here, just like your mom said. I can feel him. And for the very first time, even though I never met him, I can feel your dad, too," he said, giving voice to his thoughts.

"Yeah. Me, too," Xio replied in a choked voice. "Every time I came in here, I used to only sense my dad's presence. But after today, listening to Mom talk about them, I can feel my godfather's, too. Their spirits are here. I don't think they'll ever leave."

Raph heard her sniffle behind him, but he didn't turn around. It was one thing to admit to himself that his façade was melting, but quite another to announce it to the world. "I hope they never do."

His eyes zeroed in on the cigar box at one end of the desk. "Arturo Fuente was one of Pappoús favorite brands," he said, sniffing the faint notes of dark chocolate, molasses, and spice that lingered in the air.

"Dad's, too, of course," Xio said. "I used to sit out on the patio with him while he smoked them. My mom hated the smell, and seriously, so did I, but having that quality time with him was worth it. Don't tell my mother, but once or twice a year, I'll come in here and savor one, just to feel close to him."

"Good for you." Raph closed his eyes and allowed his mind to rewind to evenings in Santorini and in Napa when he and his brothers and their grandfather smoked together. He was sure, that like Xio, he and his brothers will continue to savor one or two Arturo Fuente in his memory.

He swallowed to ease the tightness in his throat. "Pappoús only smoked cigars with people he cared about. It's nice to know he had someone to hang out with, or lime with down here in the place where he was born."

She laughed lightly. "Yeah. According to Mom, they did a lot of liming all over the island."

Raph smiled, certain that both men had treasured the memories of their friendship for years after they last saw each other. "Do you mind if I look around?" he asked, not fully ready to leave this memorable space.

"No, go ahead. And take your time, Raph."

•   •   •

Xio closed the office door and leaned against it. She watched as Raph strolled over to her father's desk and stood behind the chair his grandfather probably sat in while he talked with her father. He rested his hand on the back of it and let out a faint sigh.

She grew still when he picked up a bronze paperweight in the shape of the Eiffel Tower, turned it over, and held it high to read the inscription on the bottom: *Malik, save the date - July 7, 1994.*

"Mom said that paperweight was the last gift your grandfather gave Dad," she told Raph. "He and Mom were supposed to go to Paris with him and your grandmother the following year."

He rubbed the back of his neck with his free hand. "I actually remember when Pappoús bought it during our family vacation. He couldn't decide between a statue of the Eiffel Tower and the Arc de Triomphe. He asked me which one I liked better. I picked the tower; maybe I thought it was taller, shinier…" His shoulders slumped. "It was the last vacation we took together before my dad and my grandmother were killed. I've always wondered what happened to it." He carefully replaced the paperweight to its spot. "Now I know."

His voice dripped with sadness, and Xio could sense his struggle to keep it together. It had only been three weeks since he'd lost his beloved grandfather, and although he had put on a brave face for them today, she knew that his emotions must still be very raw. "I'm sorry, Raph. Do you need a minute alone?"

"No," he said, quickly. "The two most important men in our lives were once close friends. It's nice to share this with you." He tapped the back of the chair before moving to the built-in shelves spanning the length of one wall.

Xio perched on the arm of the sofa and admired the graceful deftness with which he picked up and inspected various decorative ornaments, pulled books from the shelves, and scanned through them before sliding them back into place

While in the shower, Xio had thought of how easily she might have fallen for Raph if she had met him ten years ago, before she'd been broken by Toby and then Trevor. Handsome, charming, and polite, he was the kind of man a girl wanted to hold hands with in public during the day, and lie next to in private at night.

Xio wished she were as free as Akilah to let Raph know that she thought he was sexy. She wished she could smile and flirt with him, indulge in the cat-and-mouse games women and men played when they were attracted to each other. She wished she'd been brave enough to step into the energy they generated and wrap her arms around him when they were alone on the verandah.

She wished she could do it now.

Xio's hand crept to her chest, and she toyed with the ayocin pendant her botoá had given her on her sixteenth birthday. After Fitzroy's outburst at her party, Xio had been so embarrassed, she'd run upstairs to her bedroom in tears.

Her botoá had followed her, and after holding her while she cried, Kaiah had removed the necklace from a little velvet pouch, and clasped it around Xio's neck. She'd told her that the stone once belonged to one of her ancestors, and that it was magical and special, and radiated hope and love.

Xio did not know if the necklace really had magical ability, or if her botoá was just trying to cheer her up, but the moment it was clasped around her neck, she'd felt better, and had returned to her party, forgetting that her obnoxious brother even existed.

Xio only wore the necklace on special occasions, or whenever she needed a bit of courage, and always when she visited her botoá because she knew she liked to see it on her great-granddaughter. She'd tucked it at the back of her jewelry armoire so she wouldn't be tempted to wear it daily, too worried that she might lose it, or wear out its magic, rendering it powerless when she needed it most.

But this afternoon, as she'd looked for something to complement her dress, her hand had gravitated to the back of the drawer where she'd stashed the little velvet pouch that held the necklace.

And just like on the day of her party, the angst she'd been experiencing since yesterday melted away, and she'd felt a surge of confidence.

Xio's eyes moved from Raph's broad shoulders, down his back and to the subtle rise of his firm buttocks. She licked her lips at the hint of strength in his thick thighs and long legs. It was the first time she dared to admire him without risking being caught. Desire fluttered through her belly as she tried to memorize him by heart, so she could insert him into the sexual fantasies she knew would plague her in the days, weeks, and months after he left.

Her eyes followed his tiger-like strides from the shelves to a collection of framed documents on the adjoining wall—awards, honors, and certificates of excellence she and her siblings had earned over the years, including her diplomas from NYU and Princeton. Her father had loved to show off his children's talents, intelligence, and mastery in every area of their lives. Xio wished Akilah and MJ had had more time with him, and were able to build lasting memories so they could remember his love and adoration for them.

Pulling her thoughts from the past, Xio checked her watch. They had about thirty minutes before dinner, and she needed to let Raph know she would be taking him to Ynoa. There was no point in delaying the invitation any further.

A shiver of panic rocked her body at the idea of spending long periods of time alone with Raph in Ynoa, but it was unavoidable. She hoped and prayed she would find the strength to resist the sexual tension between them, help him find what he needed to know about his grandfather, spend time with Kaiah, and get back home to figure out how she was going to save herself and her hotel.

She felt the pendant grow warm between her breasts as she

crossed the room. "Raph, I'm going to Ynoa to see my great-grandmother tomorrow."

His body tensed, but he did not turn around.

"I'm allowed to take guests across the border. If you want, you can come with me instead of waiting for the application to be approved. Kaiah might have some of the answers you need. And we can help you get into Aetós to spread your grandparents' ashes," she added, coming to a stop behind him.

AT THE SOUND of those words dripping from Xiomara's sweet lips, Raph turned around, but all traces of gratitude evaporated as his eyes fixated on the wall behind her.

He felt himself sway as the hairs on the back of his neck stood on end. He was frozen, stuck to the floor.

Chapter Seventeen

TICK TOCK

"RAPH, WHAT IS IT?"

Ralph felt the heat in her touch when she placed her hand over his, but it wasn't enough to thaw the chill in his bones.

"You're freezing," she whispered in a panicked tone, rubbing her warm palms across the backs of his hands. "See, you must have hit your head when you fell. This could be a delayed reaction to a concussion. You need to sit down. I'll call our doctor."

"Óchi. No." Raph pulled his hands from hers and pointed behind her at the eagle perched in flight. His throat felt like sandpaper when he tried to swallow. "That clock," he whispered in a tight voice, staring in disbelief at the exact replica of the one his grandfather had given him.

She turned her head into the direction he was pointing. "What about it?"

He willed his heart to stop racing as he walked over to stand face-to-face with yet another mystery. Its hands were frozen at the two o'clock hour, the pendulum hanging in silence. "Where did you get this clock?" The calmness in his voice assured him that he was back in control.

"From my dad." She came to stand beside him. "It has been

passed down to the oldest child for generations. My half brother, Fitzroy, didn't want it. He said it was wood-ugly. So, now it's mine…" She shrugged.

Raph noted the tensing in her body when she spoke her half brother's name, just as she'd done yesterday in her office.

"It is rather ugly," she continued, "but it was carved from the guayacán tree. The Europeans harvested them to extinction on other islands in the sixteenth century. But here, they're sacred. Now, it's forbidden to cut the guayacán down. It's just one of the reasons this clock is so peculiar." Xio's eyes narrowed on Raph's face. "Why do you ask?"

His chest shook on a deep breath. "My grandfather gave me a clock that looks just like this one. You couldn't tell them apart if they were right next to each other."

"Really?" Her eyes widened.

"Really." Raph ran his hands over the curves and corners. He reached up and touched his fingers to the eagle's outstretched wings as though he were smoothing its feathers. It felt exactly like the one on his clock that he had run his hands over countless times with his grandfather. "Xiomara, I'm telling you, they are identical."

Raph pulled out his phone and scrolled through his photos until he found the pictures he'd taken of the clock before he had it boxed and shipped to San Francisco. He held the phone out for Xio to see. "Look," he said, pointing to the eagle, the base of the clock, the face, the same pendulum, and the same plain square side panels as he swiped from one image to the next. "Don't you think they look the same?"

"Oh my God, Raph… They do. But how could that be possible?"

"I mean— I— I don't know… Xio. He swallowed as the possibilities pounded against his brain. "My pappoús told me that my great-great-great—I don't know how many greats—

grandfather, Thaddeus, built our clock himself. He was the one who first passed it down to his son, Rapheus."

"Rapheus?" She blinked.

"Yeah, I wasn't the first, believe it or not."

She looked again at the picture on his phone, and then at the clock before running her hand over the beveled glass. She traced the eagle's claws carved into the top surface before pulling back. "This seems so unreal," she said, clutching the pendant at her breast. "They seem like the same clock. And yours has been in your family all this time, just like mine."

"Yeah, and if mine was built by Thaddeus from a tree that could only be found in Akilina when he was alive, Xiomara, Thaddeus had to have made this clock here, but…no, that can't be right…"

"What can't be right?"

"Well, as far as I know, Thaddeus Giannopoulos and his wife left Greece during the Ottoman occupation. They went to England where he started a shipbuilding company. I figured that's where he built the clock. But maybe he lived here at some point?" He shrugged. "I don't know. I know I'm grasping at straws again."

That shipbuilding company, Giannport Maritime, had been one of England's most sought-after…

Raph's jaw dropped, his eyes widening in disbelief. How could he not have seen this sooner? *Giannopoulos. Davenport.* Dear God, *Giannport* was a blend of the two families' names. That couldn't be a coincidence. He had always thought that the 'port' in Giannport was in reference to a seaport and to port wine. But he was beginning to realize that his and his family's beliefs about the origins of Giannport were built on the very same secrets that had brought him to Akilina.

The tangible evidence towering in front of him proved beyond all reasonable doubt in his mind that the Giannopoulos and Davenport families had crossed paths almost four hundred years ago. But was it in England? Was it here? Andris had told Malik that his family's connection to the island was disturbing. Could it be that the link wasn't just about the Giannopouloses, but the Davenports, too? His mind told him that he really didn't want to know the whole story while his heart warned that he would find no peace until he did.

"Raph!"

"What? Uh… so—sorry. What did you say?" He swallowed to lubricate his dry throat.

"It's okay. I thought I lost you there for a minute. I was asking you what year Thaddeus went to England? Maybe he just got hold of some guayacán timber there."

No. He wasn't going to say anything about Giannport to Xio. Not until he understood the connection. He shook his head. "Um, it was sometime in the mid-sixteen hundreds, I think."

Xio looked pensive as she crossed her arms and chewed on her bottom lip.

"What is it? I know you're thinking something," he said.

She kept her eyes on the clock. "Well, when I said it had been passed down…"

"Yes?"

"This clock belonged to Eagle Davenport."

Eagle Davenport? Shit.

"Eagle was alive in the sixteen hundreds, too. Maybe… I… I honestly— I don't know what to think about all of this." She pressed her fingers to her temples. "My head is spinning."

"Mine, too. I just can't believe that two different people would have made identical grandfather clocks as ugly and unique as these. If Thaddeus built my clock, he must have built yours. He must have made both of them. And he must have made them here. How else would Eagle have gotten it?"

"I know, Raph. I'm just—" She blew her breath out through her mouth. "It's just so weird. It's like we just poked a sleeping giant."

"That's exactly how it feels." He put his phone away. "Pappoús made me promise not to leave it in Santorini after he died. To tell the truth, when I was a little boy, I used to be afraid of it, especially the eagle with its wide opened mouth."

"I used to be afraid of it, too."

Xio pressed a hand to her chest. "Did— um…" She cleared her throat. "Did your grandfather tell you anything else about yours? All Daddy said was that it was passed down in our family. He didn't act as if it was special in any way. It was more like he was keeping it around just for tradition's sake."

"Pappoús took his role as clock custodian a bit more seriously. He asked me to help him clean it one summer when I was thirteen. Come to think of it, he was acting so strangely that day. Like he wanted to tell me something but couldn't."

"This is just so strange, Raph."

"Even stranger…that same night, I started having these reoccurring nightmares. I've never had nightmares before, not even after my dad and grandmother died," he said, his voice dropping in volume.

Xio wondered if it was on that day Andris had tried to tell Raph what he'd never been able to. "You think your nightmare had something to do with the clock?" she asked.

He spread his lips and shrugged. "I don't know, but it freaked me out." He sighed. "Earlier, before I saw the clock, you'd asked if I wanted to go to Ynoa with you. You said you could take guests across the border?"

"Yeah. My— Um— Kaiah is the dacica of Ynoa, and as her great-granddaughter, I get special privileges. New laws."

He took an abrupt step away from her. "Oh my god…wait, so does that mean you're a princess? You're even more royal than I thought when you told me that you are a descendant of Eagle's wife, Princess Ismé. Why didn't you say anything yesterday?"

Xio toyed with her braid. "It's not something I like talking about at work. I'm sorry, but when I'm there, I just like to be Xiomara Davenport, not— Besides I didn't know at the time that I would be going. And Kaiah has to approve her visitors ahead of time."

"You asked her already?"

"I told her I was bringing Andris' grandson for a visit. And that you had questions about him."

"And what did she say?"

Nothing really.

"Is she open to seeing me?" His voice was laced with hope.

"She's open to it."

"Xio, I don't know what to say. Thank you. This takes so much pressure off me, and it will save me at least three days of waiting." His eyes landed on her hands, and his breath quickened.

Realizing the provocation in the innocent hand-over-hand motion over her braid, Xio tossed it back behind her shoulder and crossed her arms. She licked her lips and watched his Adam's Apple vibrate as he swallowed hard.

As if he needed something to take his mind off what he really wanted to be doing to her, and with her, he turned and trailed his hands down the side of the clock, his fingers gliding over the dark wood like a masseuse's over golden skin.

After a few tense moments, he stepped back and turned around just as she stepped forward.

Their bodies collided for a nanosecond, but it was enough.

Chapter Eighteen

YIELD

THEY STOOD MOTIONLESS, their eyes locking and holding in silent expectation, laying bare their blazing passion for one another—a passion that had ignited the moment they met.

Raph reached out his hand toward hers, and the instant their fingertips touched, electrical jolts rippled through her body. Never had her heart raced this hard, never had it felt this heavy or been so saturated with emotions that she thought she would faint. When he laced their fingers together, she felt trapped in the energy enveloping them.

She swallowed, and clasped the pendant with her free hand, willing it to work its magic and calm her breathing, but the magnetism of Raph's nearness, the enticement in his touch, the smoldering flames within the depths of his green eyes sent her heart rate spiraling. When he pressed their clasped hands against his chest, Xio helplessly leaned in until they were so close, she could hear his heart drumming. He curled his hand around the back of her neck, drawing her even closer until their bodies fused together in the hypnotic heatwave they had triggered.

His warm breath fanned her forehead, her eyes, her cheeks. Moisture pooled in her thong—warm and sticky. She trembled when he brushed his smooth firm lips against hers, and when she moaned softly, his hot mouth opened over hers, then his tongue slid inside and enticed hers into a slow dance that sent desire throbbing between her thighs.

Her knees buckled, and she would have fallen if he hadn't wrapped his arm around her waist. He lifted her off the floor and pulled her fully into the curve of his rock-hard body.

Xio sighed aloud as her sex brushed up against the heat of his pulsing erection through their clothes, sending a sudden hunger for more of him churning deep inside her. On a sigh, she wrapped her legs around his thighs and her arms around his shoulders, clinging to him as if her life depended on being with him.

"*Nai, étsi, moró mou,*" he whispered, pressing his hips against her, and pushing her into the wall as his mouth caressed the soft flesh of her lips, kissing, nibbling, and licking them. He sucked on her tongue with the same voracity his hips were pumping into hers, thrusting the bulge of his shaft against her clit at each contact.

The pounding of their racing hearts and the harsh, uneven moans spilling from their throats swirled around Xio like the drums she so often heard beating in Ynoa—that steady, seductive rhythm to which couples performed the most ancient dance together. As the drumbeat called to her, tempted her to dance, she threaded her fingers through Raph's thick hair and tightened her arms and legs around him.

It had been so long since she was in a man's arms, so long since she'd been kissed and held and desired, so long since she'd felt life throbbing between her thighs and that deep burning inside the core of her sex. Her ache was so deep, she knew it wouldn't be long before she would be screaming Raph's name.

She whimpered in disapproval when he untangled his lower body from hers, but when she heard the metallic click of his belt buckle, followed by the scrape of a zipper, and realized that he was about to answer her call for release, her heart lodged in her throat.

"Raph," she whispered against his lips, whether in protest or encouragement, she did not know, but all logical thoughts escaped her when he gathered her dress in his hands and slowly dragged it upwards, his fingertips brazenly caressing her thighs as he trailed higher and higher, and bunched the fabric above her waist.

He released her mouth and pressed his forehead to hers, and they both glanced down to where the silky lace of her white panties drew a stark contrast to the heaving softness of her taut brown belly.

"We don't have much time," he rasped. Holding her gaze as if daring her to stop him, he sank down an inch or two, hooked his arms under her knees and raised her feet off the floor. The fire in his eyes made her heart dance with excitement as he spread her legs wide, and over his arms, then pressed himself into her quivering sex and left it there—heavy, hot, pulsing with life.

Xio cried out at the surge of pleasure it brought her.

"*Kaválisé me,*" he whispered against her mouth before capturing it again.

Xio did not know Greek, but she understood what he wanted her to do. As his mouth and tongue devoured hers, she tightened her arms around his shoulders and began to ride the ridge of his cock, gently, warily, tentatively. As his heat throbbed through her, she was caught in an undulating wave of ecstasy.

RAPH CLOSED HIS EYES, sucked precious air into his lungs, and commanded his body not to move as Xio rode him, slowly and shyly at first, her moans of absolute bliss crashing around him like ocean waves against the shore.

From the moment they'd bumped into each other, he'd

known all the resisting, and denying, and pretending they'd done was no match for the hunger that was now awakened inside them. He couldn't tell anymore if this undeniable craving for her was pure lust, or if it was his heart wishing for more than sex.

The source of his yearning didn't matter. All that mattered was that he was making her feel good, right now. And despite his promise after learning of her twice-broken heart, he was nevertheless tempted to pull down his briefs, edge her panty crotch aside, and take her hard against the wall. Or even better still, lay her down on the rug, and bury himself deep inside her tight slender body.

"Rapheus," she whispered into his mouth, as her legs began to tremble.

Raph recognized the signs of a woman on the verge of an orgasm, especially when she was in charge. He'd let Xio set the pace, and told her to ride it, and God, she was riding it. When her body stiffened and her arms and legs locked him in a death grip, he jammed his heels on the floor to keep his balance and pinned her against the wall with his hips, sealing them groin to groin, as his mouth opened and closed over her.

Her harsh cry of release echoed in his mouth as she came, and as she quivered in his arms, Raph thought of swimming laps in his pool. It was the only way he could keep himself from coming.

She went limp in his arms, and soon her whimpers quieted down to an occasional rasp of breath. He lifted his head and smiled at her closed lids shading her eyes from his. He felt like a king to have made her come so hard and fast when they hadn't even had sex. Her lips were swollen and rosy from his kisses, and he longed to drink from them again.

Her long dark lashes lifted and his heart leaped at the lingering passion in her eyes.

"I've never done anything like this before," she said.

He chuckled quietly. "You mean come in a man's arms?"

She smiled. "I've never come in the arms of a man I've only known for one day."

He was unsure if there was ambiguity in her response, but they didn't have time to discuss it. "Can you stand up?" he asked.

"I think so."

He eased her legs off his arms and helped her plant her feet on the floor.

"I don't want you to think that I'm easy, Raph, because I'm not," Xio said.

"Believe me, easy is the last word that comes to mind when I think about you. There's no need to explain. I—"

"Xio, you in there?"

"Shit!" Xio said, as she and Raph both turned toward the door at the sound of Akilah's voice coming from the hallway.

Raph hastily began to fix his clothes, fighting like mad to get his zipper up over his shaft, while Xio hastily pulled her dress down and tried to press strands of her hair back into place.

"Xiomara. Xio, are you in there still?" The door handle rattled. "Xio…."

"Did you lock it?" Raph whispered, pulling his shirt down.

"Shit, I don't think so. Wait here." Xio hurried to the door and cracked it open.

"Yes, yes, we're here. What is it?" She looked back at Raph, and seeing that he was presentable, she opened the door wider.

"Hey, Akilah," Raph said, coming to stand behind Xio.

"Hello, Rapheus. Using Dad's office to take care of some business?"

Xio cleared her throat. "Well, you know, Raph's grandfather used to spend a lot of time in here with Dad, so he got a bit sentimental. We both did. Lots of emotions coming up for him," she added, glancing up at Raph.

Akilah put her hand on the door handle, and twisted her lips as she studied their faces. "Yeah, you look pretty emotional.

Anyway, Mom says dinner is in ten minutes, so you might want to get cleaned up a bit." She closed the door.

"Nice coverup," Raph said, eying Xio warily.

"I had to tell her something. She's a teenager. She isn't stupid."

That, she definitely isn't, Raph thought, remembering his and Akilah's conversation, and her phone call with Jamon.

"Well, you heard her. We have ten minutes before Mom sends out a search party."

Chapter Nineteen

BONDING

"THAT'S A CUTE ONE." Raph pointed at a picture of a five-year-old Xio sitting on a swing, reading a book while two girls played on the seesaw behind her.

"Yeah, Xio couldn't even relax on the playground," Akilah stated, leaning into his side to stare at the photo album.

"It was a good book," Xio said from the other side of the coffee table in the family room. "I had to return it to the library the next day."

"You remember that?" Claudia asked.

Xio's lips curved in humor. "Olivia was so mad at me."

"Yes she was, and I didn't blame her." Claudia turned to Raph. "Xio had begged for a sleep over, then when we finally planned it, she realized she didn't have enough time to finish her book before the due date. So instead of playing with her friends, she spent the entire day and night reading. That's Olivia." She pointed to one of the girls on the seesaw. "You met her yesterday."

MJ pointed to a picture on the opposite page. "Mom says that's me and my best friend, Yoshi," he said over Raph's shoulder. "And that's my dad, but I was too small to remember."

Everyone grew quiet over the photo of the toddlers in a wagon being pulled along a path by Malik Sr. Raph was about to say something to the effect that he understood how they were feeling when his phone rang from where it sat on the table next to his glass of rum. He immediately picked it up when he saw who was calling. "I'm sorry, but I have to take this."

"Sure, go ahead," Claudia said. "We'll be here when you get back."

Raph picked up his drink, walked out onto the verandah, and pressed the phone to his ear. "Massimo," he said, grinning with memories.

"Rapheus. How's it going? How long has it been? Two, three years?"

"It's been a while. Didn't expect you'd call so soon. Didn't even know if you would remember who I was." Raph leaned his shoulder against a support beam and stared out at the twinkling lights of the villages on the other side of Lake Abomey. The air was fragrant with rosemary and mint from Claudia's herb garden below.

"Are you kidding me? Who could forget Pumpkin Pie?"

While at the bar where he and Massimo had met, a woman had approached Massimo, and asked if he wanted to taste her pumpkin pie, claiming it was the sweetest in London. Massimo had downed his drink in one swallow, fished out his wallet, dropped some bills on the counter, and hustled out of there. Once outside, Massimo had explained to Raph that if his wife found out that he even spoke to a woman who had propositioned him, she would cut off his balls.

They both laughed at the memory.

"How's the family?" Raph asked.

"All's well. Shaina and I are expecting again."

"Congrats, man. What's that, your third? You had two when we met. A girl and a boy."

"Yep, and I feel like an old man. What about you? Have you settled—"

"Nope," he said, cutting Mass off. He didn't even want to hear the words spoken in his ear. "Settling down is not in my life's plan." *At least not anymore.* But even as he spoke the words, he couldn't help but turn to look through the glass doors.

Since finishing dinner, Raph and the Davenports had been in the family room pouring over memories and sharing stories about the people they had lost. Claudia had pulled out some old albums and home movies—some of them dating back to before Xio and he were born—including the one of her and Malik's wedding that his grandparents had attended.

As he'd watched old footage of Claudia, Malik, his grandparents, and little Xio interacting with each other, he had been moved by the affection they seemed to have for one another. But, he'd also wondered if Malik knew that Andris never told his own family about the Davenports. And if he knew, how did that make him feel?

"Raph, that's what I used to think until I met Shaina," Massimo said.

"She must be a very special woman," Raph replied, walking to the other end of the verandah. He sat down in a woven hammock, his feet braced against the floor.

Massimo chuckled. "She actually called me a man-whore when we first me, but there is nothing like the love of a good woman to make a man change his ways. Believe me, one day, you will find her, or she will find you, as in my case. But, I'm sure that's not what you wanted to talk about."

"No, but thanks for sharing your happiness, Mass." Raph cleared his throat. "My grandfather died a few weeks ago, and—"

"Oh man, I am really sorry to hear that."

Raph took a sip of his drink. Rhum Babancourt. Claudia had told him that Andris and Malik had discovered it on a boys' trip to Haiti. It wasn't expensive, but it was good. Made from sugarcane, and aged in oak for ten years, the rum was smooth and dry, and Raph had taken an instant liking to it. To indulge in something, anything, his grandfather liked made him feel close to Andris, as though he hadn't been completely lost to him.

"Thank you, Mass. We're coping as well as we can. But I learned something yesterday that I can't quite wrap my head around. I had one of my guys looking into something, and he discovered some secret accounts that my grandfather had at Banca di Bianchi."

"Mmm. Okay. What about it? What do you need to know?" Mass asked.

"Well, one of the accounts had four hundred million euros in it. And the day after he died, someone withdrew all of it. I mean, I'm the executor of his will, and have power of attorney over his finances. But I didn't know anything about this money until I sent Declan digging for information on something else. How could he not have told me about it?" he said in an irritated voice.

"Believe me, Raph, I understand your frustration at being kept in the dark. That half brother I was in London to see when we met… I didn't even know he existed until after my father died."

"No shit! Are you serious?"

"Dead serious. When our parents die, we just have to handle the crap they leave as best we can. Unfortunately, sometimes the stink stays with you for the rest of your life. I'm just trying to make sure I don't leave any mess for my kids to deal with when I make my exit."

"Your kids are lucky to have a father like you."

"I'm lucky to have them and their mother in my life. Best thing to ever happen to me. It's nice to have someone to go home to at the end of a hard day."

The huskiness in Massimo voice when he talked about his

wife and kids denoted his love for them, and awoke a certain loneliness inside Raph.

"Anyway, what do you want to know about the account?" Mass asked.

"Can you tell me anything about it, like when it was opened, and who had access to it? I'm totally in the dark here. I'd appreciate anything you could tell me."

"Let me see what I can find out. Hold on for a sec."

"Sure." Raph took another sip of rum and looked out at the star-studded sky and thin clouds drifting across the waxing moon. What the heck had his grandfather been up to? Who was he, anyway? It just seemed as if every day he discovered another secret he'd been hiding. Raph had heard of men living double lives—having two different families in two different cities—but he never imagined that his grandfather would turn out to be one of those men.

It was tiresome, both physically and emotionally, to try to keep up with Andris' secrets, and Raph suddenly realized that if he wanted to keep himself from going crazy, he needed to let it go. He leaned back into the hammock, closed his eyes, and forced himself back from the dreaded rabbit hole.

"Hey, you still there?"

"I'm here," he said hastily, hopeful Mass could shed some light on the situation, even as his stomach cramped in anticipation of what he might tell him.

"Okay, the account was opened by Andris Giannopoulos about fifteen years ago."

Fifteen years ago? Declan had said that Andris had been bankrolling Cleon for about eight years, just around the time Cleon sold off the other vineyards. Raph had assumed that both accounts had been opened at the same time, but now...

"As you know, the account was closed a few weeks ago," Mass continued.

"Right, but by whom? Like I said, he left me in charge of his holdings." Raph placed his glass on a table and rubbed at the muscles in the back of his neck.

"Well, obviously, he gave someone else access to that account."

"Can you tell me who that could have been?"

"I wish I could, but I don't have any way of knowing that. He could have given his bank card or online banking details to anyone. He could have made arrangements in advance to have the money transferred or withdrawn upon his death."

"Can you trace the final withdrawal? I mean, that's a lot of money to just disappear overnight."

"I agree. I would want to know where it went, too, but— Hey, can you hold on a minute?"

"Sure, no problem." Feeling restless, Raph got up and began to pace in circles around the tables and chairs on the verandah. To keep himself from spiraling into a maze about the where-abouts of half a billion dollars, he allowed his mind to dwell briefly on the day he'd received Andris' letter for Xio, and how he'd thought that she was his love child. Boy, had he been dead wrong. And thank God for that.

His mind shifted to Malik's office, and the memory of Xio pinned between him and the wall while she rode him to orgasm. If she could come so hard and fast by just grinding against him through their underwear, he trembled in anticipation at the plea-sure he would bring her when his cock was buried to the hilt inside her.

Yes. He had finally accepted that he could not deny her. He'd been hesitant before, but now, he knew he would not be able to leave Akilina without having tasted her.

It wasn't a matter of *if* anymore, but of *when* they made love. He could almost feel her long smooth legs wrapped around his waist already. This was a yearning Raph never knew existed in this world. He would need the memories of Xiomara to feast on once he was back in California. He didn't want to spend the rest of his life imagining the taste of her, the feel of her clamping around his shaft, pumping the life out of him as he made her come, again and again. He wanted to feel it. He wanted to know.

Raph found himself in front of the kitchen window. Inside, MJ was carrying a stack of dishes to Claudia who was standing by the sink, loading cutlery into the dishwasher. Akilah was spooning leftovers into glass containers while Xio wiped down the center island countertop. They moved like a well-oiled machine. He should be helping them, he thought, especially since Claudia had gone to all this trouble just for him.

"Sorry, I had to sign some papers my assistant just brought me before heading home. It's been a crazy day around here."

"Thanks for making the time to talk. I know you're a busy man."

"We're both busy. But I can't imagine the pressure you're under right now."

No, you really couldn't. "So how do we go about finding out who has the money now?" Raph asked, moving away from the window.

"Unfortunately, we can't. It was transferred to a crypto account. Short of a court order or a hacker, they're practically impossible to trace."

Raph dropped down on a table as his legs gave way from under him. "So, you're saying I might never know where that money is."

"I really wish I weren't, but that's exactly what I'm saying. You'll just have to sit tight and wait."

Raph heard another phone ringing on the other end, and then a low groan from Mass. "Give me another second," Mass said, before putting him on hold again.

Sit tight wasn't something Raph did well, but in this case, he had no choice but to do just that. He couldn't do anything about Cleon or the money while in Akilina, but something told him that his cousin didn't have it. He knew Cleon didn't know anything about crypto currency. The man could hardly use a smart phone. And besides, he wouldn't have been selling off his assets if he'd just inherited—or stolen—close to half a billion dollars.

Raph sighed wearily. He had enough on his plate. Being in Akilina came with its own set of problems, intrigues, and questions that needed his full attention. He would table Cleon and the money for now.

"I'm sorry, Raph, but I have to go," Mass said, coming back on the line. "Family business at home."

"Sure. Sure. I appreciate you making time for me, Mass."

"If I discover anything else, I'll let you know. Let's keep in touch."

"Definitely. Maybe we can get together when I get back to the States. You told me so much about Granite Falls, I think it's time for a visit."

"I'd love that. Call me when you get back."

"Definitely. Thanks a lot, Mass."

Raph hung up, then emptied his glass in one long draft. He needed another.

He made his way over to the kitchen slider, but as soon as he opened the door, he wished he'd waited just a few more minutes before going inside.

"You should have brought them out a long time ago, Mom," Akilah said.

Raph could feel the mixture of anger and grief on her face as the entire family stood beside the island in the kitchen. The tension in the air was so thick, it was nearly suffocating. For the second time since coming to Eagle's Nest, he was frozen in his tracks, hoping he wouldn't be noticed, and wishing he weren't there. He closed the door behind him as softly as he could.

"I know I probably should have. I'm sorry," Claudia said. "But Akilah, those memories are painful for me, you know. And I didn't want you missing your father more than you already do.

You've seen other videos of him. We watch those together all the time."

"But this is a part of Dad's life we should have known about," Akilah argued. "Especially me and MJ. At least Xio had him for fifteen years to herself before I was born. I barely got any time with him before he died! It wasn't fair!"

She was right, Raph thought, thinking of his own father. He and Akilah were the same age when they lost their dads, and no, it wasn't fair.

"I didn't get to know him, Mom. I didn't get to have him for any of the important parts of my life. And I hate watching the video of him at Xio's high school graduation when I don't get to have him here for mine." Her lips trembled as tears rolled down her face.

MJ watched his sister's tears splashing onto the countertop. He patted her arm. "It's okay, Akilah, we'll be there."

Akilah's head shot up, her eyes glaring at her little brother. "That's not the point!" she shouted, before catching herself. Her tears fell harder. "I'm sorry, MJ. I'm sorry, I just…"

"Akilah…" Claudia eased around the island and wrapped her arms around her sobbing daughter.

Xio followed, slowly rubbing her sister's heaving back as she put her other hand around MJ's shoulders.

"I'm sorry, baby girl," Claudia said, holding her daughter tightly. "I'm so sorry that you didn't have time to get to know your daddy, but I hope you know he loved you, very, very much." Her voice cracked.

"I know, but it doesn't change anything. I miss him, so much, Mommy. I miss him…"

"We all do, baby. We all do. I'm sorry."

"I'm sorry, too," Xio whispered in a tight voice. "I wish—"

"It's not your fault, Xio. You don't have to be sorry. And Mom…" Akilah lifted her head from her mother's chest and looked into her face. "You don't have to hide Daddy from me and MJ."

"Okay. Okay. I was wrong to keep memories of him from you. From now on, I'll give you everything I have so you can get to know him better." Claudia picked up a white linen napkin from the counter and wiped her youngest daughter's tears away, and then her own.

"I'm good," Xio said, stepping back when Claudia reached out to wipe her cheek. When she turned away, she caught sight of Raph, and her face went blank.

Noticing Xio's change in demeanor, Claudia turned around. "Oh, Raph, you finished your call."

"Yes. Sorry about that. It was a friend I hadn't seen in two years," he said, stepping farther into the kitchen.

"Oh, that's nice. I hope you two had a nice catch-up." Claudia took the empty glass from his hand and walked back over to the dishwasher, placing it into the top rack and turning it on as though she'd been waiting for him.

"Thanks for a delicious dinner, Claudia, and thanks for sharing your memories with me."

"You're welcome, Raph. And you're welcome to come for dinner or lunch anytime while you're here."

Akilah straightened her shoulders and stared up at him, her misty eyes shimmering in the lights from the chandelier hanging over the island. "Don't you think for one minute that because you saw me crying that I'm soft," she stated firmly.

"Never crossed my mind." He folded his hands over his heart and nodded in a show of understanding and solidarity with her regarding new revelations about her father—things she should have know years ago.

"So what are your plans for tomorrow, Xio?" Claudia asked, diplomatically breaking the awkward silence that had descended upon them. "I was thinking you could show Raph around the island."

"I can show him around," MJ said. "I know everywhere."

"Well, as a matter of fact," Xio began, "Raph is—" She glanced warily at him and crossed her arms. "We—"

"I just thought it would be nice while you get to know each other better," Claudia interrupted.

Feeling that his presence was making Xio anxious, Raph asked, "Can I use your bathroom?"

"Of course." Claudia eyed Akilah. "I'm assuming you showed Raph where it is during the tour."

"Yes," Raph spoke up. "On the side of the stairs across from the library."

"Good." She turned to her son, and said, "MJ, come help me tidy up the dining room."

Xio couldn't keep her eyes off Raph's backside as he walked away. Her mind burned with the memories of his hard body pressing her into the wall, rocking against her, bringing her to… She blanketed her thoughts as Akilah sidled up to her.

"I would say you and Raph know each other pretty well already," her sister whispered, nudging her elbow into Xio's side. "You got real up-close-and-personal with a man who isn't even your boyfriend. *Tsk-tsk.*"

Xio gripped the cool marble edge of the island and stared blankly at Akilah. "What are you talking about?"

"I know what you were doing in Dad's office this afternoon. When Mom sent me to get you for dinner, I knocked, and when you didn't answer, I opened the door, and saw you kissing. You were so into each other, you didn't even know I was there."

Xio gave her a layered look. The sad teenager who'd been crying in her arms over memories of their dad a few minutes ago was gone. Akilah, the annoying, rascal of a sister was back. "You were watching us?" she hissed in a low voice.

"Hell, no." Akilah backed up, her face scrunched up in open

disgust. "Eww." She shivered openly. "I don't want to watch you having sex. Gross, Xiomara!" She shivered again.

"We weren't having sex, Akilah!"

"Sure looked like it to me." She leaned into Xiomara, and taunted her. "What would Daddy say if he saw you doing that in his office, hmm?"

Xio folded her arms and clenched her jaw. Akilah knew exactly how to push her buttons, but she should have known better than to be carrying on like a horny teenager in her father's office. She'd completely lost her sense of self and sanity. Her sister was right, she'd only met Raph yesterday, but she felt as if she'd known him all her life, and God help her, she loved the way he made her feel.

"You were naughty, Xio. Both of you." Akilah gave her a slanted stare. "Wait till Mom finds out. Girrrrl, the wedding invites will be in the mail the next day."

"Shush, Akilah," Xio said under her breath, glancing in the vicinity of the dining room. "You can't tell her."

"Why not? You told her when you caught me and Siyan kissing in his car last month. I was grounded for a whole week. A whole week, Xio."

"That was different. I know you don't want to believe it, but you're still a child. Siyan is nineteen and he has a reputation for..." She shook her head in vexation, more at herself than at her sister. "Just don't tell Mom, alright? I don't want to encourage her."

Since she'd broken up with Trevor, Xio had lived through enough embarrassing situations with her mother trying to fix her up, as if a new boyfriend was the solution to her two consecutive, traumatizing heartbreaks.

"To tell the truth, you could do a lot worse than Raph," Akilah whispered. "He's rich, nice, fine, and smart. I can't imagine what he sees in you, but—"

Xiomara pinched Akilah's arm.

"Ow!" Akilah giggled. "I'm only kidding!"

Xiomara sucked her teeth at Akilah's antics.

"As I was saying, it's obvious why he likes you," Akilah gave her big sister a quick affectionate hug. "BUT, I won't tell mom, I swear."

"You'd better not," Xio drawled, catching sight of her mother, MJ, and Raph chatting and laughing as they strolled back to the kitchen. He seemed entirely at home in her house, mingling with her family.

Akilah's phone dinged on the breakfast nook on the other side of the kitchen.

Raph held his breath as she went to retrieve it. He wondered it was Jamon.

"Mom, can I be excused?" Akilah said, walking back toward them. "It's Sandrine. We're working on a science project together." She held the phone up for her mother to read the message.

Raph smiled inside, sensing her effort to reassure him that she wasn't sneaking out to see Jamon.

"Go ahead. I was going to suggest that you and MJ head off, anyway. Say good night to Raph."

Akilah gave him a hug, "It was nice meeting you, Raph. See you."

"The pleasure was all mine, Akilah," he said before she pulled away and made her exit.

"I don't want to leave, Mom." MJ said.

"I know you don't, but you will."

"Raph promised to let me teach him mdambé." He looked at Raph, hope in his eyes.

"There will be no mdambé tonight," Claudia stated.

Raph was delighted to hear that. He wasn't in the mood to play with anyone tonight. That is, with anyone, except Xio.

"But, Mom—"

Claudia gave him a stern look. "You can either go upstairs to your room, or down to the game room. It's your choice." She pulled him in for a hug and a kiss on the cheek. "Just don't be here when I turn around," she warned, then headed into the family room, adjacent to the kitchen.

"Good night, Raph." MJ gave Raph a fist bump.

"Good night, MJ. It was nice meeting and spending time with you."

MJ beamed up at him. "I know you said you're not Xio's boyfriend, but I'm putting you on my Christmas list."

Xio shook her head as MJ ran out of the kitchen. She gave Raph a sideways glance. "He doesn't know what he's saying."

Raph laughed. "I know. He's just a kid."

"Now, we adults can relax," Claudia said.

Raph followed Xio into the family room where Claudia sat on the sectional, packing up the photo albums, cassettes, and DVDs on the table.

"You know, Raph, Andris talked about your father and mother, and you and your brothers all the time," Claudia said.

Raph sat down on the three-piece sectional to the left of her, while Xio sat on her right. "Really?" While he'd been watching the videos, he'd wondered why his grandparents never brought him and his brothers to Akilina with them. The more time he spent with Claudia and her kids, the more he wished that they had.

"He was so proud of you. He talked about wanting to bring you down here. I'm sorry that he never did. It would have been so nice to know you sooner. Isn't that right, Xio?"

Xio nodded. "Yeah, it would have been nice."

It brought Raph a little bit of relief to know that his pappoús talked about him and his brothers and, was proud of them. At least he wasn't hiding them. But from the hint of remorse in Xio's eyes and voice, he wondered if she was thinking that had they met sooner, she would have been spared the two heartbreaks Akilah had told him about. That thought lingered in his mind, as well.

Would he have been a different man if he'd met Xio when they were children? Would his perception of women and romantic relationships be different if they'd grown up together, grew to trust and love each other? Perhaps so, since he wouldn't have been free to meet and fall for…

"Would you like some more of that rum, or anything else, Raph?"

Raph shook himself, Claudia's question halting his descent into another whirlpool of 'what ifs'. *Yeah, he would definitely love some more of that rum.* But he had to be responsible since he was driving back to The Davenport soon. "Just some ice water. Thank you, Claudia," he said.

Chapter Twenty

NO STRINGS ATTACHED

"I'll get it." Xio jumped up and headed into the kitchen, marveling at how effortlessly Raph had integrated into her family, as if he belonged with them.

When Toby used to visit, her family had been edgy around him—as if everyone was waiting for the sky to fall, or a hole to open in the ground and swallow somebody. Not so with Raph. She was yet to feel one iota of uneasiness from a member of her family since he showed up at Eagle's Nest.

Xio fetched a blue crystal glass from the top shelf of a cupboard and made her way to the fridge. While filling it with ice chips and water from the door dispensers, she dwelled on her mother's comment about how wonderful it would have been if they had met Raph and his brothers when they were younger. Her mother's words had reminded Xio of her own earlier reflections on the direction of her life's course, had she met Raph before Toby. Regretfully, the answer to that question would forever remain a mystery.

Returning to the family room, she gave the glass of water to Raph. "I hope that's enough ice."

"Thanks, I'm sure it is." His fingers closed around hers as he took the glass, making her catch her breath. He smiled, seemingly relishing the effect he had on her senses, which he already knew she was powerless to resist.

"You still haven't answered my question about your plans for tomorrow, Xio," Claudia remarked, as Xio settled beside her and assisted in replacing the photos they had taken from the album for a closer look.

"Um, well, yeah, I forgot to tell you that I'm going to Ynoa."

"Oh. I thought you might take some time to show Raph around the island while he waits for his application to be approved." Claudia pressed a picture of a two-year-old Xio in a green dress back into place. "When did you decide to go to Ynoa?"

Lifting her head, Xio stared at the six-by-five-foot painting from Njideka Akunyili Crosby's Cassava Garden collection on the wall in front of her, while tracing her finger along the edges of the cassette in her hand.

She really didn't want to talk about Ynoa with her mother in front of Raph, because every time she thought about being in seclusion with him, visions of him pulling up her dress in her father's office sent her senses reeling. She was scared of being alone with him, because deep down, she knew what was going to happen between them, and she still wasn't sure if she was ready.

"I just thought it would be nice for you to get to know each other better," Claudia remarked. "He's not going to be here for long."

Xio moistened her dry lips and placed the cassette into its case. "Well, the thing is… I'm taking Raph with me," she said, rather nonchalantly.

"Oh. Okay then." Claudia eyed Raph, and then Xio, speculatively.

"Since Raph has to scatter his grandparents' ashes in Aetós, I figured I'd take him across the river and save him the trouble of having to wait for his application to be approved," she said, hoping to throw her mother off her scent.

"Yes, and I'm hoping your… *Botoá?*" Raph looked to Xio for approval on his pronunciation. "I'm hoping she can tell me a little more about my grandfather. Maybe she knows something about this family link he talked about."

"Well, that's nice of you, Xio. Especially with all you have going on at the hotel."

"It's no problem. I'm happy to help." *I'm doing his grandfather a favor.*

Claudia eyed her daughter. "Have you spoken to Kaiah already, Xiomara? Even though Raph is Andris' grandson, she might not want to see him. You know how she is."

"She will see him. I already told her that I'm bringing him." At first, Xio had simply told Kaiah that she was bringing a friend, but after the strained silence that had ensued on the other end of the call, Xio had told her who the friend was. Still she'd been silent, but Xio knew that her great-grandmother would have clearly said if she didn't want to see him.

"I hope you find what you're looking for," Claudia said to Raph.

"I really hope so, too. Thank you."

Claudia gathered a handful of albums and stood to her feet. "Raph, help yourself to anything you need." She glanced down at Xio. "Xiomara, help me take these to the library."

"Sure." Xio gathered the remaining albums and the box of cassettes. "We'll be right back," she said, before following her mother out of the family room.

"What time are you leaving home?" Claudia asked when they were out of Raph's earshot. "Before or after breakfast?"

Xio was tired, but she knew she had to see it through to the end. "After. I can sleep-in a little, but I have some things at Jewel Beach that I have to take care of first."

"And how long will you be gone?"

"I don't know. A few days. It depends on what Kaiah has to say." She opened the door to the library and gave a passing glance at Akilah sitting on the sofa with her feet under her, her laptop balanced on her knees, and her earbuds in.

"What about the resort? What about Stamer? Have you forgotten his threats?" Claudia asked as they walked to the back of the library and set their loads on a table.

"I haven't forgotten anything." Xio handed her mother the albums, arranged chronologically by year, to stack on the shelf.

"You can't let that man get his hands on JBR. I told you, I'll burn it down to the ground first, and I meant it."

"I know, mom, I know. But honestly, I'm just fed up with everything. I have worked so hard, and it's all falling apart."

"Xiomara, don't let me hear you talking like that. Don't you give up now, baby."

"I'm not giving up. I just need a break. I need a few days away from here, and to spend some time with Botoá. I don't know… Maybe I'll come back with some idea of how to get myself out of this mess."

"Are you going to tell Kaiah about it."

Xio verified the year on the spine of an album before handing it to Claudia. "I don't think I'll be able to hide it from her, do you?"

Claudia's snicker confirmed that hiding the truth from Kaiah was no easy feat.

"She's not going to like hearing that her grandson's legacy and his daughter's life could be destroyed because of Samuel Stamer."

"No, she will not." Xio was beginning to wonder if she should go see Kaiah at all. She wasn't sure she could face her disappointment, embarrassment, or anger, all three of which she was certain Kaiah would feel. "Mom, do you think she would…"

"Intercede?" Her mother finished her sentence. "No,

Xiomara. You know she can't do that. It doesn't matter who you are. The hotel is a private business."

Xio knew that there was nothing Kaiah could do. She was Dacica, but the private sector was just that. Private.

"But," Claudia said, cutting into her thoughts, "you are your father's daughter. God knows he always found a way to beat back his enemies."

Her mother's words generated courage in Xio. She placed a hand on Claudia's shoulder. "I'll do whatever I can to bring him down, and if I fail, I'll pour the gasoline while you light the match, okay?" She slid the last album into place and set the box of videos next to it.

Claudia smiled and touched a hand to Xio's cheek. "Like I said, you are your father's daughter."

"And my mother's, too." Xio leaned over and kissed her on her cheeks.

Claudia stretched her hands over her head, and yawned. "Oh gosh, that's my cue to go to bed."

"Of course, you've been on your feet all day," Xio said as they headed out of the library. "Would you like me to make you a cup of soursop tea, help you get to sleep faster?"

"I have some in the kitchenette upstairs. I'll make myself a cup. Make sure Akilah and MJ get to bed, and lock up after Raph leaves."

"I will, Mom. And thanks for tonight. It was really nice."

When they returned to the family room, Raph was standing at the sliders, gazing out at the darkened landscape.

"Raph," Claudia said.

He turned around, a thoughtful expression on his face. "You look tired," he said, coming to stand in front of her, "and I mean that in a very caring way."

Claudia chuckled. "I am, and I'm heading to bed. It was truly a pleasure having you, and as I said, feel free to stop by any time." She opened her arms.

Raph hugged her, the top of her head hardly making it to his chin. "I will definitely come by again, Claudia. You have a lovely family, and a lovely home."

She stepped back. "Have a safe drive back to The Davenport. But if you feel you're not up to driving, we have a guest room already made up, and two guest houses on the property, if you'll like more privacy."

"I'll be alright, but thank you, Claudia. Good night."

"Good night, Raph." Claudia turned to Xio. "Goodnight, sweetheart."

"Goodnight, Mom." Xio kissed her cheek.

"I'll get another glass of water," Raph said as Claudia made her exit. "If you don't mind."

Xio nodded, then walked out onto the verandah to enjoy the cool evening breeze. Her mind drifted back to when she was a kid, sitting out here with her parents, drinking fruit punch, and eating coconut tarts—her dad's favorite treat—the crumbs falling all over her lap.

She held on to the railing, and looked up into the sky. "I miss you, Dad," she whispered, tears springing to her eyes. "I hope you and Andris are enjoying a cigar right now."

"I hope so, too."

Xio pulled herself together at the sound of Raph's voice. He came and stood beside her, his scent making her knees weak. She willed herself to keep from falling into him.

Now that they were alone, and the din of after-dinner chatter had ceased, Xio grew conscious of the night creatures calling out to each other—crickets chirping in the hedges below the verandah, and frogs croaking from the long grass by the stream, signaling a time to mate.

The air, heavy with the smell of rain that had fallen during dinner, ignited her senses, strumming on her heart strings and causing every emotion she had been holding back to rush through her like an overflowing river breaching its levy.

They hadn't had a chance to talk about what had happened in her father's office. After Akilah had told them that dinner was ready, Xio had pointed Raph to the nearest guest bathroom, and she had gone back to her bedroom to freshen up.

"It's a beautiful night," he said, finally breaking the silence.

Xio nodded, and clasped her pendant, her throat still too tight to speak.

His gaze followed her fingers rubbing over the stone. "I've never seen a stone like that. It looks as though it's been changing color throughout the night, first orange, then yellow during dinner. And now, a deep red."

Very perceptive, Xio thought, impressed that he'd picked up on the changing colors. Most people unfamiliar with the local stone mistook it for topaz or amber.

"It's ayocin," she said, staring into his green eyes, illuminated in the soft glow of the garden lights. Ayocin was named after the little Megiri girl who found the first piece while playing on the banks of the Caonabo River, centuries ago.

"I've never heard of it," Raph said.

"Most people haven't. It's only found on Ynoa, deep in the Nacanké Mountain Range, and it's mined on a very small scale. There's gold, and copper, and other minerals, too. Our natural resources is one of the reasons the Megiri fought so hard against colonization."

"So, they knew of ayocin's existence back then?"

"Of course they did." Xio laughed at his naivety. "You westerners are so convinced that we don't know what we have, or worse, that we don't know how to take care of it. Yet, we take from the mountains, only what we need, while you strip the land bare."

"I can't argue with that." He smiled gently, his eyes fixated on the stone as if he were hypnotized by it.

"So, did you buy this gem for yourself, or did someone give it to you?"

Xio smiled, hearing the real question buried in the one he asked. "It was my sweet sixteen birthday gift from Kaiah," she answered, deciding not to toy with him. "I don't usually wear it, but it just felt right tonight."

"I'm glad you did. It looks beautiful on you." He reached out his hand. "May I—"

Xio drew back.

"I'm sorry."

Xio forced a smile. "It's just that we should be careful. MJ or Akilah could come out here at any moment. And neither of us seem to be able to control ourselves when we are alone. I don't really want a repeat of what happened earlier."

"Are you sure about that?" He leaned in, his face so close to hers that she could feel his breath fanning her forehead. "I would love a repeat, and then another, and another."

Xio grew warm, and her skin tingled as if an army of ants was crawling across it.

His eyes slid seductively to her throat where her pulse beat rapidly, then over her breasts and stomach to the quivering spot between her thighs. Finally, they moved back to her face, intense and filled with passion. "I just want to fuck you, Xiomara," he drawled, in a tight blunt tone. "And if what happened in your father's office is any indication, I'm pretty sure you want the same thing. There don't need to be any strings attached."

Xio's eyelids crash-landed, and she fell against the railing as her knees buckled from under her. Never had a man talked to her with such candor. That four-letter word he'd used was forbidden by the teachings of the church. Now, she understood why.

The sound of it, the thought of it evoked images of damp, naked bodies bucking, twisting, rising and falling together, of soft, slick flesh wrapped around something hard and hot, of moaning, and groaning, and sighs of pleasure, of earth-shattering orgasms…

No strings attached sounded perfect to her.

What Raph was proposing had nothing to do with the heart. His honesty enticed her to throw caution to the wind and revel in a good fuck or two, knowing that by the end of next week, he would leave, and that would be it. This was about satisfying the needs of the flesh, and God, her flesh needed satisfaction after a five-year dry spell and two heartbreaks by men who had never shown an interest in giving her the kind of sexual pleasure Raph already had. If what had happened in her father's office was any hint of what was to come, she knew she would be coming over and over again.

"Lucky for you, I'm a man who knows how to control himself."

Raph's voice jolted her back to their conversation. She glanced up to find him watching her with a racy look on his face. "Huh?" She'd been so deep in thought, she really hadn't heard what he'd said.

"I said, that if I wasn't a man with extreme self-control, I would have you with your panties around your ankles this very moment."

"A man who knows how to control himself, huh? Akilah and MJ are still up, you know," she said, taking the opportunity to change the subject.

"Yeah." He shrugged. "Like I said, extreme self-control."

"Akilah likes you a lot. She respects you," Xio said. "I don't know how you did it, but you won her over from the moment you met."

"I think she won me over. To be honest, Xio, I've liked hanging out with MJ and Akilah. They kind of feel like family."

Xio buried her face in her hands for a second. "Oh God, don't say that."

"Don't say what?"

"That we're family. Families don't do what we did with each other."

"You know, there was a minute when I thought we might have been."

"Might have been family?"

"Mmhmm."

"Why would you think that?"

He flashed her a cheeky smile. "When I saw what was written on the letter Pappoús asked me to bring to you, I thought you were his secret love child."

"Seriously, Raph?" She gave him an incredulous look.

"What else was I supposed to think? You know what was written on it. He called you his little daughter. I'd never heard of you, nor of any Davenport, nor of Akilina. I never even knew he'd used an alias when on island until your mother told me. I didn't know anything."

She pushed off the railing. "So, let me get this straight. When you first met me, even though you thought I could be your aunt, you still looked at me the same way you're looking at me now? Trying to undress me with your eyes."

"Oh, Xiomara, you do understand me," he said, with a mischievous curl of his lips.

"I'm surprised you even got on the plane if all that was going through your head."

"That, and a host of other things going through my head drove me to get on that plane, Xiomara. You have no idea."

"I do have some idea." She shrugged. "I know I sound like a broken record, but I just don't understand why my godfather never told you about us. Or why he didn't just tell you about… Well, about what we *think* we know about the clocks, and about Eagle and Thaddeus. Do you think he knew?"

"Believe me, that has made it to the top of my list of questions. In that same note, he told me not to be afraid of the truth I'll learn down here. Speaking of, did you read his letter, yet?"

Xio's pulse raced. She didn't know why Andris had asked her not to tell Raph, but she would not lie to him, not after what they'd uncovered this afternoon about their families' history. "Yes, I read Andris' letter."

His eyes widened. "What did he say?" he asked in a shaky whisper.

"That he was sorry he'd kept his distance all these years, and that he was proud of me. He said he still thought of us."

"Is that it?" His shoulders drooped with disappointment. "I thought there might be some explanation about this truth he sent me to find."

"He also said that when you arrived, I should make you feel at home, show you the island." It wasn't exactly a lie. By taking him to Ynoa, and to her great-grandmother, she *would* be showing him the island.

"Well, then, half of his wishes have already come true; I feel at home. You're taking me to Ynoa tomorrow. Who knows what we'll discover once we get there?"

Yes, who knows? Xio's mind raced with visions of the unknown. "I should probably warn you that it's about an hour and a half drive to Guaybana where Kaiah lives. We'll leave around four, after I'm done work. I'll text you when I'm on my way to pick you up. I'll get your number from my mom," she added, realizing she didn't have it.

He pulled his phone from his pocket. "No need to bother her. Just give me yours, and I'll text you mine."

"Is that the way you usually ask women for their numbers?"

He held her gaze. "Only the ones I already know I'm going to sleep with."

She blushed while reciting her number. "Also," she said, then hesitated.

"Also, what?"

"You need to know how to greet Dacica Kaiah when you meet her."

"What, should I curtsy?" he asked, cheekily.

She nodded. "That's a start."

"You're kidding me."

"Nope." She gently pushed him backward toward a chair.

When he dropped into it, she stood in front of him. "Now, pay attention and listen carefully, because screwing up could be the difference between her accepting you and sending you back to Akilina with your list of unanswered questions."

Chapter Twenty-One

THE DAVENPORT

*S*HE *THREADED* *her fingers through his hair and pulled him closer, opening her mouth wide to accept his ravenous kisses.*

She moaned and shivered when he rubbed the smooth pad of his thumb over her clit while his fingers tapped against the entrance of her sex as if seeking permission to enter.

"Yes, yes," she whispered into his mouth as she stroked one hand down his back and worked the other between their bodies, brushing her knuckles against his chest and inching lower until her fingers found his erection.

She palmed the broad wet head of his rock-hard cock, sliding her fingers over the veins running along its length.

"Rapheus," she moaned as a white-hot and consuming need flared in the deepest part of her. "Yes, just like that," she whispered as he slipped a finger inside her and moved it gently back and forth. "Deeper, faster," she begged, spreading her thighs wider, hooking her legs around his thighs. "Oh God, that feels so good, so good..."

"Xiomara... I need to fuck you... Please, let me fuck you, baby."

"Yes, Raph. Please..."

Bzzzt. Bzzzt. Bzzzt.

"Ahrrgg. No!" Xiomara groaned, pulled from her dream by the sound of her alarm going off.

She bit her lip as she released her breast and slowly dragged her finger from inside herself, groaning as her muscles latched on to it like it was a man it wasn't ready to release. She reached for her phone to silence the alarm when she noticed a text message from an unknown number.

Sweet dreams, Xiomara.

She didn't need to wonder who had sent the text. She replaced the phone on the nightstand and pulled the sheet up over her body.

Her dream had been much more than sweet. It was sexy and wet. She covered her face with her hands, a salacious smile curling her lips as she inhaled her own scent. Her mind spun back to the scene of her and Raph in her father's office, and then to the verandah last night. She remembered how the shock of his explicit proposal had made her body tighten, and stirred visions of wild unbridled sex.

But as Xio watched the spinning white blades of her ceiling fan, the lingering warmth of her wet dream transitioned into Stamer's threat to take Jewel Beach away from her. Yesterday, she'd deliberately stayed busy at work to keep her mind off the ultimatum he'd given her. And Raph had proved to be another welcome distraction last night.

She would rather rot in jail before marrying Trevor, but she couldn't accept a prison sentence for a crime she didn't commit. She also knew she wasn't going to hand over her family's company to that slimy piece of crap without a fight, especially not after reminiscing last night over photographs of her dad at Jewel Beach—shaking hands with guests, sitting behind his desk conducting business on the phone, and hanging Certificates of Excellence on the wall, all while glancing over his shoulder at the camera, grinning from ear to ear.

She wondered if she could find someone to buy out Jewel

Beach. Maybe her cousin, Tuolo, her aunt Zola's son, who ran Max Construction, one of the largest construction companies in the Caribbean. She and Tuolo had always been close, and though he'd never shown any interest in the hospitality business, he'd loved and respected her father, his uncle Malik, and being a Davenport, he had his share of beef with the Stamers..

Yeah. She would call Tuolo today and set up a meeting for after she returned from Ynoa.

Xio threw back the sheet, hopped out of bed, and made her way into her bathroom. Her sex still pulsed at the thought of Raph, this time, though, with the anticipation of being alone with him in Ynoa, making love under the stars in a secluded area of Kaiah's estate. For once, Xio decided she would throw caution to the wind. Once they crossed the river into Ynoa, Raph was going to get his wish—and so would she.

Two hours later, when Xio walked downstairs, she felt more confident and secure than she had in years. In her favorite orange button-down dress, she walked tall, like royalty, through the foyer. She followed her nose to the kitchen where her mother was making hot-pepper omelettes, her dad's favorite.

The house was quiet with Akilah at drum practice and MJ at archery. MJ was preparing for *Ríbaja* a ritual for twelve-year-old Megiri boys and girls to prove that that they were true *Guazabi*, or young warriors. He was excited about being a guazaba, especially since he was in line to become Dacique of Ynoa, one day. All daciques and dacicas were formidable warriors. Even Kaiah, in her day.

"Hey, Mom," she called, setting her bag on the island, and going over to stand next to her mother at the stove, the spices coming from the frying pan making her mouth water.

Claudia smiled at her daughter. "Hey, baby." She picked up a plate from the countertop and arranged Xio's omelette next to a slice of wheat toast and a serving of fresh cut fruit. "How did you sleep?"

Xio blushed as she poured herself a cup of coffee from the pot near the stove.

"That good, huh?" Claudia said, lifting an eyebrow.

"Stop it, Mom." She took her cup to the fridge, added sone almond milk, then followed her mother to the breakfast nook.

"Here you go, baby." Claudia placed the plate on a bamboo mat across from her own mug of coffee.

"Thanks Mom." Xio set her coffee next to her plate, sat on the stool, arranged her napkin on her lap, and picked up her knife and fork. "This is so good," she murmured on her first bite of the omelette. "Sure you don't want to come work for me at Choréta?"

Claudia laughed at the suggestion that Xio's father had posed to her many times. She sat on the stool facing Xio, leaned forward, and said, "So, what do you think of Raph?"

"He's okay." Xio shrugged and broke off a piece of toast.

"Just okay? Oh please, Xiomara. Even Akilah picked up on the vibes between the two of you."

Xio froze, her fork suspended in midair. "What… What did she say to you?"

Claudia shrugged. "Just that she thinks you like him, but that you're afraid."

Xio let out a long sigh. "Yes, Mom. I am afraid. I don't think I can take another heartbreak. Besides, we live worlds apart." She took her first sip of coffee.

"I'm just saying, it wouldn't hurt for you to brush off some cobwebs if—"

"Mom, come on…"

Claudia raised her hands, and backed away. "Okay, okay, I'm done." She took a sip from her mug. "By the way, have you read Andris' letter, yet?"

Xio took a bite of her toast, then leaned back in her chair. "I have."

"Well, what did it say?"

"It's in my bag. You can read it."

Claudia walked over to the island and got the letter from Xio's bag. She returned to her seat, pulled it from the envelope, and began reading it.

While Xio ate her breakfast, she kept one eye on her mother, watching her expression turn from excitement, to sadness, and finally understanding. By the time Claudia folded the sheets of paper and put them back into the envelope, there were tears in her eyes.

"That is so sad," she said, tapping her fingers against her cheeks to catch her tears. "Poor Andris." She shook her head in sorrow. "And all this time I thought he didn't care, anymore."

Xio placed her hand on her mother's. "It was just too difficult for him. Like he wrote in the letter, he failed his own family, too. And last night, Raph told me that Andris hardly spoke about Karena and Xander after they died, even to him and his brothers." Xio got up and took her dishes to the sink.

Claudia followed. "So, that's why you're taking Raph to see Kaiah. Because Andris asked," she said, returned the letter to Xio's bag.

"Yes, and it's a good thing he did, because it gave me a reason to go see her. I just need her right now, you know, with the Stamer stuff and all."

Claudia brushed strands of hair from Xio's face and tucked them behind her ears. "I know. The two of you have had this special bond since you were born. You are her little princess."

Xio looked at her watch and picked up her bag. "I have to get to work."

"Me, too. I have a fitting at the boutique at nine-thirty." Claudia followed her down the hallway toward the garage.

"Where are my bags?" Xio asked of the weekender and the backpack she'd left in the iabora last night.

"I had Meka load them into the Range Rover."

"Okay, thanks." She kicked off her slippers and slid on a pair of black leather heels.

"Give Kaiah my love, and you have a nice time with Raph," Claudia said as Xio opened the door.

"Sure. Bye, Mom." Xio gave her a quick kiss and fled.

SEVEN HOURS LATER, Xiomara parked in the carport next to Raph's Jeep and turned off the engine. She rolled down her windows and admired The Davenport's landscaping.

No one visiting the estate now would believe that only three years ago, weeds and shrubbery were choking the gardens and fallen fruits were rotting on the ground, attracting rodents that made their homes in the trunks and branches of the trees. It had cost Xio more than two million dollars to hire rotating landscaping teams who were still working to restore the beauty of the estate after Fitzroy had neglected its upkeep.

Xio jumped when a green lizard landed on her windshield, eying her warily, as if rebuking her for being in its way.

"Shared space, buddy," she murmured, as it scurried down the hood and disappeared. Xio checked her watch. "Shoot." She adjusted the black cap on her head, climbed down from the Range Rover, and made her way toward the villa.

Before leaving the hotel, she'd texted Raph to let him know she was on her way to pick him up. He hadn't responded, but she hoped he was ready, or close to it.

If she wanted to avoid driving along the remote, winding mountain roads in the dark, they needed to get going. Last night, she'd told Raph to check out Cuyás Sports in Anacaona for hiking gear and some warm clothes. The nights were chilly high in the Nacanké Mountains where he was headed.

Xio spotted a black duffel bag, a black backpack, and a blue velvet case on a chair by the front door. *Good*, he was packed. Without thinking, she turned the handle and opened the door.

She stepped inside, removed her sunglasses and her cap, and laid them on the table at the entrance. She would later blame her impulsiveness—doing the very thing she warned her employees against ever doing—on her need to get on the road and into Ynoa before nightfall.

But for now, her breath solidified in her throat at the sight of a butt-naked Raph on the sofa, his long, muscular legs spread wide in front of him. His head was pressed against the back of the sofa, his eyes closed, and groans slipped through his parted lips, as he stroked his cock.

Xio stood rooted to the floor, her eyes fixated on the spot between his legs. Her body grew warm and tight and her sex vibrated to his rhythm, as if he was thrusting up inside her—in—out—in—out—filling her up.

"Xiomara…" he whispered.

Well, at least she didn't have to wonder who he was fantasizing about. She moaned softly.

His lids flew open, and although his body stilled, he did not get up nor release his erection, nor did he say one word. He glanced down at his hands and, for a second, his face colored in embarrassment, but then his piercing gaze moved back to her face. His eyes dared her to leave. Or were they compelling her to come over and take what she wanted, what they both wanted?

Desire rolled through her. All she had to do was walk over, climb on, and ride him. She didn't have to say a word.

She felt the heat of his gaze raking down her body, silently enticing her to get naked with him. Her heart drummed in her ears.

It was as though she were on autopilot. She could not stop

her feet from toeing off her sneakers, her hands from lifting her shirt over her head, or her fingers from pulling her yoga pants and panties down to her ankles.

When she stood, and stepped out of them, Raph's eyes fastened on the spot between her thighs. Xio walked slowly toward him while unclasping her bra. Her breasts sprang free, and her nipples immediately grew harder. She wiggled her bra off and dropped it on the oak table in front of the sofa.

They stared silently at each other with a kind of uncertain familiarity, as if they had been here in this time and space before.

He reached for her hand, and without hesitation, Xio allowed him to pull her forward. She straddled him, using his hand as leverage. Butterflies fluttered in her stomach at the initial contact of his smooth hard thighs against the softness of her own. His eyes held hers as if reassuring her that she was doing the right thing, that she could trust him to bring her out alive on the other side.

When he pressed his arms into her back, pulling her closer, she trembled from the feel of her nipples brushing the silky hair on his chest. He tugged at the elastic holding her ponytail in place, and she shivered as her hair fell on her shoulders and down her back, his hands following, lightly brushing against her skin and sending tingles of ecstasy racing through her. He pressed her face into the side of his neck with one hand, while he cupped her buttocks with the other, easing her closer still.

Xio exhaled sharply as their sexes meshed and he began rocking against her, gently and slowly, his shaft brushing her clit at each stroke. She remembered the feeling of riding him yesterday, but today, with no barriers between them, the sensations were magnified a hundredfold as she slid up and down his ridge.

One last thread of caution infiltrated the haze of yearning, telling her that it was not too late, that she could back out before anyone got hurt, but their heavy breathing, rumbling through the air like the roar of the Yacao Waterfall, chased her apprehensions away.

Her arms wrapped around Raph's shoulders and, as her orgasm hit her full force, she pressed her mouth into his neck to stifle her scream. The waves of ecstasy were still crashing through her when he reached between their legs and lodge himself at the entrance of her sex.

With his hands around her waist, he penetrated her in one long upward thrust, locked his arms around her and began thrusting slowly, deeply, and urgently, filling her with each powerful stroke, stretching her body, forcing her to accept and welcome him.

Their moans of pleasure filled Xio with a depth of sexual desire she had never experienced before. There was so much, almost too much of him. He grew harder, bigger, and hotter inside her, sending lust rippling through her in one powerful wave after another. Hungry for more, she pressed her knees into the sofa, tightened her arms around Raph's neck, and began to ride him like a sex-starved nymph, until her body vibrated from the white-hot pleasure rolling through her.

"Rapheus…" she cried out, clutching at his hair as ecstasy numbed her mind.

His rhythm grew more erratic, his groans harsher. His hands moved up to her shoulders, and he pushed her down hard as he slammed into her with one last desperate thrust. His arms became steel bands around her body, holding her in place. A long, low growl erupted from his throat, then he stilled, throbbing deep inside her. Her sex clamped around him as he groaned out his release.

They held each other, trembling uncontrollably, gasping for air, their hearts beating hard and heavy.

Even after she felt Raph slide out of her, Xio remained where she was. She wasn't certain her legs would bear her weight if she tried to stand. With every breath she took, it felt as if Raph was still inside her, taking her with power and purpose. She wondered if that feeling would ever go away.

Xio felt him stir, his arms still wrapped around her, one hand on her shoulder while his other rested in the hollow of her back. She waited with bated breath for him to say something, break the ice, but he didn't. She felt the muscles in his neck contract as he swallowed. Maybe she should say something, apologize for walking in on him masturbating, but that would sound foolish, pointless. Embarrassing.

Her body felt utterly weak and ragged, as if she had been making love for hours.

Lovemaking, she thought on a ragged sigh. There had been no kissing, no caressing, no foreplay involved. She and Raph hadn't just made love. They'd gone at each other like animals, only interested in satisfying their own lust.

Chapter Twenty-Two

CRAP

FLATTENING her hands on the back of the sofa, Xio eased her upper body away from Raph's. Sweat glistened on their skin; a drop fell from one of her nipples into the curling hair on his chest.

He dropped his hands to the sofa and stared at her, as if he too was unsure of what had just happened between them. It was wild, and she loved his streak of freakiness. It was what they both wanted to happen from the moment they met, so why did it feel so awkward, so out of place now that the heat and the lust had been quenched?

Had Raph planned this, knowing she was on her way to pick him up? He said he was a man with self-control, so was this his way of getting what he wanted after all? Or had the same force that had driven her to take off her clothes, walk over to the sofa, and mount him, also stripped him of his self-control?

Shivers rushed up her spine as he brushed strands of damp hair from her cheeks and tucked them behind her ears.

"Xio, I— I want to—"

"No." *No.* She was not going to have this conversation while she was in his arms, naked, and smelling of him. She needed time to think about what had transpired, and assess the barrage of feelings that had popped up along the way.

"We really need to get on the road," she said, abruptly scooting off him and planting her socked feet on the floor. She snatched her bra from the table and picked through their clothes—lying in a sinful heap on the floor—for her own, then raced up the stairs.

After a quick shower in the bedroom farthest from the primary suite, Xio hastily put on her clothes, grimacing at the feel of her damp panties against her skin. She wrapped a towel around her wet hair and sat in a chair in the bathroom to both gather her thoughts, and to give Raph time to get himself together and dressed, before they had to face each other again.

"Are you okay, Xiomara?"

Xio started at the sound of Raph's voice on the other side of the door. "I'm fine." She didn't remember locking the door, and she held her breath, willing him not to turn the knob and walk in.

"I thought you might want your hair tie."

Xio stepped to the door and cracked it open. Without meeting his gaze, she took the elastic dangling from his finger, then closed the door. Unwrapping the towel from her hair, she draped it over the rack and stood in front of the mirror. She combed her fingers through her damp hair, twisted it into a ponytail, and secured it. It wasn't as soft as when she used her brand of shampoo and conditioner, but it would do until she got to Ynoa. At least she was able to wash away Raph's scent.

When she finally went back downstairs, Raph was standing at the front door, and fully clothed in white chinos and a blue T-shirt, holding her sunglasses and her cap.

"Do you want anything before we leave?" he asked, handing over her belongings. "Water, something to eat?"

"I'm good, thanks. I have water in the car. Plus, Kaiah is

going to feed us when we get there." She put on her cap and arranged her sunglasses over the visor.

"I don't want her going through any extra trouble for me."

She smiled. "It's not for you, Raph. It's tradition. Megiri feed their guests. It would be considered offensive if she didn't."

"Gotcha," he smiled. "Good to know."

Anxious to leave the scene of the crime, Xio stepped outside to the tunes of doves cooing over the sound of Raph closing and locking the door.

"Your grandparents?" she asked, pointing to the velvet case.

He nodded, lifting the case, the backpack, and the duffel bag from the chair.

Xio took the lead down the steps, but as she walked across the courtyard, she stumbled.

Raph's hand on her elbow kept her from falling. "Whoa, you okay?" Concern rang in his voice.

"Yeah. I tripped on the stone slab between the gravel." Her nerves were working against her, for sure.

He released her, but the electricity that had passed between them lingered. Even though they had just satisfied their lust, the urgency to do it again was still there. She continued to the carport, every step she took reminding her of Raph thrusting inside her with force and urgency.

"I'm looking forward to the drive and seeing some sights," he said behind her.

"Yeah, it is beautiful."

"It sure is."

His tone made her turn her head, and just as she'd suspected, his eyes were fixed on her ass. "You have a one-track mind, Raph."

"Don't all men?"

"Not all, just most." Xio continued walking, the thought of him watching her ass, sending tiny tremors through her.

"A Range Rover Defender," he said, as they reached the carport.

"Yeah, my little Lexus would never get us where we need to go. Not all of the roads across the river are paved. In the mountain villages, people still walk, and some use horses or donkeys to get around. You need some serious wheels to get to Xiobayo."

"Xiobayo?"

"The territory where Guaybana is, where Botoá lives."

"Nice, nice." Raph circled the black SUV.

"How does it handle?" he asked, standing beside her at the back of the vehicle.

About as well as I just handled you. "It handles well," she said, too chicken to voice her lewd thoughts. "It belonged to my dad, so when I drive it, I feel like he's with me."

"I get it." He nodded.

"It's unlocked," she said, realizing he still had his luggage in his hand.

He opened the swing gate and tossed his backpack and duffel bag in next to Xio's backpack and weekender. "A sleeping bag?" he asked, curiously.

"For your hike up Mt. Cayacáo. If it rains, the ghauts could overflow and parts of the trails might get washed out. If that's the case, you and your guide might have to spend the night in one of the caves."

"Caves? Is that safe?" he asked, closing the swing gate and then opening the back door to place the velvet case in the foot well.

She gave him an incredulous look. "Five hundred years ago, they were used to shelter those who could not fight in the wars against the French and British. There are caves all over the island. Your guide will have no problems finding one, if he needs to."

Xio got into the vehicle, fastened her seatbelt, fired up the engine, and put her hand on the gearshift. She waited for Raph to climb into the passenger seat beside her and fasten his seatbelt before backing out of the carport.

As they drove away from the villa, she felt relaxed enough to address the elephant sitting on her chest. "About what happened just now…"

He cocked an eyebrow. "Oh no, you were a virgin."

"Don't be silly." She was relieved he was making light of it. "I have never had sex with someone I wasn't in a relationship with."

"Why do you feel you have to explain yourself, Xiomara? We are two consenting adults. We're allowed to act on our feelings, you know. You don't owe anyone an explanation, not even me."

Xio drove through the exit gate of the resort and took a right turn onto Island Main Road that would take them east to Abomey Highway. "I know, I know, but it's true."

"Like I said, you don't owe me an explanation. Let's not talk about it, anymore." He pulled his sunglasses from atop his head and placed them on his face.

Xio's heart pinched at the thought that he was shutting her up and out. She put her sunglasses on, too, the need to ask why he didn't want to talk clawing at her throat. But when he pressed his head against the headrest, and his mouth tightened considerably, she knew the subject was closed. In all fairness, when he had tried to discuss it earlier, she had practically run away. She had her reasons. Now, it was Raph's turn to clam up, leaving her to wonder about his.

As she turned right onto Abomey Highway, and into the flow of traffic, she thought back to The Davenport. That was the first time she had come during sex, and when her first orgasm had hit, it had shocked the hell out of her, making her reassess the beliefs about her own sexuality that she'd come to, years ago.

She had never come with Toby, and after finding out what he had been doing behind her back, she'd realized why. And Trevor had never cared if she was satisfied or not. Most nights, he would just roll over and fall asleep after he was done with her.

But Raph? He'd made her come three times in about fifteen minutes. It was as if her body was making up for all the orgasms she should have been having all these years. Xio was bursting to tell someone that she had finally come with a man inside her.

Inside her…

"Crap!"

Xio slammed on the brakes as reality punched her in the gut.

Chapter Twenty-Three

DOUBLE CRAP

RAPH'S EYES flew open as his body lurched forward and the seat belt tightened across his chest. He pushed his sunglasses to the top of his head and turned to Xiomara. "Everything alright?" he asked.

"I'm sorry." Her hands gripped the steering wheel. "A car was about to cut me off."

She kept her eyes on the road ahead, not glancing at him for even a second, signaling that she wasn't being truthful.

They were headed east on Abomey Highway that would take them to the Boni Bridge, and over the Euka River. He checked the side mirror. There was a long line of cars behind them. Last night, during the lesson on how to greet the dacica, Xiomara had told him about *Sakétebon*, the annual harvest and food festival that was taking place in Arijua this weekend. He'd seen posters while walking around Anacaona yesterday. It was a big event, and lots of people from Akilina crossed the river to attend it. "Are you tired?" he asked, looking over at her. "We were up late last night."

She moistened her lips nervously. "I'm not tired."

Well, good for you. He'd hardly slept. That dream about being bound with vines and tossed into the ocean had tormented him again, with more intensity this time. But he was used to functioning with little sleep. "If you want, I can take the wheel. You'll just have to tell me where—"

"I'm fine, Rapheus, I know—"

"Incoming call from Olivia Baker," a voice announced through the vehicle's speaker.

"Sorry, I have to take this," she said. "It's probably JBR business."

"I get it. Business stops for no one."

She retrieved her earbuds from the center console and slipped them into her ears. "Hi, Liv… No… I'm just getting to the Boni. Yeah, that's right… I'm sure… I'll explain when I get back… Sure, if those dates are still available, but they need to decide quickly. We can't keep our vendors waiting. If she wants, she can…"

As Xio talked with Olivia, Raph thought back to their heated encounter. Never one for pillow talk, he usually feigned sleep or conjured an excuse to make a quick exit. Sex, for him was little more than scratching an itch. But what he'd done with Xio was far more than that. Yes, they had been driven by lust, but as he'd held her in the aftermath, he'd wanted to tell her how amazing, sweet, and sensual she was.

He was relieved when she'd shut him up, then ran upstairs to the bathroom, thus preventing him from saying something he would later come to regret. He didn't want to lead her on. But, as they crossed the bridge over the rushing Euka River, he realized that his growing difficulty in resisting her was likely due to increased oxytocin levels challenging his self-restraint.

He'd been thinking about her all day, looking forward to the moment she would come to get him, and wondering what they would talk about on the drive into Ynoa and, more importantly, when he would be able to see her naked. While waiting on the front porch for her, Raph had gotten so worked up, he'd thought it best if he released some tension before getting into her car.

He'd gone back inside, stripped off his clothes and made himself comfortable on the sofa, stroking his cock with visions of Xiomara riding him, her long black hair cascading down her back. When he'd opened his eyes to find her standing at the door watching him, he'd felt embarrassed at being caught.

He'd tried to get up, to say something, but his body had felt heavy, like bags of wet sand were pinning him down. His cock was throbbing so hard, and the blood pumping through his veins so hot, he'd felt that if he didn't feel her sliding up and down on him, he would explode into a thousand pieces.

When Xio walked over and straddled him, the world, as he knew it, had collapsed and disappeared. He was no longer in the villa. He wasn't even in Akilina. He was nowhere, yet every-where. He heard nothing, but the ragged sound of her breath, saw nothing, but her sweet, shapely body atop him, smelled noth-ing, but her woman's scent. And then, when their passions were unleashed and they labored to quench their thirst for each other, he'd felt nothing, but the tight, hot cavern of her sex swallowing him whole.

When he'd felt his orgasm building in his groin, and knew he couldn't hold himself back any longer, Raph had tried to lift her off him and pull out, but the same energy that had kept him frozen in place when he'd first seen her in the doorway, had kept her locked on him. He could not have pulled her off of him if his life depended on it.

Riding her bareback was so damned wild, and hot, but coming inside her, or any woman, was a line he hadn't crossed since one reckless night in college. Having to accompany his one-night-stand to the pharmacy for the morning-after pill had been enough to scare him straight. And if Xiomara turned up pregnant…

Raph's stomach flipped. He did not even want to think about

the fallout with her family when she started showing. How would he manage a life between San Francisco and Akilina? What if she had the baby and didn't tell him? After all, he had made it quite clear that their getting together was a no-strings-attached affair.

As much as he didn't want it now, Raph knew that he would take on the responsibility of raising his child. He'd grown up without a father and he would never wish that pain on anyone. Despite his resolve to not have children, he couldn't bear the thought of his child living an ocean and a continent away and wondering where, or who, his father was.

To keep himself from plunging down a rabbit hole, he opened his phone and checked his email. There were several from Declan. The meeting for the Graystone Mall project in Portland had gone well. The property owners were eager to finally sell, but they wanted to meet with Raph first. Afraid they might sell to a rival at a higher bid while Raph was unavailable, Declan had sweetened the deal with an additional million, and they had signed without giving it another thought. After scanning his inbox for anything that couldn't wait until he got back from Ynoa, he checked his text messages.

The first one was from his mother. She wanted to know where he was and when he was coming back. It was timestamped around the time he and Xio were lost in each other. Knowing she would keep texting and start calling if he didn't respond, he tapped out a lengthy text about running an errand for Pappoús, and that he couldn't tell her what it was or where he was, but that he was okay and not to worry. He loved her, and would be home on Saturday. The next message was from Sebastian. He was visiting L.A. with some friends in two weeks and wanted to know if they could stay at his penthouse.

"You're getting some business done, too?"

Raph sent off a reply to Sebastian that he'd be glad to see

him. "Just checking my messages," he said, then put his phone away.

"Must be good news. You look happy."

Happy? He didn't think so, but it had been so long since he'd been happy that he'd forgotten what it felt like. "My COO, Declan, closed a deal on the purchase of an abandoned mall in Oregon. It's in a low-income neighborhood, and a lot of people lost their jobs when it closed. We've been trying to get the owner to sell for years now, and he finally agreed."

"What are you going to do with it?"

"Well, the structure itself needs a lot of work. Years of sitting empty has taken its toll."

"Believe me, I know what that's like. Once people move out, insects and all kinds of animals move in."

"Exactly. But it still has good bones, and the location is great. Our team has been doing some research into the needs of the community. It's a food desert, so we're angling to get a few grocery stores and dedicate some space for a farmer's market. The roof itself will be turned into a pollinators' garden… I'd like to build two additional floors for mixed-income housing. We'll see what city hall lets us get away with."

"Wow. How long will all that take?"

"It's hard to tell. Sometimes the red tape ties our hands for years longer than anticipated. And it depends on the number and complexity of environmental and safety issues we encounter. We did a similar project in North Jersey, and that community is thriving now. It gave us hope that what we'd done was a good thing. Hopefully, the folks in Portland agree."

"I did a little research on G3," she said, giving him a quick glance.

"Did you, now? What did you find out?"

"That you are environmentally friendly and only take on projects that benefit the communities you develop. My dad used to cringe when he heard of prime real estate being sold off to wealthy foreigners on other islands, especially after a devastating hurricane, with promises to build better homes. Many locals realized, too late, that they couldn't afford to live in their own neighborhoods, anymore. Sure, they can work in them as housekeepers or garderners, but when the sun sets, they catch the bus back to their villages and just pray the next hurricane passes them by. But imagine…" Xio added, slamming the heel of her hand into the leather-covered steering wheel, "when elections come around, they vote for the same corrupt politicians with all their broken promises."

"Well," Raph said, "to be honest, we weren't always so mindful of our impact on the world. When we first started out, we were like most other developers—in it to make money, regardless of how it affected the surrounding communities. And believe me, we still invest in our fair share of luxury projects, but we try to find balance."

"What changed?"

"My conscience, I guess. Like your dad and your government, we didn't like the idea of displacing people, making it impossible for them to stay in the homes their families had lived in for generations because we built another, completely out-of-place luxury condo complex. Hundreds of these buildings are still empty across the country, while entire families are living out of their cars, in shelters, or on the streets. After a while, we just couldn't live with ourselves."

"You and your brothers, you mean? I'd like to meet them one day."

He watched her from the corner of his eye. When Claudia had voiced that desire, it had felt like a natural next step. After spending time with her family at Eagle's Nest, Raph had liked the idea of continuing and strengthening the friendship between the Davenport and Giannopoulos families. But what had just happened between him and Xio was sure to complicate matters, and he knew it was bound to happen again. As long as he kept his emotions under control like he'd been doing all his life, he was sure he could handle it.

You keep telling yourself that, his heart mocked.

"I'm sure you will one day." There was a high likelihood she would meet his brothers after he told them about Akilina, that Pappoús was born here, and that their father had visited a few times.

Checkpoint Ahead, Raph read on a sign over the highway as the Caonabo River came into view. It was wider, and calmer than the Euka, and from his window, Raph could see women in white dresses and head cloths washing clothes on the river bank while children splashed nearby. "Why are they washing their clothes in the river?" he asked, glad to have something else to talk about. "They don't have washing machines in Ynoa?"

"Washing clothes at the river is a spiritual ritual."

"Oh?"

"The Megiri believe that the river goddess, Atabey, rids their clothes of any toxins or malicious intent they might have picked up during the day, and replaces them with good omens and good health."

Discomfort rattled Raph as an awkward silence ensued.

"Wait, so you really thought we don't have washing machines in Ynoa? Are you going to ask me if we have indoor plumbing next?"

"Well, no," Raph said, "but I won't lie. The question had crossed my mind."

Xiomara shook her head. "It's amazing how ignorant the world is about indigenous culture. You know, our people had already built underground sewage systems while Europeans were still throwing their shit out of windows onto the streets below. We've been practicing our traditions longer than yours have even existed, and still the world thinks we're so backwards and simple-minded."

"I wouldn't go so far as to think you're backwards and

simple-minded, Xio. I just— I guess I just don't understand Akilina… Or Ynoa."

"What don't you understand about it?"

"Well, why the separation between the two sides of the island? Why aren't foreigners allowed in Ynoa without permission? Are Akilina and Ynoa like two separate countries?"

"No, it's one country, but in the fifties, when the Guaitiari wanted to open to tourism, it was decided that they could only do so if some territories remained closed to foreigners. Dacica Naima didn't want the Megiri customs and rituals to become a spectacle under the western gaze as it had in parts of the Americas and Africa. She didn't want our women showing up in the pages of National Geographic to be gawked at and studied by undergraduates who would never bother to come here and learn about the Megiri for themselves. She gave the Guaitiari permission to open the three western territories, Akilina, Canae, and Lacanoix. They called this new region Akilina, since Akilina was the largest of those districts, and decided that the Caonabo River would serve as a natural border between the open and closed regions."

"And the eastern region?" he asked. Traffic slowed to a crawl as the checkpoint booths, about a half mile ahead, came into view.

"It's still called Ynoa," she replied.

"Ynoa, Ynoa. Like New York, New York."

"More or less. Although the two regions themselves don't have any political importance," she added. "Decisions are made by our Dacica at the advice of The Council, which is made up of twelve sub-chiefs."

Raph was silent as he tried to wrap his head around the distinctions.

Apparently, sensing his confusion, Xio continued, "The island, our country, is called Ynoa. That's what's on our passports. But as far as ninety-nine percent of tourists are concerned, we're Akilina, because that's all they know. The airport is in Akilina, and that's where the vast majority of hotels are. Most people fly into Akilina and never venture out to any other part of the island. Most of them don't even know that the island is actually called Ynoa. They have a vague awareness of the Megiri living in the mountains to the east, but as long as they have their beach chairs and their rum punch, they don't really care where they are. To the outside world, we are just Akilina."

"Yeah, I guess a beach is a beach."

"Exactly, and their blissful ignorance suits us just fine." She eased the SUV forward.

"And so, what? The Megiri just stay in Ynoa?"

"No… I mean, most Megiri live in Ynoa, and for the most part the Guaitiari live in the west, but it's not a rule."

"But, can the Megiri leave Ynoa if they want to?"

"Of course, they can. And Guaitiari live in Ynoa, as well. You have to remember that Ynoa was never colonized. The French and British tried and failed to take our land—this small patch of earth where my African ancestors could live free from oppression. My people fought against all odds, bled and died, to protect this island and our culture from the most powerful armies in the world. And we won. The Council honors the sacrifices of our ancestors by continuing to protect our people from the misguided values of the globalized world—to ensure there is always a place for us."

His pappoús must have been aware of the rich, complex cultures of the people who lived on this beautiful island, and yet he had kept it a secret from his grandchildren. Why? The more Raph learned about the island, the more in love he was with the place. "What's the Megiri view of the outside world? I mean, if people aren't allowed in, how do they…" He couldn't think of the right words to phrase his question without sounding insulting. "How do they learn about outsiders?"

"Raph, it's not as though parents here don't allow their children to read books or watch TV or learn about the world beyond our waters. Megiri go to university abroad, or to Akilina for work. It's up to each person to decide to what degree they want to live within the limits of our traditions."

"Do a lot of people choose to leave?"

"I don't know if it's a lot, but sure, people do leave. The important things is that we are raised in the richness of our own culture, knowing the full, honest history of our people… and it's a very proud history." Xiomara stopped and swallowed. "It is very difficult to walk away from that," she said. "Knowing where you came from and who you are is invaluable. It is something that not every descendant of slaves can claim to know."

"And do you? Do you know who you are?" he asked, mesmerized by her storytelling.

"Yes, Raph, I know who I am. I've known ever since I was a child. Every Megiri learns about their history through oral accounts."

"Through the BÓ'Ro… BÓ'Roco who keeps the histories. I think I read something about that in the library. Did I pronounce that correctly?"

"Almost," she said, smiling sweetly. "But, yes, that's right. You're learning. Keep that up. Knowledge impresses Kaiah. And speaking of…" Her voice faded and she leaned forward, her brows knitted together.

"What is it?" Raph followed her gaze. They were one car away from the checkpoint.

"Kaiah's car is here," she said, pointing to a black Mercedes-Benz SUV parked in front of a small building a few yards beyond the gate.

Raph recognized the premium G-Class model. "Does she usually come to meet you?" he asked

"No," Xiomara sighed, her fingers curling around the steering wheel. "But it's not her. It's her *hajime*, head of her private guard. And it's not a good sign."

Part II

THE CONNECTION

Chapter Twenty-Four

WAWU

Xɪo ᴄᴀᴍᴇ to a stop at the border gate and rolled down her window.

"Hey, Xio," the young man in the booth shouted.

"Hey, Diogo. What's up?"

Diogo flashed her a big grin. "Girl, you know what's up. You get more beautiful every time I see you. When are you gonna let me take you out on a date?"

"You forget we're cousins? And even if we weren't, you still wouldn't have a chance."

"Ouch! Girl, you're as mean as a bucket of crabs." Diogo laughed, then stretched his neck out of the booth, his long black hair partially hiding his face as he stared at Raph. "Is he your new boyfriend?"

"You're too fast, Dio."

"Apparently, not fast enough. I'm still chasing you," he said on a grin.

They might have been joking, but the thought of another man wanting her infuriated Raph.

"Welcome to Ynoa," he said to Raph. "I'm sure Xio will show you a good time."

She already has. "Thank you, Diogo."

Diogo pulled his head back inside the booth and said to Xio, "I guess the chief's car is here for you."

"Yep. Tell Auntie Loida I say hello if I don't see her," Xio said, rolling up her window.

Dio waved her through, but as soon as the guardrail opened, a guard in a black and gray uniform emerged from behind the booth and motioned her over to the side of the road.

"What's going on?" Raph asked.

"I don't know." She unbuckled her seatbelt. "Wait here. Do not get out of the car," she warned, staring at him.

"Okay," he said, when he realized she was waiting for a response. "I won't get out of the car."

She hopped out and closed the door.

Raph turned and looked through the rear window at the guards moving from one vehicle to the other, checking the IDs and travel documents of every passenger. Many of the stopped cars were occupied by people who looked like him. *So this was how it felt.* It wasn't pleasant being targeted or placed under suspicion, simply because of the way you looked.

His gaze shifted to Xio as she approached the Mercedes and began talking with the man who'd emerged from it. After a short exchange, he handed her a sheet of paper. She glanced down at it, frowned, and then said something to him. The man handed her a phone, and she walked to a railing overlooking a deep lush ravine, with her back to the road.

His stomach tightened when, after a few minutes of talking on the phone, Xio turned and glanced in his direction. She did not look pleased, he thought, as she walked back to the Mercedes and handed the cell to the man. After another short conversation, she headed back toward him.

"Is there a problem?" he asked, as she climbed back in.

She closed the door and dropped the piece of paper in the console between their seats. "I can't take you to Xiobayo."

The knots in his stomach tightened. "But you said Kaiah was expecting me."

"I did say that. But sometimes Kaiah can be… She just has her own way of doing things, and she isn't ready to accept you."

"What was the point of coming to Ynoa if she refuses to see me?"

"I didn't say she's refusing to see you. I said she isn't ready." She paused on a sigh. "Well, what she said was that you aren't ready to see her."

"*I'm* not ready to see her? I'm here, aren't I?" He threw his hands up in frustration. "What's the point of—"

"Raph," Xio warned in a low tone, "you should keep your voice down and mind your body language. They are watching us, and if they detect an ounce of antagonism, they will put you in a police car and send you back to Akilina tonight. That would defeat the entire purpose of you being here. Not to mention, it would probably make it impossible for you to cross the river again."

"I thought you said this wasn't a police state."

"It's not. And neither is it *your* state. This isn't your land. You're an invited guest here, and you need to act like one, otherwise you'll be asked to leave."

"In a police car?"

"Well, there aren't any taxis running, and I'm still going to Xiobayo, so…" Xiomara shrugged. "Yeah, in a police car."

Raph glanced through the windshield, and sure enough, two officers were standing behind the Mercedes, looking in their direction. Irritation gnawed at him. He was not used to following orders. But Xiomara was in control here, and he would have to follow her lead if he wanted to get anywhere.

It would be wise of him to remember that Kaiah was not just Xio's great-grandmother and a former friend of his grandparents. She was the Dacica of Ynoa—their chief. She had the power to not only send him back to Akilina, but also to kick him off the island. Nevertheless, he hated to accept that an old woman was asserting power and control over him, and that there wasn't a damn thing he could do about it. At the end of the day, *he* needed to see Kaiah. She had no need to see him.

"Do we go back to Akilina tonight?" he asked

"No. We'll continue on to Wawu."

"Where?"

"It's the main town in Arijua."

He groaned inwardly at the thought of being set back an entire day.

"I understand your frustration, Raph, but everyone is on high alert this weekend."

"Did something happen?"

"Two nights ago, a French journalist tried to climb a security fence into Zatona, the territory east of Arijua. When he filled out his visitor's application, he concealed the fact that he was a journalist."

"What will they do to him?"

Her lips twisted ruefully. "It's a very serious offense. The last time someone entered Ynoa illegally, they tied him to a post at low tide."

"Jesus."

"Rapheus, I'm kidding." She chuckled at the terror on his face. "We're not animals. No, he'll probably spend six months in jail and be fined as much as a hundred thousand euros. They'll keep him in jail until his fine is paid, so it might be longer if he or his publication can't come up with the funds. And of course, he will be banned from ever coming back to the island. It's just not worth the risk."

"They do not play around here, do they?" he murmured.

"No, they don't.

"What's up with that guy?" He pointed to a guard escorting a passenger from the small building, and over to a police car.

"Who knows? His papers weren't right, or something. We

need to get going," she said, buckling her seatbelt. She slowly pulled back onto the road, and instead of taking the lane that would take her to the southeast highway into Xiobayo, she went north, following a sign that read, *Wawu Coast*—the Mercedes hot on her tail.

"Some people just won't take no for an answer," she continued, once they merged into traffic. "People think they have a right to invade your privacy however and whenever they want. Having permission to visit a country does not mean you have permission to exploit its people."

"Speaking from a bad experience?" he asked, at the hint of ire in her voice.

"Over the years, there have been a few guests who knew who I was. People get weird around celebrities and royalty. It was just awkward trying to run a hotel when your guests are scared to interact with you, or feel uncomfortable or intimidated around you. Or worse, are trying to butter you up."

"I can imagine." Raph was all too familiar with people being nice to him just because they wanted something from him.

"It didn't bother my dad," Xio continued, "but I made it clear to my staff that nobody was to treat me with any reverence in front of guests."

"Will you still become Dacica when Kaiah…"

"When Kaiah dies? No." Her lips puckered. "I am next in line since my grandmother and my dad are gone, but I've always wanted to follow in my father's footsteps and run JBR. I can't do both."

"How does Kaiah feel about that, about you not succeeding her?"

"Not happy, but she respects my decision. And it's not like I'm her only option."

"Right, there's Akilah and MJ. Are they interested in the job?"

"Akilah isn't, but MJ is."

Raph smiled. "I think he would make a great leader. He's strong, smart, determined, and very protective. No uninvited guayanki would get past the border." He laughed, even as he held his stomach remembering MJ's vicious kicks.

Xio joined in his humor. "MJ is really excited about his training. When he turns twelve, next year, he is going to live with Kaiah, so she can start teaching him what it really takes to be Dacique."

"Does your mom have any say in the matter? I mean, I can't imagine my mother sending one of us to live with a relative when we were twelve. She ended her marriage when my step-father suggested she pack us off to boarding school."

"Well, it's a small island," she said, taking a right turn off the highway. Lush mountains dwarfed them on both sides. "It's only an hour and a half between Eagle's Nest and Xiobayo. Plus, Mom understands that it's what MJ wants. When she married Dad, she knew that there was the possibility that one of us could become chief at some point. MJ is his father's son, so…"

He sensed that she did not want to talk about it anymore, so he changed the subject. "So, if we're not going to Xiobayo, what are we going to do tonight?" he asked. His disappointment over not seeing Kaiah tonight was still high, but the promise of a night alone with Xio, of getting to take his time with her in a bed, lifted his mood almost as much as the breathtaking view of the Atlantic Ocean as Xio rounded a bend at the top of a hill.

"About that," she said. "Kaiah told me to take you to a hotel in Wawu. But Garayx, the guy behind us, will drive me to Xiobayo."

Well, there goes that idea. Raph wanted to kick something. The frustration over his well-laid plans falling apart was mounting inside him. "Do you have any idea how long she'll make me wait?"

"Maybe a day, or two. It depends on a lot of things, and the journalist problem does not help one bit."

"Maybe if I spoke with her directly, she might reconsider seeing me tonight, for my pappoús' sake, at least."

She paused before answering. "I told her why you came, Raph, and that you need to scatter your grandparents' ashes in Aetós, and get back to your life in San Francisco, and…"

Even though he did want to get back to his life, he didn't like hearing it from her. "And…" he prompted at her hesitance to continue.

"Look, I get your frustration, but Botoá is a complicated and busy woman. She's not easily persuaded to do anything. She acts when she's ready, and her word is final. I have learned that the best way to get anywhere with her, is to do as she says."

"Fine," he said with a little more irritation in his voice than he'd intended. He put up his hands in defeat.

"Kaiah said that you need to understand Megiri customs, so I suggest you visit the Museum of Megiri History," Xio recommended in a soothing voice. "I think what Kaiah is trying to teach you most of all is awareness. She said you weren't ready. So, get ready," she emphasized. "Let her see that you're preparing yourself to receive whatever stories she will tell you."

His impulse was to exhibit the same dominance he would in his boardroom. But he had enough sense and respect for Xiomara, his grandfather, and himself, to show restraint. He took a deep, calming breath. "If learning about the Megiri is the ticket to seeing Kaiah, I guess that's what I'll do."

"See, that wasn't so hard, was it? I'll call you when I get to BÓ-Caneye, and I'll try to come see you tomorrow."

"I look forward to that." The anticipation was already rolling through him.

"Kaiah sent this for you." She picked up the sheet of paper the security guard had given her and handed it to him. "It's your visitor's pass to move around Arijua since I wouldn't be with you. Don't leave your hotel room without it."

"Like the American Express card?" he asked with a grin as he shoved it into his pants pocket.

"I'm not kidding, Raph," she said in a serious tone. "A police officer can stop you at any time and ask for your papers. Not having it will be cause for suspicion, and you will be immediately sent back to Akilina. Kaiah obviously does not want that to happen."

The lack of control, the sudden change of plans, and his driving need to find answers sooner rather than later, made him want to demand to be seen and heard. However, considering the recent event with the journalist, and the man being arrested at the checkpoint, he understood the precaution. "You're right, I'm sorry. I'll keep it with me. And would you thank Kaiah for me when you see her?"

"I will." She reached over the gear shift and laid her hand on his thigh.

The gesture was genuine and reassuring, and it reached into the corners of his heart that had been barricaded against the tenderness of a woman for years.

I know what you gave up. His pappoús' words flooded his thoughts.

Raph tried to shut out the conflicting emotions swelling in his chest. Common sense told him to pull away from her, but desire compelled him to lace his fingers through hers, and so he did. He was quickly realizing that when it came to Xiomara Davenport, desire was going to win out against caution every time.

Caution and desire. Shit.

Raph untangled their hands and, shifting in his seat, he turned sideways to face Xio. He cleared his throat. "Xio, we need to address another issue."

"Huh?" she asked, twisting her lips. "What issue is that?"

"We didn't use a condom. And we haven't talked about it," Raph said in as guarded a tone as he could. It wasn't a topic he ever had to discuss, especially not after the fact.

She slowed to a stop as they approached a four-way intersection and took a quick glance at him. "I'm on the pill."

He exhaled. "Good, we're safe."

"Well, from pregnancy, yes, but…" She paused as she eased up off the brakes and moved forward.

"But what?" he asked.

"Well, when was the last time you were tested?"

"I always use condoms."

"You didn't today. And that wasn't my question."

"No, *we* didn't today. I think you got a little carried away."

Xio smirked at that. "*I* got carried away?"

"Correction, we both got carried away in the moment. But I get tested every six months. My last one was just a couple of weeks ago. I'm all clear."

"Every six months? Damn, how many women are you sleeping with?"

"Not as many as everyone thinks. I'm not out there picking up one-night-stands every weekend, you know." *Only every other weekend.* "But a man needs to let loose every once in a while."

He felt her body tense. Damn, that was insensitive of him. He should know better than to talk so nonchalantly about sleeping around after he'd learned what her exes had put her through. "You don't have to worry about catching anything from me, Xio. And just to be on the safe side, we'll use condoms moving forward."

Xio sucked her teeth and cut her eyes at him. "So, you're assuming you'll have more opportunities?"

"Are you saying I won't, Xiomara?" he asked in a silky tone, trailing a finger down her bare arm.

Xiomara came to a stop under the hotel's front portico. Through her rearview mirror, she noticed the Mercedes pull up behind her. "I'm not saying anything," she told Raph, giving his hand a quick squeeze before letting him go.

Within seconds, the doors opened, bringing their conversation to an abrupt halt.

Chapter Twenty-Five

BÓ-CANEYE

IT WAS STILL LIGHT when Garayx turned off the mountainous highway that ran through the territory of Xiobayo, the ruling chiefdom of Ynoa, and cruised through the village of Lebo where Xio used to spend a lot of time when she was a child.

As they passed the first circle of houses around the batey, she recalled visiting those homes and playing with her cousins and friends, while women went about their daily chores—hanging clothes to dry in the sun and wind, grinding cassava for the week's supply of bread, weaving mats and baskets for home use, gifts, trading, and sale, and tending to the younger children. Men secured hammocks between trees, raked leaves, hoed gardens, and carved smoking pipes and musical instruments for the next Rocotiéri.

Leaving the village behind, Garayx turned onto a long, flat stretch of road. Lagoons split the natural landscape on each side. From the back seat of the Mercedes, Xio's eyes swept over the ragged hills and deep ravines that comprised the twenty-acre estate.

She remembered the children from Lebo coming to the estate and how they ran around in nothing but their underwear, and the men and women who attended them wearing only *naguas* and *inaguas*—breechcloths—around their hips.

Xio's smile dwindled as her recollection of those happy childhood memories reminded her of the many reasons foreigners were not allowed beyond Arijua. Outsiders perceived their way of life as backwards and primitive. In 1873, when Joseph Owens, a man who thought of himself as the American Charles Darwin, visited Ynoa and published a piece that described the Megiri as just that, Dacica Eweda closed the island to foreigners. It wasn't until the 1960s that visitors were allowed back. And still, the only territory east of the Caonabo they were allowed to travel to was Arijua, and no farther without a special permit. Those were seldom handed out.

Her heart pounded as the Mercedes approached BÓ-Caneye, and the *Kú*—the sacred temple. Everyone who came to BÓ-Caneye to see Kaiah had to pass through the Kú and pay respect to the dacica and her ancestors, and that included anyone in the chief's family who did not live on the estate. The Megiri believed in the influence of evil as strongly as they believed in the influence of good, and passing through the Kú was also a way to prevent evil spirits from entering the chief's private quarters.

Garayx came to a stop in the stone courtyard of the Kú. "Welcome home, Princess Xiomara," he said, upon opening his door.

"*Hahom*," Xio thanked him in Megiri. She waited while he walked around the vehicle to open her door. Her legs wobbled a little as Garayx helped her down from the SUV and up the twelve limestone steps. "*Tain tireiro*," she said, wishing him a good night as he bowed and retraced his steps to the SUV.

Xio nodded to the door attendants, Yumax and Tysil, as they opened the double mahogany doors to the iabora. They were not allowed to speak when on duty, but they smiled at her. She smiled back, knowing that one night before she went back to Akilina, they would be sitting around a fire on the back lawn, cracking jokes and reminiscing about childhood memories over roasted corn and platters of grilled lobster and coconut cream.

Inside the iabora, the attendant on duty, a young woman Xio did not recognize, and who was dressed in a short brown cotton inagua and a matching *tagana* covering her breasts, bowed in reverence to her. The woman gestured for Xio to sit on one of the two mahogany benches along the wall, then knelt on the floor and removed her sneakers and socks.

She placed a bowl of cool water in front of Xio, washed her feet gently, then dried them with a soft cloth. As the woman set the bowl and towel aside, Xio was about to thank her when she remembered her position on the island, and that for this young woman, it was an honor to perform this act of service in their sacred temple.

The woman led her to the white wooden door leading into the temple, opened it, bowed to her princess, then stepped back.

Xio entered the palatial Kú, and although she could not yet see her, she knew that Dacica Kaiah was seated on her sacred *dujo,* a centuries-old throne crafted from the guayacán tree in the shape of a crouching man. The dujo was raised up on a dais with three white, wraparound limestone steps leading up to it.

Twelve *rabori,* both male and female warriors from each tribe, who had volunteered to serve their dacica, were strategically positioned around the steps, blocking her view of her great-grandmother. A full quiver, along with a bow, hung from each of their left shoulders, while in their right hands, they grasped spears with sharp copper tips pointed toward the ceiling. Their embroidered breechcloths, the feathers in their hair, and the gold and ayocin jewelry that adorned their fully painted bodies never ceased to amaze Xio. As usual, she felt as if she'd entered an ancient world where time continuously stood still.

Behind the dujo, two black rock columns supported a twelve-foot-wide by three-foot-tall plank of guayacán wood that bore the carved likenesses of the twelve Megiri gods. Beneath it sat twelve Zemis that housed the spirits of the most revered ancestors from each chiefdom.

Xio startled when the rabori tapped their spears three times in perfect unison on the steps, then parted their ranks to reveal their chief, seated regally upon her dujo.

Kaiah was dressed in a white cotton robe, expertly embroidered with bright colored threads, and adorned with beads, chips of gold, ayocin, and jasper at the waist and hem. Around her neck, she wore a three-tier choker of whelk-shells, but most significantly, the *Guanín*, a round medallion made of gold, silver, and copper—a symbol of her authority and position as a chief—suspended from a thick gold rope.

From beneath her feathered crown, dripping with ayocin gemstones, each gleaming a different hue in the light filtering in through the glass windows, her thick gray hair cascaded down her chest in two thick braids that coiled in her lap like sleeping cobras. Kaiah's hair, like that of most Megiri women, had never been cut. It was their crown of glory, and for women of royal lineage, it was also a symbol of their position in their villages. Slender, at five feet, three inches tall, she was stoic and regal, her piercing brown eyes, and her strong rectangular face, though wrinkled with age, was as beautiful and graceful as it was in her youth.

Finally, when Kaiah lifted her hand from her lap and gestured for Xiomara to step forward, she walked barefoot across the polished mahogany floor. But before ascending the steps, she stopped and bowed to silently pay respect to the bones of Kaiah's ancestors, neatly packed in a large zemi basket at the base of the dais. Some of those bones were centuries years old, and some were more recent, like Xio's father, her grandmother, and Kaiah's late husband, Orocobix—Xio's great-grandfather.

Lifting her head, she climbed the steps to the *dais*, dropped to her knees, and kissed the ayocin ring on Kaiah's forefinger. Even though Kaiah was her great-grandmother, Xio was still required to show her the honor befitting her position, especially in the presence of others.

Kaiah tapped Xio's forehead, signaling that her reverence had been acknowledged, and then rose to her feet.

Xio stood and waited for Kaiah to speak.

"Xiomara, *d'nanichi*," she finally said, her eyes lighting with a bright smile.

"Botoá." Xiomara leaned in and kissed her on both cheeks, then held steady as Kaiah returned the tender show of affection.

"*Anegwaha?*" Kaiah asked.

"*Tainwei*, Botoá," she lied. All was not well, but she held herself in check in front of Kaiah's rabori.

"And your mother and siblings?" Kaiah gave her a puzzled frown.

"Everyone is doing well." She dropped her gaze and boxed her lips.

Kaiah waved her hands, the bands of gold bracelets dangling from her wrists jingled as her arm swayed. The rabori filed out in two lines, disappearing through an open door behind the dais.

"Come, my child," Kaiah said, taking Xio's hand and walking with her to the right side of the Kú. Two guards standing at either side of a pair of double doors opened them and bowed as Kaiah and then Xio stepped into another iabora.

Xio slid her feet into a pair of her own sandals she knew had been brought from the house by the woman who had helped her earlier, while Kaiah continued through to her dressing room where her personal attendants would remove her ceremonial attire.

As she waited for Kaiah, Xio paced the tiled floor as the anxiety and anger about Stamer began to bubble to the surface. To say she was scared of the outcome if she didn't find a way to stop Stamer was an understatement. With her mother, she'd been able to contain her feelings, but with her botoá, it was a different story. Kaiah had a sixth sense, and there was no use pretending or trying to hide her feelings.

She stopped pacing as Kaiah emerged from her dressing room, wearing a loose blue dress and a pair of brown sandals. Her braids had been twisted into a bun and pinned on top of her head. The chief had retired for the night, and in her place stood the sweet, old woman whom Xio was proud to call her great-grandmother.

"*Rahe*." Kaiah touched a cool hand to Xio's face and smiled with deep affection, her eyes twinkling in the light from the wall lamps. "You're so beautiful."

"I take after you, Botoá," Xio replied with a catch in her voice. She pressed her lips against her great-grandmother's forehead, drinking in her earthy scent. The thought that these tender moments would inevitably come to an end deepened the angst in her chest.

"Sweet child," Kaiah astutely said, searching her face. "I haven't heard my ancestors' calls. I'll be here a little while longer."

"Promise?"

"I promise. Though I must confess, I'm a little weary."

"You still have a lot of fight left in you, Botoá, and that gives me hope." Xio kissed her again.

Kaiah hooked her arm through Xio's and led her from the iabora. "Tell me how MJ's training for Guazabi is coming along, and how Akilah is doing in school."

Xio felt as if her botoá was deliberately distracting her from her own problems by asking her to talk about her siblings. As they strolled through the breezeway toward the courtyard that connected the Kú to BÓ-Caneye, she brought her up to date on the lives of the youngest Davenports.

Night had fallen, and in the darkness, Xio listened to the crickets in the grass and the roar of the Ubón Waterfall, which fed the lake behind Kaiah's house. "MJ really enjoys archery. I think he could hit a bullseye with his eyes closed," Xio said, as they walked through the lighted courtyard.

Kaiah chuckled. "His great-grandfather was the master of archery during his time. MJ has inherited that talent, I suppose, and his yanchi tells me he's doing well in mdambé. I'm so proud of him. Your father would have been proud, too."

"Yes." Xio refrained from telling her that MJ was so good, he'd taken down a man three times his size without breaking a sweat. "Akilah's doing alright, I think. Did she tell you she's the new president of her school's career club?"

"No! She didn't tell me that." Kaiah squeezed Xio's side. "How wonderful for her! She's so sharp, that one. Like her Botoá."

Xio held her tightly as they climbed the steps of the great house and onto the vast wooden verandah. "You know Akilah, Botoá. She changes her mind every other day."

"It's good to have choices and to not be afraid of moving on if your original plan isn't working out," Kaiah offered, as they stepped inside the residence.

Xio felt as if her great-grandmother was hinting at Xio's two failed relationships that Kaiah had forewarned her about, but she bit her tongue. She didn't want to give her the satisfaction of having been right, though right she was.

"I hope you're hungry. Mara has been in the kitchen all day," Kaiah said as they sat on the cushioned bench in her iabora.

"Actually, I am," Xio responded as two attendants appeared from behind a white curtain and knelt before them.

Chapter Twenty-Six

CONFESSIONS

After they had eaten in silence for a few minutes, Xio rested her fork on her plate, turned to Kaiah, and asked, "Botoá, why wouldn't you see Raph? You knew he wanted to ask you about his grandfather. He's just trying to get some answers about his family. Truthfully," she admitted, "I have questions, too."

Kaiah took her time chewing and swallowing her grilled fish, tapped the corner of her mouth with her napkin, then took a sip of wine before meeting Xio's gaze. "Not all truths are to be revealed at the whim of the seeker, Xiomara. Take what happened between you and Rapheus for instance. I'm curious, but I haven't asked."

Xio didn't have to wonder how her botoá knew. She had the gift of sight. Had she seen them in her father's office yesterday, and then on the sofa in The Davenport today? She lowered her gaze.

Kaiah leaned into the table and touched Xio's hand lying on the white tablecloth. "I didn't need to see you and Rapheus to know what happened between you. I smelled him on you the minute you walked into the Kú."

But I took a shower and washed my hair. Apparently, not well enough, she thought, averting her eyes, even though she detected no condemnation in her great-grandmother's expression.

The Megiri didn't have hang-ups about chastity and virginity. When a woman reached the age of consent, which was seventeen, she could have as many, or as few, lovers as she desired. Polygamy was customary for both men and women, and safe sex was highly encouraged with condoms. Other methods of birth-control were available free of charge for both sexes.

Salacious visions of her and Raph riding bareback filled her with reawakening desire. She sipped her wine, her body aching to feel him again.

"If you continue to dwell on what you don't want me to see, you will give me a portal into your thoughts. That's the nature of my gift," Kaiah warned.

Xio took a bite of Mahi Mahi and immediately turned her thoughts to Stamer, though, she didn't want to mention it at the table when staff could be lurking just outside the door. She knew they could never speak of anything they heard or saw in BÓ-Caneye, but Xio didn't want anyone to know about her impending demise. She felt foolish enough as it was without being at the receiving end of pitiful glances from her great-grandmother's staff.

Setting Stamer aside until they were alone, she decided to test Kaiah's memory. "Botoá, I've been meaning to tell you something since we sat down, but…"

"What is it, Rahe?" Kaiah asked when Xio hesitated.

She wondered if she should wait until Raph got here.

"You know you can always tell me anything."

Xio closed her hand around her pendant. *No.* She couldn't wait. She needed to know. "Mom invited Raph to dinner last night, and she brought out some old videos and photos of his grandparents with her and Dad and me."

"That was nice of her. I'm sure he enjoyed seeing this side of them."

"He did, but as you can imagine, he was shocked to learn that they had a life down here that his family didn't know about."

She simply nodded.

"I showed him Dad's office, because, you know… Well, his grandfather and Dad spent a lot of time there. But when Raph saw Eagle's clock, he froze, Botoá. It was like he'd seen a ghost. He told me his family has one just like ours. He showed me pictures and all. He said Andris told him that the clock was made by Thaddeus Giannopoulos almost four-hundred years ago, which got us thinking that Thaddeus must have made both clocks, and that there must be a connection between our families. Plus, Mom said that the last time Andris was here, he told Dad that he'd discovered a disturbing link his family has with the island. Do you know anything about it?"

Xio's brows furrowed as she realized that Kaiah hadn't reacted to anything she'd just said. She hadn't even blinked while Xio was talking. "Did you know about the clocks? Tell me Botoá… Was it really Thaddeus who made Eagle's clock?"

Kaiah sat back and folded her hands over her stomach. "I cannot tell you anything, Xiomara, not until Rapheus gets here."

"So, you do know something," she pressed.

"I do, but as I said before, all will be revealed in time." Kaiah took a sip of water.

"Raph told me the clock used to give him nightmares when he was a child."

Kaiah's head dipped slightly with interest. "Like yours?"

What? She'd never told anyone about them. "How do you know about my nightmares, Botoá?" she asked, dropping her hands to her lap to hide their shaking.

"The morning after your sixteenth birthday at Eagle's Nest, I got up very early, and was reading in your sitting room when I heard you gasping for breath. I knew immediately what it was. But tell me, Rahe, how old were you when you had the first one?" Kaiah asked.

Xio reached for her stone again as anxiety tumbled through her. It was seventeen years ago that she had broken the sacred law, and although she knew she was too old to be punished, the disappointment she anticipated she would see in her botoá's eyes made her feel like she was a child again. She dropped her gaze to the table. "I'm sorry, Botoá."

"About what, Rahe?"

Xio lifted her face. "I first had the dream when I was thirteen. It was after Rocotiéri… Some of us went into a burial cave."

"Xiomara Jewel Davenport!" Kaiah's body stiffened and her lips tightened.

Tears welled in Xio's eyes. "I'm sorry," she said again, "That's why I never told you, or anyone else. I knew what it meant. I knew that I had angered Maketaori Guayaba. I was scared and I didn't want to get anyone in trouble." Xio pressed both hands into her chest, trying desperately to still her wildly racing heart.

Without saying another word, her great-grandmother stood and shuffled her petite body around the corner of the table. She pulled Xio's tear-dampened face into her soft bosom, placed her hand over Xio's forehead, and began to murmur, just as she did when she prayed to the zemis. When she removed her hand, Xio realized the pain in her chest had vanished.

Xio marveled at the magic in her great-grandmother's touch. Her botoá always knew how to ease her mind and body, and make her feel at peace with the world.

"Now it's time for my confession," Kaiah said.

"What confession?"

"When I heard you moaning in your sleep, and gasping upon awakening, I knew you had been shadowed."

"You did? Why didn't you ever say anything to me about it?"

"I'm sorry, Rahe, but I knew that the source of the dream was buried deep, somewhere dark and forgotten, and I did not want to say anything to you until I'd spoken with Katone, our shadow guide. She advised me not to question you about it. She told me that the truth will be revealed in time."

That's exactly what you just said to me about Raph. Xio remembered spending time at Katone's home with her granddaughter, Isa. On one of her visits with Isa, Katone had asked Xio how her dreams were coming along. At the time, Xio thought she was referring to her dreams of following her father into the hotel business. Everyone was aware of that. Now, she wondered if Katone had sensed the shadow following her long before Kaiah had known about it.

It didn't matter anymore. She was more interested in the meaning of her dream and whose pain she was reliving. "When will it be time to talk about my dream?" she asked, glancing up at Kaiah, still standing beside her.

"I don't know, Rahe."

So, her botoá didn't know everything after all.

Kaiah smiled. "Xiomara, you are too young to worry yourself over time. It is only when you get to be my age that time becomes a thing you must fight, both for and against. I will tell you and Rapheus what I know when he is here."

"When will that be?"

"When he is ready. Rapheus needs to understand our people and our history, before he can understand his own."

"He only has a few days here, Botoá."

"Then we shouldn't have to wait too long for him, should we?" Kaiah winked playfully. "In the meantime, you will keep an old woman company, yes?" She touched Xio on the cheek.

Xio's anxieties melted as she pressed her cheek into Kaiah's warm, weathered palm. "Yes, Botoá." After all, spending time with her great-grandmother was the reason she had come to Xiobayo in the first place.

Kaiah clapped her hand. "Let's have tea and dessert in the

sitting room. I sensed there is another reason you came to see me."

Yeah, and it was only a matter of time before it came tumbling out of her, Xio thought, following Kaiah out of the dining room.

"So, Xiomara, what is it that troubles you?" Kaiah asked, only after Mara had poured their lemongrass and mint bush tea, served one of Xio and Kaiah's favorite desserts, Budin de Pan, and left Kaiah's private sitting room, closing the door behind her.

Finally, and truly alone with her great-grandmother, Xio pulled her bare feet beneath her and curled into the chair with her bread pudding in her lap.

The room was small and cozy, and a standing fan rotating in a corner kept them cool, the low hum drowning out the sounds of the night creatures in the gardens. Mt. Cayacáo loomed over them in the moonlight against a starry sky.

"It's about Stamer," she said, bracing herself for what was to come.

Kaiah cocked an eyebrow as she placed a bite of pudding into her mouth. "What has he done this time?"

"Well, you know Jewel Beach was in a lot of trouble a few years ago."

"Yes, between Fitzroy and Hurricane Julie, she was almost lost."

Xio noticed the acerbity in Kaiah's voice when she spoke her great-grandson's name. But who could blame her? Fitzroy has always been a scourge on their family name.

Long before he left the island, Kaiah had banned Fitzroy from BÓ-Caneye after he had stolen a priceless bracelet that had belonged to her mother, Dacica Naima. Luckily, Sherylyn had found it before Fitzroy could sell it in Sint Maarten, and it was returned to

Kaiah. At the time, everyone had thought Sherylyn's good deed was merely an attempt to get into Kaiah's good graces after putting Xio's father through hell during their divorce. Kaiah was nevertheless grateful to her, but she was also furious and embarrassed by Fitzroy.

"Rahe," Kaiah prompted softly.

Xio refocused her attention to the kind, wrinkled face. "You know that almost every bank I went to denied my loan application. And those that approved it offered me interest rates and terms that were so horrible, I would have only fallen deeper into debt and probably lost JBR, and everything else in the process."

Kaiah took another bite of pudding, but said nothing.

Xio swallowed and, placing her dessert on the table, she planted her feet on the floor, and her elbows on her thighs. She clasped her hands and stared into her steaming cup of tea. "Trevor offered me a loan through his father's bank, and it was a great offer," she explained. "He said he was trying to make up for hurting me, but he said we couldn't let his father know because he wouldn't have approved."

She raised her head and met Kaiah's gaze that seemed to ask, *And you believed him?*

"I was desperate, Botoá. But Jewel Beach bounced back, and I was meeting my obligation every month. I was on track to fulfill the demands of the loan, and even go beyond that to pay it off faster than expected."

"Then what is the issue?" Kaiah took a sip of her tea.

Xio curled her toes into the soft fibers of the lambskin rug, her anger building. "Two days ago, Samuel came into my office accusing me of fraud."

Kaiah's eyes turned stone cold. "Fraud? What kind of fraud?"

"Bank fraud."

"How is that even possible? You would never do anything like that."

"No, I wouldn't. And I didn't, I swear to you." Xio sat up and crossed her arms over her stomach. "But I was stupid enough to allow Trevor back into my life. Last week, he came to my office begging me to give him a second chance."

"And did you?"

"No. I would never marry into that disgusting family." Bile rose to her throat at the thought.

"You should have never been in bed with them in the first place," Kaiah said in a soft voice.

Xio knew she wasn't condemning her, but rather pointing out the obvious truth that everyone, except Xio, had seen from a mile away.

"But, I suppose you were hoping for a different outcome," Kaiah added, her lips tightening. "What did Trevor do when you refused him?"

"While I was in the bathroom changing for my boxing class, he switched out the contract that I had signed with one he and his father had doctored to make it look like I had inflated my assets to get the loan."

Kaiah's nostrils flared, and her hands balled into fists on her lap.

Xio's anger and fears grew as she watched her ninety-four-year-old great-grandmother fight to contain her wrath. Part of her suddenly wished she hadn't troubled her with her stupid mistake.

Finally, Kaiah unclenched her fists and looked sternly at Xio. "What does he want?" She raised a finger. "No, I know what he wants. What are his terms?"

"Marry Trevor and give him fifty-one percent of Jewel Beach, hand it over for a couple hundred thousand dollars, or go to prison. He said even if I choose prison, the hotel would eventually be put on the market and he would buy it." She wiped the snot running from her nose with the back of her hand. "He gave me thirty days to decide. I don't know what to do, Botoá. I..." Unable to hold back her sorrow, Xio scooted off the chair and over to the two seater where she fell into Kaiah's arms, sobbing into her lap.

"There, there, my sweet Jewel. There, there," Kaiah crooned in a soothing voice as she brushed Xio's hair back from her face with one hand and stroked her back with the other. "It will be okay. It will be okay."

Xio held on to her botoá and let the sadness, the anger, and the humiliation over falling into the Stamers' trap wash over her. When she finally sat up, she wiped her face on her napkin. "I think I really just needed to hear that," she said, smiling weakly at Kaiah. "I'm sorry, I didn't want to burden you with this."

Kaiah covered Xio's trembling hands with her own. "I wish you had listened to your mother and stayed clear of that family."

Xio nodded, no longer able to defend herself. "I know. I know. And now I could lose Daddy's legacy. He must be so disappointed in me."

"You did what you thought you needed to do. There's no use crying over it now."

"I can't help it. I feel so…so lost."

"Well, Rahe, what are you going to do to find your way again?"

Xio shrugged. "I don't know. I was hoping you would tell me what to do."

"You have three options before you. Which do you think is the best?"

Xio sank into the cushions and stared across the room at the potted purple orchid, her botoá's favorite flower.

"Are you going to marry Trevor?" Kaiah asked.

Xio shook her head.

"Are you willing to go to jail?" she asked again, moving the process of elimination along.

She shook her head again.

"Then you have made your decision."

"But I don't want to sell. That resort has been in our family for generations, ever since Eagle opened the boarding house. Only a Davenport will be able to take care of it."

"Yes," Kaiah said with a heavy sigh. "But nothing lasts forever, does it?"

"No, but it might have lasted longer if I hadn't been so stupid."

Kaiah placed her hand under Xio's chin and lifted her face. "You are not stupid, Xiomara. You're just too trusting and ready to forgive and forget the wrongs of others."

"But you've always told me that forgiveness is better than anger and hate."

"There are some people you forgive and take back into your arms because they are worth your love. Then, there are others, like the Stamers, who you forgive, forget, and stay away from." She paused. "Is it the end of your world if you lose Jewel Beach, Xiomara?"

Xio dug her nails into her palms. Kaiah wasn't a Davenport, so maybe Jewel Beach didn't mean as much to her as it did to Xio. Hell, she didn't even know if it meant much to Akilah and MJ, and since she was so unlucky in love, she might never have children to pass it on to. "I just don't want him to win," she said.

"Who said anything about winning? He might have bitten off much more than he can chew this time."

"What do you mean by that?"

"Just that I've lived long enough, heard enough, and seen enough to know that most people regret receiving the things they covet."

As Xiomara tried to puzzle out Kaiah's meaning, Mara opened the door.

"They are ready for you, Dacica." She bowed her head, and stood waiting for Kaiah's word.

"Why don't you go upstairs. You look like you could use some rest. Maybe the answer will come to you in your dreams."

"What about you, Botoá?"

"I have to join a call to decide what to do about that French journalist. It seems as though his government is very eager for him to return home." Kaiah smiled amusingly and lifted her elbow for Xio to help her stand. She glanced down at the table. "Eat your pudding, Xiomara," she said with a gentle smile. "A lot can happen in twenty-eight days."

Yeah, like Stamer and Trevor could drop dead.

"And one more thing, Xiomara. You are not to speak to Rapheus until he arrives. Do you understand? No calls. No messages."

"Yes." Xio felt like a child on time-out, but rules were rules, and she knew better than to argue with the chief in front of her staff.

Kaiah turned to leave, then stopped and looked thoughtfully at Xio. "Why don't you take Rapheus to Aetós? Be his guide on the hike."

Xio twisted her hand in front of her. "Why would I do that? I have my own problems to deal with. I came to Ynoa to spend time with you, Botoá, and try to figure out how to fix them. This is as far as Andris asked me to take Raph. I don't have time to—"

"I understand, Rahe, but in my ninety-plus years on earth, I've learned that sometimes the solution appears when you aren't even looking for it. Give yourself some space, go breathe some fresh mountain air, and I'm sure that by the time you return, you'll know what to do." She smiled at Xio affectionately. "Now finish your dessert and go to bed. *BÓ-Hupia-tí*, Rahe."

Xio kissed both her cheeks. "BÓ-Hupia-tí, Botoá."

Chapter Twenty-Seven

SPECIAL DELIVERY

RAPH JUMPED awake at the loud pounding on his hotel room door. He opened one eye and glanced at the bedside clock. Who the hell could be knocking at this hour in the morning, and with such impatience? Was the hotel on fire? He didn't smell any smoke.

"Coming!" he yelled at the persistent knock, groaning inwardly that his *coming*—deep inside Xio's warm, succulent body—had been rudely and unwelcomely interrupted.

Instead of the nightmare that had haunted him the night before, last night he'd had the wildest dream of making love with Xio on a secluded, black sand beach. It was even hotter and sweeter than what they had shared in The Davenport.

With a grunt, he stumbled out of bed, grabbed the robe from the foot bench, and shrugged into it on his way to the door. He yanked it open, blinking as the bright light from the corridor bulbs blinded him. "What the—"

He checked his anger at the sight of a stern faced Garayx. His straight, jet-black hair, peppered with strands of gray at the temples, was pulled back and twisted into a long single braid.

"Mr. Giannopoulos?" the hajime said, looking up and down the hall, "I need you to come with me now."

Raph frowned and pulled his robe tighter about him. The breeze coming through the open hall window was chilly, especially at this time of day. Xio wasn't lying about how cold it got over here at night. "And where are we going?"

"To Xiobayo."

Two days ago, Xio had promised to call when she arrived in Xiobayo. She'd also promised to come back to see him yesterday, but he hadn't heard a word from her all day.

He'd texted to ask where and how she was, and his follow-up call had gone straight to voicemail. He hadn't bothered to leave a message. What would he say? *I miss you? I'm burning for you? I'll show you mine if you show me yours?*

Despite his frustration, his sleep deprivation, and being as horny as a toad, Raph couldn't say he hadn't enjoyed himself in Wawu.

On the first day here, he'd been waiting on the steps of the Museum of Megiri History when the doors opened at ten o'clock, and had spent three and a half hours learning about a side of Caribbean history that he had never heard of.

In middle school, he'd been taught next to nothing about any South American or Caribbean indigenous people. What little he did learn, often framed their history in a way that justified historical injustices against them and their continued marginalization.

But those old school textbooks and their convenient truths had been written by outsiders. Here, in Ynoa, the Megiri still controlled the narrative.

After working up an appetite walking the rooms of the museum, studying images of Megiri gods and goddesses, learning about their customs, and admiring pottery and other art works, he had taken full advantage of the Food and Agricultural Fair taking place this weekend. He'd strolled the park grounds, sampling stews and dumplings, barbecued meats, freshly caught grilled fish, and cassava breads and cakes.

The flavors—clove, ginger, nutmeg, vanilla, garlic, cinnamon, coconut, and hot peppers—had danced in his mouth. He'd bought jars of tamarind paste, bundles of cinnamon sticks, vanilla pods, guava cheese, and bottles of hot sauce for himself, his mother, and each of his brothers. Raph wanted to remember this day once he was back in San Francisco.

From the craft stalls, he'd picked out ayocin studded earrings and gold bracelets for his mother, and for Petra, a purple, hand-sewn dress made from locally grown and spun cotton.

Back in his hotel room yesterday evening, after a hot shower, Raph had opened his laptop, and spent the rest of the night combing through the initial reports of a multi-million-dollar project Tele had landed in Denver before crawling into bed, exhausted, and falling into a sweet dream about Xio.

He had hoped Xio would have returned to drive him to Xiobayo herself, but beggars couldn't be choosers, and the thought of finally having an audience with Kaiah eased his disappointment. Yes, he was relieved that the waiting game was over, but why was he being whisked away at 5:30 in the morning?

"The Dacica will explain everything when you arrive," Garayx said, as if reading his mind. "I have already checked you out. I'll wait for you in the car." He turned and walked toward the stairs without any further explanation.

Raph closed the door, shrugged out of his robe and jumped into the shower. He shaved quickly, collected his clothes and personal items from around the room, slid into a pair of dark blue slacks and the white button-down shirt he'd had the good sense to iron and hang the night he'd checked into the hotel. After grabbing his phone and charger from the nightstand, Raph took one last look around to make sure he hadn't forgotten anything before closing the door.

The sun came up shortly after they left the hotel. They drove south into Xiobayo, passing village after village as they traveled around the mountainside, climbing up steep hills one minute, then cruising down lush valleys the next.

Raph had tried to engage Garayx in conversation, but the man had given only curt responses. He wanted to ask him if he'd ever met a Greek man named Andris Giannop— Aetós, or his wife Kerena, but convinced that he wouldn't get much out of him, he instead let his thoughts wander to the unique access he was being given to this world, and quietly watched it all pass by through his window.

The Megiri were early risers, so Raph was not surprised to see several stands already set up along the roadside where vendors sold and traded fruits, vegetables, cold drinks, and home-made goods.

Even though Xio had warned him of what to expect in the most protected areas of Ynoa, as they traveled further south and deeper into the heart of Xiobayo, Raph felt as if he'd been trans-ported back in time. Near naked men and women walked along the roadside carrying baskets of goods on their heads. Older villagers rode bareback on horses and donkeys laden with sacks of fruits and vegetables.

Garayx pulled off the mountainous highway and cruised along a flat stretch of road. Anxiety crept through Raph as he tried to recall every little detail of what Xio had told him about the proper way to greet the chief. He wished that he'd taken notes.

Don't mess up, don't mess up, he thought, as the Mercedes finally came to a stop in the courtyard. Raph looked up in awe at the massive mahogany doors of the Kú, his heart sinking that Xio wasn't there to welcome him. He wondered if she even knew that her great-grandmother had sent her head of security to whisk him away from Arijua before the break of dawn.

"I hope your ride was pleasant, Mr. Giannopoulos," Garayx said.

Raph met his gaze in the rearview mirror. "It was. *Hahom*."

The man's lips cracked on a slight smile. "I'll get your door." He hopped out and walked around the vehicle.

The chilly mountain breeze wrapped around Raph when Garayx opened his door, but as he stepped down into the stone-cut courtyard, the early morning sun peeking through the treetop warmed him.

"Welcome to BÓ-Caneye, Mr. Giannopoulos," Garayx said. "Your bags will be taken care of," he added when Raph took a step toward the trunk. "Dacica Kaiah is waiting for you." He gestured toward the steps leading up to the Kú, before getting back into the Mercedes and driving off.

His task of delivering his passenger to the chief was complete, while Raph's journey was just beginning. As he ascended the steps, he wondered, and worried about the answers awaiting him inside.

<h1 style="text-align:center">Chapter Twenty-Eight</h1>

RAHECICA OF YNOA

RAPH STEPPED barefoot through the white door and into the Kú.

The first thing he saw were the twelve armed warriors with the flag of Ynoa painted on their bodies, standing in a protective circle on the steps of the dais, obscuring the dacica from his view, and bringing the images he'd seen in the museum springing to life before his eyes.

Xio was still nowhere in sight.

A few seconds, later, the warriors tapped their spears on the floor three times, then stepped apart, giving him his first-ever live view of Dacica Kaiah, poised stoically on her dujo. She wore a multicolored robe, an elaborate feather headdress, and the guanine—her symbol of authority—around her neck. To the left of the dujo was a small round table with what looked like a folded orange sarong on top of it.

Adrenaline coursed through Raph's veins as he stood with his hands flat against his thighs, his head bowed, and his eyes fastened on the chief's hands resting on two thick braids in her lap, just as Xio had instructed him.

He could feel her assessing him, trying to determine his character, but raising his eyes to meet hers before he had been officially accepted was a sign of arrogance and disrespect.

Raph had met some of the most powerful people in the world—men mostly, some of them taller and larger than him—yet he had never been intimidated by any of them. But Dacica Kaiah, a petite woman and a family friend, unnerved him. He was out of his element, no longer in control. Here, in Ynoa, she possessed all the power. And as the silence and the suspense dragged on, he was certain that she was testing his patience, one of the lessons she'd left him in Arijua to learn.

Xio had told him that some people got this far, only to be turned back for jumping the gun when they thought the chief was taking too long to address them. At this point, Raph didn't care if she kept him here all day. He would be patient until the end.

When she finally raised her hand, indicating that he could step forward, he walked across the wood floor on unsteady legs, climbed the steps of the dais, dropped to his knees, and kissed her ring.

Kaiah tapped his forehead, then rose to her feet in one gracefully fluid motion that belied her age.

When Raph stood up, he found her looking right through the core of him, opening doors he'd tightly shut, unwrapping secrets he'd hidden away, seeking out hurts he'd carefully masked. He'd been eager to meet her, but now that he was in her presence, as she continued her silent probing into his innermost thoughts, Raph suddenly had the feeling that he had set foot on a path that would change the course of his life forever.

Her face was strong and wise—that of someone who knew things he would never be able to comprehend. Her cheekbones were high, her forehead flat, her nose small and pert, and her chin, resolute and angular. Her skin was now wrinkled and spotted with age, yet wisdom resided between each fold. Her thick braids hung from her crown, almost to her knees. And though ninety-four years old, she stood firm and erect.

She took his hands in hers, wrapping her age-worn fingers around his in a firm welcoming grip. "Rapheus Xander Sebastian Giannopoulos, grandson of Andris and Kerena, you are exactly as he said. Strong, confident, and determined." Her voice was uncompromising.

It touched Raph deeply to hear her call him the grandson of Andris and Kerena. He squeezed her hands, grateful that she had finally agreed to accept him. "Dacica Kaiah, it is wonderful to meet you at last. How are you?"

"As well as an old woman can be." She released him and waved her wrists in the air.

The warriors immediately filed out and disappeared through a door at the back of the room.

Raph wondered if they'd ever had to use their weapons to protect her.

"How was your stay in Arijua?" Kaiah asked.

"It was nice. Thank you for asking. And thank you for arranging it," he replied. "There was so much I didn't know until yesterday. I mean, I didn't even know Ynoa existed until a few weeks ago."

Her eyes grew somber, and she breathed deeply and slowly while pressing her hands into her chest. Her voice faltered when she spoke. "Even though death is a journey we must all take, I was very grieved when I learned of Andris' passing. He was a *taiguaitiao*, a very dear friend. Not only to me, but also to my grandson, Malik. I had not seen him in many, many years, but he was still my friend."

"Did you know my father? Claudia told me that he visited the island a few times."

"I did meet your father." She chuckled. "He was not keen on our little island."

"Claudia told me," Raph said, smiling.

"In spite of his dislike for island life, I remember him as a very polite and sweet little boy. Kerena was always trying to entice him to come down with them, but eventually I told her to leave him alone. You cannot force a person's spirit." She cleared her throat. "I've missed Kerena, just as I've missed my own daughter and grandson."

Raph choked back a rush of sadness. "I wish I'd known about you and the Davenports, but Pappoús only told me about Akilina moments before he died."

"That would have been nice, but you're here now to honor his dying wish. I'm sorry for the early wake-up call this morning, but I have to leave for Huguay shortly. And you need to get to Aetós before the full moon."

"Yes. Day after tomorrow."

"That should give you enough time to settle in before the ceremony." She paused, her eyes grilling into him before she spoke again. "Before you leave, there is someone I must introduce to you."

"My guide?" he asked.

Amusement flicked in her eyes. "Yes, your guide," she said, settling herself on the dujo.

Recalling Xio's instructions and what he'd learned at the museum, Raph promptly and carefully backed down the steps of the dais to the floor.

Kaiah bestowed him with a smile, tinged with appreciation at his knowledge about Megiri customs, then clapped her hands twice.

Raph's knees buckled when the Megiri Princess emerged from an archway at the side of the room.

She was painted from her neck to her feet in patterns of red, white, and golden-brown hues, but her face was bare, and he feasted on the desire radiating from her beautiful brown eyes. Atabey, the supreme mother of fresh water and fertility was painted on her stomach—her belly button acting as the goddess' open mouth. Raph envisioned dipping his tongue into that tiny opening, again and again. Her hair, parted in the middle, fanned her cheeks, and cascaded down her shoulders, spreading over her breasts like a curtain of thick black silk—high, full breasts that Raph had been dreaming about, just an hour ago.

She wore only a red cotton inagua secured around her hips by a brown silk ribbon, and a red bougainvillea flower in her hair.

"Mr. Giannopoulos." Dacica Kaiah's voice broke into his erotic thoughts. "I present my great-granddaughter, *Rahecica* Xiomara Jewel Davenport of Ynoa." She turned to Xio and extended her hand. "Rahecica Xiomara, Rapheus Xander Sebastian Giannopoulos."

As Xio glided seductively toward him, each sway of her hips making his pulse beat faster and faster. Raph could feel Kaiah's watchful gaze on his face, analyzing his reaction. But there was nothing he could do about his growing arousal. She was damned hot.

He inhaled deeply when she stopped in front of him and licked her lips, slowly and invitingly. She smiled up at him with an innocence she did not possess—not one ounce—and allure rose from her body in waves, wrapping around, and filtering through him.

He had no idea what all this meant. It hadn't been part of his museum experience, and Xio hadn't explained it to him the other night. Logic told him to run, get the hell out of BÓ-Caneye, out of Ynoa, and off the island. But passion kept him grounded—kept his eyes locked on the drop-dead beauty standing in front of him.

"Mr. Giannopoulos," she said, extending her hand with a huge ayocin ring on her forefinger.

Not knowing what to do, if he was even allowed to touch her, he stood frozen, his gaze darting warily between Xio and Kaiah.

"My ring," Xio whispered. "You have to kiss my ring, say my name, and bow as you release me."

Shit. He had to bow to her, too? He took her hand. "Rahecica Xiomara." His voice shook, and so did his body as he followed her instruction. His lips lingered a little too long against her skin as he gazed deeply into her eyes.

Pulling her hand free, she removed the flower from her hair and, raising up on her toes, tucked it behind his ear, sending a wave of desire through his core when her warm fingers brushed his neck and her knuckles his cheeks. He could feel the pulse of her heart in her touch, beating in time with his as the familiar hypnotic field between them began to grow, pushing them toward each other.

"*Rahu*! Children!" Kaiah's assertive voice shattered the moment. He snapped back to reality and stepped away from the princess.

She'd called them children, and that's exactly how Raph felt —like a horny teenager who had come to pick up his prom date and who, after seeing her, couldn't wait to get her somewhere dark and private so he could do things with her he knew their parents wouldn't approve of. Only in this case, he'd already done those things with Xio, and the memory of those moments were dancing across his mind. Judging from the look in Xio's eyes, he knew she was thinking about them, too.

"Rahu," Kaiah repeated, gentler this time. "Now that you have been properly introduced, I can dispense of my role as chief."

She picked up the sarong and, descending the dais, she offered it to Xio who, in one fluid motion, wrapped the cotton fabric around her body and tied it behind her neck.

Disappointing, but probably for the best. As much as he'd enjoyed the view, at the end of the day, he'd rather not be standing in the chief's presence with a raging hard-on for her great-granddaughter, the princess of Ynoa.

"Excuse me while I remove my ceremonial attire," Kaiah said, before walking away.

"What is she up to?" Raph flared his hands down Xio's body as his eyes feasted on her. "I mean it's hot and sexy as hell, and I almost came in my pants when I first saw you, but—"

"I know," she said, catching her bottom lip between her teeth, making his shaft twitch. "I saw the shock on your face."

"When you told me you were a princess, I didn't expect you would be *presented* to me, and certainly not like this. What does all of this mean?"

Xio played with the ayocin ring. "We have just been betrothed."

Raph blinked, and his head jerked involuntarily. "I'm sorry, what?" His throat suddenly felt dry. "Did you... Did you say... Betrothed?" He raked his hands through his hair and stepped back, putting some distance between himself and a future that had just been sprung on him. "Is this for real?"

"Yep. That flower behind your ear sealed the deal." She moved closer to him, her hips snaking slowly from side to side. "Why? Don't you want to marry me?"

"Xio, that— Um that's a big step." *I'm not ever marrying anybody,* was what he wanted to say. But that was too harsh, especially after what had happened between them.

"Fine then." She snatched the flower from his ear and returned it to her hair. "The engagement is off! And you can leave." She pointed to the door. "Now, before the chief gets back."

"No, no, it's not that I wouldn't— I mean... You're lovely, Xiom— Rahecica Xiomara. It's just that... I wasn't expect—"

Xiomara laughed out loud, obviously taking wicked delight in his discomfort. "Relax, Raph, I'm only kidding," she said, placing a reassuring hand on his arm.

Raph's shoulders immediately dropped with relief. He wasn't used to being put on the spot like that. *You are a sexy little devil...*

"You can breathe easy. It wasn't a betrothal ceremony. It was Kaiah's way of honoring you, by introducing you to her family in all their glory. Well, in all *my* glory." She spun around, the sarong billowing to reveal her toned, painted thighs.

She was so freaking hot, and if there wasn't the possibility of the chief walking in on them, he would have had her up against the wall like he'd done in her father's office, only this time, there would be no teasing her. He would be buried deep inside her tight wet… He cleared his throat. "You certainly are glorious, princess."

"I told you already, you don't need to call me that," she admonished.

"Oh, but I think I do. Tell me, what's the significance of the design?" he asked, his eyes sliding appreciatively over her body.

"A princess' body is painted to ensure that the guest she's presented to doesn't try anything inappropriate with her. After the presentation, she would be checked by a rahami to make sure the design was undisturbed. In the old days, violating a princess was reason to go to war."

"So, you're painted between your thighs, too?" His eyes narrowed devilishly.

"Yep," she said, her lips twisting in humor, "which means you can't touch me since we're not heading for the altar. You've got to be on your best behavior, Rapheus."

"Sorry to disappoint you, princess, but that ship has sailed. I don't think you'll be able to keep me from touching you. I would do it right now if your botoá wasn't nearby. I would hate for her to know what we've been up to."

Xio chuckled. "Unfortunately, that ship sailed, too. Kaiah knows we've had sex."

His eyes bulged and his mouth dropped. "Jesus, Xio, I can't believe you told her."

"I didn't have to tell her anything, Raph. Her exact words

were, 'I smelled him on you the minute you walked into the Kú.'"

Raph blushed.

"You don't need to be embarrassed. She's not going to—"

"Rahu."

Raph turned as Kaiah called from the back of the Kú. She was wearing a green embroidered dress and her loose hair fell around her shoulders like a gray cloak. No longer in her ceremonial robes, she looked like a sweet old lady whom any child would want to cuddle up to.

He felt his face turning red, embarrassed that she knew he'd had sex with Xio. Even though he'd learned the Megiri were liberal when it came to sex, he nonetheless felt a tinge of unease in her presence, now.

"Come," she beckoned to them. "Mara is preparing breakfast. We can talk in the courtyard until it is ready."

Chapter Twenty-Nine

BRIDGE OVER TIME

"You didn't tell me how lovely it is here," Raph remarked, as he and Xio stood in the courtyard garden between the Kú and BÓ-Caneye, breathing in the fresh mountain air.

"You never asked."

True. He'd been too preoccupied with finding answers to his myriad of questions to consider the island's natural beauty and the locals' connection to it. It was like living in the center of a rainforest, he thought, appreciating the sight of a frothy waterfall cascading down a rocky hill into a lake, just a few yards ahead. Green mountains and valleys encompassed the scene, adding a touch of serenity to the surrounding. "Did you spend a lot of time here when you were a kid?" he asked.

She nodded, gathering her wind-tossed hair into a ponytail and securing it to the top of her head with an elastic she had grabbed from a table on their way out of the Kú. "My grandmother brought me every month for Rocotiéri, and my dad brought me over a lot on weekends."

"What's Rico—cor...?"

She smiled at his attempt to pronounce the word. "Ro-co-ti-eh-ri is a story-telling night. In every village, under the full moon, villagers gather in the batey to celebrate it. And sometimes neighboring villages would join together."

"The batey is the ceremonial park in the center of every village, right? I learned that at the museum.

"That's right. Anyway, on Rocotiéri, there's music and dancing and a lot of food. We give thanks to our ancestors and gods and goddesses for their protection. But the most important event of the night is when the BÓ'Roco—that's the storyteller—stands in the front of the batey and chants the history of the village."

"So, will they have Rocotiéri in Aetós when we're there?" Raph asked.

"Definitely. Rain or shine."

Raph wondered if his pappoús ever attended a Rocotiéri. He smiled at the thought of it. The more he learned about Ynoa's customs, the more he understood why his grandparents loved it here so much. It was rich in culture, and the people, from what he'd learned at the museum and observed at the food festival, were very friendly and welcoming.

Raph was surprise when Kaiah quietly appeared between him and Xio, laced her hand through his arm, and rested her head against his shoulder, as if it were the most natural thing in the world. He relaxed into her embrace, imagining that this is how it would have felt to cozy up with his grandmother, had she lived to see him become a man.

Kaiah pointed a bony finger at the scenery. "That's the Ubón Waterfalls, and that's Lake Nori."

"Beautiful." Raph's breath caught in his throat when Xio's hand brushed against his side as she curled it around Kaiah's waist. He prayed for the strength to resist her pull on him in the presence of her great-grandmother.

"And this," Kaiah added, "was your grandparents' favorite spot when they visited me. We spent many wonderful moments in this courtyard, just sitting quietly and enjoying the beauty of the gods."

Raph gently squeezed her frail hand, his heart warming toward her. "I can tell those moments were very special for you, and for them. Thank you for sharing, Dacica Kaiah." He swiped the back of his hand across his misty eyes and smiled down at her.

"If there was time, I would tell you stories about them."

"That would have been nice." At least he had gathered a few special memories about their time down here to take back home to his family.

"I would have loved to hear them, too," Xio remarked.

"Perhaps, we will make time before you fly back home, then." Kaiah tilted her head back and gave him a warm smile.

"Oh, that would be awesome." He resisted the desire to kiss her forehead. *Too soon.*

Kaiah sighed, then abruptly stepped out of their embrace. "Come," she commanded, walking ahead of him and Xio.

She sat on a bench beneath a cherry tree, and motioned for them to sit on the one in front of her that faced the waterfall and the lake. "I know you have many questions, Rapheus," she began, "however, my knowledge is limited. I will give you the answers I have, but others can only be found in Aetós. Where would you like to start?"

Raph sat down, feeling a ball of nerves gather in his throat as he thought of the question that had been bothering him for the past three weeks. "Dacica Kaiah, do you know why Pappoús never told me or my brothers about Akilina?"

She shook her head. "I'm sorry, Rapheus, I do not know. But I suppose Andris had his reasons."

Reasons, he had taken to his grave, Raph thought, his heart sinking. He wished they'd had more time…

"Maybe his reasons will be revealed as you learn more about

his time in Ynoa," Kaiah offered, as if sensing his struggle to accept that he had hit a dead end with that question.

Xio cleared her throat. "Speaking of learning more… Botoá, last night when I told you that Raph and I have identical clocks, you didn't seem surprised. You just brushed it off and changed the subject. So, what's the story behind them?"

"You knew about the clocks?" Raph asked bemused. "Pappoús told me that Thaddeus Giannopoulos built mine, and Xio said that her clock was made from the guayacán tree that could only have been found on Ynoa at the time."

"What exactly is your question, Rapheus?"

Raph swallowed the lump in his throat. "Was Thaddeus ever on Ynoa?"

"Yes," Kaiah forthrightly responded. "Not only was he on the island, he also lived here for twenty-four years until he died."

Raph's back went ramrod straight. "What? He died here? We always thought he and his family died in a flood in England. That's the story that has been told in our family for generations."

"Well, I don't know anything about *that* story, Rapheus, but your grandfather told me that Thaddeus lived and died in Ynoa."

Lie number one from his family history debunked. Raph leaned forward, trying to control the quiver in his voice. "So he did tell you something."

She crossed her legs and leaned against the arm of the bench. "He did, the last time he was here."

"What did he tell you?" Xio asked.

"The last time I saw Andris, he was very agitated about seeing the clock."

Xio grabbed his hand, her eyes widening. "Oh my god, Raph. You remember my mom said that the night Andris was at Eagle's Nest for dinner, he ran out of dad's office and the house without an explanation. Daddy had just inherited the clock that year, and had it put in his office. Andris must have seen it for the first time that night."

"Yes, I do remember Claudia relating that story."

"That is exactly what happened, Xiomara," Kaiah confirmed. "Andris came to see me the next day, but I had no idea what he was talking about. I didn't know anything about identical clocks." She shrugged slightly. "I sent him to see the BÓ'Roco in Aetós where he was born."

Raph scooted to the edge of his seat. "The BÓ'Roco? The storyteller?"

Kaiah nodded.

"What did he tell him?"

Kaiah's focus stretched beyond Raph and Xio to the verandah where the staff was setting a table for their breakfast, her face pinched in concentration. Finally, she brought her attention back to them. "I don't know everything, but when Andris returned from Aetós, I felt fear and sadness and anguish in his spirit. Whatever he learned in the mountains, changed him. He wasn't the Andris I had known for thirty-odd years."

A chill ran down Raph's spine, and he fought the urge to get up and pace—the only thing he knew that would keep him from being swallowed whole. But that might be too distracting for Kaiah. He forced himself to stay seated as a sinister question raised its head: *What had spooked his grandfather so much that he'd taken it to his grave?*

"Botoá?" Xio coaxed. "What did Andris tell you?"

"I'll try to recount as much as I can." She took a deep breath. "Andris first explained how his ancestor, Thaddeus, ended up in the Caribbean." Kaiah looked at Raph. "I'm sure you're familiar with your own history of the Ottoman Empire's occupation of Greece."

"I am."

"And about the Janissaries?"

"What's that?" Xio asked.

Raph turned to Xio. "During the Ottoman occupation of Greece, twenty percent of Greek boys between eight and twenty years old were taken from each family and forced to convert to Islam. Some were trained for government service, and others were placed in a military group known as the Janissaries, an elite army of slaves, who were forced to fight their own people and protect the sultan."

"That's terrible," Xio murmured.

"After Thaddeus' older brother was taken by the Janissaries," Kaiah continued, "Thaddeus' father... I'm sorry, I don't remember his name. He joined a militia group to fight the Turks and was killed in battle. The mother died soon after, leaving Thaddeus as the sole caretaker of his two-year-old brother. He was only sixteen, himself."

Jeez. He was just a kid.

"Six years later, the Janissaries came for his eight-year-old brother, and rather than let them have him, Thaddeus killed the soldiers. Well, he thought he'd killed both of them, but one survived. In any event, Thaddeus took his little brother and his new bride, Amaryllis, and boarded a ship for England."

So Thaddeus did leave Greece for England. At least that part of his history was true.

"Why didn't he stay there?" Xio asked.

"When the soldier Thaddeus thought he had killed reported to the authorities, the Turks put a price on his head. Dead or alive, they wanted him back in Greece. Sometime after they'd been living in England, Thaddeus got word from a friend in Greece that the Turks knew he was in England and were coming for him."

"So, they went on the run again." Xio perched on the edge of her seat.

"That's how they came to Ynoa." Raph said.

Kaiah shook her head. "Barbados first, and then Ynoa. When he arrived, because of a two-hundred year old prophecy about a guayanki who would destroy the Megiri, Thaddeus was allowed to stay, but secluded in the mountains until the Dacique felt he could trust him and his family. Thaddeus named their village settlement Aetós."

So, Thaddeus brought a little bit of Greece to Ynoa. But, Barbados... "Wait a minute. Was Thaddeus on that boat with Eagle, the one that came from Barbados?" he asked through the constriction in his throat. *Was he one of the four guayanki I read about in the library?*

Kaiah nodded slowly. "Not only was he on that boat, but he'd built it. It was because of him that Eagle and the others were able to come to Ynoa that night."

"Were they friends on Barbados?" Xio asked.

"Yes, very close friends."

Oh my god, Raph thought, not only was Aetós a town in Greece, but it also meant 'eagle' in Greek. Before he could elaborate the point, Kaiah spoke again.

"Eagle's clock was a gift from Thaddeus. It was a symbol of that friendship."

She should be smiling while telling them that. *Why wasn't she smiling?* His stomach twisted into knots.

"Botoá?" Xio's voice was barely a whisper as she stared at the ground beneath the cherry tree, her face scrunched up in thought, and her steepled fingers tapping against each other "Was it Thaddeus who, um—" She cleared her throat and raised her face to Kaiah. "Was Thaddeus the guayanki who betrayed Eagle?"

Betrayed Eagle? "What betrayal? What are you talking about?" Raph blurted out, watching the muscles in Xio's neck vibrate.

She sighed, and turned to face him. "It's one of the first things we learn in school on Ynoa—the story about Eagle's guayanki friend who betrayed him. The betrayal was so terrible," Xio continued, lowering her gaze, "that the guayanki and his entire family were erased from our history."

Raph's anxiety burned a hole through his stomach. He

wanted to excuse himself, to find a quiet, dark corner and absorb what he was hearing, but the weight of this new information kept him firmly planted in his seat.

Xio turned to Kaiah. "So, was it him, Botoá?"

She held Xio's gaze. "Yes, Rahe, Thaddeus was the guayanki who betrayed Eagle." Kaiah answered as if she'd been waiting a long time to get it off her chest.

Raph slumped against the back of the bench. *A betrayal so bad that Thaddeus was written out of Megiri history?* The thought of it made him sick to his stomach. This had to be the disturbing link his pappoús had promised to tell Malik about.

Xio shifted in her seat—uncrossing and recrossing her legs as she edged away from Raph. Even her shoulders seemed to box him out. Her body language said it all. Just a few days ago at Eagle's Nest, Xio had told him how proud she was to be a Davenport, the descendant of a man who was revered throughout the island. She had promised to help him get to the truth of his family history, but those truths were now spilling into her life in ugly ways.

No wonder his pappoús had been distressed after hearing such a story. No wonder he hadn't been able to face Malik after his last visit. The guilt and shame must have been too much to bear.

He needed more answers. "Dacica?" he asked, humbling himself. "How did Thaddeus betray Eagle? What was so bad that his name was written out of history?"

"I do not know, Rapheus. No Megiri knows, and Andris never told me. The only remaining living person who knows that truth is the BÓ'Roco in Aetós."

They sat in silence, seemingly engrossed in their own thoughts and speculations about what could have happened between the two men who were once close friends. Only the gentle sounds of the breeze passing through wind chimes on the verandah kept them in the present. Raph was grateful when Xio spoke, breaking the quiet discomfort.

"Botoá, weren't there two Greek boys on the boat with Eagle?"

"Yes."

"Was one of them Thaddeus' brother?"

"No, Rahe, they were his sons, Neopheus and Telepheus. They were born in Barbados."

Barbados, not England. Raph wiped his sweaty palms along his thighs, his eyes fixed on Kaiah. "If his brother wasn't on the boat from Barbados, what happened to him? Did the Turks catch him and take him back to Greece?" *Please say, no.*

"No."

He released the breath he'd been holding.

"Thaddeus left him in England with the family he had been working for. They never saw each other again."

Oh, that was just as sad. He could only imagine the life-long pain they must have suffered after their separation. He would die if he ever had to leave one of his brothers anywhere, never to see him again. "Did Pappoús mention the family's name?" he asked.

Kaiah's eyes bore into his before she spoke. "He did not. Like many of us whose family members were stolen, bought, and sold, you will forever carry the burden of knowing you have family somewhere in the world who you'll never ever know, never ever meet."

That stung, but she was right. Raph had always been conscious of the possibility that his ancestors were somehow involved in the Atlantic slave trade. The fact that the Giannopouloses were shipbuilders in England during that period lent validity to his speculation. Even if the ships they'd built had not carried human cargo, they almost certainly carried goods that were the product of slave labor. The realization, and Kaiah's insinuation, left a sickening taste in his mouth. "Did my grandfather tell you how and when Thaddeus and Eagle met?" he asked, steering the conversation into a more palatable direction.

"It was a couple years after Eagle was taken to Barbados. Because he spoke many languages, including English, the plantation owner used him as an interpreter at the docks where Thaddeus built and mended ships. That's where they became friends."

"And then he betrayed him," Xio said, keeping her eyes on Kaiah.

An awkward silence followed.

"Dacica Kaiah," Raph asked tentatively. "Did Pappoús tell you how he found out that he was born on Ynoa?"

"He told me that he found his real birth certificate among his father's things after he died."

Raph wondered where those things were, and if there was more information waiting to be discovered. "It must have been shocking for him to learn the truth about where he came from."

She stared at him for a long silent moment. "None of us are who we think we are, Rapheus. Sometimes we think we want to know the truths about ourselves until we find them, at which point we have to make the difficult decision of denying them and continuing to live a lie, or embracing them for better or worse."

An ominous feeling washed over Raph, and he couldn't help but think that her words about what to do with the truth, once found, were directed specifically at him.

"Raph." Xio gently tugged at his hand.

Certain that all hope of ever holding her again had gone up in flames, he reluctantly faced Xio, only to find empathy and warmth.

"You are not Thaddeus, and I am not Eagle," she said tenderly. "We cannot live our lives in the shadows of the dead."

"I've told you everything your grandfather told me," Kaiah said, looking at both him and Xio. "The rest you'll find in Aetós. I have gifts for you, Rapheus," she added, "something I think you will appreciate. Remind me after breakfast."

"I will. Thanks. And thank you for bridging the gap between my present and past, Dacica Kaiah. Even if I don't find all the answers in Aetós, at least I know how my family is connected to the island."

She beckoned for Raph and Xio to stand in front of her, and when they did, she took each of their hands and clasped them together in hers. "BÓ-Hupia-tí, Rahu. May Guabancex give you safe passage." She uttered a prayer in Megiri, then released their hands.

As if on cue, a woman approached them from behind the low branches of the cherry tree, bowed to Kaiah, and informed her that breakfast was ready.

Xio pulled Raph aside as the woman helped Kaiah stand and assisted her across the courtyard.

"Xio, what does BÓ-Hupia-tí, mean?"

"May the great spirits of our ancestors be with you."

"I have a strong feeling we'll need them."

"Me, too," she whispered.

Part III

TO AETÓS

Chapter Thirty

ANCESTRAL PATHS

RAPH'S PACK was heavy with gifts Kaiah had asked him to take to Mitayna Luyaron, and the porcelain urn that held his grandparents' ashes, wrapped inside a blanket to keep it safe. Xiomara carried their mats and sleeping bags, and a couple days' worth of dried food in her pack.

With each step in his grandfather's old boots—his gift from Kaiah—sadness creeped through him. The backpack he carried had also belonged to his grandparents. From the moment he'd strapped it to his back, Raph had been keenly aware that the pack they once carried up the mountain was now carrying their remains to their final resting place. But most specially, was the fact that his pappoús had entrusted him with the sacred honor of being his sole pallbearer.

"I miss you so much, Pappoús."

Tears stung his eyes, and his throat grew parched and tight. On a shuddering breath, he stopped and pulled his water bottle from the side compartment of his pack. As he raised it to his lips, the forest, heavy with the scent of wet moss, seemed to come alive with bird song, parrots calling to each other from high in the trees, and the sound of ground lizards scurrying across the forest floor. He could make out a sheep bleating from somewhere within the dense brush. Raph lowered the flask and closed his eyes, allowing the sounds of nature to ease the pain in his heart.

There you go, to mikró mou gio, he could almost hear his grandfather's voice whispering on the wind, and his fingers stroking his forehead like he used to do in the years after the accident that changed all their lives—calming him, giving him the strength he needed to continue this most difficult task.

"I won't let you down, Pappoús," Raph whispered in a choked voice. After a few more calming breaths, he returned his water to its slot, and hurried to catch up with Xio.

They were forty-five minutes into Stone Mountain—*Cibao* in Megiri—walking a meandering path with lush ferns dancing in the wind on either side of them. Veteran trees lined the trail, their exposed roots crisscrossing the path while their branches interlaced overhead to form a dense canopy, shading them from the mid-morning sun. The smell of decaying wood and mud filtered through the cool breeze.

Raph didn't mind sharing the narrow path with the few people going back and forth to their homes in the villages between Guaybana and Aetós, or the occasional herd of goats or sheep crossing from one side of the forest to the other. But he was a little annoyed at having to share Xio's company with Fijalí, her body artist, who lived in a village an hour up from Guaybana. After having to contain himself in the Kú when Xiomara appeared wearing Fijalí's work of art on her naked body, he wanted nothing more than to have her to himself.

He'd been following a few paces behind, listening to them talk in Megiri. He hadn't known Xio was fluent in the language. There were a lot of things he still didn't know about her.

Isn't that the way you prefer it with women?

It was. The less he knew, the faster and easier his exit strategy. But after Kaiah's revelation, he found that there were no limits to what he wanted—needed—to learn about Xio, Ynoa, and whatever had transpired between their ancestors, all those years ago.

The time spent on the trail while Xiomara talked with Fijalí had given Raph the head space to think about Thaddeus—at first a hero in his eyes—who had fought off two Janissaries to save his young brother from a life of slavery under Ottoman occupation. Thaddeus had risked everything in the name of family—from Greece to England and Barbados, and then Ynoa. But the darker truth was that Thaddeus was a man capable of murder.

Given that the Megiri had wiped his name from history, even after he'd built the boat that brought Eagle and company to Ynoa—to safety—and fought with them, side by side, against the British and French, he shuddered to think what other dark deeds Thaddeus could have been capable of. What had he done to Eagle, and would Xiomara be able to face him once they learned the truth in Aetós?

The questions intensified his urgency to be alone with her. This could be the last day they had before the burden of Thaddeus' sins overshadowed them, tarnishing their emergent bond.

What the hell did you do, Thaddeus?

Raph frowned, a nauseating despair sinking into his belly. He was surely walking an ancestral path that both Thaddeus and Eagle had walked many times, four hundred years ago, a path that led right into the epicenter where the terrible events had taken place. For each step he took toward the base of Mt. Cayacáo, Raph wanted to take three back.

"Rapheus!"

"What?" Startled, Raph stubbed the toe of his boot against a loose stone on the trail and went flying forward, catching himself just before he hit the ground face-first. He regained his balance and straightened his backpack. His fists curled around the straps to steady his shaking hands and hide his embarrassment.

Up ahead on a small incline, Xio and Fijalí were standing on the side of the path with puzzled looks on both their faces. The voice that had called his name hadn't sounded like Xio's. It was more like the spirited echo of a young girl, a million light years away. But it couldn't be, he told himself. He was just too deep inside his head, too far into the past, and his mind was playing tricks on him. He took a deep breath and closed the distance between him and the women.

"Are you alright?" Xio's eyes searched his face. "You sounded a little vexed there."

"Sorry, I didn't mean to snap." He raked his fingers through his hair, brushing the errant curls back from his forehead. "I was lost in my own head. You startled me, that's all."

"I'm sorry. I've been ignoring you, but I don't see Fijalí often and it was nice to catch up. We've been friends since we were kids."

"I get it." He gave Fijalí a warm smile.

"Her village is down there." She pointed to a narrow path leading away from the trail they were on. "She wants to tell you goodbye, and that she hopes you liked the painting she did on my body."

I love your body. I want to feel it shaking under me again. "I did. I do. It's very beautiful." He smiled at Fijalí, and said. "You're very talented."

Xio translated his message, then blushed at Fijalí's response.

"What did she say?"

"She said you have a strong, beautiful body and she would love to paint it." Her eyes roamed lazily down his body then back to his face.

"You should know." He held her stare, her eyes telling him everything she felt, everything she wanted from him. "You rode this beautiful body like you owned it. Translate that. I dare you."

A hint of challenge appeared in her eyes before she turned to speak to Fijalí.

Fijalí clapped a hand over her mouth and her eyes widened

in shock. They both laughed before she said something to Xio, hugged her, then, shaking her head in amusement, turned down the path that led to her village.

"What did you tell her?"

Xio wrestled her water bottle from the side pocket of her backpack and unscrewed the top. "Exactly what you told me to," she said with a sultry grin.

"You did not!"

"I did. I also told her that you have a nice, thick cock, and that I was dying to ride it again. She said that she doubted it could be any bigger than her second husband's, Tarvo." Xiomara raised her water bottle to her mouth and took a long drink, watching his stunned reaction from beneath lowered lids.

Chapter Thirty-One

UNDER THE GUAYACÁN TREE

When she lowered the bottle, his eyes gravitated to a drop of water glistening on the side of her mouth like a pearly drop of cum. Up until this moment, Raph had no idea that such a mundane image could evoke racy thoughts in him, but it did. And when her tongue darted from between her succulent lips and flirtatiously licked at the drop, Raph's brain went into overdrive.

He was lying on his back, naked, and an equally naked Xio was kneeling between his parted legs, her hard nipples brushing the hairs on his thighs, her slender fingers wrapped around his shaft as the tip of her tongue grazed the head, teasing and tempting him to come in her mouth.

With a low groan, Raph reached out and pulled her up against him—hard—just like he'd wanted to do the moment she'd walked into the Kú wearing nothing but a strip of cotton. If she was still wearing that instead of her tight green leggings, all he would have had to do was unzip his fly, lift the cloth, and ease himself into her.

Xio's eyes burned with lust. Her water bottle slipped from her fingers as she wrapped her arms around his neck, and pressed her body into his.

It was all the consent Raph needed. He lowered his head and brought his mouth just centimeters from hers, inhaling her sweet, hot breath, and releasing the heady rush of excitement it sent through him. "How about you ride it right now?" he asked, huskily.

Xio hissed on a sharp breath as his lips lightly teased the soft contours of her mouth. "Oh God, yes," she begged. She curled her fingers into his hair and pulled his head down. "I want you right now," she rasped, opening her mouth and giving herself freely to the fierceness in his kiss as she moved her hips against him.

Their breaths were hard and ragged as the familiar fire reignited between them, and that undeniable and irresistible pull that had been suspended for two days came back in full force. He moaned into her mouth when her hand slid between them and she delicately curled her fingers around his erection straining against his shorts. He gripped her arm as she teased him, the blood draining from his brain, making him grow under her touch.

After the quickie on the sofa in The Davenport, he'd promised himself that their next time would be slow. He wanted to spend hours caressing, licking, and teasing her, and exploring every inch of her body, searching out her most pleasurable spots until heat and passion consumed them both. But this was neither the place nor the time to carry out that fantasy.

Under the teasing manipulation of her fingers, his throbbing cock was begging to be released. Raph swiftly scanned the forest and spotted a large tree with a trunk wide enough to hide them from the trail.

He ripped his mouth from hers and, ignoring her groan of protest, took her by the hand. He marched her off the trail, dead leaves and undergrowth crunching beneath his hiking boots as he pulled her toward the tree that seemed to be whispering his name. What the hell had happened to the level-headed, focused man who'd landed in Akilina four days ago?

Her lips were wet and swollen from his kisses as she pushed her backpack off her shoulders and dropped it beside his on a soft layer of golden yellow flowers. Just as in The Davenport, words were unnecessary. Their eyes alone revealed the deep desire burning within them both. Their chests rose and fell rapidly as their hands reached for their waistbands, pulling their layers down just enough to get the job done.

Xio braced her hands against the tree trunk. She glanced over her shoulder, her eyes laced with impatience while her tongue slid temptingly over her beautiful lips. The provocative invitation was too much for Raph, and his cock pulsed impatiently in his hand. He moved behind her, brushing her long braid to the side.

She was already wet as he moved into her slowly, inch by inch, giving her time to adjust to him as he watched himself disappear between her tight folds. She pushed back into him, egging him on until he was buried to the hilt. Raph drew back ever so slightly, eliciting a small whimper from her open, pouting mouth, and then slid back in, again, and again, building their pleasure with a slow and steady rhythm he knew would soon escalate into madness.

She groaned deep and hard, and her sounds of pleasure rumbled through him. He'd never been with a woman this sensual, this sexy, this insatiable. It made him feel like a virile jungle king, a potent forest god whose only edict in life was to please the woman whose body he was currently buried inside.

She was pushing back into him with force and speed, turning his slow rhythm into a wild dance, twisting her hips to get more of him, to angle his shaft where she needed him most, while his name, falling from her lips, echoed across the forest.

Driven by a shot of mad lust to conquer and devour her,

Raph wrapped both arms around Xio's waist, hauled her off the tree and held her flush against his stomach. She reached back, locking her arms around his neck as he continued to thrust into her. The friction was incredible, and he gave himself over to the luscious sensations of riding Princess Xiomara Jewel Davenport of Ynoa, burning in the feel of her velvety walls clasping around his cock.

"Oh, god, that feels so good," she whispered.

Raph slid a hand around her, letting it roll off her breasts and down her heaving stomach to her sex, and began working his fingers over her slick clit, rubbing against her in time with his thrusts. He dropped his mouth on her neck and licked her salty skin as she jerked and shivered in his arms.

"Harder. Deeper. Faster. Make me come."

As he bucked recklessly against her, she moved her hips in a slow circle, grabbing his backside, making him work harder and faster to push in and out of her. He slammed into her again, and again, and again…

"Xiomara," Raph whispered, as he felt her body go tight as a bowstring. Then her sex spasmed uncontrollably, sending powerful pulses through his cock. As he felt the familiar tingling in his spine, he crashed into her one last time before pulling out and coming on the foliage at their feet.

Feeling his knees about to give out from under him, Raph turned and dropped his back against the rough bark of the trunk, still holding Xio's quivering body tightly against his belly. He closed his eyes and reveled in the rhapsodic sensations as they fought to bring their breathing under control.

Silence hugged the breezes cooling their damp skin. The creatures in the jungle had gone quiet, as if the world had been shaken off its axis by the force of their passion. A flower fell on Raph's arm, still wrapped around Xiomara's stomach.

Xiomara took the flower in her hands, stifled a laugh, then tossed it to the forest floor. She glanced down at it, then let her laugh rip out of her as she pulled out of Raph's arms and struggled to pull up her underwear and pants.

Raph nervously did the same. "What's so funny?" he asked, zipping his fly as she doubled over in laughter.

She turned, still holding her stomach. "It's a guayacán tree, Raph."

"Am I supposed to know what that means?"

"The guayacán tree is the tree of life. Couples who are having fertility problems have sex under it and then carve their initials into the trunk."

"Oh, Jesus." Raph laughed as he looked up at the canopy of golden flowers. "Of all the trees in the forest, I had to choose this one," he said, pulling Xio back into his arms. "Good thing we aren't trying to start a family, so no carving of names for us." He nuzzled his nose into her neck. He had been tempted to cum inside her again, but it seemed as though he'd been right to err on the side of caution. Lots of women had gotten pregnant while on the pill. He wouldn't want to tempt the Megiri fertility goddess.

"Good thing." She wound her hands around his waist, and laid her cheek against his chest. "I've never had sex in the open like this, but I liked it."

"I liked it, too." He locked his arms around her and stroked his hands down her hair. It was the first time they'd hugged, but somehow it felt more intimate than sex, certainly more intimate than the unrestrained fucking they'd been doing. He loved the lazy, tender feel of her in his arms, her heart beating to the slow rhythm of his. She was becoming an addiction, and he worried that he'd have to fight through withdrawals when he got home.

"We should get going." She pulled out of his embrace.

"Yeah, I guess we have six hours of hiking ahead of us." He helped settle her pack on her back before strapping on his own and followed her back to the trail. The sounds of birds squawking and insects buzzing filled the air again, as though the forest had returned to life. Xio's water bottle, now empty, was exactly where she'd dropped it, lying in a pool of muddy water. He picked it up and tucked it into the side pocket of her pack, then removed his and offered it to her.

She drank down a good portion of his water, then wiped her hand across her mouth as she handed back the flask. He smiled, wondering if she knew it was a tantalizing drop of water on her lip that had started the madness they had just been lost in. He quenched his own thirst, then put the bottle away.

"There's a water source about a mile up where we can fill up, and a few small farms nearby where we can pick fresh fruits. We'll stop for lunch at BO'Acú."

"What's BO'Acú?"

"It's a lookout."

"What does it mean?"

"You'll know when you get there." She moved ahead of him, the trail too narrow for them to walk side-by-side. "Except for the peak on Mt. Cayacáo, it has the best view of the mountain range," she said. "You can see Lake Kitha, the biggest lake on the island, that supplies fresh water to a lot of villages in Ynoa, and on a very clear day, you can see St. Emilia to the south. You'll enjoy it. Trust me."

I'm already enjoying the view. "I trust you," he confessed, following behind her, taking care to step around the loose stones in his path.

He did trust her, and not just about the lookout—something he could never say about any of the women he dated.

But you're not dating her.

True… Which was probably why he trusted her. She was not a pretender; she had no calculated agenda to hold on to him. He enjoyed being around her, not just for the wild sex, but because she was genuinely lovely, intelligent, sweet, and passionate.

She had a way of soothing his anxiety while simultaneously making his heart race with excitement. She was a fighter and a protector—especially of her younger siblings—much like he had always been of Neo and Tele.

Xio, like their mothers, Claudia and Jordan, who had found themselves widowed at a much younger age than expected, prioritized the needs of her family above all else, even in the face of personal grief.

She was the kind of woman every man wanted. The kind he would choose if he was the marrying kind. *He wasn't.* Yet, in the heart of his denial, a burst of loneliness surged into his soul, and he found himself fantasizing about sharing his world with Xio, and being the man she needed.

This place was doing something to his defenses, opening parts of his heart that he had hidden away, and showing him how lonely and unexciting his life really was, making him wish for things he shouldn't be wishing for.

"Hey, Raph."

Raph pulled himself back from his desperate fantasies. Xio had stopped a few feet ahead of him on a flat stretch. Dry plant pods dusted the ground and vines curled around tree trunks in suffocating loops on both sides of the trail. A green praying mantis clung to a low-lying branch over her head, watching them.

Raph checked his watch. They'd left the guayacán tree about thirty minutes ago. "You need a break already?" he asked in a jesting tone. "You did come hard back there, so I'll understand if your knees are a little weak still."

She sucked her teeth and rolled her eyes, making him laugh. She planted her hands on her hips. "You're the one lagging behind, so maybe your knees are weak and you need a break."

Raph caught up to her, and the faint, lingering smell of sex made his cock stir. "My knees are weak, Princess Xio. They go weak every time I think of you. And I'm lagging, just to watch your fine ass moving under those tights." He held her by the nape, tilted her head back, daring her to resist him.

"You could lose your head for talking to a princess like that," she challenged, her tone mockingly authoritative.

"I have no problem losing my head, as long as it's buried deep inside your tight sweet body." He brushed his thumb along her bottom lip.

"No, not that head. I wouldn't dream of taking that from you." She caught his thumb between her teeth and smiled wickedly. "I can smell myself on you."

"Likewise." He tilted her head back another fraction. "You need a bath."

She licked her lips, her eyes growing wide and dark with desire, and her breasts rising and falling under her t-shirt.

"Xiomara Davenport, you are very dirty…" He pulled her up against him. Their sexes collided, sending a new wave of heat rushing through him.

"You're making me wet again," she whispered, reaching under his pack to squeeze his ass. She held him tight and pressed her sex along the hard ridge of his cock, just like she'd done in her father's office.

As he read the temptation in her eyes, Raph imagined them standing right here in the middle of the trail, their packs still on their backs, her pants and panties around her thighs, and his cock thrusting inside her through his unzipped fly.

He licked her neck, loving the salty taste of her, and moved the tip of his tongue behind her ear. He sucked and teased her earlobe, encouraged by her soft moan, and the heat and pressure of her clit against him.

"Oh, god, that feels good," she panted, lifting a leg and hooking her foot around his thigh.

Raph smiled, feeling like a god to have found one of her pleasure spots.

"Open my fly," he whispered. He eased her foot back to the ground, then hooked his fingers into the top of her tights.

As her hands moved to his waistband, the sound of voices

echoed in the stillness. "Damn." Raph glanced over Xio's shoulder to see two men in naguas rounding a bend about twenty yards away. They carried baskets of green bananas on their heads.

As the men got closer, Xio turned around and stood close to him to help hide his erection. But her ass rubbing up against him was just as tantalizing as her clit. *Lord, have mercy.* He placed his hands on her shoulders and edged her to the side of the trail as the men reached them.

"*Tau mautia,* Rahecica," they both said, bowing to their princess, only as deeply as their baskets allowed.

"Tau mautia," Xio replied.

They repeated the words to Raph.

"It means 'good morning'," Xio told him.

"Tau ma—mutia," Raph said, eliciting smiles from everyone at his butchered attempt to speak their language.

The younger one, who looked to be around twenty, spoke to Xio in Megiri. The only word Raph understood was 'Fijalí', before they were on their way again, their soggy sneakers squeaking as they walked.

"Who are they?" he asked, when Xio turned around.

"Fijalí's husbands."

"I thought so when I heard her name mentioned. Which one is Tarvo?" he enquired, remembering Fijalí's remarks about the size of his cock compared to her second husband's.

"The younger one. He's twenty. Fifteen years younger than her. Her first husband, Roque, is forty-three. They got married when Fijalí was seventeen. She and Tarvo have been married for a year now."

"Lucky woman."

"They work on Kaiah's farm," she said, clearly ignoring his quip. "They said to be careful at the creek up ahead. Tarvo fell in and Roque had to pull him out. That's why their sneakers are wet."

Tarvo was probably thinking about getting home to fuck his wife, and lost his balance, Raph thought. He kept it to himself as Xio abruptly left and walked on ahead.

He looked up to find the praying mantis still hugging the branch, watching him. "Peeping Tom," he muttered. "At least I get to keep my head after we mate. That's a lot more than I can say for you." He straightened his pack, his crotch, and his clothes, and chased after his guide, falling into step beside her on the wide path. "You alright, Xio? You seem upset."

"Not at you, Raph," she answered, not missing a step.

"Then at whom?" he asked, as they came to the bend where Raph had first seen Fijalí's husbands. Fractured spider webs drifted in the breeze.

"Not at anyone. It's just that I have to be careful how I act in public, especially when I'm in Ynoa. Sometimes I forget who I am. Thankfully, Tarvo and Roque are friends who would never tell anyone what they just saw. It could have just as easily been someone else, not so eager to keep my secrets. I'm expected to behave in a certain way, and having sex in public isn't acceptable. It isn't acceptable for anyone. Even what we did under the guayacán tree was risky." Xio smoothed her braid over her shoulder. "I keep losing my head when I'm around you."

"I'm sorry. And I get the whole losing-your-head thing. It's the same for me. But I'll keep my hands to myself in public from now on." He thrust them into his pockets to make a point, and gave her a sorry, puppy-dog face.

She laughed, and poked him playfully in the side. "Back there, I had stopped to tell you that there's a lookout called Kabun Amé before we get to the water source and the farms."

"And what does Kabun Amé mean?"

"It means three waters. There are walnut trees on the way, so we can shake some loose to snack on."

They reached the wide, shallow creek, and carefully chose their path around moss-covered stones and over the swiftly moving waters that carried fallen leaves and twigs down the mountain.

"It's about twenty minutes off the trail each way," she continued, "but the view is breathtaking, and I think it's worth the detour. We'll still have time to get to Aetós before sunset."

Raph was losing himself in a fantasy world where every day could be an adventure with this woman, but he immediately snapped back to reality, and paid attention to where he was stepping before he slipped and fell into the creek like Fijalí's young husband.

On the other side of the creek, the trail narrowed into a meandering dirt path where pink and white wildflowers pushed their way through the dense greenery, their petals bobbing in the wind.

"Step it up, Raph," Xio said, sprinting ahead of him. "We're not going to get anywhere with your lazy-ass lagging. You can bring up the rear again," she added, turning for a second to throw him a devilish look.

Bringing up the rear was slowly becoming his favorite thing to do in Ynoa, Raph thought, his eyes glued to Xio's tight ass and long legs. He could not wait to have her on her back, those legs wrapped around his waist, and her ass cupped in his hands as he rode her into oblivion. He reached down and adjusted his cock again as it tried to stand in agreement.

Xio knew that if Fijalí's husbands hadn't happened upon them, she would have let Raph take her right there on the trail. What the hell was wrong with her? She had never been this reckless with her reputation. She couldn't afford to be irresponsible with an impressionable teenage sister who had no qualms about stirring up trouble. Xio was always the level-headed sister, always two steps ahead and thinking about how her actions might reflect on her and her family. Raph was quickly turning her into the kind of woman she couldn't afford to be—careless and carefree.

She noticed two birds on a branch overhead, scanning the forest before fluttering away over the treetop. She envied their freedom to soar and live their lives the way nature had intended, while she was facing the possibility of jail time or humiliation for losing her family's legacy.

And she couldn't figure out which was worse. Her botoá had said that a lot could happen in twenty-eight days. But what if nothing happened? What if when her time was up, she still didn't know what to do? She could see the headline now:

PRINCESS XIOMARA CONVICTED OF BANK FRAUD

She had loved Trevor once, and marrying him would at least keep her out of jail and in charge of Jewel Beach. Trevor would have fifty-one percent, but she might still be able to call the shots, and she wouldn't have to suffer the humiliation of losing her family's business outright.

And you trust what that lying lizard told you? Really, Xiomara! You can't trust anything that comes out of that man's mouth. What if he backs you into another corner and demands eighty percent? You know how he works. He always finds a way to sink his teeth in deeper.

On the other hand, what if I marry his treacherous son, bring him up to Kabun Amé the day after our third anniversary, and push his spineless, cheating ass off the ledge? Accidentally, of course. According to Megiri law, everything he owns would be mine.

"Hey, where are you?"

In jail for murder.

Raph bumped his shoulder into Xio's, yanking her from her happy thoughts of pre-meditated murder. *Shit.* Is this what she'd come to? *Atabey, help me.*

She smiled at Raph, whose eyes seemed to have come alive

within the greenery of the rainforest. "Sorry. Was just thinking about business."

He shook his head. "Nope. I set aside business for a couple days to enjoy this. A first for me. You should try it," he said with an arched brow.

Xio chuckled. "Remember, I can come here anytime I want."

"Show off," he chided, bumping her again. "Tell me about Kabun Amé."

"I think it's just one of those things that you have to see for yourself, but I'll try…"

Chapter Thirty-Two

SHARING

THE VIEW from Kabun Amé was well worth the diversion, just as Xio had promised.

Raph sat on a ledge, chewing on a handful of sweet walnuts with his feet dangling over the craggy rock face. Below, the Amiche River eddied around boulders and fallen trees as it snaked its way south through the valley.

Xiomara was beside him, cracking walnuts between two rocks, her feet swinging over the ledge and strands of her hair flirting on her forehead and cheeks. God, she was beautiful, sexy, and as sweet as the walnuts she'd been feeding him. He watched as she pried the whole succulent nut from its shell, broke it into two halves, gave him one, and slid the other into her mouth.

"That's the last one for now," she said, brushing the shells over the ledge into the river below.

"Thanks. You're a great nutcracker, you know." He popped his half into his mouth.

"Don't worry. I'll be gentle with your nuts when I finally have them in my hands." She threw her head back in laughter.

Xio was as natural and real as they came, and Raph marveled at her unrestrained joy. Her laugh was melodious, and sweet, and in that moment, he realized that he had never had so much fun with a woman he was having sex with.

The brisk breeze, infused with the crisp mist from the waterfall on the opposite side of the ravine cooled his skin and refreshed his body after their three-hour hike. The rhythm of the river and the waterfall, and the whirling wind seeped into the very core of his soul. The experience was exhilarating, yet tranquil on the same wave. What he felt was tantamount to a spiritual awakening and, magical, was the only way to describe it.

"Told you it was breathtaking, didn't I?"

He knew that she had anticipated his reaction to seeing Kabun Amé, and it was spot-on. "That really doesn't begin to describe it. If I died right now, I would leave this world a happy man."

"Yeah, it's amazing. Every time I hike up here, it takes my breath away. It's like seeing it for the first time all over again."

"You do this hike often?"

"Akilah, Malik, and I usually come up here when we visit Botoá. Sometimes we bring picnics, or books, or headphones to listen to music. It's just a nice place to spend some quiet time. There's a legend about this lookout," she added. "Want to hear it?"

"Please."

"Okay. Well, BÓ'Nimini, the god of spring waters, lived on the other side of Mount Cibao." She pointed behind them. "He guarded a lake called Life of Spring Waters which was the source of all bodies of water on the island."

"So he was like Poseidon, god of the sea and water," Raph interjected.

"I guess." She shrugged. "Now, BÓ'Jike, the god of forest and earth, lived on this side in front of us. He made sure the soil was fertile, that the trees grew and produced fruit, and that the animals had grass to graze."

"So he was the gardener?"

"I suppose." She chuckled. "One day, BÓ'Nimini sent his son, Amiche, to ask for the hand of BÓ'Jike's daughter, Nera. Amiche and Nera fell in love instantly, but BÓ'Jike refused him."

"Why?"

"BÓ'Jike was afraid his daughter and only child would forget him if she married Amiche, and moved away to the other side of the mountain."

"I guess he hadn't yet heard of texting and video chatting."

Xio chuckled. "Amiche was grief-stricken, and on his way home, he cried so much that his tears blinded him, and he got lost. He wandered around Cibao for many moons, growing weary, hungry, and thirsty, because the portion of spring waters inside him was rapidly depleting. He would perish if he couldn't drink from Life of Spring Waters."

"And so he died, and now he's a ghost god, doomed to wander the woods forever."

Xio poked him in the side, making him jump. "Would you let me finish?"

"Don't I always?" he drawled, turning to peer at her.

"Does everything have to be about sex?" she shook her head in feigned impatience. "Anyway, just when Amiche thought he would wither into nothing, Nera appeared in the rustling of the wind, and told him to throw his spear at the mountain. Amiche did what she said. The mountain split open, and the water from Life of Spring Waters rushed into the gorge and replenished him.

"When BÓ'Jike saw that he could visit his daughter without going all the way around the mountain, he allowed them to marry. They made Kabun Amé their home, and to make sure that no one ever got lost in the mountains and died of thirst, Amiche created many more lakes, rivers, and waterfalls around the island so that there would always be landmarks and a supply of fresh water. And when there's drought on other islands, we give our water away freely and eagerly."

"That is a sweet love story," Raph said.

"Yeah. I love telling it."

"I can tell. We should have lunch here."

"Are you hungry already?"

Only for you. "No, it's just that the view is so amazing."

Xio checked her watch. "It's tempting, but it's just a couple more hours to BO'Acú. It's a little over the halfway point to Aetós and closer to the caves in case the rains come. There's a rest area with tables and benches so we'll be more comfortable instead of sitting on hard rocks here. And take my word for it," she said, as she inched back from the edge of the cliff and jumped to her feet. "You'll have a real bird's-eye-view of this part of the island from there."

"I take your word for it." Raph tossed the last of his walnut shells into the wind and stood to his feet.

"Here, let me." He helped her into her pack, strapped on his own, and took one last look around Kabun Amé, promising himself that this would not be the last time he would look out over this view.

Back beneath the cool covering of the rainforest's canopy, Raph had an overwhelming need to reach out and take Xio's hand or wrap his arm around her shoulders. But their chemistry was like nothing he'd ever had with anyone else, and he knew that touching her would start another fire, and he'd promised to keep his hands to himself.

She'd said that it was her first-time having sex outside. But he still hadn't been her first, and the thought of another man touching her, bringing her the kinds of pleasure he'd brought her was making him crazy with jealousy. Akilah had given him some insight into Xio's past relationships, but how much could he really trust the word of a fifteen-year-old?

"Hey, Xio? Have you had any serious boyfriends before me?" he asked, trying to mask the jealousy in his voice.

Her head snapped around, and a smirk lifted one side of her mouth. "Oh, so you're my boyfriend now? And serious, *seriously?*"

"You know what I mean."

"Yeah, yeah. Yes, there were two. So? Why do you ask?"

He shrugged. "Just curious about why you broke up. I mean, I can't imagine why any man would walk away from you. If I—"

"Who said they walked away from me? Maybe I walked away from them." She let out a nervous huff of air, her lips parting briefly.

"You're right... I shouldn't have assumed." Raph hadn't expected her to be this sensitive about it, and he immediately regretted opening his mouth. "Xiomara, you really are amazing, just for the record." That was all he'd really wanted to say in the first place, but Xio seemed not to hear him, or perhaps not to care.

The uneasy silence that had settled between them was soon veiled by the swiftly moving river in a ravine somewhere up the trail.

Several feet ahead of him, without pausing, or saying a word, Xio stepped confidently onto a narrow rope bridge swinging lazily in the mountain wind, as though she were still on solid ground.

A lush, green wall of ferns, thick vines, and mangled tree roots on either side of the pass dropped hundreds of feet below to rushing white waters, and the cool, misty air was teaming with swallows and the insects and dragonflies they hunted. Earlier, he had clearly overstepped with Xio by asking her about her exes, but a misstep here, from this height, would be fatal. Raph held tightly to the taut rope railings with both hands and gingerly made his way across the rough wooden planks.

Though her eyes were fixed somewhere into the trees, Xio had waited for him on the other side of the ravine, and once he was safely across, she walked with him, side-by-side, their boots faithfully gripping the wet rocks in their path. Just when Raph thought they might walk the rest of the way to Aetós in silence, Xio finally spoke.

. . .

"THE LAST TWO guys I slept with told me that I wasn't any good in bed." Even though there was no need to confess to him that they were the *only* two guys she had slept with, Xio had decided that after the unbridled passion she and Raph had shared under the guayacán tree, she felt no shame in sharing what Trevor had said to her when he had tried, and failed, to justify his cheating.

However, she couldn't talk about Trevor without talking about Toby, and she hadn't talked with anyone about Toby for years. Remembering what he had put her through brought the embarrassment and self-loathing to the forefront, and filled her with anger for being so blind and stupid. But now, as Xio waited for the familiar anxiety to settle in, for the bile to rise to her throat, and her stomach to cramp, there was nothing. She felt nothing—not even a twinge of unpleasantness—at the thought of Toby.

Satisfaction and triumph began to move through her like a warm bath, and there was little she could do to stop the Cheshire cat grin from spreading across her face. Sometime in the last couple of days, sometime since she'd been worn-through after talking about Toby with her therapist, Xio had finally released herself from the hold he'd had on her—more like a grip around her throat, really. And it was all because of Raph.

Raph had made her feel sexy, sensual, powerful and, most of all, desired. Even though she barely knew him, she had been able to trust him with her body in ways she had never trusted Toby or Trevor, even during the best moments of their relationships.

Raph was different. He'd been honest from the start about what he wanted from her. That, in itself, had created a trust between them that she hadn't thought she would ever be able to find with a man. There were no expectations or promises, and neither was pretending that it would lead to anything. It was what it was. Raw, primal sex.

She was no longer bound by feelings of distrust and insecurity. Raph had brought out a side of Xio that she never imagined she had. He had turned her into a lustful goddess, and she was beginning to love the power she held over him.

"Hey, Xio," Raph said in her silence. "You don't have to talk about it if you don't want to. It's really none of my business."

"No, it's fine," she finally said. "I don't mind talking about it." *Damn, it even felt good to say that.* "I fell for this guy, Toby, during my freshman year in college. He was my first. I thought it was going to last forever, but, obviously, it didn't, since I'm here in Ynoa having this conversation with you."

"How long were you together?"

"He broke up with me in my senior year, a few weeks after my dad died. So three years and a couple months."

"Jesus Christ. Talk about shitty timing."

She could see the questions burning behind his eyes—questions he was too reluctant to ask. If he had asked her about her failed relationships a few days ago, she would have been too embarrassed to tell him the truth. She realized, now, that what Toby had done to her wasn't her fault, and she had nothing to be ashamed of. She was still guarding her heart, but for different reasons than before.

"Well," she continued, appeasing his interest, "I'd say we broke up, but as it turned out, we were never a serious couple as far as he was concerned."

"What do you mean? You were together for three years, weren't you?"

Xio pried her thumbs under the straps of her backpack and shifted the weight on her shoulders. "While I was here, attending my father's funeral, taking care of my sister and brother and making sure my mom was eating, someone sent me an email with a photo of him and another girl making out at a party. When I got back to New York, I confronted him about it, and without even trying to deny it, he told me that I was a virgin conquest."

"What!"

"Yep. He and some of his shitty frat brothers had this pact. Every semester, they bet on how many virgins they could get."

"Son of a bitch!"

"I wouldn't bring his mother into it. The two times I met her, she was kind to me. Anyway, Toby said that they usually ditched the girls right after, but I was a 'special case'."

"What is that supposed to mean?" Raph ducked to keep from walking into a low-lying branch.

"I was a rich girl who came with perks. He got free vacations to Akilina. He got to take my car to North Carolina when I came home on breaks, and the last two years we were together, he lived with me, rent free, in the apartment my parents were paying for. He enjoyed all the other luxuries my family provided. He would have kept it going until he graduated. Maybe even longer, who knows."

"Some people have no fucking boundaries. Did you ever find out who sent you the email or who the girl in the photo was?"

"I didn't care who the girl was then, and I still don't. His deception didn't have anything to do with her. And besides, he had hooked up with dozens of girls while we were together, sometimes in my apartment."

"That's disgusting."

"And the email could have been from anyone—although if I ever find out who, I'd probably kiss them for keeping me from wasting any more of my time. But so many people on campus knew about it. All of his friends and some of mine. I even got a few sympathetic looks from professors after we broke up."

"Oh my God, I'm so sorry."

"As if losing my dad wasn't bad enough, I felt like all of New York was laughing at me. I almost dropped out of school, Raph. It was awful."

"It sounds awful. *He* sounds awful. Why were you even with this guy?"

"Seriously, Raph?" She shot him a dubious look. Never again would she feel embarrassed by a man's actions. "He told me that he loved me. And I believed him. I learned a little too late in life, that men will tell women all kinds of things, just to get their clothes off."

"I have never lied to a woman to get her into bed," he said "And I've never cheated, Xio. My relationships are short, I'll admit, sometimes very, very short, but I've never cheated."

His reiteration was not lost on her. He wanted her to know that about him. "I believe you." She had only known Raph for a few days, yet she trusted him. She'd known Toby for three years, and… "Even after three years, I didn't really know Toby Warner," she said, voicing her thoughts.

"Toby Warner. Even his name is stupid."

"Anyway, in the end, the thing he was most upset about was getting kicked out of my apartment. Could you believe he threatened to sue me when I wouldn't give him thirty days to find another place?"

"Yeah right, you would have had him buried. He didn't know who he was messing with."

"It wasn't even like that. I wasn't the businesswoman I am now. I still thought I loved him and I didn't want things to end. But at that point, I just couldn't bear the humiliation, or the fact that the person I was living with didn't show one ounce of sympathy for me after I lost my dad. His insensitivity to my grief was the only thing that kept me from begging him to love me. And, to add insult to injury, as he was walking out the door, he turned back and said, 'You were never any good in bed, anyway, bitch. It was like fucking a dead fish'."

"Son of a bastard. What a dick."

Xio laughed, and when she realized that it was the first time she'd ever laughed after recounting that pain, she laughed even louder. She was so over it. That piece of trash had no more power over her. "Yeah, he was a bastard, a real dick like his father. He actually told me his father said he wanted more than a half-breed, N-word Indian for his son—even if she was rich."

"He should be strung up by his balls."

"I think he is, metaphorically, five days a week. Last I heard, he was teaching math at a middle school in Maryland."

"You couldn't pay me enough to go back to middle school. It sounds like fate took care of Toby."

"That's exactly what I thought. Although, I wonder what kind of values he's teaching those kids. I hope he has changed for their sake."

Even for the man who had publicly humiliated her, who had been so cold in the aftermath of her father's death, Xio still found a way to let her compassion win out against hatred.

Kaiah had instilled in her the importance of empathy, even towards those who seemed like monsters, as past traumas could shape their actions. While she believed Toby's father played a significant role in his behavior, she also understood that empathy didn't excuse his actions.

That's what therapists were for.

"So what happened with Trevor? Was he the two-timing bastard your mother was raging about when she barged into your office the other day?" Raph asked.

Her eyes narrowed in his direction. "What do you know about Trevor?"

"It's a small island?" He curled his hands around the straps of his pack. He'd asked about Trevor without thinking.

"Rapheus. Where. Did. You. Hear. About. Trevor."

She was no longer asking him.

"Um… I, uh…"

Xio halted in her tracks, jammed her hands on her hips, and turned her head to the sky, her eyes closed in vexation. "Akilah told you about me and Trevor, didn't she? I can't believe she would tell you that— Agh! It is none of her damn business!" She threw her hands into the air and stomped her feet along the path. "I'm gonna wring her little neck like a yard chicken when I get home."

Raph quickened his pace to catch up with her. "Hey, hold on. Hold on, Xio!"

"What!" She stopped abruptly, her hands folded over her chest.

"It's not all Akilah's fault."

"What do you mean it's not *all* her fault?"

"I overheard her on the phone before you got home."

"Who was she talking to?"

Shit. This was not going well. "I promised her I wouldn't say anything, so please don't get mad at her."

"Who was she talking to, Raph?"

He could lie and say he didn't know, but knowing that Xio had trust issues when it came to men, he opted to tell her the truth. "A kid named Jamon. They were talking about Trevor hurting you. And then later, Akilah—she just sort of volunteered the information."

"Fuck! Son of a bastard!" She slammed her fist into her palm, and marched on ahead.

She had turned into a fire-breathing dragon just like her mother, Raph thought, chasing after her. "I should have stopped her when she was volunteering the information, but I didn't. After what your mom said about the two-timing bastard you were about to marry again, I can't say that I wasn't a little curious."

She stopped and gave him a blank look.

"Okay, I was very curious. Very, very curious to know why someone would 'screw you over', as Akilah put it. Xiomara, I'm sorry, but from the moment I met you, I wanted to know more about you. No, from the moment I heard about you. But when I first walked into your office, I—"

Xio sighed, her shoulders relaxing by miles as she listened.

"Forgive me. I shouldn't have pried." He shouldn't have encouraged Akilah to gossip about her sister, either, but God help him, he was already smitten, and wanted to know everything he could about her. "But I am still curious."

"Fine. What do you want to know?" She started up the trail again, at a much slower pace this time.

"Well, was it love with Trevor, too?"

"Yes." The word seemed to scrape its way out of her mouth against her will.

"I did love him. That's the sad part. We grew up together and were always friends. I thought he would be different from— I just thought he would be different." She threw her hands up in apparent exasperation. "I thought I could trust him with my heart since I'd known him my whole life—or thought I did. I came back home after I finished my MBA, and within a few months, we were dating. Less than a year later, we got engaged, and two months before the wedding, I found out that another woman was six months pregnant with his child."

"Ouch."

"Yeah. That hurt. I felt like such an idiot."

"They're the idiots."

"Maybe, but when the only two men you've ever dated cheat on you… When one says you're no good in bed, and the other one tells you you're cold, as in Trevor's case, you start to wonder if there's some truth to what they're saying."

"Xiomara, I'm sorry those guys made you feel like that. But, trust me, there is nothing wrong with you. And there is certainly nothing wrong with the way you make love."

"I thought we were just fucking, Raph."

Raph stopped and reached for her arm. He turned her gently to face him. "Whatever you call it, it was good—better than good. It was amazing, and I'd be willing to bet that those jackasses told you that you weren't any good because they weren't any good. They said those things because they wanted to hurt you, not because there was any truth behind it."

His body trembled on a deep breath. "I shouldn't have said that I just wanted to fuck you. It was crude. What we did was not crude, and I take it back. I have never burned for a woman the way I have been burning for you, and you are the best I've ever had. I think you've ruined me for other women," he added, his voice shaking with the soul-pounding truth. He dropped his hand as he felt heat rising between them, and the sound of voices behind them.

He looked back to see a little girl and two women emerge from a narrow path off the main trail. A little black puppy followed behind them.

"Taiguey," the women said, as they power-walked past him and Xio.

"Taiguey," Xio answered back.

The girl smiled at Xio, her little feet moving double time to keep up with the women, while the puppy took up the lead.

"Why did you get so furious when I told you who Akilah was talking to?" he asked, when the women and child disappeared through the thick forest. "Who is Jamon, really?"

She tightened her jaws, then spat out the words, "He's Trevor's little brother."

"Oh." He wanted to pry, but the look on her face told him that it was best not to.

"What about you?" she asked, turning the spotlight on him. "Have you ever been in love?"

His chest tightened. *Be honest with her. She's been honest with you.* He took a moment to figure out how to respond. "Yes, I was in love once, and I got my heart broken." There, he'd shared something with her that he'd never shared with anyone else.

Yet, his pappoús had known. He'd told Raph that he knew what he'd given up while he lay on his deathbed. How he knew, was yet another thing that would forever remain a mystery.

"What happened?" Xio asked, as they picked their way down a steep slope.

I walked away so she could be happy. Unwittingly, Raph's mind traveled back to the moment he'd happened upon her soaking in the Jacuzzi on the rooftop of his penthouse, a glass of red wine in one hand, and the other holding her phone against her ear. Her voice, her words… *"I don't know how to tell Raph, but I'm in love with someone else, too. I don't want to hurt him…"*

"Raph, what happened?" Xio asked again.

He shook his head, killing the memory. "She said I was emotionally void," he answered in an emotionless voice.

"That's harsh, and for the record, I don't think you are emotionally void."

She held his arm for balance as they bounded over a highway of tree roots crisscrossing the trail, sending a cozy feeling flowing through him and extinguishing the remainder of the angst he'f felt at the unsettling memory.

"Emotionally void people don't care about other people," she said, letting go of his arm. "You care about my little brother and sister and you don't even know them."

I care about you, too, Xio. He couldn't bring himself to tell her, couldn't admit it. He didn't need complications in his life. "Maybe I was emotionally void back then. It was the only way for me to stay focused, and accomplish everything I wanted to accomplish."

"You mean building your business."

He brushed his fingers through his damp hair. "Something like that."

"How long were you together?"

"Not long." He watched loose pebbles they'd disturbed with their boots spin down the slope in front of them.

"Were you happy with her, before you broke up?"

She was getting too close.

"I mean, even though Toby turned out to be a douche, I was

still happy in the relationship. I guess happiness is relative. It comes and goes in different degrees and stages."

True. Today, he was swimming in bliss. He was happy walking beside Xio. He was happy a few hours ago when he'd taken her on the side of the trail, and he was hoping for more happiness with her tonight. In a cave or a hut, it didn't matter, just as long as he could satisfy her the way he really wanted to.

Chapter Thirty-Three

DETOUR

RAPH MARVELED at the view from the summit of BO'Acú, the second highest peak in the Nacanké Mountain Range.

Rivers and lakes meandered through the rainforest, waterfalls plunged down hillsides, villages dotted the valleys all the way to the Atlantic Ocean, and billowing clouds drifted lazily across a deep blue sky. It was, indeed, the most breathtaking scenery Raph had ever witnessed.

He leaned against the smooth surface of a massive boulder, its center boasting a sizable naturally carved orifice—large enough for three adults to easily fit inside. Jagged fragments, resembling eyelashes, framed the top and bottom areas of the hole, creating the illusion of a giant eye overseeing this side of the island. This unique geological landmark, serving as a symbol of guardianship for generations of islanders, had inspired the name for this mountain—BO'Acú, or Big Eye, as Xio had finally translated for him.

They had made it to the summit about forty minutes ago, and after a leisurely lunch, Xio had offered to pack up so he could get one last view before they had to leave this spectacular and peaceful place behind. Raph had to say that the longer he admired the landscape, the more he felt at one with Ynoa, like he belonged here, or at least was here at some time in the past—a feeling that baffled him.

He was certain that his grandparents had stopped here on their way up and down the mountain to Aetós, but had his great-grandparents been here, too? Was that the reason he felt at one with the place? How many times had Thaddeus and Eagle rested on this ledge together before Thaddeus' betrayal? Raph wondered on a slightly less uplifting note.

He turned at the sound of Xio's footsteps approaching from the picnic area secluded by thick brushes behind him.

"You're enjoying yourself, still?" she asked.

"I am. It just blows my mind that I'm related to people who lived on this island hundreds of years ago. Makes you wonder about your ancestors' footprints in the places you visit around the world."

"I know what you mean. It's the same feeling I got when Kaiah took me to Benin when I was sixteen. She wanted me to walk in my ancestors' footprints, to get a sense of where I came from. Then the summer before Dad died, we went back as a family. MJ was too young to remember, but Akilah still talks about it."

"Can you believe we have this history in common? One ancestor from Africa and the other from Greece who arrived here together?" He shook his head, still bewildered at the link between their two families.

"Yeah, it's pretty crazy, but so is this weather," she said, tilting her head back, her eyes narrowing in concentration as she studied the clouds. "There are storm clouds on the horizon, and the wind is bringing them straight toward us. We gotta get going!" she exclaimed, hurrying back to the picnic tables.

Raph pushed off the eye and scampered behind her. "I don't see any rain clouds."

"Believe me, they are there, and it's only a matter of time before they catch up to us."

She pulled two ponchos from her pack and dropped them on the table. She then looped her arms through the straps of her pack, settled it on her back, then fastened the clasp across her chest.

"Maybe it will blow over quickly," Raph said, strapping on his pack.

"This isn't like the quickies we have in Akilina. In these mountains, it pours, sometimes for days." She pulled her poncho over her head and arranged it over her backpack in lightning speed.

"Where are we going?" he asked, swiftly donning his poncho.

"To the nearest system of caves along the trail. We need to get to shelter before the trail washes out," she said, taking up the lead.

Raph took one last look around and followed, hot on her tail. He prayed he wouldn't slip and break his neck as he picked his way down the muddy path. He was glad he'd taken Kaiah's advice and worn his pappoús' waterproof boots instead of the sneakers he'd brought with him, and that he and his pappoús wore the same size shoes.

They had been speed-walking for about thirty minutes when a raindrop landed on Raph's nose, then another on his arm, then in the blink of an eye, it was as if heaven was done playing around, rolled back its curtains, and inundated earth with a torrential downpour.

"This way," Xio shouted through the roar, as she cut off the trail down a narrow path. "Hurry up!"

"There they are." Xio pointed to a wall of black rocks jutting out from the side of the mountain ahead of them.

"I see them," Raph shouted. They'd fought gravity, crawled

up the trail on their hands and knees, using exposed roots and vines to keep from slipping in the deluge. It had been a hard climb, balancing the need to hurry with the need for caution. One misstep could have resulted in a serious, or even fatal fall.

Xio darted into the cave with Raph right on her heels. They both doubled over, hands on their knees, struggling to catch their breath.

After a few seconds, Raph stood upright and pulled his poncho off, dropping it to the floor. He wiped his hand down his face and blinked a few times as his eyes adjusted to the darkness. He finally spotted Xio a couple feet in front of him, wringing water from her braid with one hand while trying to remove her poncho with the other.

He walked up behind her, and she silently raised her hands to allow him to pull off her poncho, and then lowered them so he could remove her pack.

"Thank you," she said, turning to face him, her nearness in the dark, cramped space sending butterflies fluttering in his belly.

"No, thank *you* for getting us here safely, Xio. You are an exceptional guide."

"Well, I do try to excel in all areas of my life," she quipped playfully.

"You don't just try, baby, you actually do excel in everything. Take my word for it."

"Word taken."

To keep himself from stripping her naked and proving his point before they had a chance to clean up, Raph turned and set her pack on a huge boulder with a flat surface near the door, serving as a makeshift table. He removed his own and placed it next to hers, then flexed his shoulders and stretched his back, happy to be rid of his load.

"Does it still hurt?" Xio asked, coming to stand beside him. "From MJ's kick, I mean."

"No, it's good. I've been icing it for two days," he replied, gathering their ponchos and hanging them on stone pegs jutting from the wall of the cave. "It's just nice to be rid of the weight for a few hours."

"Yeah, it is." She pulled a flashlight from her pack and clicked it on, flooding the cave with light.

Raph looked curiously around. There were no animal droppings, spider webs, or any of the other odious elements typically associated with caves. "Nice. There's a fire pit," he remarked when Xio flashed the light over a circle of soot-stained rocks in the center of the chamber.

"Of course, people use these caves all the time." She pulled a dry cloth from her pack and handed it to him. "You can wipe down the pallet and lay out our mats and sleeping bags while I light a fire."

Raph eyed the plank of wood supported on four two-foot posts on the inside wall, just beyond the fire pit. It looked long enough to accommodate his height and wide enough to sleep two comfortably. "Yes, Ma'am." He liked taking orders from her, he realized, walking over to do her bidding. He was beginning to like a lot of things about Xiomara Davenport.

From the corner of his eye, he watched her place the flashlight on the ground, gather an armful of wood and kindling from a pile near the cave's entrance, and arrange them in the pit like a pro.

The fact that she had given him the easy chore while she tackled the more challenging one wasn't lost on Raph. The women he usually dated would have been standing around wringing their hands and complaining about the rain, their wet hair, ruined makeup, and the dark cave, while he did all the heavy lifting.

But you like women who are helpless, or at least pretend to be, just so you can control the relationship, don't you?

After he finished wiping the dust from the pallet, Raph turned around to find Xio standing at the cave's entrance, watching the rain fall through the trees, a hair brush under her arm while she unbraiding her hair. He walked up behind her and placed his hands over hers.

She lifted her face and frowned. "What are you doing?"

"Unbraiding your hair," he said, threading his fingers through the sections she had already undone.

"Have you ever unbraided hair before?"

"No." He removed her hands and placed them at her side. "I've done a lot of things this week that I'd never done before."

She chuckled. "Okay. You can brush it when you're done, then.

As he loosened the braid, Raph experienced a kind of caring for a woman he hadn't felt for a long time. It filled him with longing, but also dread, if he were being honest with himself. "So, how many times have you been here?" he asked, trying to keep himself from admitting what was missing in his life.

"Many."

"Alone?" He couldn't see her face, but he could feel her smile.

"No, never alone. I've been here with my dad, Olivia, and some of my cousins over the years. But I haven't been up since I came back from college. I've been too busy with the resort to make the time."

"Yeah, I can understand that. I'm sorry if my… If all this *stuff* is getting in the way of your work. I know you hadn't planned on spending two days in the mountains when you have a hotel to run."

"Honestly, Raph, I didn't think I could afford the time off. But I realized I needed to get away from some of the madness. Besides, I love it up here."

With the braid undone, Raph took the brush from her, and began brushing her hair, beginning at the tips, and working his way up to her scalp like he'd seen other women do.

"You sure you haven't done this before?" Xio asked.

"I'm sure," he replied softly. The tenderness of brushing her hair was affecting him more than he'd anticipated. "Tell me about this place, why you love it so much," he said, needing to steer his mind away from dangerous thoughts.

"I feel at one with nature here." Her voice was soft and husky. "This place connects me to my history. The Megiri and Guaitiari fought in these mountains. They used the caves to shelter the old, the sick, and children who were too young to fight in the wars. These mountains were a natural defense against the colonists. And once the wars ended, many of the older people stayed and lived out their lives in these caves. Kaiah comes here to consult the spirits when she needs to make a difficult decision, or when she just wants to be alone. She stayed here for weeks after both my grandmother and my dad died."

"Kaiah climbs up here, at her age?"

"No silly. Her pilot flies her in on her chopper."

"Oh, okay. I can see that. I wonder if Eagle and Thaddeus spent time here together," Raph murmured.

"I bet they did. Maybe they slept in this very cave."

"Totally possible." He ran the brush through her hair one last time, then gently released the strands, letting them cascade down her back. "All done."

She combed her fingers through her tresses. "No tangles. Nice job."

"That'll be a hundred, please." He held out his hand.

She slapped it, mischief dancing in her eyes. "That's less than what a guide gets paid, and since this guide comes with extra benefits, I'd say you owe me."

"Fair," he replied on a chuckle, pushing his hands into his pockets to keep from pulling her close and capitalizing on those extra benefits.

They stood quietly, watching the curtain of rain falling over the entrance of the cave. And in those quiet moments, Raph could almost sense his ancestors' spirits from four hundred years ago, and more recently as a couple decade, and he knew in his heart that his pappoús and yaya overnighted here on their way to Aetós when they were young enough to make the climb.

"I guess I should light that fire before it gets too dark," Xio finally said. She walked over to her pack, took out a lighter, then sat in front of the pit and lit the kindling. Holding her hair back from her face, she gently blew on the small flames until they grew and ferociously licked at the logs.

Raph hadn't even realized that he had grown hard watching her until he felt the restriction against his shorts. He got their mats and sleeping bags, and took them over to the pallet, laying them out as the roaring fire cast shadows on the walls.

"Now, to the second order of business. We need to clean up." Xio left the fire pit and walked to her pack. She retrieved two towels and two pairs of flip-flops and laid them on the table before dropping down on the floor to unlaced her boots.

Raph sat next to her and removed his boots and socks. "I don't see a tub of water anywhere. Are we supposed to shower in the rain?"

"Not a bad idea, but no. Don't you smell it?"

Raph sniffed the air, breathing through the heavy scent of mountain rain, and sure enough, there was the faint smell of sulfur in the air. "Is there a hot spring in here?"

"Yep." Xio stood and, hooking her thumbs into her waistband, she pushed her pants and panties down to her ankles, and stepped out of them. She then reached for the hem of her shirt and pulled it over her head along with her sports bra, dropping them on the floor.

Raph's throat swelled up with emotions as she stood naked in front of him, her long hair draped across her chest and the fire casting dancing shadows over her enticing body. She was so beautiful, so lovely.

"What, are you suddenly shy now?" she taunted, twirling a strand of hair around her finger. "It's not like we haven't seen each other naked before." She reached for her flip-flops and slipped them on.

"I'm not shy. I'm just trying to talk myself out of picking you up and laying you out on that pallet before we clean up," Raph said. He stood and lifted his shirt over his head, dropping it on her bra.

Her eyes followed his every move as he eased his shorts and briefs over his hips and down to his knees. She moaned and licked her lips when his erection sprang up against his belly. "Hmm," that's nice, she murmured, as he finished undressing and stood naked before her.

"Hmm, indeed." Keeping his eyes firmly fixed on the thatch of dark hair between her thighs, Raph slipped on his flip-flops and picked up the towels.

Xio turned on the flashlight, laced her fingers with his, and led him through the tunnel.

"XIOMARA, THIS IS... OH MY GOD..." Raph whispered, his breath catching as he stood mesmerized in front of the aqua-blue pool, steam rising like clouds above its hot surface.

"Yeah, I know." Xio set the flashing on the ground and pulled a small box of matches from a metal tin tucked inside a wide ledge, cut into the wall. She struck one, and lit the oil lamps hanging from hooks bored into the cave's walls, illuminating the chamber with a soft, glowing amber light. She kicked off her flip-flops,' and said, "Now, get in. I'm tired of smelling you."

Raph laughed. "You're no bed of sweet-smelling roses, you know. I've been downwind of you all day." He placed the towels on the ledge.

"Oh, stop complaining," she teased, gripping his hand. They approached the pool's edge with cautious steps, and eased themselves into the water, little by little, allowing their bodies time to adjust to the heat.

"Ohhhh my God," Raph drawled when he was waist deep. "I can actually feel my muscles relaxing."

"That's the idea." Xio let go of his hand and sank down to her chest. She closed her eyes as the hot water soaked into her pores, soothing and cleansing her—body, mind, and soul. She couldn't imagine sharing this experience with any other man but Raph.

Raph's heart throb at the temptingly beautiful picture Xio made with her luscious dark hair floating in the water and clinging to her bare brown shoulders. All day, he had been fantasizing about running his hands up and down her naked body, but as he observed her now, what he felt was beyond lust.

Something had shifted today, and the thought of sharing more than a bed with her did not scare him as much as it had a few days ago when he was laying down his no-strings-attached rules.

He laced his fingers with hers and closed his eyes, knowing that this moment, deep in the cave with Xio, was what he would remember most when he was back in San Francisco.

You still think you can just walk away from her, don't you?

Chapter Thirty-Four

SEDUCED

ALL TOO SOON, or maybe not soon enough, they were back in the warm cozy chamber with a gentle, flickering fire casting bouncing shadows on the walls.

Raph placed the flashlight on the makeshift table, then turned around. Xio was standing near the fire pit, clutching the thin white towel to her chest, her eyes large and luminous. Though unspoken, the anticipation of their lovemaking hung palpably in the air.

His eyes slowly roved over her as if he was seeing her for the first time, curious about what lay beneath that towel, even though he already knew. His desire for her had grown stronger throughout the day. But rather than seek immediate gratification again, he'd found himself craving a more profound, thorough, and emotionally engaging connection, especially after hearing about the two jerks who'd hurt her.

"Are you hungry?" she asked, taking a step toward him.

Only for you. He closed the distance between them. "You're so beautiful, *agápi mou.*"

You realize you just called her your love, right?

His body trembled as he accepted the truth he'd been

denying from the moment her image appeared on his computer screen in San Francisco. In his heart, he had felt her, had known her, like his pappoús had said.

Embracing this revelation should scare him, chase him out of the cave, but something kept him grounded. It wasn't just the fear of being caught in the rain or lost in the jungle at night; it was a deep inexplicable need to be with Xiomara, show her how much he burned for her, cared about her.

"I'm hungry for you. Let me look at you," he said through the tightness in his throat.

Xio sensed Raph's eagerness. Something had changed between them the moment he'd laced his fingers with hers in the hot spring. Time had seemed to pause, and the air had crackled with electrical energy, whispering tantalizing promises over their skin.

In this moment, she felt at ease with Raph, free from the fears of judgment or ridicule she'd been holding on to. With that assurance in mind, she released the towel and allowed it to fall in a soft pile at her feet.

Raph swallowed hard as his eyes moved slowly from her face to the delicate curve of her smooth shoulders and the rise and fall of her breasts, then lower to her taut belly, the sloping dip of her belly button, over her swelling hips, and then to the patch of dark, damp hair at the apex of her thighs. He couldn't wait to run his palms along her skin and feel her fall to pieces under him, but he'd promised himself he would take his time tonight. He was sticking to that promise, even if it killed him. He wasn't about to leave Ynoa with her thinking he didn't know how to properly make love to a woman.

He cupped her chin and tilted her head back, allowing his eyes to caress her face, to burn her mesmerizing eyes into his memory. His stomach tightened with nerves as he bent his head and pressed his lips to hers, gently kissing her soft flesh.

She moaned into his mouth, her breath warm and sweet as

she curled into him, her hard nipples pressed into his chest as her arms wound around his neck. When her lips parted, Raph slid his tongue inside and wrapped it around hers, and together they danced in the sweet sensations pulling them deeper into that chasm of delight they both knew so well. How did he ever get this lucky? he wondered, at her eager response to him.

Xio threaded her fingers through Raph's hair, allowing herself the pleasure of his fervent kiss, stoking a fire so deep inside her belly that her toes curled. This kiss was different from their first one—demanding and ravishing. This was sweet and tender, and it made her shudder. Urgently needing more, she unwrapped the towel from around his hips and curled her fingers around his erection. It was hot, hard, and heavy in her hand.

Raph groaned, lifted his mouth from hers, and stepped back, pulling himself free.

"Not yet," he murmured at the look of surprise and frustration in her eyes. "We're taking this nice and slow, Xiomara. No quickies tonight," he said in a deep, gravelly voice.

Xio's eyes feasted on Raph's strong shoulders and arms that would be holding her tight as he moved fervently inside her, the silky mat of hair on his chest that her nipples would be nestled against, and his rock-hard stomach that would be pressed into hers as their bodies moved to a silent rhythm, pushing each other higher and higher until they surrendered to the flames they would ignite.

Raph licked the soft flesh of her neck, pulling the skin between his teeth and lapping it with his tongue, working his mouth up her neck and behind her ear. Her knees buckled from the sheer sweetness of his wet tongue strumming the erroneous zone he'd discovered today. His hands on her waist kept her steady as he kissed his way around her neck and to her other ear, making her sex contract at the thought of his face between her thighs, his tongue licking her clit.

Fire roared in her bones as his mouth trailed down her neck, roaming over the top of one breast, kissing the nipple, and running his tongue over the pebbled knob before sucking it into his mouth, while his hands moved up and down her back, her sides, and her buttocks.

He groaned, and took more of her breast into his mouth, sucking gently, yet firmly, the feel of her nipple brushing against the back of his mouth sending an unending series of tingles from the hard tip, straight to the core of her sex. "Rapheus," she called, clinging to his shoulders, trembling with desire.

In response to her call, he ran his tongue along the bottom of her breast, then up the side to the other, giving that nipple the same delirious attention as the other.

He lifted his head and smiled at her, his green eyes electric and passionate in the firelight, his mouth rosy and wet from sucking her. Then he dropped to his knees on the towels at their feet.

Raph marveled at Xio's sex, swollen, and glistening. Her arousing scent made his mouth water, but he fought the need to dive right in. *Patience.* He had to exercise patience tonight.

He held her gaze while his hands roamed slowly up her legs toward the back of her knees, loving the way her knees buckled, the soft sighs slipping from her lips, and her warm hands gripping his shoulders as she shivered from his caresses. She was so sensuous, so sexy, *so… everything…*

He gave her time to regain her balance before he continued trailing his hands farther up her smooth, toned thighs, watching the play of emotions on her face while her sexy whimpers urged him on, giving him assurance that he was doing the right thing. He glided higher, moving inward, until his fingers were coated with the warm juices trickling down her thighs. He tapped the pads of his thumbs against the soft folds covering the entrance to her body, and she uttered a low groan, her grip on his shoulders tightening.

Xio's head sagged forward, and her hair fell across her face, obscuring it from his view. Perfectly fine, he thought, giving all his attention to the view at eye level. He licked the sides of her clit, his tongue gliding through her wet warmth. His cock throbbed in anticipation, jealous of his tongue giving her pleasure. He ignored the call to take her to the pallet and fill her. He wanted Xiomara to experience a man on his knees worshiping her, letting her know how amazing she was.

Xio moaned as Raph's hot breath stirred the wispy curls on her sex, and his tongue slid up and down, licking the sides and undersides of her clit like no man had ever done before. The white-hot heat was unbearable, and her body bucked as waves of desire whirled through her, robbing her of her strength to stand, to think… Her hands closed around Raph's head and, placing her right foot on his thigh, she pushed her hips into his face. "Oh God," she moaned when the tip of his tongue finally flicked her sensitive knob.

"Yes," he groaned in response, easing a finger inside her and stroking her slowly, gently, swirling and thrusting, while his tongue strummed against her clit.

"Raph…" she whispered, clutching at him as her body took on a life of its own. She rotated her hips, bucking and quivering, seeking more, demanding more and, as the ache intensified and her breathing grew harsher, he eased another finger inside her, intensifying the friction, multiplying the blissful sensations.

"Come, Xiomara. Come in my mouth. I want to feel you, taste you…"

At his command, the walls of Xio's sex tightened around his fingers. Liquid fire poured through every cell of her body. Her legs shook uncontrollably, and her breath came out in gasps. She stiffened for a moment as the pleasure built, and then she screamed his name as a powerful orgasm whipped through her, forcing her surrender to the pleasure he elicited from her.

He kept his mouth on her and his fingers buried in her tightness until she stopped trembling. When she collapsed against him, he stood and, lifting her into his arms, he placed her on the sleeping bags he'd so carefully laid out.

"You are so sweet and hot. Absolutely gorgeous," he whispered, settling down beside her. Fire and tenderness swelled in his chest. He would always remember her this way—her silky black hair spread out on the gray sleeping bag, her beautiful brown eyes, dark and begging him to touch her again, but willing to wait because he'd asked her to be patient. For that, he cherished her. He wanted to soak up everything she offered him, and lavish her with all he could while this cave was theirs.

All he wanted to do was please Xiomara, and he knew that once he entered her, he would never want to leave. He'd never been this famished, never felt this kind of appetite for any other woman. Maybe it was the reality that this was the only night he would have with her, and if that was the case, he wouldn't waste one precious second of it. He crouched over her.

Xio inhaled sharply when Raph's lips fluttered over the delicate hollow of her neck, dropping soft, feathery kisses on her skin, while his warm hands cupped her breasts, kneading them gently in his palms. She moaned feverishly as warmth spread through her system, weighing her down, pulling her into a dreamlike state, lifting her out of her body where she could do nothing but feel what her lover was doing to her.

She sighed in pleasure as his mouth blazed a slow hot trail across her chest, kissing, nibbling, and licking her breasts and nipples as his right hand reached between them. She moaned as he eased a finger inside her again, gently thrusting back and forth as his thumb caressed her clit.

Xio hooked her legs around his and rushed her hands up and down his shoulders and back, growing bolder at the feel of his muscles flexing under her palms. She squeezed his buttocks and thrust her hips to the rhythm of his hands igniting the fire between her thighs once more while his mouth sucked hungrily on her breasts. He teased, licked, strummed, and nibbled, pushing her closer and closer to a shuddering climax that took her by storm, pulling her into a sea of ecstasy that threatened to drown her.

She was still panting from her orgasm when he lifted his head from her breast and moved up over her. His eyes were glowing with passion, hunger, and lust, his lips wet from her, but deep in the recesses of his eyes, she saw a tenderness she never expected. He gazed at her as if he knew her in all her flawed perfection, and yet he wanted her.

"Now," he breathed, as he pulled his finger from inside her, but before she could utter a cry of protest, she felt the head of his shaft at the entrance of her sex. He held it there. His stomach convulsed and his body trembled over her as if he was fighting the need to thrust and claim her as his own.

She closed her eyes to prepare for the impending feelings of having Raph inside her.

"Look at me, Xiomara" he said in a husky voice.

Xio opened her eyes and the passion she saw in the emerald depths of his moved her to her core. He was the most irresistible and sensuous man she'd ever met, and he was hers for the night.

He rubbed the tip of his shaft against her.

"Oh God," Xio groaned as he slowly pushed inside, stretching her... He pulled back and thrust again, and again, sinking deeper with each succeeding stroke until he was buried inside her to the hilt. She felt every vein in his shaft as he lay still, filling her. Her flesh quivered around him, welcoming him, cherishing him, thanking him for this night of tenderness and intimacy.

He clasped her hands in his and brought them down on the mat above her head, intertwining their fingers as they moved together under a blaze of fire that inflamed their hearts and threatened to engulf them alive, and yet they continued to love, slowly, gently, and intensely, taking each other to passionate heights, neither of them knew existed.

Xio's body tightened and quivered around him, creating such a friction between them, she thought she would explode. And as her climax gripped her, Raph pushed his tongue into her mouth, moving with the same rhythm and gentleness he thrust into her sex, until it became too much and their bodies begged for more from each other.

"Yeessss," she groaned.

He thrust deeper and harder, their cries of pleasure lost in the sound of rain beating down outside the cave, and the shadows of their entwined bodies dancing on the walls inside it. Never had she experienced anything so erotic, so magical…

She felt herself spiraling into a universe that stripped her of all knowledge of Xiomara—the woman she knew—and transformed her into a goddess enveloped in Raph, floating on a cloud with him, dipping and dancing with him, breathing him, inhaling him, melding into him… She held him closer as more earthshaking tremors swept through her, clutching his hands to keep from soaring off into the black rock above them. "Rapheus…"

She wrapped her legs higher around his waist and gave herself over to the delightful fire pulsing through her. Their bodies fused and danced as one, communicating in the language of love, arousing hunger in each other as they rode out the hot storms of desire that came and went in mysterious magical waves. The sensations of him moving in and out of her were so intense, sweet, and fiery, she began to sob, and in response Raph cradled her face and kissed her, swallowing her cries while continuing to move with her, and soon she was falling to pieces in his arms again.

"Xiomara…" he called out in desperation.

Xio opened her eyes and her heart lurched as she took in the sight of his magnificent body, glistening with sweat, his mouth agape, his eyes rolled back. He was beautiful to her.

Without missing a beat, Raph hooked his arms under her

thighs and swung her legs over his shoulders, opening her wider, allowing him to move deeper into her, filling her completely with his massive length. His thrust grew more vigorous, more tumultuous, and less controlled as his pleasure demanded release. Placing her palms flat against his chest, Xio caressed the rippling muscles beneath his damp skin as her insides gripped him, sucking him deep, making him growl out his ecstasy.

"Yes, Rapheus..." Xio felt every quickening inch of him, trembling, quivering as their hips locked together. She fought to hold back her climax, waiting for him, wanting to be carried away in the sea of delightful euphoria with him, crash with him upon the edge of love's enchanting shores.

"Oh, fuck..." Raph dropped his head beside hers on the mat and groaned deeply. He felt Xio's tight, slick body gripping him, tugging at him, milking him as her orgasm spiraled, sending shock waves through every nerve in his cock. It felt like it was on fire, throbbing and pulsing in her velvety heat, tilting his world on its axis.

Blood pounded through his veins, throbbed in his cock, rushed to his heart. "Oh my God, Xiomara!" he roared, as his orgasm ripped him apart, knocking down barriers he'd so carefully erected, laying him bare and vulnerable to the woman beneath him as he unraveled in a burst of exquisite sensations. He collapsed on top of her, pinning her to the mat, his body jerking from the shock and force of his orgasm.

And as the rain poured down in torrents on the earth outside, Raph emptied himself into Xiomara, their cries echoing around the cave.

A LOG CRACKLED and shifted in the fire pit.

Raph rolled onto his back with Xio in his arms. He couldn't believe he was hard again after only a short nap. It was as if his body was refusing to quit wanting her. And he was okay with that, he thought, arranging Xio on top of him, her legs between his, and her cheek on his chest. He picked up the sleeping bag that had fallen to the floor and spread it over them.

Xio moaned sleepily and burrowed deeper into his arms.

He kissed the top of her head, relishing the steady beat of her heart against his, and the softness of her body in his arms. She felt perfect, too perfect, he realized, now that he was spent and could think more clearly. Although every cell in his brain was telling him to place her back down on the mat, zip her into her sleeping bag and get into his own, Raph was welcoming the thawing effects she was having on his heart.

He would allow himself this little bit of…whatever it was he was feeling tonight. They would be in Aetós tomorrow, and who knew how their feelings for each other might change then.

Oh, so you have feelings now, Mr. Emotionally Void and Unavailable?

Oh, yes, he was having feelings—fierce and overpowering ones. He didn't want them. He couldn't handle them, yet they persisted on making their presence known.

"You alright, Xio?" he asked, needing conversation to keep himself from tumbling down his dreaded rabbit hole.

"Yeah," she said sleepily. "Just tired. You wore me out."

Raph could feel her smiling into his neck.

"Don't get me wrong, I loved every second of it. I'm not complaining."

Raph laughed. "I never thought you would," he said, caressing her back. Raph had never made love like this before. He'd never had a woman who made him want to. A woman who satisfied him and made him hunger for her in the same breath. "You're just so damn sweet, and I couldn't get enough of you," he said, giving her the simplest truth.

"The feeling's mutual." She lifted her head and rested her chin on his chest. "You're beautiful when you come."

He laughed out loud. "I don't think any woman has ever used that word to describe me."

"I doubt that. You're beautiful in many ways," she murmured, tracing a finger along the outline of his mouth, down his chin and neck and coming to rest over his heart. "Especially here, and here," she drawled, continuing her brazen trail down to his stomach and below... She closed her hand around his cock. "Look at you, hard again." She giggled.

He brought her hand to his lips and kissed her palm, savoring the lingering scent of their lovemaking. "I'm always hard around you."

"And I'm always wet around you, so... Uh oh..."

"What?" He raised up on his elbows and looked in the direction she was staring. "Oh, the fire is dying. I'll take care of it." He eased from under her, and left their warm bed.

Xio watched lazily from the pallet as he gathered logs from the pile, took them to the pit, and strategically placed them on the fire. They'd been making love, napping, awakening, and making love again as the afternoon had turned into night. No wonder her body felt like a truck had run over it.

"I don't know about you, but I'm starving," she said, getting off the bed and walking over to the table.

"Actually, I'm famished, too," he said.

She pulled a small silver camping pot and two packets of dried soup from her pack. She shook the packets in the air. "Chicken noodle, or split pea? And we have some rolls from breakfast to go with the soup."

"Chicken noodle. It's the best on rainy days," he responded, stoking the fire until it was roaring again.

"Chicken noodled it is." She poured water from her water bottle into the pot, and then took a long sip. She handed the bottle to Raph, who had joined her at the table.

"Will we have enough to get us to Aetós?" he asked, screwing on the lid after quenching his thirst.

"There's a cistern on the other side of the cave. With all this rain, it's probably overflowing."

"Compliments of Amiche?" he asked with a wide grin.

She laughed and slapped his butt. "Nice one, Raph, but no. It was built for hikers and campers. And since someone stockpiled the dry wood we have tonight, before we leave tomorrow, we'll have to bring in some logs so they can dry out for the campers who come after us."

"Of course." Raph watched her dump the dry chicken noodle packet into the pot and stir it with a wooden spoon. "So, is Aetós the nearest village to this cave?"

She nodded.

"What if someone else comes by, looking for a dry place for the night. Are we supposed to share? I don't mean to sound selfish. but—"

"No one will come here once they see the fire. And there are other caves around." She walked to the pile of wood and pulled a flat iron grate from behind it. She took it over to the pit, balanced it on the stones, then set the pot down on top.

Feeling a slight chill, Raph dug into his pack and fished out two T-shirts. "Here you go." He helped Xio into one, and after putting on the other one, he wrapped his arms around her. *God, she felt so good*, and she looked good in his shirt.

They stood quietly behind the fire, keeping one eye on the soup and the other on the dark, stormy night beyond the cave.

As he breathed in her essence, Raph's hunger for Xio began to build anew, and soon his cock was pulsing against the hollow of her back. She pushed back, trapping it between them and wiggled her body, sending him spiraling into a vortex of lustful madness. Turning her around, he edged her over to the slab of rock, grabbing their towels from the floor on the way. He pushed their packs to one side, spread the towels on the surface and, lifting Xio up, he sat her down upon them.

Their eyes locked as he pulled his shirt off her, then raised his hands as she pulled off his. She spread her legs at the same time her hand clasped around as much of his erection as it possibly could.

"You're so big," she whispered, glancing down as she began to stroke him, sliding the pad of her thumb over the head. "You like that," she asked in the sexiest, huskiest voice he'd ever heard on a woman.

"I love it."

"I love your cock, Raph. I just love the way you make me feel, the way you make me tremble, the way you make me come when it's deep inside of me." She stroked him faster, sliding her hand up and down, back, and forth, sending excitement careening through him.

He filled his palms with her breasts, kneading them and loving the feel of her nipples hardening in his hands. "And I love the way you stroke me, Xio, like no other woman before you. It's the sweetest feeling in the world."

His stomach contracted and desire crept up and down his spine when her other hand cupped his balls, massaging gently as her other continued their up and down, and round and around motion on his ever-growing shaft, squeezing, releasing, clenching. She tortured him, pushing him to the edge of delirious elation, only she had the power to do.

"Oh, God." He threw his head back and pulled air into his lungs, fighting the need to come in her hands. He needed to be inside her.

Calling on his reserve of self-control, Raph removed Xio's hands from around him, and placed them on his shoulders. "Hold on." He spread her thighs farther apart, then placed her feet, one at a time, on the edge of the rock, rendering her totally vulnerable and at his mercy.

He saw a flash of fear in her eyes. "I won't hurt you," he whispered, curling his hand around himself. "Trust me. Don't look away from me."

She shivered when he placed the head of his shaft at her opening, then whimpered as he drove slowly into her in one tight motion, creating a tantalizing friction in every cell in her sex.

"Oh… God." Her hands clutched his shoulders and her eyes rolled back in her head, her mouth opened in pleasurable delight.

Raph breathed deeply as he glanced down at their joined flesh, then back up at her face. He wrapped his hands around her waist and held her tightly. "No," he whispered when she thrust her hips. "Just clench your walls around me."

"I can't," she said on a nervous tremor.

"You can. When you feel me pulse like this…" He pulsed his cock. "I want you to tighten your muscles. Clench and hold me for as long as you can. Do it again, and again, and again…"

He gazed deeply into her seductive eyes, feasting off the hunger and the fire she exuded as he began to pulse inside her, groaning aloud at the sensation of her wet heat clutching him like a thirsty leach, driving passion and desire deeper into the very core of his being.

His grip on her hips tightened. "Oh God, Xiomara. Yes, baby, just like that. That's it, Xio. Suck me… Hold me… God, you're so tight. That's so fucking good…"

Raph shivered in pure bliss as the succulent walls of her sex contracted around him when he flexed, drawing him deeper into wetness, then releasing, only to drag him back in again. His pulses increased and so did her contractions. Their heavy breathing filled the space and the fire roared behind them as the hot tide of passion hurled them into an abyss where only true lovers dared enter.

Xio moaned, and when he felt a contraction, much more powerful than any she'd had with him, and the tingling racing up his spine, Raph knew it was time. He gathered her close, pushed deeper still, locking them eternally together and flexed his cock, holding his climax while she drew tight as a bow string. He surrendered to his, only when her muscles collapsed around him, and his cock was bathed in her sweet warm essence.

"I love you," they cried together.

Those three simple, yet life-changing words were ripped from the deepest parts of their beings as they clung to each other, gasping, each wondering, hoping that the other hadn't heard.

But they had heard. Both of them. And they knew they had to face the consequences.

As he slid out of her, Raph's heart raced at her beauty, her sexiness, at the remnants of their desire shimmering in her sable brown eyes. He loved her, but he'd never intended to tell her. He hadn't even been thinking about love when he heard the words tumbling out of his mouth. But, no, it wasn't his mouth. It was his heart. That's where it had come from. *What now?*

Xio's heart pounded furiously as she gazed into the heat of Raph's eyes. He looked like the Greek god she'd thought he was when he first walked into her office. Never did she imagine that less than a week later, he would be standing in front of her naked, his eyes laced with lingering passion, gazing at her expectantly after telling him that she loved him.

Never did she think she would be foolish enough to put her heart at risk, set herself up for pain. Maybe it was something men said when the fire was too much for them to handle. But that didn't explain why *she* had said it.

"I heard you," he said, breaking the silence.

"I'm sorry. You said no-strings-attached. I don't want to complicate things."

He uttered a skittish laugh and took her hands, bringing them to his lips. "Oh, my sweet Xiomara, I'm afraid that things are already complicated. Things got very complicated in your father's office." He kissed her fingers one at a time. "Those rules I laid down that night were more for me, than for you." He placed his hand under her chin and gazed deeply into her eyes. "And don't pretend you didn't hear me say that I love you. I do love you, Xiomara. Like I've never loved another. I'm man enough to admit it, but I'm also honest enough to say that I don't know what it means for us moving forward."

Xio suppressed the disappointment in hearing that he didn't see them walking off into the sunset together. "I understand," she said. "We are from different worlds. My home is here in Akilina, and yours is in California. Maybe it's enough that we know that we love each other."

"Maybe." He leaned in and kissed her lips.

"Our dinner," she exclaimed, pushing him away, and jumping to the floor. "It's burning."

He was burning, and he had no idea how he would cool himself off.

RAPH LAY on his back with Xio in his arms and a sleeping bag over them. "Tell me about Aetós," he said, combing his fingers through her hair while her fingers toyed with the hair on his chest.

"It's beautiful. It's nestled in the valley below Mt. Cayacáo, with the Bari River running by. The people are very friendly. And everything in the village is powered by the Yacao."

"What's that?"

"The Yacao is the tallest waterfall on the island. It's the mother of all waterfalls at seventeen hundred and ninety-eight feet high. Depending on which way the wind is blowing, you can hear the rush for miles around."

"I'm excited to see it, but how do the villagers stand that constant roar day in and day out?"

Xio appreciated Raph's genuine interest in her people, her heritage, and her culture. Unlike Toby, who was solely focused on what he could gain from her during their three and a half years together, Raph asked thoughtful questions and showed a sincere curiosity.

"Did you fall asleep on me?" Raph asked, squeezing her.

Xio giggled. "I was just thinking…"

"About what?"

"About love."

He briefly glanced off into the fire pit before bringing his gaze back to her. "I love that I love you, Xio. I really do."

Xio felt the power of his love in his touch and in the way he was looking at her with the firelight dancing in his eyes, but she also felt hesitation in him.

"Anyway," she said, laying her head back down, "for the people who are born and raised in Aetós and the surrounding villages, it's all they know. Don't you think they wonder how Americans can sleep or find any peace in big cities? When I first moved to New York, I couldn't stand the constant noise. Every night, it was something else—car alarms, garbage trucks, police and ambulance sirens—you know. I couldn't hear myself think. I felt like I was going crazy, but I got used to it, and eventually I started to love city life."

"Do you miss living in the States at all?" he asked, maybe too hopefully.

The idea of leaving all of this—these mountains, her family, and a sense of community—had once seemed absurd to Xiomara, but she was beginning to fear that she wouldn't be able to survive the humiliation of losing Jewel Beach to Stammer. That sense of community was a double-edged sword. Everyone on this small island would be in her business, whether she wanted them there or not. "I wouldn't want to live anywhere else in the world," she said. At least she was still sure of that.

Xio's answer made Raph confront the stark reality that they were from two different worlds. They had come together physically and emotionally tonight, and he'd let his guard down by fantasizing about falling asleep in her arms and waking up next to her every day for the rest of his life. Those fantasies had led him to confess his love. And although he genuinely meant every word he said to her, his past experience in the matter made him cautious.

It was one thing when two people were secluded together with sexual tension flying high and lust numbing their brains, but it was another when they were confronted with the drama and pain the real world hurled at them—threatening, and often succeeding in destroying the affection that had brought them together in the first place. As beautiful and exciting as it was to love Xio and to know that she loved him, Raph had to remember that what they were sharing in this cave was just a detour from their real lives.

It was just a lovely fantasy.

And knowing that he might not have this opportunity again, Raph meant to take his fill of Xio tonight—all night, and into the morning. "I'm hungry for you again," he said, rolling over, so she was beneath him.

"Mmm," she hummed when he rubbed his erection into her belly. "You're hard as a rock again."

"Told you, I'm always hard around you." He kissed her lips, then slid his tongue into her mouth as she sighed in pleasure.

After a few minutes of their tongues dancing the tango, she rolled him over, so she was on top. "My turn to taste you," she said. "And baby, I'm gonna lick you and suck you until you scream my name and beg me to stop."

"Don't think I will ever beg you to shop, but show me what you got, baby. I'm not bashful," he said, grinning.

Smiling wickedly and salaciously, Xio kissed her way down his hard, muscular body, slowly, softly, and lightly as he he'd done to hers.

When Xio's fingers closed around his cock, and her warm, wet lips brushed the head, Raph sucked vital air into his lungs and curled his toes. He grabbed a fistful of the sleeping bag to keep from leaping off the pallet from the intense pleasure of having Princess Xiomara Davenport's hot mouth wrapped around him, engulfing him in flames that, until this moment, were unimaginable to him…

Part IV

ILLUMINATION

Chapter Thirty-Five

AETÓS

THE SUN HUNG high above Mt. Cayacáo when Raph and Xio finally started out on the last leg of their journey. Neither had been eager to leave their little love haven, but Mitayna Luyaron was expecting them, and the full moon would wait for no one.

What happened in that cave last night was beyond Xio's wildest imagination. When she started out on this journey with Raph, love was the last thing she'd expected to find. But it had blossomed within her, overflowing in abundance with the knowledge that Raph loved her. He loved her, and she loved him with every fibre of her being.

But you might not be around to enjoy that love…

Xio clenched her jaws. What Raph had told her yesterday about Akilah talking with Jamon on the phone about her, had sent her blood curdling. If Samuel Stamer thought that Jamon and Akilah would be a repeat of Trevor and her, he didn't know her little sister.

Akilah might be a lot of things, but she wasn't gullible or stupid, and she was as fiercely protective of her family as Xio was. But most significantly, she didn't trust people like Xio tended to do. She could spot a lie, ten miles down the road, and she seldom forgave or forgot wrongs, even though she might pretend to. Jamon might think he was in charge of that relationship, but Xio knew her sister, and she knew when Akilah was done with Jamon, he will wish he'd never tangoed with her.

"How much farther?" Raph asked, pulling her from her bittersweet thoughts.

She took a breath of composure. "Once we get to the other side of the next hill, we'll be able to see Aetós. Then it's a half hour climb down to it. Are you excited to see where your grandfather was born?" She already knew the answer, but she needed something to keep her mind off Stamer and his rotten sons.

"It's exciting, but sobering, too." Raph brushed locks of hair from his forehead. "Hey, I know you said we shouldn't live in their shadows, but I hope whatever we learn in Aetós doesn't change the way you see me."

"Why would you say that?"

"Because sometimes the truth is too much to handle. What if once you hear the whole story about what Thaddeus did to Eagle to cause his name to be written from history, you start to see me as the enemy. Whatever it was, it couldn't have been anything to be proud of."

Xio searched his face, and her pulse quickened at the fear she saw in his eyes. It was the first time she'd seen him vulnerable, and her heart ached for him. "That was a long time ago, Raph," she said gently. "You don't know what Thaddeus did, or why he did it. I don't see the point in worrying about it until you know. It's not going to change what happened. And I can't hold you accountable for the actions of a man who has been dead for centuries."

"You're right, but whatever it was, it kept my grandfather away from Akilina, from a place and people he loved, and it drove him to keep secrets from his family."

Xio could see the angst in him, and she wished there was something she could do to ease his worry. "Raph, if you—"

"Could you tell me about Eagle?" he asked, changing the subject. "Back at BÓ-Caneye, Kaiah said that he was multilingual. Did he come from a wealthy family."

Despite a need to soothe the anguish eating away at him, Xio was happy to talk about something and someone who grounded her in the knowledge of who she was. "He did. Before he was Eagle, he was Prince Idí of Béhanzin, and heir to the throne of the Kingdom of Allarda."

"Whoa… What? You're kidding. How did a prince end up on a slave ship bound for Barbados?"

"His father's second wife and her son sold him into slavery so that he could take the throne."

"Damn… He did that to his own brother?"

"Some people would do anything for power and money." *Boy, didn't she know that, all too well.*

Xio thought of Eagle, a seventeenth-century Allarda prince, chained in the hold of a slave ship. He would not have known where they were taking him, or what would happen to him, but Xio was certain he'd known that he would never see his family again.

She imagined him standing here in the Nacanké Mountains, decades later, watching other slavers sail by, filled with pain, and hate, and the determination to free his people—Xio's people— from the horrors of slavery. "The sad irony is that by selling him, Idí's brother and his stepmother saved his life," she admitted.

"How's that?"

"Well, a few years after he was sold in Barbados, Eagle met a woman from Allarda who told him that his entire family had been massacred by a rival, a year after Idí disappeared. There was no home for him to return to."

Raph couldn't fathom the pain Eagle must have felt to have lost his country, his family, and his throne, only to be further betrayed by a friend he'd made while enslaved.

More than ever, he wanted to turn on his heels and run for

home, but when Xio laced her arms around his waist, he felt as though he were already there.

"I'm glad I could be here with you," she said.

"I'm glad, too. I can't imagine sharing this with anyone else."

As they walked in silence again, Raph wished the hike to Aetós had taken longer. He wanted more time with Xio. He wanted to memorize her voice and every square inch of her body, to make love to her over and over again with no where to be, and no one and nothing to distract them.

"There she is. There is Aetós." Xio said as they came to a cliff overlooking a narrow valley.

The valley, with the Bari River running through its center, was hugged by a low-hanging, almost mythical fog.

"Beautiful, isn't she?" Xio whispered in his ear, her soft breath against his skin.

He smiled into her eyes. "The most beautiful thing I've ever seen."

WHEN THE TWO HAJIME, standing guard at the village entrance, saw their princess approach, they bowed and greeted her with their hands crossed over their hearts. Then, without further delay, they took their guests' packs and strapped them onto their own backs.

Relieved to be free from his weight, Raph stood silently by as the men spoke to Xio in Megiri. After a minute of rapid exchange, one said something to a little girl standing near the gate, and she ran ahead, while Xio, Raph, and the hajime followed her leisurely.

"Mitayna Luyaron was expecting us yesterday," Xio said. "They sent the little girl ahead to let her know that we're here."

"We haven't offended her, have we?" Raph was desperate for everything to go smoothly in Aetós.

"No, not at all. I'm sure they would assume that the rain held us back." Xio placed her hand on his back. "Raph, don't worry. Everything is going to be alright."

They followed the men past beautiful homes where laundry flapped on lines between trees. Groups of women weaved baskets; others ground maize, and the delicious smell of cooking followed them, making his stomach growl.

Along the river, women washed clothes on the banks, as he had seen them do in the Caonabo on their way to Arijua, while a dozen men and children were working to smoke fish behind them. The thud of axes chopping into wood drew Raph's attention farther up the riverbank, where a group of men were hollowing out logs. Younger boys stood nearby, watching intently. "Looks like canoe-making school is in session," Raph remarked.

"Yep. Like basket weaving, wood and stone cutting, and pottery, the skills are passed down from generation to generation. And," she exclaimed, sweeping her hand in front of her, "we're at the batey."

A crowd was gathering around the dirt clearing. Since they were familiar with their princess, Raph knew their curious stares were directed at him, the strange guayanki.

Xio waved to them as they crossed the batey, but Raph fixed his eyes on the green and brown painted mud home ahead, and Mitayna Luyaron, a stout, middle-aged woman, sitting on a dujo at the edge of her verandah.

"Just follow my lead when we meet her." Xio said.

"Will I have to take my shoes off? Oh God, I hope not," he added under his breath. "They must smell so bad."

"No, not this time." Xio giggled. "We'll have to bathe before we're allowed into her home, though."

"You're kidding."

"I'm not. It's customary after a long journey. Who knows what kind of spirits we picked up along the way? She'll send us to the waterfalls."

Not a bad place to wash up, Raph thought.

Mitayna Luyaron wore a long yellow robe and a thick gold rope around her neck with an ayocin pendant resting in the valley between her buxom breast. The necklace, her gold nose ring, and her bangles, shone in the morning light.

Three men in long blue robes stood on her right side, like soldiers at attention, and five children stood to her left.

"Are those her husbands?" Raph asked Xio in a low voice.

Xio nodded. "I didn't know she had three. She only had one the last time I visited."

They stopped in front of the caneye and bowed before the chief.

"Welcome to Aetós, Rahecica Xiomara of Ynoa. BÓ-Hupia-tí," Mitayna Luyaron said, rising from her dujo as a courtesy to Xio.

"BÓ-Hupia-tí, Mitayna Luyaron." Xio bowed her head.

The chief turned to Raph. "Welcome, Rapheus, grandson of Andris," she said, with a smile that crinkled the corners of her brown eyes.

"BÓ-Hupia-tí, Mitayna Luyaron." He bowed as Xio had done.

When the chief sat back down, the oldest of the three men came down the steps and bowed to Xio. "BÓ-Hupia-tí, Rahecica. It is our honor to have you."

"Thank you, Orion." Xio gave him a warm smile.

Orion reached out a hand to Raph. "Welcome, Rapheus. I am Orion, first husband of Mitayna Luyaron."

"Thank you, Orion."

The second and third husbands, Matuku and Ciro, who looked considerably younger than their wife, paid honor to their princess, and then introduced themselves to Raph. After they had stepped back into line, and the chief had introduced her children, she dismissed them all with a mere nod.

Xio beckoned the two hajime who had met them at the gate. The men set the packs at their feet and Xio retrieved the two parcels Kaiah had sent and presented them to the chief.

"Thank you for bringing them all this way. Your botoá is a true friend. How is she?" the chief asked.

"She is well. Getting up in years, but still as spirited as ever."

Luyaron laughed heartily. "I'm half her age, but we've had good times together. I hope for many more in years to come if it pleases the hupia." Her bracelets jingled as she waved her left hand in the air. Two women emerged from inside the caneye and took the packages inside.

"How was your journey?" She looked from Raph to Xio, then back at Raph.

"It was—enlightening." Raph didn't know how to put into words all that had happened in the last twenty-four hours. Certainly not words that he felt were appropriate for the chief.

"There will be more enlightenment tonight."

Her tone filled Raph with uneasiness.

The chief rose from her dujo. "You will be staying at my caneye. I have two rooms prepared for you. Rahecica Xiomara, do you remember the way to the *Calichi*?"

Raph turned to Xio and she answered the question in his eyes.

"Calichi is the nickname for the Yacao Waterfalls. It means fountain of the high mountain."

Mitayna Luyaron held out her hands. "I would like to have the ashes of the soul you brought home and his beloved wife."

Tension swirled through Raph, but before they completely unraveled him, Xio touched his arm, steadying his nerves.

"They need to prepare your grandparents for their journey into the afterlife," she informed him.

"How? What are they going to do to them?"

"The BÓ'Ajari, the village priest, has to communicate with them to make sure they find their ancestors who are waiting for them across the great river."

"I should be there with them."

"Only priests talk to travelers. He will return them. You brought them a long way, and you have every right to be wary, but I promise, they'll be waiting in your room when we get back from the pool."

Raph found reassurance in Xio's voice and tenderness in the face of Mitayna Luyaron. He retrieved the urn from his pack and placed it into the chief's hands.

"I was just a girl when they first came to our village," she said, holding it against her bosom. "I am sorry for your losses."

"Thank you, Mitayna Luyaron." Raph could scarcely contain the emotion choking his voice.

She smiled. "You will be painted tomorrow afternoon."

"I will? Why?" Raph asked.

"Your grandfather chose you to assist him on his journey into the afterlife, so you will take part in the ceremonies. But tonight, you will sit with BÓ'Roco Wotani Bithithian, your family's memory guide. Tomorrow, we will scatter their ashes."

"I meant to explain all of this to you last night, but…" Xio said, under her breath.

"Because there are two souls who need assistance. You will need to choose someone to guide Kerena into the afterlife," the chief added.

"I don't know anyone here."

"You know me," Xio said, raising her hand. "I will stand as Kerena's guide, if you will accept me. It's up to you."

"Of course. I accept. Thank you, Xio. Thank you for doing this with me. I couldn't have asked for a more perfect partner."

The chief smiled. "There are clean robes and sandals for you at the Calichi. When you return, Piia, your attendant, will serve you lunch, and show you to your rooms. At sunset, I will take you to the RaRoco to meet BÓ'Roco Wotani Bithithian. He has the answers you seek." She bowed to Xiomara, turned, and disappeared into her caneye, the curtain of beads at the door rattling as she parted them.

"The RaRoco is the House of Memories where people go to learn about their family history," Xio explained in response to the apparent look of confusion in his eyes.

Boy, had she learned how to read him in the five days since he'd arrived on the island. The thought made him uneasy.

Chapter Thirty-Six

BÓ'ROCO

BÓ'Roco Wotani Bithithian was a short, thin man with a bald head. His brown eyes were exceptionally sharp and assessing under hooded sockets, Raph thought, as he and Xio sat across the table from the old man in the dimly lit room of the RaRoco.

The air was heavy with the smell of tobacco and the dried herbs hanging from the thatched roofing. Raph breathed through the panic rising in his chest, and his toes curled over the brown and white woven mats beneath the table.

"Thank you for seeing us, BÓ'Roco Wotani Bithithian," Raph said, his apprehensions growing at the prospect of what he was about to learn.

"Yes, thank you," Xio echoed, her voice sounding as shaky as his.

The memory guide stared at them while stroking his chin slowly. "I have been waiting to tell your story for many years."

"Did you know my grandfather?" Raph asked, wondering if he was the one Andris had sat with.

"I know your grandfather, Andris, son of Rapheus."

Raph thought it odd that he spoke about his pappoús in the present tense, and that he called Raph son of Rapheus.

"My father, BÓ'Roco Wotani Kabynthian, was Andris' guide through the past. I will be yours." He picked up a maraca from the table, shook it once, then replaced it.

A boy, about eight years old, and wearing a knee-length white robe, emerged from behind a colorful beaded curtain. He carried a tray with four bamboo cups and a clay pitcher. Without saying a word, or looking at either Raph or Xio, he set the tray on the table and poured water into the cups.

"This is my son," the BÓ'Roco said. "He is in training to become BÓ'Roco Wotani Biandakhabo. My father was the eighth, I'm the ninth, and my son will be the tenth memory guide in my family," he said with a hint of admiration in his voice. "He is here to listen, learn, and memorize the facts as I speak them, so that after I'm gone, he will be able to guide those who seek answers into the past." He gestured to his son to sit next to him, then eyed Raph and Xio. "Have you sat with a BÓ'Roco before?"

They shook their heads.

"There are rules that you must follow. You will ask your questions and the truth you are seeking. Once I begin recounting your history, you may not interrupt. It is critical that the BÓ'Roco in training hears the story in its entirety without interjections. Once I have told your story, I will shake the maraca, and give you time to reflect on what you've heard. If you have more questions after your reflection, I will answer them if I can. Understood?"

"We understand."

He sat tall on his stool and folded his hands on his lap. "What truth do you seek?"

Raph placed his hands on his thighs and pressed down to hide the trembling in his legs. "Four weeks ago, on his deathbed, my grandfather told me that he was born on Akilina. He asked me to come here and scatter his and my grandmother's ashes at Aetós. He said he was sorry for not telling me something that he should have. He said he tried, but that it was too hard, or something like that." Raph paused and closed his eyes as he felt himself slipping back into that woeful day, the smell of death permeating the room.

Xio's hand on his arm pulled him back, and he again fixed his gaze on his guide. "When I got to Akilina, I learned that on his last visit here, he discovered that our family has a link to the island that goes back hundreds of years."

The BÓ'Roco nodded.

"When I was thirteen, my grandfather asked me to help him clean an old clock that has been in our family for generations. He told me that it was built by Thaddeus Giannopoulos, over three hundred years ago. That night, after cleaning the clock, I started having a nightmare that lasted for a few months before it stopped completely. In the dream, I—"

His memory guide raised his right hand. "I tell stories as they are told to me, Rapheus. I do not interpret dreams."

Raph nodded. "Dacica Kaiah told me how Thaddeus ended up on Ynoa, about the boat that he'd built to bring Eagle and the others from Barbados, and about the friendship between Thaddeus and Eagle." He paused. "How many questions am I allowed to ask, BÓ'Roco Wotani Bithithian?"

"As many as you need, Rapheus."

"I want to know about Thaddeus' betrayal of Eagle." Fear knotted in his throat. "What was so bad that he was written out of Megiri history." Raph licked his dry lips. "And I'm hoping you can tell me how my great-grandparents, Arsenios and Giulia, heard about Akilina. Do you know why they came here?"

The memory guide took a sip of water from his cup, folded his hands on his stomach and fixed his gaze on the wall behind Raph and Xio.

It was so quiet inside the house, Raph could hear the trickling of water against rocks from the brook outside the open window behind the guide.

"I will answer your second question first. I will tell you as it was told to me. But please leave your questions until I pick up the maraca, indicating I've reached the end."

Raph nodded, his throat too tight to speak. He placed his hand over Xio's lying on her lap, and calm seeped into his heart.

BÓ'Roco Wotani Bithithian began in a slow baritone voice. "In the year nineteen twenty-six, the day before Arsenios Giannopoulos was to travel to Italy from Greece to purchase vineyards for his family's company, his father, Visilios Giannopoulos, told him that he had found some journals that belonged to Thaddeus Giannopoulos. The journals were written while Thaddeus was living in the village of Aetós in the Nacanké Mountains of Ynoa, and that from the journals, Visilios learned that the story they had been told about their family's history was a lie. Visilios promised to tell Arsenios more when he returned from Italy.

"While Arsenios was in Italy, he fell in love with Giulia Metti. But Arsenios and Giulia were already promised to others from families as powerful and wealthy as their own. They were torn between duty and their love for each other.

"Then, fate decided the course of their lives when Giulia became pregnant. Fearing what would happen if their families discovered their affair, they ran away to Ynoa, believing they would be safely hidden here. Four months after they arrived, your grandfather was born in this village of Aetós."

Wotani paused and breathed deeply. Then he closed his eyes, reached for the maraca, and shook it. "Now, you may ask your questions," he said, raising his lids.

Raph didn't know where to start. He'd gotten the answer to one of the first questions he'd had after his grandfather died, but now, there were so many more. "Did my grandfather mention the journals when he met with your father? Do you know where they are now?"

"Andris did not know anything about the journals until he met with the BÓ'Roco. And I do not know where they are now."

"But, if Andris didn't know about them, how do you?"

"Arsenios Giannopoulos shared this story with the BÓ'Roco when he came to Aetós."

"Do you know when and why Arsenios and Giulia left Ynoa? If they were hiding from their families, why did they return to Greece?" They had to have returned at some point, Raph thought. *At least that much must be true.*

"After their son was born, Arsenios wrote home to tell his father that he had a grandson. A year and a half later, he received word that his father was dying, and Arsenios took his son and his wife and left Ynoa for Greece."

Raph reached for his cup, and drank from it. Once he replaced it on the table, the young BÓ'Roco refilled it from the pitcher.

"Do you have more questions, Rapheus?" BÓ'Roco Wotani asked.

"I just wish I knew where the journals are. Your father didn't ask my grandfather if he had any idea where they could be?"

"BÓ'Roci can only relate what we witness, and what we are told. We do not ask questions of our seekers."

"It is forbidden for BÓ'Roci to ask questions," Xio said. "There are some truths that seekers never want revealed."

"So there are questions I may never have answers to?" Raph curled his fist on his thigh.

Their silence answered him.

Raph would love to get his hands on Thaddeus' journals, especially because there might be information about his life in Greece, England, and Barbados. But he had no idea where to begin searching. He and his brothers had inventoried everything at the estate in Santorini after Andris died. He would surly remember coming across four-hundred-year-old journals.

"Are you ready to hear the story of Thaddeus?" BÓ'Roco Wotani Bithithian asked.

Raph turned to Xio, giving her an apprehensive smile. "We're ready," he said.

Wotani took a deep breath, then began speaking slowly, in a clear, crisp voice. "Thaddeus and Amaryllis Giannopoulos and their two sons, Neopheus and Telepheus, arrived in Ynoa in sixteen-forty. In sixteen-forty-five, Amaryllis gave birth to twins, a boy and a girl. The daughter died shortly after birth, but the son survived. They named him Rapheus Sebastian."

Rapheus Sebastian? Raph knew that he and his brothers had been named after Thaddeus' sons, but hearing the names now sent a chill down his spine. *So Rapheus was born in Ynoa, not in England, as he'd been told.*

"Three years later, a daughter was born to Eagle Davenport and his wife, Rahecica Ismé. They named her Xiomara Quetia."

Xio tilted her face toward Raph. *Rapheus and Xiomara? Three years apart? What a strange coincidence...*

"In sixteen-fifty-five, when Rapheus was ten years old, his mother, Amaryllis, died. Eight years later, Neopheus and Telepheus left Ynoa for England, leaving Rapheus alone here with their father. They took with them a clock that Thaddeus had carved from the guayacán tree."

Okay, so they did live in England, but did they really die in a flood? Or was that a made-up story, too?

"As Rapheus and Xiomara—the children of two taiguaitiao—played and grew together, they fell in love, and in sixteen-sixty three, they were married, and lived together in Allarda. Rapheus referred to Xiomara as his *Jewel*, because she was a jewel given to him by the gods.

"Rapheus was a fearsome warrior," Wotani continued. "He and his father, along with Eagle and the Megiri led many raids on the other islands when our people fought the guayanki to protect our lands. They helped many of the enslaved Guaitiari escape. and brought them back to Ynoa.

"One night, during a raid on Barbados, Rapheus disappeared."

Raph and Xio stiffened in their seats.

"When Thaddeus returned to the boat, he was badly beaten. He told the raiding party that he and Rapheus had been attacked by a group of guayanki overseers. A fight broke out and they were separated in the commotion. After hiding in a sugarcane field, Thaddeus came back to the boats hoping to find Rapheus safe and waiting.

"Though the raiding party, many of whom were Rapheus' friends, wanted to stay and search for him, the cover of darkness was fading, and they had to leave the beach. A man named Daniel Davenport, who lived in Barbados, and who helped plan the raids, was a friend of Eagle and the Megiri. He promised to find Rapheus and bring him to Ynoa."

Thank God they had help. And Davenport? Raph watched Xio from the corner of his eye. *Was she related to Daniel, too?*

"Rapheus' friends went back to Barbados the next night. They searched for him and hoped to get word about his whereabouts from Daniel, but without success. It was as if he had vanished. Jewel was devastated. She wept for her missing husband, refusing to eat, and unable to sleep for days. She sought comfort from her parents, and those who loved Rapheus. On the eighth day of Rapheus' disappearance, Eagle brought Jewel to Aetós to visit his friend and her father-in-law. Thaddeus was grief-stricken over the loss of his son, and hadn't left his house since that terrible night."

Raph could only imagine the hell he was in: first losing his parents and older brother in Greece, then his little brother in England, his daughter and wife here in Aetós, and his two oldest sons who'd left for England. And on top of all that, his youngest son—the only family he had left—was missing, presumably dead. *The poor man.*

"They found Thaddeus lying on the floor of his hut. He hadn't eaten or bathed since the fateful night. Eagle later said that Thaddeus had the eyes of a wild boar who'd been wounded. They spent the night with him, trying to give him comfort since he was now alone in the world.

"Two days later, during the early morning, Eagle and Jewel said their goodbyes, and left Thaddeus' hut. As they walked through the batey toward the village gates, Thaddeus came out of his house with a bow and shot a poisoned arrow at Eagle's back. Jewel screamed as her father fell to the ground, the arrow's tip piercing through his chest."

Xio pressed her hand to her chest and groaned as pain ripped through her heart. *Her dream... This was her dream.* Thaddeus had launched the arrow, but it wasn't meant for her, as she'd thought. The pain she felt at waking was Jewel's broken heart over losing her husband and watching her father writhing in agony on the ground with an arrow lodged in his chest, fired from the bow of his best friend, and knowing she might lose him, too. Tears filled Xio's eyes.

BÓ'Roco Wotani continued. "Eagle was badly wounded, and though the poison did not kill him, it weakened his body, and he was never the same. Thaddeus was taken before the Council of Elders that day. He gave no defense for his actions when questioned, and his immediate execution was ordered. He was taken to a cliff, bound by ropes, and tossed into the ocean."

Pain moved slowly through Raph's chest and curled around his lungs as he was sucked into his nightmare, gasping, and choking, and trying to free himself from his cords. Why had he been chosen to relive the man's nightmare?

"The following day, Jewel's grandfather, Dacique Kufko, demanded she be married to a Megiri warrior. Her family, and the Council of Elders reasoned that her husband had abandoned her and that his father had tried to kill hers. They told her that the two-hundred-year-old prophecy of the guayanki coming to destroy them had come true in Thaddeus and Rapheus, and that in order to prevent further harm to their lives and customs, all traces of the guayanki had to be wiped from their history. Dacique Kufko decreed that no one was ever to speak their names again. Jewel was married before sunset that day."

Raph's heart dropped to the pit of his stomach when Xio pulled her hand from his and turned her face away. Now that they had learned that Thaddeus had tried to kill Eagle, would she hold his ancestor's sins against him?

BÓ'Roco Wotani again closed his eyes and breathed deeply before picking up the maraca and shaking it.

To give himself time to process what he had heard, Raph fixed his gaze on a wooden totem with figures of various Megiri gods carved intricately into it, standing in the corner of the hut. *Why had Thaddeus shot an arrow at his friend's back in the middle of the batey with so many witnesses around, when he could have killed him in secrecy during the two days Eagle spent at his hut? Could losing Rapheus really have driven him to that level of madness? Did he think Eagle had something to do with Rapheus's demise?*

Finally, with his heart racing in his chest, Raph turned his gaze to the BÓ'Roco, and asked the first in a long list of new questions. "BÓ'Roco Wotani, where was Rapheus all this time? He obviously didn't…die." *My existence is proof of that.*

Xio turned around at his question, but she didn't look at him, nor did she close the space she had created between them.

"The story that Thaddeus told the raiding party the night Rapheus went missing was not true," the guide said. "Rapheus and Thaddeus were not attacked by overseers and separated from each other. They were arrested by a pair of British soldiers and taken to jail. A young officer, eager to be noticed by his superiors, told Thaddeus that in return for not hanging his son, he must kill Eagle Davenport."

My god. Xio's chest burned. He'd done what any father would have done, she realized now. Tears streamed down her face, and she blindly reached for Raph's hand.

"You see, you must understand that there was a price on Eagle's head, and he was wanted by the British, dead or alive," Wotani said, his voice catching just a little as if he felt the sadness of the situation. "Eagle was recognized as one of the fiercest warriors on Ynoa, defending the island from the British and French, and leading raids on Barbados and other British-controlled islands."

Raph and Xio could feel the rapid pounding of each other's hearts through their joined hands. They squeezed, offering each other courage and strength.

"The ambitious officer beat up father and son, then released Thaddeus, giving him fourteen days to bring proof that Eagle was dead, or Rapheus would be executed. They warned him that if he told the Megiri, and they attempted a rescue, Rapheus would be shot."

Jesus, Raph thought. *And to make matters worse, he couldn't tell anyone, because he knew they would try to spring Rapheus from jail, and that would just bring about his immediate death.*

Raph didn't have to wonder why Thaddeus shot Eagle in broad daylight and, in front of witnesses. There was no way he could kill Eagle and smuggle the proof of his death off the island to Barbados in time to save his son. He didn't want to go on living. It didn't matter what he did, his son would hang. He'd probably remained silent at his trial to spare Jewel having to imagine Rapheus hanging from the end of a rope. He was damned if he did, and damned if he didn't. *What an impossible choice...*

The memory guide's voice brought Raph back to attention. "While waiting in jail, unaware of the deal that had been struck between the officer and his father, Rapheus was able to escape when a fire broke out one night. He went to the home of Daniel Davenport, where Daniel hid him for two nights."

Relief flooded Raph. *At least Rapheus and Jewel would have a second chance. But who was this Daniel Davenport? One at a time, Raph. One at a time.* "Did he return to Ynoa once he escaped?"

"Yes. With Daniel's help, Rapheus did find his way to Ynoa. But he did not receive the welcome he was expecting. On the beach that night, three of his friends were standing guard. They were happy to see him alive, but warned him of the danger that awaited him. The men told Rapheus what his father had done to Eagle, that Thaddeus had been executed, and that his Jewel had been married only one day before. He was told that The Council of Elders had lost all faith in the guayanki, and did not want any living on Ynoa. If found, he would be killed on sight.

"Rapheus was heartbroken that his father was dead, though he was prepared to fight for the love of his life. Knowing that he would be killed if he tried to see Jewel, his friends encouraged Rapheus to leave Ynoa quickly.

"Insistent on going inland to see his wife and his father-in-law, and desperate to tell them what had happened to him, and that he had not abandoned his Jewel, Rapheus tried to fight them, but he was overpowered by the men who were determined to save his life. Rapheus was knocked unconscious and carried back to Daniel's boat. The next morning, silent, inconsolable, and despondent, Rapheus boarded a ship with Daniel, and sailed for England. He never returned to Ynoa."

"And he never saw Jewel again?" Raph's voice was filled with his soul's anguish.

"No, they never saw each other again."

"What about—" Xio stopped, remembering that only Raph could ask questions of the BÓ'Roco in Aetós. Her family's memory keeper was in Allarda. "Ask him about Jewel," she whispered to Raph, tugging at his shirt sleeve. "Ask if anyone ever told Jewel the truth… That Rapheus came back for her."

"Well, did they?" Raph asked anxiously. "Did Jewel know that Rapheus didn't abandon her?"

Wotani shook his head. "No, the princess was never told that Rapheus had returned to Ynoa, but..." He paused, cleared his throat, and took a sip of water. "Five months after she was married the second time, in sixteen-sixty-five, Jewel gave birth to a son. She named him Rapheus Sebastian after his father."

Xiomara's jaw slackened at the revelation that Jewel, her ancestor and namesake, had a child with Rapheus. *Did that mean...*

"But the baby," Wotani said. "The baby, Rapheus Sebastian, died within hours after he was born. Jewel did not speak again for two years."

So a heartbroken Rapheus left Ynoa without ever knowing that Jewel was pregnant with their child, Raph thought. He wasn't sure if he was more relieved to know that he and Xio couldn't be related, or heartbroken to know, that not even their child had managed to survive this tragedy.

"In sixteen-sixty-seven, two years after the loss of her first child, Jewel gave birth to her second child. And after two years of silence, as the child slipped from her body, Rahecica Xiomara Quetia, Rapheus' Jewel, cried out his name and that of their dead child three times. She died with her second child still lying between her legs. She was nineteen years old."

Xio was unable to stifle her cry, and a guttural moan vibrated in her throat.

Raph clasped her hand between his. "But, wait a minute." He shook his head in confusion, his grief and concern for Xio suddenly overshadowed by an impossibility. "If she never knew, how do *you* know? If Rapheus never made it back to Aetós, how do you know what really happened that night of the raid in Barbados? How do you know the truth behind why Thaddeus tried to kill Eagle?"

"Daniel Davenport."

There was that name again. Raph looked to Xio. "Are you related to this Daniel Davenport?"

"I'll tell you all about him later," she said, wiping her nose on the inside collar of her shirt. "Just let him finish telling the story."

Okay. Raph nodded to the memory guide.

"Once they arrived in England," he continued, "Daniel took Rapheus to his home, and took great care of him as he tried to locate Rapheus' brothers, Neopheus and Telepheus. After finding them, he left Rapheus with his family and returned to Barbados. Three years later, he overheard a conversation in Bridgetown, and learned what Rapheus had never been able to tell him in the aftermath of his grief. Daniel learned that Thaddeus had been arrested along with his son, and that Rapheus would have been hanged if Thaddeus did not bring proof of Eagle's death.

"Understanding why Thaddeus had betrayed Eagle, Daniel came to Ynoa seeking an audience with Dacique Kufko. He told the dacique what he had learned, though, the truth had come home too late for Jewel. She never knew that Rapheus had not abandoned her."

She died from a broken heart. Xio's heart pounded as Jewel's pain over losing Rapheus flooded her being. It was incomparable to what hers would be when Raph returned to San Francisco. At least she would know where he was, and that he was alive and safe. Jewel never had that peace of mind. She never even knew why her father-in-law had tried to kill her father.

"Did Daniel and Rapheus remain friends?" Raph asked.

"I know that Daniel and Rapheus remained friends. And I know that Daniel never told Rapheus that Jewel had been pregnant and that she and their child had died. Daniel believed that Rapheus' state of mind was too fragile to bear the burden of truth. He believed such knowledge would have pushed him to take his own life."

Raph shook his head, feeling bereft and desolate. "I can only imagine Daniel's own state of mind when he learned the truth.

He must have been racked with guilt for keeping Rapheus in Barbados one extra night, instead of bringing him straight to Ynoa after he escaped from jail."

Xio gasped. "Oh, my God, Raph, you're right. I never even thought of that. Rapheus might have been too late to save his father, but he could have kept Jewel if he'd returned in time to tell them the truth, give insight into what Thaddeus had done." Her throat swelled with an acute sense of loss for everyone involved in the heartbreaking plot.

"Do you know what happened to Rapheus in England?" Raph asked, no longer confident in the stories he had been told about anyone in his family.

"Rapheus worked for the shipbuilding company that his brothers had started, and to keep the memory of his Jewel, and his true home alive, they named the business Giannport."

"Oh my God," Xio exclaimed, staring at him wide eyed.

He nodded. *So, that's when it happened—the blending of the two family names.*

Wotani continued. "However, in sixteen-seventy-six, a great flood swept through London, and Neopheus and Telepheus were killed along with their families.

At least that part of my family history is true. But in light of all that Rapheus had already lost, the tragedy of that flood must have surely magnified his grief a thousand folds. *How could anyone bounce back from so much sorrow?*

"Then in sixteen-eighty-eight, twelve years after his brothers and their wives and children died, Rapheus Giannopoulos, the only surviving son of Thaddeus, moved to Greece, where he alone continued the Giannopoulos bloodline. He was forty-three years old."

As he held Xio's hand in his, Raph began to understand the debt of gratitude he owed Rapheus for his existence. His throat swelled, and he instinctively turned to Xio.

They held on to each other as their bodies wracked with sobs.

They cried for their ancestors, young lovers torn apart who, almost four hundred years later, seemed to be reaching out to them, begging them to finish their story. Now, they understood the reason for the uncontrollable passion between them, their burning need to be together, and inability to stay away from each other.

This was their destiny, though they could not give Rapheus and Jewel the blissful life they had been deprived of, the happily-ever-after they deserved.

Finally, their sobs ceased, and the faint murmur of water washing over riverbed rocks soothed their minds. They lifted their heads and gazed into each other's eyes, their hearts saying so much, yet not enough of the things they were too afraid to speak out loud.

Raph and Xio had not heard him get up from the table over the sound of their cries, but BÓ'Roco Wotani Bithithian's smile was gentle as he walked over to them from a cupboard at the edge of the room. He sat down and, reaching across the table, he held Raph's hand and dropped a pendant into his palm. "This belonged to Rapheus," he said.

Xio gasped at the sight of the ayocin stone burning orange in the low light. She reached for hers and closed her hand around it.

"Rapheus and Jewel choose matching ayocin gems as a symbol of their love for each other. Warriors didn't wear jewelry when they went out on raids," Wotani said. "Rapheus left his at home the night he was kidnapped. When there are no family members to pass such items down to, they are given to the BÓ'Roco for safekeeping until someone comes to claim them. It was offered to Arsenios, and he refused it. And when it was offered to Andris, he asked my father to keep it until he returned. But he never did. So it is yours now, Rapheus, if you will take it."

Raph closed his hand around the pendant, feeling the energy

of his ancestor seep into his soul, the love he had for Jewel, just as pure and intense as the love Raph had for Xio.

BÓ'Roco Wotani pulled an envelope from the pocket of his robe and held it out to Raph. "Two years ago, when he made arrangements for his ashes to be scattered here at Aetós, Andris sent this letter to the RaRoco, asking that it be given to you, should you ever visit your family's BÓ'Roco."

Raph stared at the envelope, overwhelmed at the sight of another letter from his grandfather. He never thought he would hear from him again.

"When Dacique Kufko heard the true story about the events of that night," the memory guide said, "he was saddened, and changed his decree to allow the BÓ'Roci to speak of Thaddeus and his family, only when a son of Rapheus returns. You are the third son of Rapheus to return to Aetós. You are the third to hear this story that the BÓ'Roci have kept secret for four hundred years. You must now choose what you will do with the truth." He paused. "Do you have any more questions, Rapheus?"

Raph lifted his head. "No. I don't. Thank you, BÓ'Roco Wotani Bithithian," he said, the gratitude and appreciation he felt for the man, and what he'd done for him, heavy in his voice. "Thank you for everything."

He nodded and smiled. "My son will bring you tea. Stay as long as you like." He stood to his feet, bowed to Xio and then to Raph. "BÓ-Hupia-tí, Rahecica Xiomara, daughter of Jewel. "BÓ-Hupia-tí, Rapheus, son of Rapheus."

Raph and Xio stood and, bowing in respect, said, "BÓ-Hupia-tí, BÓ'Roco Wotani Bithithian," then watched silently as the memory guide walked out of the room.

Raph stared at his name on the front of the envelope in his grandfather's neat handwriting, and then at the pendant—gifts from beyond the grave, both of equal importance to him. He placed the envelope on the table and fastened the gold chain around his neck. The instant the stone touched his chest, he felt the last block of ice melt away from his heart.

"We have something of both of them," Xio said in a choked voice, reaching for hers. "We will carry on their legacies."

Raph watched her through his blur of tears. "I love you, Xiomara," he said, pulling her into his arms and holding her tightly.

"I love you too, Rapheus."

They held each other for a few quiet moments, closing their eyes and opening their hearts to receive the energy, the love, and passion their ancestors had for each other, and hoping that their love would also last beyond the grave.

Raph opened his eyes, then easing Xio out of his arms, he picked up the envelope, opened it, and flipped through the four sheets of paper. "It's in Greek," he said.

"Do you want some tea while you read it?" Xio asked.

He looked around the sparsely furnished room. "No. I think I need some air." He folded the pages and pushed them back into the envelope.

"You want to go back to the caneye then?"

"Yeah, that sounds good." Raph pulled Xio back into his arms. "Will you sit with me while I read it?"

"Of course. We're in this together now."

Chapter Thirty-Seven

FULL CIRCLE

MARCH 15, 2018

My Dear Rapheus,

If you are reading this letter, it means you made it to Aetós, and have heard the truth about Thaddeus and the history of our family's link with the Davenports. As you can tell by the date, I am writing this letter following our most recent family tragedy. I will be mailing it to our family's BÓ'Roco with instructions to give it to you if you ever make it there.

You see, even as I put pen to paper, I am still unsure about telling you a story that I heard about our family after your father and grandmother were killed—a story that has been a burden on my heart for the past twenty-five years.

I don't know if I'll ever have the heart to tell you, Rapheus, but since life is so precarious, I thought I should at least make certain that the story doesn't die with me. I'm ninety-one years old, and I am the only living Giannopoulos who knows the truth. Who knows how much longer I will be here. You and your brothers have a right to know the truth about our family, so I'm also writing a letter to Xiomara, asking her to help you. My attorney will deliver it after I'm gone, whether or not I have already told you. This letter might be unnecessary, but just in case...

I imagine you are wondering why I never told you about Akilina. The truth is, I wanted to tell you. I tried to tell you that day when we cleaned the clock together in my bedroom. It was the reason I asked your mother to send you to Santorini ahead of your brothers. But I couldn't, Rapheus. You were too young to be burdened with a story so tragic, or the weight of having to fulfill a four-hundred-year-old destiny on an island in the Caribbean. I thought I would tell you when you got older, but it didn't get any easier. You were off to college, enjoying your life. I thought of telling you after you graduated, but then you were focused on launching G3, and then you fell in love.

You had created your own destiny, Raph. You were happy, and I didn't want to upset your world. After I heard about Rapheus and Jewel's tragic love story from BÓ'Roco Wotani Kabynthian, I was plagued with regret for having named you Rapheus, especially knowing that little Xiomara, whom I love like a granddaughter, was descended from Eagle Davenport.

When BÓ'Roco Wotani Kabynthian told me that my father, your Great-grandfather Arsenios, had been pressured into naming me Rapheus and leaving me in Ynoa to fulfill the destiny, I understood, then, why he falsified my birth certificate and never told me about Ynoa. He was trying to protect me, like I was trying to protect you. I wanted you to choose your own path in life and not be bound by the deeds and promises of your ancestor.

But after your heart was broken, you gave up on love, and began building walls around your emotions and retreating behind them. I wondered if perhaps your destiny was indeed in Ynoa. I don't know…

Once again, our world has been turned upside down with Helena's tragic death, and fear shadows my heart. You've always been a skeptic, Raph, much like your father, only believing in what you can see and touch, and always needing proof. I am afraid you will think the story is the rantings of an old man who's losing his mind, just as I thought about Wotani Kabynthian. I think the only way to convince you that Rapheus and Jewel's love story did occur on this mountain is to plant you right in the middle of it with Xiomara. Hence my letter to her, asking that she accompany you on the journey when you do show up to scatter your grandmother's and my ashes—which I hope you will.

I'm not telling you what to do with the truth you've uncovered. Whether or not you decide to pass it on to the next generation or keep it to yourself is up to you. As you're aware, Thaddeus' two oldest sons and their wives and children died in England. So, if it wasn't for Rapheus, the son who, like me, was born in Aetós, Ynoa, the Giannopoulos bloodline would have died with Neopheus and Telepheus and their families.

Rapheus, I know you carry the guilt of Helena's death, but you're not responsible for what happened to her. She chose her path, and you must choose yours.

I did not send you and Xiomara on this journey together to fall in love, but I believe you two were born to love and care for each other, just like Xiomara and Rapheus before you.

It is with a peaceful heart that I say goodbye for the last time, but know that I will always be with you and your brothers and your mother and Petra. When you are sad, I'm right there brushing your fears away from your brow, and when you are happy, I'm standing beside you, enjoying a cigar with your father and a glass of wine with your grandmother.

With all my love and blessings for long life, happiness, and a clear path for the future of our family.

Your Loving Pappoús,
Andris

RAPH'S HEART pounded in his chest as, for the first time in a long time, he knew what he wanted. He wanted Xio and she needed to hear him say it. Even though he'd told her that he loved her, he hadn't committed to being with her, sharing his life with her under one roof. It was time she knew he was all in.

He turned and cradled her face in his hands. "I don't want us to end up like Rapheus and Jewel, living unhappy lives apart from each other. I'm not willing to live without you, Xiomara."

Tears rolled from Xio's eyes into his palms. "I don't want to live without you, either." Xio hesitated before she said what she needed to. "But there's a slight chance I might have to. Not by choice."

His eyes narrowed and a mixture of fear and confusion shadowed his face. "What do you mean? What are you saying, Xio?"

Xio got up and began pacing, the reality that she could lose Raph starker now that she knew for certain she had him.

"Xiomara." Raph stood in front of her. "What is it, hon?"

Xio glanced up at him. "It's Stamer."

"The man who you told me is threatening to call in your loan?"

She nodded. She'd opened up to Raph about Stamer over a breakfast of instant oatmeal this morning. But she hadn't told him everything, only that he'd threatened to call in her loan over a technicality in the contract.

"I know you refused when I offered help, but things are different between us now, Xio. Your loan would be taken care of with one phone call to my bank."

"It's not that simple, Raph." She crossed her arms. "It's not about the loan. It's about me going to jail for a very long time."

"What?" His hands were firm on her shoulders. "Xio, what do you mean you're going to jail?"

The uncertainty in his eyes was like a knife to her heart. According to Andris' letter, he had already lost one woman he'd loved, and she could see fear of history repeating itself on his face. Maybe she should have told him before she let things get this far, before he fell in love with her, and was ready to change up his life to be with her.

"Xiomara, talk to me, damn it! What did that bastard do? I swear to God I will fucking kill him."

Something snapped inside Xio at his anger, his rage, his instinct to stand beside her in battle. It was exactly what she needed. Pity and sympathy would have made her feel pathetic and would have hacked away at her newly restored self-confidence.

Holding Raph's inflamed gaze, Xio rode that ferocious wave, and as the story tumbled out of her mouth, her resolve to fight grew stronger and more urgent. By the time she got to the three options she had been given, the wave of emotions had evolved into a forceful tsunami, ready to swallow Samuel Stamer whole.

"Bastard!" Raph's eyes glowed like shards of green fractured glass, and his jaws clenched tightly as he fought to contain himself. "No wonder you blew a gasket when I told you who Akilah was talking to on the phone. But I don't think you need to worry about her. She's in charge of that relationship, believe me."

Xio chuckled. "I know. And, I'm not marrying Trevor, just so you know."

"Of course you're not." His eyes softened.

"And I'm not just handing over my family's company to him, either. I'm taking him to court for blackmail."

He pulled her into his arms. "*We're* taking him to court. I will be with you every step of the way. I'll be in the courtroom every day with you."

Xio struggled out of his embrace. It was time to get practical. "I don't know how that's possible, Raph, when you're going back to San Francisco. I mean, even if I win and manage to keep myself out of jail, I can't leave my home, my family, and Jewel Beach. I have to keep my father's legacy alive. There's no one else to do it."

"You don't have to leave. I'll move to Akilina."

Xio held her breath, savoring the words that breezed over her ears. "What about G3? Can you just walk away from it?"

"I wouldn't be walking away from it, really. It's the twenty-first century. I can work from anywhere. My COO, Declan, can manage things when I'm here. I'll fly up when I need to."

"What about your brothers?" Xio asked, throwing everything into the ring before she allowed her heart to accept what he was proposing. "Won't they think you're abandoning them, and the company you built together?"

"They'll understand, especially Tele." He chuckled. "He

knows that everyone and everything else takes a back seat when you find true love. Plus, he owes me."

Xio wondered if the slight note of unresolved tension in his voice had anything to do with Helena, the woman, whose death Andris had told Raph he wasn't responsible for. Was she the same Helena Tele had married? There was still so much she didn't know about Raph's experiences regarding his relationships with women. But she knew that in time, when he was ready, he would open up to her about his broken heart. In the meantime… "And your mother?" she asked.

"Will dance at our wedding."

Xio brushed away the happy tears pooling in her eyes. "I can't wait to meet your family."

"They will love you," he murmured, tucking strands of her hair behind her ears.

"Like you love mine."

"Exactly. We will be one big happy family. Giannport has already established that eternal bond. By the way, you promised to tell me who Daniel Davenport was, and how Prince Idí ended up with his surname."

"Oh, yeah, I did promise. Well, in short, Daniel worked on the ship that brought Prince Idí from Africa. It was his first time working on a ship. He didn't know it was a slaver, and was horrified at what he saw. He was in charge of the captives, and when he realized that Idí spoke English and several other languages, he started questioning him about his life. He promised to help him return to his home in Africa, but when that was no longer feasible, he did the next best thing and helped him and Thaddeus escape to Ynoa. Daniel spent the rest of his life helping other enslaved people escape. So, in honor of all he'd done for him and others, Eagle, with Daniel's blessings, adopted the surname Davenport, and my family has been carrying it ever since."

"Wow, that's quite a story. I can't wait to hear the full

version." Raph shook his head. "This all seems so surreal, like we're living inside a dream."

"I know. And speaking of dreams. If you don't mind my asking, what was your nightmare about? And you said it reoccured for months after that first time?"

His entire body shuddered and his face contorted as if he were in pain.

"I'm sorry. Maybe I shouldn't have asked."

He placed his hands on her shoulders, and looked into her eyes. "No, it's fine. And yes, I had it for months, then it stopped for about twenty years. I'd forgotten about it, then it returned on my first night in Akilina."

The same night hers had resurfaced after a seventeen-year absence, Xio thought. *Coincidence?*

"I—" Raph swallowed. "I dreamed about what happened to Thaddeus. It's as if I was reliving every second of his horrific death sentence. I'm bound by tree roots and tossed into the sea, and as I plunge downward, the roots tighten around my body and choke me. I wake up gasping for air and trying to expel sea water from my lungs. It always feels so real."

"Oh my God." She pressed a hand to her chest. "I'm so sorry, Raph."

"Yeah. But I don't think I'll ever have it again, now that I know Thaddeus' story. It's as if he wanted me to find the truth about what happened to him."

"I know the feeling. I've been having nightmares about Jewel since I was thirteen."

He tipped his head to the side, his eyes widening with curiosity. "Really? What's yours like?"

She licked her dry lips. "I'm a young woman, walking through the village. I'm very happy because I have something to tell my husband when I get home. But when I reach the door of my hut, an eagle flies in front of me and then falls to the ground with an arrow launched in its chest. I always wake up with an excruciating pain in my heart, and gasping for air, like you."

"Oh no. Xio." He pulled her close, his hands gently caressing her back.

"I always thought the eagle had taken the arrow meant for me. But I now know that it was actually *Eagle* absorbing his daughter's sorrow, helplessly watching her whither away. My pain was Jewel's heartbreak over losing her husband and her baby, and the fact that she never got to share the happiness of her pregnancy with Rapheus. She had nothing else to live for after they were taken from her."

"So sad and heartbreaking, even after three hundred years," Raph said. "I wonder why, of all the people in our families through the centuries, you and I were chosen to relive their pain?"

Xio took a deep breath and stood back from him. "I don't know. But, when a person dreams about an event in an ancestor's life, the Megiri calls it shadowing. We were both shadowed, so Thaddeus, Rapheus, and Jewel's story could be told. Now, they can all rest in the peace they so very much deserve."

Raph nodded in agreement. "If I didn't believe in destiny or things beyond this world before, I do now. Wholeheartedly," he said in a tremulous voice. "Just think of it, without knowing Rapheus and Jewel's story, your great-grandmother and my grandfather named us after them. You and I are meant to be together, Xiomara Davenport. There is no doubt about it."

"I feel it in my heart, too, Rapheus Giannopoulos, whole-heartedly." Xio's heart overflowed with joy as she gazed up at the man she was born to love, and who was born to love her. Their fates had been sealed the moment they entered this world, long before they knew the other existed.

She tilted her head and gave him a slanted look. "Did you say something about a wedding? I think you're skipping a few steps, like—"

"Oh, we'll get there," he said, cutting her off, pulling her into his arms, and capturing her sweet lips with his.

THE FOLLOWING DAY - AFTERNOON...

Xio hugged her great-grandmother, and rested her cheek on her shoulder as they sat together in the batey, watching the sunlit waterfall pour into the pool where she and Raph had bathed yesterday. It seemed she had lived through ten lifetimes since then.

She had been awakened this morning by the sounds from Kaiah's helicopter, kicking up dust and pebbles in the batey.

During breakfast, Xio and Raph had shared what they had learned from the memory guide with Kaiah. They had also told her about their dreams, and she had confirmed that Thaddeus, Rapheus, Jewel, and Eagle could now rest in peace, and that Raph and Xio would never have those nightmares again.

As Xio breathed in her botoá's lilac fragrance, she was taken back to when she used to visit her in Xiobayo as a little girl. When Kaiah was available, they would sit in the courtyard in the morning and watch the sunrise, and then in a gazebo in the evening and watch it set.

It was times like these that Xio wondered if the madding crowd and the rat-race life beyond Ynoa was even worth it.

"Are you happy?" Kaiah asked, stroking her arm.

"I am, Botoá. Happier than I've ever been in my life. I love Raph so much, and he loves me. He's staying in Akilina."

Kaiah laughed. "I am not surprised. He seems like a good man, polite, and very charming. I would expect nothing less from someone who had Andris as a role model. You have been hurt, Xiomara, by men who couldn't appreciate you, but you have another chance at happiness. I know in my heart that Raph is the right man for you."

"He is more than right, Botoá. He's perfect for me."

"I do believe that." Kaiah raised Xio's head from her shoulder. "Now, Rahe, have you decided how you will deal with that treacherous bastard?"

Xio laughed. She loved it when she had Kaiah to herself, when the chief was just her great-grandmother with a very sassy mouth. "I'm going to fight. I'm not marrying his stupid son, and I'm not going to jail. I'm taking him to court. I don't know yet how I can prove he did what he did, but I have to trust that my character will speak for me, and that his will speak for him."

Kaiah smiled as she nodded her head. "Good. I wanted you to come to that decision on your own before I tell you a little story."

Xio squinted. "A story? What kind of story?" Xio wasn't sure how many more revelations she could take.

"A bittersweet one about your father and Sherylyn."

"Oh."

"Do you know why your father divorced her?"

She shook her head. "I just figured it was a bad marriage, and that they decided to call it quits, like many couples do."

"*Humph.* If only it was that simple."

"It wasn't?" She blinked in bafflement.

Kaiah sighed and glanced away as if she was both relieved to finally unburden her heart, and regretful for having to speak of it. Finally, she faced Xio again. "When Fitzroy was five, Malik overheard a phone conversation between Sherylyn and Stamer. They were making plans to meet somewhere."

Xio sat up straight, her hand over her gaping mouth. "She was cheating on Dad? Did he tell you?"

"Yes, and no. But he didn't have to."

"Right. You just knew."

Kaiah's eyes hardened. "There was nothing insightful about what I knew, or did not know. I took one look at that boy in his hospital crib, and knew he was not my blood. I could not sense my ancestors' spirits in him."

Xio's jaw dropped and her eyes widened. "Fitzroy isn't my half brother? Oh my God!" She slapped her hand to her chest, unexpected delight jumping inside her. She couldn't have been happier to know that she wasn't related to that thieving scumbag. "So Sherylyn was having an affair with Stamer all through her marriage with Dad?"

"It started before they were married. When Malik confronted her, she denied it at first, saying it was just business. Malik knew she had no business with him. But he kept asking until she finally broke and told him that she had been seeing Samuel for just as long as she'd been with Malik."

Xio shook her head slowly, her stomach turning. She could strangle that woman. "Mom was right," she murmured. "Samuel has always wanted what Dad had."

"Envy is the worst of sins."

"So when Sherylyn married Dad, did she know Fitzroy might not be his?"

"Well…" Kaiah began, pausing and twisting her lips. "I summoned Sherylyn to the Kú, and questioned her."

Oh God, Xio thought. Sherylyn, who was from the Chiboni tribe, knew that lying to the chief in the Kú was tantamount to lying under oath before Congress in the States. She could go to jail.

"She claimed she didn't know who'd gotten her pregnant," Kaiah continued, "but since Stamer was already married, she told Malik the child was his."

"Unbelievable! Daddy went to his grave, not knowing that Fitzroy wasn't his son." She tightened her jaws as anger boiled in her.

"I told him, Rahe. He refused to believe it. He said he wanted to forgive and forget, and make his marriage work. It's a small island, and he didn't want to get caught up in a scandal. And he did love that boy."

"Yeah, that was before he grew up to be a real—you know what," Xio murmured.

"I believe deep down in his heart, he knew Fitzroy belonged to Stamer, but he needed a son to carry on his name, and Fitzroy was all he had at the time."

"Why didn't they have more children?"

"I do not know, Xiomara." She laughed. "But I'm happy they didn't. I could not stand that woman after what she did to my grandson—causing him to drop his head like a whipped dog every time he saw Stamer. I think that's the reason he finally filed for a divorce. He couldn't live with the fact that Stamer was having an affair with his wife."

"Does Stamer know Fitzroy is his?"

"I do not know that, either. But bringing it to his attention is in your hands now."

Xio frowned. "What do you mean it's in my hands? Stamer and Sherylyn will just deny it. His cheating on his wife isn't enough to bring him down. I don't have any proof."

"Rahe, there is always proof, if you dig deep enough. And I dug deep into that baby's mouth, and swabbed his little cheeks while he lay drooling and kicking and grinning up at me from his crib."

"Botoá." Xio burst out laughing at the image of the dacica swabbing the cheeks of an innocent infant. "How did you get Stamer's DNA to do the paternity test?"

"That was easy. His gum-chewing habit was his downfall. I fished a few wads of gum out of the waste basket after a dinner party at Eagle's Nest."

Xio pressed her hands to her mouth and just shook her head. She was speechless.

"So, you don't have to dig for evidence. I did it all for you."

Kaiah pulled an envelope from inside the book she'd been reading when Xio joined her. She glanced down, rubbing her wrinkled hands across the front of it. "I've been sitting on this for thirty-nine years, just waiting for the right time to use it."

Xio gaped at the plain white envelope. It was all the evidence she needed to bring Stamer down, and to think it was always within her reach. Her father had never asked for help, so Kaiah had never given him the proof he needed. And maybe it was best. Like Kaiah said, deep down in his heart, he must have known, but he'd chosen to deny it.

"Once we leave this mountain," Kaiah added, "you and I will sit down with a bottle of wine, and I will give you some more ammunition to use against him."

Xio kissed her great-grandmother's cheek. "Thank you, Botoá. Thank you so much."

Kaiah patted her on the knee. "Do not open it now. Wait until you get home when you can concentrate on your next move and plan your attack."

Xio laughed. Her botoá was not to be messed with. She placed her hand to her heart. "All of a sudden, there is so much happiness in the world."

Kaiah stroked Xio's cheek. "There's always been happiness in the world, Rahe. Most people just don't know how to tap into it."

* * *

RAPH ARRANGED the white cotton inagua around his hips, then stared at his reflection in the mirror, inspecting the designs that had been painted on his body for the ceremony at sunset. His artist had explained the various elements, and why they were required.

The Greek flag on his back and the flag of Ynoa on his chest represented the two places Andris had called home. An image of the rising sun on his left cheek and the setting sun on his right signified the souls' arrival into one realm and their departure into another. A circle with four squares inside it was painted on his forehead. Each square contained a symbol representing one of the four stages of life—infancy, youth, adulthood, and old age. His arms and legs were covered with figures representing air, fire, earth, and water, along with the frog, the Megiri's symbol of creation.

Raph's thoughts turned to Xio in the adjacent room of the bohio. The four phases of the moon were being painted on her face to serve as Kerena's guide through the afterlife. She would also have a Greek flag on her back, but since Kerena was not born on the island, in place of the flag of Ynoa on her stomach, Xio would bear an Eagle—the most revered bird with the ability to soar between the physical and the spiritual worlds.

In the last few days, Raph had gone through a transformation, a spiritual awakening, an awareness of the connections between everything and everyone around him. He'd come to Akilina, thinking he knew so much about everything, including who he was. And in digging for the truth about his family's history, he had discovered his true self in the six-year-old little boy who had shut himself off from the world, bottled up his emotions, and existed in a prison of guilt, regret, and hurt. He had found healing, along with the love of a woman who took his breath away.

Raph smiled as he thought of his future with Xiomara. He couldn't wait to start their life together, to introduce her to his mother and his brothers.

His smile dulled as he thought of his brothers.

Pappoús had said it was up to him to keep what he had learned to himself, but Raph knew he could not do that. He had to share everything with his brothers. It was their history, too.

They had as much right to it as he did. The cycle of silence would end with his grandfather.

His hope was that they would accept and embrace the truth, just as he had done.

Chapter Thirty-Eight

BÓ-HUPIA-TÍ

THE SMELL of whole lamb and goats roasting in open pits permeated the night air.

Raph held the urn in one arm, while his other arm was wrapped around Xio's shoulders. She looked beautiful in her white cotton inagua and a tagana.

They stood a few feet behind the stone zemis at the front of the batey, waiting for the signal from the *mayohuacán*—the Megiri ceremonial drum—indicating that the moon had emerged from behind the mountain, and was visible in the sky. He'd never met a more patient people, he thought, looking around at the crowd. Even the young knew better than to speak during a soul's transitional ceremony.

Dacica Kaiah and Mitayna Luyaron, in ceremonial headdresses and robes, along with the priest and the memory guide stood in front of the effigies with their backs to the crowd. They would lead the procession through the village toward the place where his grandfather was born and where his and his wife's ashes would be released into the river.

Raph hadn't expected the entire village to come out to say goodbye to a man most of them had never met, or were too young to remember the last time he was here. But Xio had told him that it was simply because he was one of them, and because it was Rocotiéri.

He observed the rows of dancers in traditional costumes of colorful feathered headbands, woven grass and reed skirts of varying colors held around their waists by decorative embroidered belts.

He wished his mother and brothers and Petra were here to see this honorable send-off for their beloved pappoús and yaya. He wished he'd thought to record it, so they could watch it when he got home.

Suddenly, the boom of the mayohuacán echoed across the valley. Raph, along with everyone else, looked to the mountains where a full moon hung low over the top of Mt. Cayacáo, casting its light across the dark gradient sky.

A perfect night, a perfect moon, a perfect setting to scatter his grandparents' ashes.

On the second boom, a rhythm of gourd instruments— guïros, maracas, and rattles, along with ocarinas and bamboo flutes—filled the air with music. On the third boom, the villagers started chanting for the dead, and the dancers came alive, stomping their feet in place, and twirling their decorated bodies in the moonlight, their bangles and anklets jingling to the beat.

His heart pounded and his soul danced to the music as they began the procession, each step taking him back to his childhood and the wonderful times he'd spent with his grandparents in the nursery, on the playground, at the beach, and later on, with his grandfather sailing the Aegean Sea, having coffee while watching the sunrise, and traveling around the world together. He'd wept for them, mourned for them, and now, he celebrated them.

The procession finally came to a stop at the site where Andris had been born, the spot where his childhood home once stood.

Through blurry eyes, Raph watched as the chief, the sub-chief, and the priest formed a semi-circle in front of a mango tree. Beneath its branches rested a funeral ark filled with fruits, vegetables, bows and arrows, clothes, and household items—everything a soul might need for daily living in the afterlife.

Raph admired the moonlight shimmering on the surface of the Bari River behind the ark, and the black and white canoe on the bank with an unlit torch at the bow and one at the stern. He thought of Arsenios and Giulia, playing with Andris along the river banks and attending Rocotiéri during the eighteen months they'd lived here.

"They're waiting for you," Xio whispered.

He wiped his tears away, and then hand-in-hand, they walked up to the ark. With a steady hand, Raph carefully placed the urn inside the glass compartment at its center.

The mayohuacán sounded two times, then the priest raised his arms in the air, a wood carving of a frog in one hand and a carved eagle in the other. He turned his face toward the moon and said in a loud voice, "Andris Sebastian Giannopoulos and Kerena Phoebe Mitrou, son of Ynoa and daughter of Greece. You arrived on earth, mounted on the sunrise and swayed by air, fire, earth, and water. You danced, you loved, you gave, and you received. Tonight, you make your exit, guided by the light of the moon. BÓ-Hupia-tí."

"BÓ-Hupia-tí," the crowd chanted.

The mayohuacán boomed again, and BÓ'Roco Wotani Bithithian set a large tome on the back wing of the ark and then began reciting the names of twenty generations of Giannopouloses, starting from Rapheus, son of Thaddeus, and ending at Andris son of Arsenios. The drum boomed a half-beat after each name was called.

When the BÓ'Roco was finished, the BÓ'Ajari picked up the urn and held it over his head, the gold and silver bands around the porcelain dazzling in the moonlight. "Andris Sebastian Giannopoulos and Kerena Phoebe Mitrou, son of Ynoa and daughter of Greece, may Mother Frog grant you the power to travel between worlds, mounted on Father Eagle. BÓ-Hupia-tí!"

"BÓ-Hupia-tí."

Three men and three women picked up the ark with all its contents. They carried it down to the canoe and placed it carefully inside before pushing it into the river. One stayed to hold the canoe while the others retreated to the banks. A group of children, dressed in white robes, and carrying black and white baskets filled with petals, created a colorful path from the spot where the ark had been resting all the way down to the canoe. They emptied their baskets into the water, then ran back to the banks.

Everyone's love and reverence touched Raph deeply, bringing a new well of tears to his eyes. He wiped them away, blinking rapidly.

The priest presented the urn to him and Xio, who cradled it in their hands like it was a newborn baby, and amidst the continuous rumble of the drum, the melody of the band, the undulating bodies of the dancers, and the chants of the crowd, they walked barefoot on the path of petals toward the canoe and waded waist-deep into the water.

It was chilly, but neither of them flinched.

Raph removed the cover, and with Xio's help, he tipped the urn, sprinkling the remains of his grandparents and her godparents into the river. As the water ferried away the ashes, Raph's throat tightened with the love and happiness he'd shared with them. Finally, they covered the urn and placed it into the canoe. The torches were then lit, and the canoe untied.

"Safe journey, Pappoús and Yaya. I love you." Raph waved at the canoe drifting down the river. He would remember them with joy and happiness, instead of grief and sorrow.

"Goodbye, Pappoús and Yaya! We'll miss you!"

Raph froze. Was he hearing voices above the music and chanting?

"Oh my God, Raph, it's your family."

"Uncle Raph! Uncle Raph!"

Raph turned, and his jaw dropped at the sight of his family emerging from the crowd. Kaiah walked slowly behind them. "Your family is here, too," he said, pulling Xio out of the water with him.

Raph picked up Petra in his arms, and they all moved in for group hugs.

"Uncle Raph, I missed you," she said, toying with his pendant. "Where were you?"

"Right here, Petra. I missed you, too." Raph kissed her on the cheek and put her down.

Piia, their attendant, emerged from behind Kaiah with two white robes draped over her arm. She helped Xio into hers while Raph put on his own, grateful for the barriers from the cold.

When Piia disappeared back into the crowd, he turned to his family. "How did you get here? I wasn't expecting you."

"I got a call two days ago," Neo said, nodding in Kaiah's direction. "She said our grandparents requested the entire family's presence at the scattering of their ashes on some Caribbean island. I thought it was a hoax. When I couldn't get a hold of you, I called Declan. He told me that it wasn't a hoax, and that you were already here."

"Imagine my shock and joy to be able to say goodbye to Andris again." Jordan added. "It was a lovely send-off in such a lovely place with the waterfall, the mountain, the river, just beauty everywhere."

"It was lovely," Claudia said. "Aetós came through for her native son and adopted daughter."

"She sure did." Kaiah glanced off across the river.

"So where have you guys been hiding?" Raph looked from his brothers to his mother. "I mean, you couldn't have hiked all the way up the mountain today."

"Dacica Kaiah flew us up in her chopper this morning," Neo answered for everyone.

"Botoá," Xio drawled, "I can't believe you kept this from us all day."

"We wanted to surprise you," Tele said.

"Well, you did a good job of it. Did you stay at Bo-Caneye?"

"They've been staying with us," Akilah responded to Xio's question.

"And Petra went to school with me, yesterday," MJ said.

"Yeah, it was fun, Uncle Raph." She glanced up at her father. "Can we stay, Daddy? I like it here."

Everyone laughed, then Tele said. "I'll think about it, baby."

"Are you going to introduce us?" Jordan's eyes were trained on Xio.

"Oh, I'm sorry. Um… Mom, Neo, Tele, Petra, this is Xiomara. Xio, my family."

Raph watched as his mother hugged her tightly, and his brothers shook her hand, telling her how lovely it was to meet her. He loved that they immediately took to Xio, and she to them. It would make telling them about his decision to live in Akilina easier.

Jordan smiled at Xio. "Xiomara, Dacica Kaiah told me you helped Raph find his way to Aetós to send off Andris and Kerena. Thank you for doing this."

"It was an honor. They were my godparents, and the few memories I have of them are pleasant ones."

"So we've been told," Neo said. "Thank you for helping my big brother," he added, tossing Raph a suspicious look, as if he knew something was going on between him and Xio.

"You'll have lots of time to catch up," Kaiah interjected. "Let's gather around in silent honor of Andris and Kerena as they continue their journey to the other side."

And so, the group of ten stood arm in arm on the banks of the Bari River and waved goodbye to Andris and Kerena under the guiding light of the full moon. Even after the music ceased, and the canoe had disappeared from sight, they remained silent for a few extra moments in the calm and peace of the night, honoring the souls they'd been fortunate to know, and would forever love and cherish.

Raph's heart was filled with joy as he watched the tear-stained faces of every member of the Giannopoulos and Davenport families, and Dacica Kaiah. This was his family now.

Xio's arm tightened around his waist, and she brushed her leg subtly against his, as if she knew his thoughts. He smiled down at her, warmth and love illuminated by the moonlight in her eyes. He wanted to shout his love for her from the mountaintop.

But this was not the time or place. Soon they would all know that he had been seduced by the passion of the most beautiful woman in the world. He squeezed her close to his side, and when she laid her cheek against his chest, he kissed the top of her head, and smiled.

Thank you, Pappoús.

Epilogue

SUCKER PUNCH

Two weeks later...

Bypassing her personal parking space at the front entrance of Jewel Beach Resort, Xio drove around to the side of the main building, and pulled her Lexus into the employee lot.

She shut off the engine and stared at the envelope on the passenger seat. For two week, she'd been sitting on the bombshell her botoá had given her, strategizing how to play her hand to maximize the impact of her delivery. Plus, she enjoyed watching Stamer squirm as he waited for her response. She would have stretched it out until the very last day when her clock ran out, but fate forced her hand this morning.

She had awakened to over a dozen frantic voice and text messages from Fitzroy, begging her to call him back ASAP. His pleas were followed by a detailed voice message from his mother, Sherylyn, urging Xio to wire money to Fitzroy, so he could pay off some gambling debts he'd racked up at a race track near Dallas, Texas. According to Sherylyn, Fitzroy had told his bookie that he owned shares in Jewel Beach Resort, and that he would pay him as soon as the money was deposited into his account.

Sherylyn was afraid of what they might do to her son if Xio didn't help him.

Like it was her problem.

"The nerve of those two!" she yelled, recalling the stress her mother had been under when Fitzroy had taken her to court over Eagle's Nest, seven years ago. Xio had gone to Sherylyn and begged her to talk to her son, to get him to back down so their little sister and brother wouldn't be forced out of their home.

"He's your father's son, and he has just as much right to that estate as you and your sister and brother," Sherylyn had told her.

"But they are children," Xio had pleaded. "We could lose everything."

"That's not my problem," Sherylyn had snorted, before slamming her door in Xio's face—the door to the million-dollar beachfront villa Malik had coughed up in their divorce settlement.

And now, Sherylyn had the audacity to ask Xio for help, conveniently forgetting that her son had forced Xio to sell her birthright—the land her father had gifted to her—proceeds from which both Sherylyn and Fitzroy had benefitted.

It was time to take out the trash and rid herself of this odious waste once and for all.

She pulled the visor of her cap down over her forehead, straightened her sunglasses, picked up the envelope, and exited her car. Instead of using the employee entrance where she might run into her staff, she hurried along a path to the back of the building, her sneakers barely making impact on the steppingpingstones.

She ascended a flight of stairs to a small balcony connected to her office, and unlocked the door. Once inside, she removed her sunglasses, unmanned the alarm, then instructed the front desk to send Stamer up as soon as he arrived. She fished her phone from the pocket of her white shorts and called her cousin,

Dylan, JBR's head of security, to let him know she was in her office.

Dylan had agreed to stand outside the door in case Stamer tried to pull anything. Although she'd never heard of Stamer getting physically violent with anyone, she was taking no chances. You never knew how a cornered fox will react, or how much pressure any one person could take before they snapped.

Xio was initially going to meet Stamer at his bank, but at the last minute, she'd decided to bring the game home. She felt more comfortable on her own turf, surrounded by the portraits and the spirits of her ancestors. Plus, once she was done with Stamer, she could immediately call Raph before he went into lockdown for a four-hour meeting.

God, she missed him so much, it hurt. She sat down in her desk chair as visions of them in that cave rushed to the surface of her mind. They had made love several times in several places since then—under waterfalls, in pools, in cabanas on the beach in the middle of the night when guests were asleep, in the hammock in her backyard when her family was out, and under the stars with a crackling fire to keep them warm.

But when Xio thought of that night in the cave, her body burned with the hottest, fiercest fire. Raph had taken her to such pleasurable heights and in so many positions. She was still trying to fathom how her body had succumbed to his demands. What a sex god the man was. And he was *her* sex god for the rest of their lives.

She glanced over at the sofa where they had made love two days ago, minutes before she'd driven him to the airport for his flight back to San Francisco. She moaned softly, remembering how he'd taken her from behind while she leaned over the back of the sofa with her skirt hiked up to her waist and her panties around her ankles. Xio had learned that day in her office, that passion escalated exponentially when she was forced to stifle her cries of pleasure. *God, that was wild and erotic.*

She couldn't wait for Raph's return next week, so they could begin planning their future together.

The sharp knock on her office door ended her daydreaming. She clutched the edge of the desk and took a deep breath.

By the time the second impatient knock sounded, she was back in control. She picked up the envelope, rose from the chair, and walked across the floor, her mind going back to a few weeks ago when she'd been reluctant and afraid to meet with Stamer.

She was anything but reluctant or afraid today. It would be nice to say that this would be the last time she'd ever see his face, but that was an impossibility on their small island. She would see him, but he would be the one dropping his head like a whipped dog every time their paths crossed.

She placed the envelope on the conference table and opened the door. "Come in," she said.

When Stamer stepped inside, she closed the door and, hurrying ahead, positioned herself between the conference table and the giant whiteboard she'd used during a late meeting with her department heads, last night.

Instead of addressing her deliberate attempt to block him from advancing further into her space, Stamer thought it more appropriate to, as he liked to put it, advise the youth in professional ethics. "Xiomara, what are you wearing? This is a place of business. You have better training than this. Malik—"

Xio pinned him with a repulsive stare. "Don't you *dare* talk about my father. Don't let me hear you utter his name ever again." She was in no mood for his mind games or his useless opinions. There was no need to play nice with him.

He gave her a bemused stare, his mouth hanging wide.

"And another thing," she added, "*you* don't qualify to give me advice about anything. Keep your counsel for your own litter. God knows they need it." Xio was surprised at the placidity in her own voice, but then again, she had already released her anger, so nothing he said or did would have any effect on her.

He pushed air noisily through his mouth. "I don't know what your problem is, Xiomara, and I don't have the time to squabble with you today, so let's get to the point. There are only two reasons you would call this meeting. You're either signing over Jewel Beach to me, or you've decided to marry my son to keep yourself out of jail." He toyed with his mustache, a vile grin etched on his face. "I don't think you want to give up total control of your business, so I'll say it's the latter."

Xio placed her hands on her hips and fixed him with a stern stare, reminiscent of a principal confronting an insolent student. "Are you absolutely certain that those are the only two reasons I would summon you to my office, Samuel? You can't think of any others?"

He stiffened, clearly taken aback at her stance. "You seem very arrogant and self-assured, all of a sudden. Am I missing something?" he asked, his voice rife with indignation.

You're missing a lot of things. Xio allowed her gaze to wash slowly over him, from his neatly cut hair to his starched white shirt, navy blue tie, his tailored gray suit, and polished black leather shoes. That was Samuel Stamer, prim and proper on the outside, but stinking rotten on the inside.

"I'm through playing your little game, Xiomara," he said, with rising ire in his voice. "You either tell me why I'm here, or I'm leaving. And the next knock on your door will be the authorities coming to arrest you."

"Hahaha." Xio sighed, then said, "You can drop the superior act and your stupid threats. I'm not afraid of you. You can't hurt me, anymore." She crossed her arms, delighting in her power to strip him of his. "But your wife sure can hurt you."

"My wife? What does Angelica have to do with anything?"

He'd obviously forgotten, so Xio was happy to jog his memory with the bit of history her botoá had given her after they left Aetós. Kaiah had told Xio to pull out all the stops and blast him into the ethers. "Your grandparents came to Akilina from Montserrat, and like many other families who migrated here, yours worked hard to make something of themselves and contribute to the community. Our families had always been—"

"Is this going somewhere?" he asked, brandishing his hands. "You haven't told me anything I don't already know."

Xio held up her hand. "Don't be rude. This is still my office, and you have better training than that," she said, throwing his jab right back at him. "Like I was saying, our families had always been friends until your jealousy and your greed drove a wedge between us. And now, the chicken that was born from your envy has finally come home to roost."

"What chicken? What are you talking about, Xiomara? You sound like a crazy woman."

Xio took a deep breath, then calmly and slowly stated, "Your chicken's name is Fitzroy. He is your son."

He coughed and clawed at his neck, the blood and confidence draining from his face as he shrunk an inch or two before her eyes.

"Yeah, I thought that would knock the wind out of your sails," Xio said, reveling in the same smug satisfaction he had portrayed when he thought he had her cornered.

"Fitzroy is your son," she repeated, thrusting her dagger deeper as he speechlessly grappled with the knowledge that his secret was no longer a secret. "Judging from your reaction, I'd guess that you knew he was a Stamer all this time, yet you let my father raise him as a Davenport."

Finally, his head jerked up, his face a glowing mask of rage, and his eyes bulging from their sockets. He lunged at her with his fist raised as if he was going to strike her. "You lying, crazy, little bitch. If I—" Stamer stopped suddenly as if he'd slammed into a brick wall. He staggered backward, his eyes wild with confusion and fear.

At that precise moment, Xio felt her ancestors' spirits building a wall around her, shielding her from this pile of raw fish guts that had been lying on the pavement for three days with flies buzzing around it. Their presence, and Dylan standing outside the door, ready to barge in and take him down if she sounded the alarm, emboldened her even more. Besides, she would have easily taken him down. After all, she took kickboxing lessons, and she was trained in mdambé.

She stared into his cold dead eyes. "You are nothing, Samuel Stamer. You are small and insignificant. You're a coward and a bully who married into wealth and status that you don't deserve. Earlier, you asked what your wife had to do with anything? Well, this is it. Akilina Bank and Trust does not belong to you, even though you act as if it does. It was founded by Timothy Salamon, your wife's great-great-grandfather," she said, refreshing his memory with the other tidbit Kaiah had given her.

"If Angelica ever finds out that you not only cheated on her, but that you also had a child with another woman, she would divorce you and have the board explore some new options where you are concerned. You will lose everything, and your crooked tired old ass will be tossed out on the hot sand."

His cheeks swelled up like a puffer fish. "If you ever breathe a word of this nonsense to anyone, I swear, I will—"

"You will what, Samuel? What are you going to do?" She picked up the envelope and approached him. "You have always wanted what my father had. Well, here!" She slapped the envelope against his chest, and immediately took a step back from him. "You can have the boy he raised."

Xio watched as he quietly and methodically folded the envelope and shoved it into the pockets of his pants, without even opening it to verify her claim. The bastard already knew the truth, she thought, shaking her head in disbelief. She wondered how many other children he'd fathered behind his wife's back.

"Anyway," she said, "let's move to the next related topic on the agenda. Since it was Fitzroy's despicable character and mismanagement of my family's business that caused me to fall victim to your sick schemes, I'll say we're even. However—"

"Even? You call that even? You owe Akilina Bank and Trust eight million dollars, Ms. Davenport. You can't—"

"Shush!" She raised her hands. "*You* don't tell me what *I* can or can't do. *I* make the rules now."

When he shut his mouth, she dropped her hands. "Now, as I was saying, I was tempted to tell you to eat your eight million dollars for dinner, but I'm a professional. I pay my debts, so I will continue to pay back that favorable loan you and Trevor so kindly bestowed upon me."

"Of course. I wasn't suggesting that you would default on your loan."

Not so fast. Xio smiled. "However, there will be some slight changes in the conditions."

His forehead wrinkled. "What kind of changes?"

Xio's smile widened at the caution and civility in his tone. "I'm so happy you asked, Mr. Stamer." She clasped her hands in front of her chest. "As you are aware, the old contract stipulates that as JBR's profits increase, so will my monthly installments, up to a certain rate. That is no longer the case," she said, shaking her head. "My monthly installments will remain as they currently are, and my interest rate will decrease one and half percent for the duration of the loan."

"But it's already so low, Ms. Davenport. That would mean…" His eyes darted left and right as he ran the numbers through his brilliant mind. "It would take…" He pressed his hand into his chest, and sweat beaded his forehead. He was clearly panicking at the facts that it will take almost twice as long to get back his eight million dollars, and that his bank will lose a gargantuan amount of money at this ridiculously low interest rate. He slumped against the table, swallowing convulsively. "My bank will… I will…"

"Lose?" Xio spoke the word he couldn't bring himself to

utter in reference to himself. "I know. But look on the bright side," she said, cheerily. "It's still a win-win, right? Isn't that what you told me a few weeks ago when you were here in my office setting out the rules that would insure I lose my family's company?" She suppressed the laughter bubbling in her chest. "Furthermore, I expect to have the new contract with those two changes—and those two changes only—on my desk, by two o'clock on Monday afternoon. No need to prolong this process."

He stood upright and adjusted his tie and jacket. "My board will never approve this loan."

"You're a go-getter, Mr. Stamer!" She punched the air with her fist, cheering him on. "You make people do exactly what you want them to. Right? I believe in you."

Xio could smell the fear and humiliation oozing out of him. Never before had he been bent over a table, exposed and vulnerable, and especially not while a powerful woman with a bullwhip stood behind him. He did the summoning, the threatening, the harassing, the beating-down of the underdog. Well, he could choke on a dose of his own medicine. Now, he knew how others felt when he threatened to destroy their lives, or did so without warning.

He licked away a layer of white foam from a corner of his mouth. "What are you going to do with the information about your bro... About Fitzroy?"

Wouldn't you love to know. She trembled on a deep breath as she turned and gazed at her father's portrait on the wall. That boy who wasn't even his son had caused him so much grief, pain, and shame. She brought her gaze back to Stamer. He didn't deserve an answer, and being near him made her skin crawl. She felt soiled. And although it gave her great satisfaction to watch him stew, it was time to end it. But there was one last thing she needed to say to him. "By the way—"

"Please, Xiomara. What are you going to do with the information?" he asked again.

Well, since he said please, this time. Xio shrugged. "Whatever, I like, Samuel. I might put it on the evening news tonight. I might wait until next week, or next father's day so you and Fitzroy can celebrate. Or maybe the next time he or Trevor gets in my face. So you'd better keep them on short, tight leashes."

He pressed his lips together, nodded, and dropped his gaze to the floor.

Xio studied him, standing in front of her, deflated and sucker-punched in the gut, like she had been when he was threatening to destroy her and her family's lives if she didn't bend to his will. She could tell him that she would keep silent—though only for her father's sake. She would not make her dad look like a fool for not figuring out or accepting the truth, that Fitzroy wasn't his. But she would not give Stamer that satisfaction.

From this day forward, he will exist in a perpetual bubble of fear and paranoia, wondering when his world will come toppling down around him. This card, Xio would keep to ensure he never came at her or her family, ever again.

"By the way," she said, picking up from where he'd interrupted her, "your son is in quite a bit of trouble. You should speak with his mother."

His head jerked up. "What kind of trouble?"

She shrugged nonchalantly. "Not my problem, but I suggest you make it yours, quickly. If anyone asks me why I won't help my brother, I would have to tell them the truth. I won't lie for you and Sherylyn. My father spent his entire life cleaning up Fitzroy's messes. It's your turn now. The Davenports are done with you and your worthless sons, all three of them. Which reminds me, whatever scheme you were cooking up for Akilah with Jamon, it ain't happening. And, please, do me the favor and tell Sherylyn to stay out of Davenport business, or else..." Xio walked to the door, and opened it. "You've been served your just desserts, Samuel Stamer. Enjoy." She dusted off her hands.

Without uttering a sound, Stamer walked out of her office,

and out of her life, his tail tucked between his legs like a whipped dog.

Xio closed the door, and collapsed onto the edge of the table. She dropped her face into her hands and sighed long and hard. For the first time in three years, maybe seven, Xio felt free, and with that freedom came a sense of empowerment. She had stood up to Stamer, the biggest bully on the island. She could take on anybody and anything now.

She got up and walked over to her father's portrait. He had placed a lot of trust in her, and that made Xio's heart swell with satisfaction that she had brought him justice. As tears stung her eyes, she placed two fingers against her lips, and then pressed them to her father's forehead.

"Everything went okay?"

She pulled herself together before turning around to see Dylan standing just inside the door, his muscles bulging under his shirt. He reminded her of The Rock—big white smile, bald head, and all. "Things are better than okay," she replied, walking over to him.

Dylan only knew that she had discovered something about Stamer that would make him back down, but he didn't know what. The fewer people who knew, the better chance Xio had of keeping Stamer in check. "I chopped him off at the knees," she said, perching on the edge of the conference table.

"I'll say. He hobbled down the steps like he was walking on stilts. You sure he can't come back to hurt you?"

"No, he's done messing with me, with anyone with the last name Davenport."

"And you're not going to tell me what he did to you, or what dirt you got on him?"

She pursed her lips and shook her head slowly. "I can't."

"Okay." He nodded. "So, tell me about Raph. When are you two tying the knot?" He pinched her arm. "I'll have to dust off my best suit. It's been a while since we had a wedding in this family."

Now, that was something Xio was happy to talk about. Grinning, she pulled Dylan down on the table beside her, and hooked her arm in his. "As a matter of fact, I was thinking about asking you to walk me down the aisle. Of all my…" She paused at the knock on the door.

"Are you expecting someone else?" Dylan asked.

"No."

He shot to his feet, and halted her attempt to get up. "Let me check, in case it's Stamer returning with a new bag of tricks. I'd love to punch that idiot in the face, just once," he said, fisting his right hand.

Xio grinned as he marched to the door. She heard a woman greet him, then instructed him to sign something.

"What is it?" she asked, as he came back with a large white envelope in his hand.

"It's from Kalneh and Hamat Law Associates in Allarda," he said, handing it over. "You think Stamer set his lawyers on you to try to shake you down."

"I definitely know it's not from Stamer's lawyers. He is vain and cruel, not stupid." Curious to know who had sent it, she took the envelope over to her desk, picked up her letter opener, sliced through the seal, and retrieved the contents. "Oh my God!" she exclaimed, at the letter clipped to the top of a stack of papers.

"What is it?" Dylan peeped over her shoulder.

"It's from Andris… Raph's grandfather—my godfather."

"Damn, news from the grave? What does it say?"

Xio walked around her desk and sat in her chair. She wanted to read it first before sharing it with her favorite cousin.

MARCH 15, 2018

Dearest Xiomara,

I don't know when this letter will reach you, or if you will have met my grandson, Raph, by the time it does. You may not have any memories of the old man who loved you when you were a child, but I, your godfather, have never stopped loving you.

I purchased the plot of land your brother sold, and the plot you sold, too. I know Jewel Beach has seen better days, and I can only assume that you were forced to sell land in order to support the resort. However, I am aware of the significance of these properties to your family. They once belonged to your father, and to Eagle, and they should stay in your family. I could not sit by and allow someone else to purchase them.

All one hundred acres now belong to you. Along with those parcels of land, I am also gifting you five acres of beachfront property in the territory of Obijax, and five in northern Akilina. Kerena (your godmother) and I had hoped to build homes on them one day, but fate saw otherwise. You should find the deeds enclosed in this envelope from my lawyer.

Xiomara, I hope this brings you a measure of peace and comfort to know that this part of your father's legacy remains intact. It's the least I could do after turning my back on your family.

With love,

Andris Aetós-Giannopoulos

P.S. If you are unsure about the claims I have made in this letter, please share it with your mother, with my love and deepest apologies for letting her down. And if Rapheus has not yet made it to The Davenport, reach out to him at his company, G3, in San Francisco. Tell him that his pappoús is still waiting to return to his Ra.

TEARS ROLLED down Xio's cheeks onto the pages. She quickly wiped them away so the ink wouldn't smudge. She would treasure this letter forever.

"Is it bad news?" Dylan asked, from the other side of her desk.

Too emotional to speak, she unclipped the letter from the rest of the stack, and handed it to him. While he read it, she flipped through the deeds, her heart overflowing with gratitude.

She couldn't wait to tell Raph that they had the perfect plot of land on Mt. Aymaco to build their dream home—the very land her father had gifted her upon her birth.

The first part of their journey together had begun with Andris' death. The second part would begin with his gifts, his love, and his blessing.

The End

A Note from the Author

I have always wanted to write a romance series set in the Caribbean, primarily because I was born on a small island in the Leeward Islands, and I wanted to share my culture with my readers. But after seeing Marvel's Black Panther, I had a "What If?" moment.

I thought, What If, like the fictitious African country of Wakanda, whose culture and lifestyle had never been touched nor influenced by Westerners, there was an island in the Caribbean that was never colonized by Europeans? What if the Taino, the Kalinago, the Arawak, and other indigenous peoples to these islands were left to practice their way of life without outside influences and ideology?

And so the South Caribbean island of Akilina, along with the indigenous Megiri (based on the Arawak, Kalinago, and Tainos) and the Guaitiari (a culture born from the blending of several African tribes) were born.

In order to create Akilina and the Megiri and Guaitiari cultures in a way that honored the ancestors, I had to do a lot of research. Research on the raids conducted by the indigenous nations on the colonists, life in 17th Century Africa and the tribal wars between emerging kingdoms, life in the colonies for both the enslaved, those who enslaved them, and the abolitionists and sympathizers who helped men and women escape to freedom, the language of the Taino and Arawak peoples, and much more. I especially studied the history and survival of the Kalinago of Dominica.

I have only grazed the surface, but I hope that what I incorporated in these pages gives you a glimpse of what life could have been like if Akilina existed.

Not only does Seduced by Passion relate Raph and Xio's steamy and emotional journey to happily ever after, but it also sets the stage for the second and third books in the series that follow Raph's brothers, Neo and Tele, as they find and fight for love in Akilina.

Writing Raph and Xio's story was an emotional roller-coaster ride. I laughed and cried with them as their story unfolded and the island of Akilina developed a life of its own.

I hope you enjoyed reading Seduced by Passion as much as I enjoyed writing it and getting to know all the dynamic, funny, and charismatic characters on this pristine island. As always, your reviews, ratings, and comments are appreciated. I would love to hear from you.

Love,
    Ana

P.S. Turn the page to read the first chapter of **Consumed by Desire - Book 2** in the series, and continue the Giannopoulos family saga with Raph's brother, Neo, and his love interest, Cali, as they begin their journey to happily-ever-after on the magical island of Akilina…

Consumed by Desire

CHAPTER ONE

JUNE, Akilina...

Neo's gaze drifted toward the head of the table where his brother, Raph, and his lovely fiancée, Xiomara Davenport, were seated. Seemingly oblivious to the guests gathered for their rehearsal dinner, they exchanged smiles and glances with each other, their bliss radiating throughout the room where warm light spilled from crystal chandeliers.

Taking a sip of his wine, Neo surveyed the reception hall as servers cleared the tables in preparation for dessert. Centerpiece vases overflowed with palm leaves, orchids, and hibiscus, and a few young children played hide-and-go-seek behind the soft pink and cream silk drapes. The hall, filled with the honored couple's closest family and friends, was alive with conversation and laughter, the clinking of silverware against precious porcelain, and traditional Megiri music playing softly in the background.

It had been a beautiful evening, one that should have had him riding on cloud nine along with his family. Instead, Neo was poignantly reminded of all that was missing in his own life. The emptiness was amplified by his cousin Nikolas, seated to his right, who'd been flirting shamelessly with his date throughout dinner.

To his left, Xiomara's aunt and uncle, who would soon be celebrating their fifty-fifth wedding anniversary, seemed just as lost in each other's presence as the young bride and groom-to-be.

Feeling a tap on his shoulder, Neo looked up into a pair of green eyes that mirrored his own. His brother, Tele, the youngest of the Giannopoulos triplets towered over him. "What are you doing?" he asked, noticing the chair Tele had brought with him.

Ignoring his question, Tele turned to Nikolas. "Hey, Niko, you mind if I pull in here for a sec?"

"Sure, cousin," he said, as he and his date scooted their chairs over the tiled floor to make room.

As Tele slid into the vacant spot, Neo set his glass of Tanama Halhira on the hand-printed tablecloth. The local wine, named for the small white butterflies that pollinated the flowering grapevine, had been a hit that night, and Neo had already asked Xiomara to secure a crate for him to take home to New York.

"What a feast, huh?" Tele asked. "I feel like a stuffed goose."

Neo's taste buds still savored the succulent roasted duck, pounded yams, and garden salad—all bathed in red-currant sauce. "I know what you mean." He wondered if he'd have room for the black cake, fresh fruit, and Champagne that were now being served.

"You ready to roast him?" Tele nudged his head subtly toward Raph.

Neo had been working on his best man speech all week. "When have you known me not to be ready? What about you?"

"I'm ready enough. But you know me, I'm quick on my feet." Proving his point, Tele turned to the waiter who had stopped behind them, seemingly thrown off his game by the sudden seating change that Tele had orchestrated. "Hey, thanks, I'll take that." He took one of the dessert plates from the tray and, helping himself to Neo's dessert fork, carved out a large bite. "Oh, my god, this is so good," he mumbled with a mouthful of the spiced fruit cake.

Neo eyed his brother as he chewed slowly, swallowed, then took a second, even larger bite. He shook his head, praying he never looked quite as gluttonous as his younger brother did wolfing down his cake.

Five minutes younger than Raph, and two minutes older than Tele, Neo was the middle of the Giannopoulos triplets. While not identical, they were close enough in appearance for people to mistake one for the other: tall, muscular, olive skin, dark hair, square chins, and classic Grecian noses. Those who failed to look closely missed the subtle features that set them apart.

Neo smiled as he recalled the countless failed attempts he and his brothers had made at tricking their mother when they were kids. When they were eight years old, she had finally sat them down and explained that since the moment they were placed in her arms, she could always tell them apart by Raph's fuller, rosier lips, Neo's slightly lower nose, and Tele's dimpled smile. They had all inherited their maternal grandfather's green eyes, but Raph's were a deeper shade than Neo's—though both were speckled with amber—and in a certain light, Tele's appeared more blue than green.

Their personalities, Neo thought, couldn't be more different. Of the three brothers, Raph was the cautious and protective guardian, navigating life with a measured seriousness and an unwavering sense of responsibility and stability. He was a steady anchor, ensuring the safety and well-being of those he loved. Tele was mischievous and playful, and operated with an air of mystery, cloaking his intentions, while strategically assessing both short and long-term consequences.

Meanwhile, Neo, although often accused of being impatient, flowed with the tides, opting to embrace life's meandering path, rather than resist its inevitable changes. He was a peacemaker who preferred to diffuse tension with humor and charm rather than anger.

"I still can't believe Raph is getting married tomorrow," Tele said.

"Tell me about it." Their stoic brother, who had always sworn off committed relationships, had inadvertently stumbled into the kind of love and happiness Neo longed for. Hoping his turn would come sooner rather than later, and determined to embrace his brother's happiness as though it were his own, Neo swiped his stolen utensil out of Tele's hand and forked his dessert. He groaned as the rich cake melted in his mouth. "Jesus, this *is* good," he mumbled.

"Right? Told you."

"Hello. Can I have everyone's attention, please."

A hush fell over the room as Dylan, Xio's cousin and Master of Ceremonies, took the floor.

"I want to thank you all for coming out to celebrate the upcoming nuptials of my dear cousin, Xiomara, and her chosen life partner, Raph." He tapped his stomach. "I don't know about you, but I'm absolutely stuffed with one of the best meals I've ever had."

"They'll have to roll me out of here," someone shouted from the back, making everyone laugh.

Dylan continued. "We heard speeches from the bride's family during cocktails, and now it's time to hear from the groom's. The first to take the floor will be Neo, Raph's brother and best man, followed by their other brother, Tele. Finally, we'll hear from Jordan, mother of the groom—without whom we wouldn't be here tonight. So now, without further ado…" Dylan walked over and handed off the microphone to Neo.

Neo knew all eyes were on him, but he kept his gaze fixed on Raph and Xio—their glowing smiles giving him encouragement. "Good evening," he said, standing to his feet.

"Good evening," the guests called back in near-perfect unison.

He cleared his throat. "I'm going to confess that Tele tried to get me to make this speech more of a roast than a toast. And although I considered it, I know that this once-in-a-lifetime love between Raph and Xiomara deserves better. So, friends, family, though I have a keen memory of my brother's bachelor days, you'll be spared the details this evening."

"Your brother thanks you," Raph called out.

Neo relished the look of relief on their mother's face. "Raph. I never thought we'd see the day you would be so eager to take the plunge into married life."

"I didn't know it either, until Xio." Raph placed an arm around Xiomara and kissed her cheek.

"And Xiomara, on behalf of the Giannopoulos family, thank you for saying yes to my brother."

"Of course, I said yes. Just look at him!" Xiomara cupped Raph's cheek, turned his head, and kissed him so passionately on his mouth that even Neo blushed.

Neo loosened his tie, and when the whoops and hollers subsided, he continued. "So, tomorrow's the big day, and I can't help but feel a mix of emotions. There's happiness, a touch of nostalgia, and maybe even a bit of envy, because between the two of us, you were the least likely to tie the knot." He took a deep breath and steadied his voice. "You, Tele, and I have been through a lot. After we lost Dad, we depended on each other. We took turns comforting each other, and as we got older, we leaned on each other for guidance on how to navigate the world without him in it. The love that grew out of our loss made us stronger… brought us even closer together. We formed a bond that was unbreakable, and that bond has been our rock ever since."

Neo paused and blinked back stinging tears as his mother and Raph openly dabbed their eyes with their napkins, and Tele sniffled next to him.

"Raph, you've always been the leader, even when we were kids. We looked up to you then, and hell, we still do. Seven minutes older, or not, you took the lead, protected Tele and me at school and on the playground, and taught us how to stand up for ourselves. Because of you, the bullies thought twice before messing with us, and since we looked so much alike, nobody dared pick on any of us, just in case they were messing with you.

"As we got older, people continued to mistake us for each other, which led to some very interesting encounters, particularly with the ladies. As a matter of fact, I remember one such encounter in Boston when…"

Neo grinned as chairs creaked around the room—their occupants leaning in closer for the juicy details. Raph, however, stiffened in his seat, sending Neo a dagger stare.

"Just kidding, Raph," he teased. "Your secrets are safe with me."

"As yours are with me, little brother," Raph retorted, his tone laced with both humor and caution.

"Anyway," Neo continued amidst the disappointed groans from guests who'd hoped to hear more, "tomorrow, you're starting a new chapter and a new family with Xiomara, and just as you've been our champion…" He smiled reassuringly at their mother and placed his hand on Tele's shoulder as he heaved a heartfelt sigh. "I know that you will love and protect her and the life you build together, because that's just the kind of man you are."

Neo pulled a piece of paper from his left jacket pocket and unfolded it. "As only those closest to me know, I've been writing poems since middle school. It's very rare that I share them, but tonight, to celebrate new love, I'd like to read one I wrote for you, Raph and Xiomara." He swallowed the lump of nerves in his throat and began.

In the realm where stars softly gleam,
A tale of love, a heartfelt dream.
As two souls embark on wedded bliss,
Let these words convey the depth of this.

To my brother, steadfast and true,
In love's embrace, both old and new.
As you stand together side by side,
A journey begins, a joyous tide.

In laughter shared and tears embraced,
In every challenge, together faced,
May your days be filled with loving light,
And brilliant passion consume your nights.

And as you dance through time, hand in hand,
Let the rhythm of your hearts be your accompanying band.
In this chapter, as husband, wife, and friend,
I pray your love story never ends.

So, here's to love, to laughter, and more,
To the journey that lies beyond life's open doors.
To Raph and Xio, forever entwined,
A union blessed, two souls combined.

Neo picked up his glass of Champagne and, raising it, smiled at his brother and his lovely fiancé. "To Raph and Xio."

It had been ghostly quiet while he'd read his poem, and it had taken every ounce of his strength to hold himself together, but relief washed over Neo as the room erupted into applause, and the guests echoed his sentiments with "To Raph and Xio!" Many stood, toasting the happy couple. And as he returned his poem to his pocket, Neo, forever plagued by a hopeless romanticism that had directed his steps ever since he was a child, hoped that his own, once-in-a-lifetime love story was still waiting to be written, and that when the right woman came into his life, it would be every bit as beautiful as the love he and his family celebrated tonight.

"Dynamite, bro," Tele praised, when Neo sat down. "How am I supposed to top that?"

Mischief tickled the corner of Neo's mouth. "You can't."

LATER THAT NIGHT, Neo leaned on a high-top table in the corner of the room, impatiently counting the minutes until he could abandon the party for the solitude of his guest house at the Davenport's estate.

As people posed for photos with the happy couple, Colibri, the globally renowned Megiri band, played the rhythmic beats of *Guariyambe*, the popular Ynoan music, blending the sounds of traditional instruments, such as ja'baos, maracas, ocarinas, and drums, with the more contemporary keyboard, and electric bass.

"Hey, Neo!"

Neo turned as Akilah, Xio's sixteen-year-old sister and maid of honor, came up behind him.

"Hey, Akilah. Don't you look lovely tonight," he said, admiring her fully embroidered jumpsuit—one of her mother's masterpieces, he was certain.

"Why thank you, good sir." She gracefully spun around on her tiptoes. "You don't look so bad yourself. I wanted to ask if you're good for the *Areito*, or if you wanna practice one last time."

"I think I've got it down." The Areito was a traditional cere-monial dance, typically accompanied by historical songs. As they were celebrating an upcoming marriage, a professional story-singer would render a love ballad that weaved together Xio and Raph's family histories, while Neo and Akilah performed the dance.

"You sure?" Akilah asked, with a skeptical twist of her lips. "Because we can sneak into the back."

"I'm sure. They'll be talking about us for weeks to come."

"Okay, but I'm warning you right now, if you make me look

bad in front of all these people, I'll make you work to earn my forgiveness."

"Knowing you, I'd be in debt for the rest of my life."

"Just as long as you know what's at stake."

Her mother called her impatiently from across the room.

"I'm coming, Mommy!" she yelled over the music. "Ugh. I gotta go meet some more off-island relatives whose names I'll probably forget by the end of the night. See you on stage?"

"See you there, Akilah."

As Akilah hurried off to fulfill her duties, Neo looked toward the door when it opened. Even though at this point, he knew she wouldn't be walking through it, disappointment and irritation washed over him.

"Everyone is still talking about your poem."

He turned at hearing Tele's voice behind him. "Thanks, man."

"But I think that scare you gave Raph was my favorite part," Tele added.

"Yeah, I had him there for a second, didn't I?"

"Boston was a riot, man. I wonder if he will ever tell Xio." Tele's grin widened.

"I wouldn't, if I were him. There are just some things from your past that should be forgotten."

"Yeah right, as if any of us could forget that."

The corners of Neo's mouth lifted in a languid smile as he recalled the incident that took place a few years ago when they were all in Boston on business.

Neo had been sitting in the restaurant of Hotel Andreas, scanning the morning paper, when a woman came up behind him, placed her hands on his shoulders, and whispered in his ear, "Last night was amazing. I think— No, I *know* that was the best fuck of my life. You're a god in bed."

Neo had merely lifted an eyebrow. Tele had brought Petra, his three-year-old daughter, on the trip and wouldn't have been entertaining women in his suite, so Neo knew he'd been mistaken for Raph. He'd turned around, hoping in vain that the woman would realize her mistake once she got a good look at him.

"I'm in town for one more day. Maybe we could see each other again tonight," she'd said, her brown eyes bright with foolish hope.

"Sure, why not?" he'd replied, with a wicked grin. "Same time, same place?"

"Yes! I'll meet you at— Oh my god," she'd whispered breathlessly. "There are two of… *Three* of you!" Her mouth had hung open as she stared wide-eyed over his head.

Neo had turned to find his brothers walking their way, his grin deepening at the mortified look on Raph's face at seeing his one-night stand at their breakfast table.

Raph had merely glanced at the woman as he sat down, the blank look on his face indicating that he had probably forgotten her name—as was typical with Raph.

"Uh…which one of you did I sleep with last night?" the woman had asked, her eyes and a pointed finger darting between them.

"All three of us," Raph had said nonchalantly, as he reached for the porcelain coffee cup their waiter had immediately filled upon his arrival.

The woman's hand had gone to her throat, and her face had turned peach-red. "Oh god," she whispered. "You're all… Oh my god…"

"No, no, I'm sorry, I'm only joking," Raph had said, mercifully. "You slept with me. Just me. And you were fantastic. Thank you." He had winked at her over the rim of his cup, then picked up the paper Neo had abandoned, silently dismissing her.

"Thanks, I think," the woman had said, then turned and walked out of the restaurant, her head high, as she tried to maintain some semblance of dignity.

Neo had shaken his head disapprovingly at Raph. "Now, why

did you go and do that after I painstakingly arranged another hook-up for you tonight? She said it was the best fuck of her life. She actually said you were a god in bed. Tele, did you know our brother was a *god* in bed?"

Tele had laughed. "I just hope it doesn't go to his head. He might fall over if it gets any bigger."

"I told her it was a one-time thing. But since she obviously can't tell us apart, you are welcome to have her tonight. See if you can top me," his brother had said, with not an ounce of emotion in his voice.

"No thanks, I already have a girlfriend," Neo had reminded him.

"Well, that's not my problem, but I'm sure Brooke would be pleased to hear you say that." Raph had placed his napkin on his lap as their waiter approached with a basket of warm pastries.

"You are one cold, conceited jerk, you know that?" Tele had piped in.

Raph had given Tele a stone-cold stare. "*You*, of all people, have the nerve to call me a jerk? Are you forgetting…" His voice had trailed off as Petra and her nanny entered the restaurant and headed their way.

Neo had sighed in silent relief that they were all spared yet another rehashing of past misdeeds and misunderstandings between Raph and Tele. There was nothing to be done about it now.

"Mr. Emotionally-Void-and-Unavailable has found true love."

Tele's voice brought Neo back to the present. "Yep," he agreed. But the fact that *that* cold, conceited jerk, whom he loved with all his heart, was getting married before him, was a hard pill for Neo to swallow.

"I thought it would never happen for him," Tele continued. "But here we are." He pulled two glasses of wine from a passing waiter and handed one to Neo. "Here's to Raph and Xio."

"Yep, to them." Neo took a small sip just as his phone buzzed in his pants pocket. He anxiously pulled it out, but tension tightened in his belly as he read the message.

> I'm sorry, Neo, but I can't do this. I'm tired of pretending.

Neo clenched his jaw and shoved the phone back into his pocket. *So it's like that, huh?*

"What's wrong?" Tele asked. "Is it—"

"I need to get some air," Neo said tightly. He set his glass down on the high-top table behind him and headed for the nearest exit.

THE NIGHT AIR was warm and heavy with the scent of jasmine as Neo meandered the grounds of Jewel Beach Resort, the award-winning luxury hotel on the Caribbean island of Ynoa—known to tourists and outsiders as Akilina. It was here, only fifteen months ago, that his brother had met Xiomara, the owner and CEO of the resort that had been in her family for generations.

"Everyone's in love tonight," Neo muttered, as he crossed a footbridge over the adults-only swimming pool where he couldn't help but notice one couple enjoying their moonlit dip, perhaps a little too much for the public eye.

He shook his head. Who was he kidding? If he could be doing the same thing with a woman he loved right now, instead of walking alone through one of the most romantic, luxury resorts in the world, he would be. He believed in love, and he wouldn't begrudge anyone theirs, he thought, as he continued across the grounds, putting as much distance between him and the couples.

As he followed a gravel path, the sound of waves crashing on the white sand beach gradually gave way to that of a live band echoing through the night. Neo followed the music until he found himself in front of what looked like a brand-new wooden sign. Pelican Pier Beachfront Bar was painted on it in a cool, laid-back, blue font, beckoning guests to relax and leave their worries behind.

Eager to do just that, Neo stepped off the path and made his way across the sandy-floored bar. The smell of grilled seafood, cannabis, and seaweed filled the air, taking Neo back to spring break in college when he, his brothers, and their friends would throw parties like these on California beaches, doing things they knew they shouldn't, but were too young to care.

Peals of laughter erupted from one of the cabanas surrounding the bar. Around an open fire pit, small groups lounged on blankets and cushions, their conversations punctuated by the crackling flame. On the small stage, a jamming, all-female steelpan and string band dared the audience to stand still. As they leaned into every beat, seemingly one with their instruments, bodies on the dance floor rocked and spun in a chaotic blur of lights and color.

Here, among these blissful strangers, Neo thought he might be able to hide from the demands of Raph and Xio's wedding preparations long enough to process what had been eating him since he'd arrived in Akilina two weeks ago.

He scanned the bar for a seat, but it seemed every stool was occupied. He was just about to signal a bartender when he felt a gentle tap on his arm. He turned around to find identical twins smiling up at him, streaks of purple running through their blonde hair. Their eyes were bloodshot and hazy, likely due to the influence of weed—legal on the island for anyone over twenty-one—or alcohol, or more than likely, a combination of the two.

"Hey there, you lookin' to buy us a drink?" one asked in a deep southern drawl.

Neo narrowed his eyes. They looked like they were barely out of college, and he wondered if they were experienced enough to handle the kind of tryst they seemed to be looking for—maybe or maybe not. Either way, they were too young for his taste.

"So?" the other asked. "What d'ya think?"

Neo didn't need trouble with twins tonight, especially ones who were probably so messed up, they couldn't tell themselves apart. All he wanted was to buy his own drink, find a seat somewhere, and get lost in his thoughts. "Sorry, not tonight, ladies. I think I'd only be in your way," he said politely, offering them nothing more than a bland smile.

"Are you sure? We do everything together, if you know what I mean." One winked at him while curling her manicured nails around his arm.

Neo knew exactly what she meant. "I'm very sure," he said with a bit more gravity this time, removing her grip on his arm.

"Whatever," she snorted, and yanked her sister away.

There was a time when Neo wouldn't have dreamed of passing up an opportunity like that. In fact, he'd have given anything for just five minutes with the Barton sisters in high school. In truth, there was no reason he couldn't bury his angst between a pair of those long, tan legs, and then roll over to bury them a bit deeper into the next, equally sexy pair. But Neo wasn't trying to bury his problems—he just wanted to think.

Before the twins were even out of sight, he spotted another eager catch on the other end of the bar. She raised her glass and gave him that come-and-get-me smile.

This is too easy, he thought. Neo wasn't vain, but he wasn't stupid either. He knew he looked good, especially in his Prada suit and a fresh cut. And he imagined that without lifting a finger, he could bed just about anyone he wanted at the bar tonight.

There was something wild and wanton in the air at Pelican Pier and, reluctantly, he realized that if three women had already made a play for him before he'd managed to order a drink, the solitude he sought wasn't likely to be found here—at least not on this night. Thinking that Cove Lounge in the main building might better suit his somber mood, Neo gave up on catching the bartender's attention and turned to leave.

That was when he saw her, just as a cool breeze lifted the hem of her yellow cotton dress ever so slightly, revealing a pair of smooth, toned thighs. The heavenly vision, like something out of a nineteen-fifties film, pulled the air from Neo's lungs, and stopped him in his tracks. Frozen and helpless, he watched her through the crowd, dancing in the moonlight.

She held a drink in one hand while the other twirled freely above her head. Her black tresses brushed her bare, creamy shoulders and fell down to the delicate hollow of her back. She was beautiful and beguiling, and she seemed to radiate amidst the crowd, as if the moonlight shone only for her.

Neo's chest tightened as her slender body rocked to the rhythm of Bob Marley's "One Love", and a barely audible groan vibrated in his chest as he imagined her beneath him, rocking to the rhythm of his hips.

A wild fluttering that started deep in his belly worked its way up to his throat, his breathing hardening and quickening fiercely. Mesmerized, and with a longing to be nowhere else in the world but here, he signaled the bartender and ordered a bourbon and soda, never once taking his eyes off her.

With his drink in hand, Neo headed toward an empty chaise lounge closer to the stage and the siren on the dance floor. He sank into the cushion, loosened his tie, and sat back to enjoy the show.

With each graceful movement, her spell over him grew stronger and his soul burned hotter. The sexy, commanding sway of her hips, her uninhibited smile, the way she seemed to float through the air—it was irresistibly alluring, awakening something deep within him, and stirring emotions he'd long forgotten. Her presence enveloped him, wrapping him in a cocoon of longing and desire. It was a connection unlike anything Neo had ever experienced.

Suddenly, as if sensing she'd attracted a voyeur, she stopped dancing and scanned the crowd. When she finally spotted him—when their eyes finally locked—a surge of electricity coursed through Neo, making his ears ring with nervous anticipation. Motionless, she held his gaze as time itself stood still, and every scent, every sound, everyone, and everything around them faded into darkness.

Just as Neo felt he might combust under the heat of her gaze, she tore her eyes from him. Then in three fluid motions, his mystery girl placed her drink on the edge of the stage, reached for the hand of a petite, dark-haired beauty nearby, pulled her close, and began grinding her body against hers. Mystery girl number-two seemed confused by the maneuver, but Ms. Wild and Sexy whispered something in her ear, then slapped her on the ass. *Hard.*

Neo nearly choked on his drink. Who *was* this woman?

Whatever she'd said had caused her friend—or so Neo hoped—to clamp her hand over her mouth, stifling a laugh. But as her laugh subsided, the friend lifted her arms over her head, and began to work her small body like a professional belly dancer.

Damn. Neo moaned. "One Love" had finished, and the two women were now locked hip to hip, working their bodies seductively against each other to a slow, rhythmic tune.

Neo was hard as an elephant's tusk, but he couldn't look away—couldn't bear the thought of her not being within sight. His manhood pulsed as she and her partner leaned their upper bodies away from each other, their dark hair swaying behind them like heavy, silk drapes. Neo's skin tingled as he imagined those silky strands brushing against his bare chest as the object of his desire leaned over him, kissing her way down his body toward his…

When three other women, all stunning in their own right, entered the circle, it became clear to Neo that Ms. Wild and Sexy was not at all on her own—she was on a girls' trip. It was hypnotic, and the wildest, sexiest thing Neo had ever seen. He wasn't the only one who thought so. Others on the dance floor had circled around them, cheering on their licentious display.

It wasn't long before a man, wearing nothing but a pair of white swim trunks, got behind one of the women. He grabbed her hip with one hand and pulled her into him, causing his drink to spill all over both of them. She pushed his hand away, but the asshole grabbed her again, carelessly pulling her long braids, and began grinding on her backside.

Neo was searching for a place to put his glass down, ready to leap to her defense, but before he could get to his feet, she turned, kneed him in the groin, tossed her braids over her shoulder, and without missing a beat, got back to dancing with her friends.

The man, clearly too drunk for his own good, dropped his glass and, clutching his balls with both hands, hobbled off the dance floor with his tail between his legs.

Neo watched with curiosity as Ms. Wild and Sexy shook her head when her dance partner whispered something in her ear. Soon, all five women were huddled together, then, all at once, black, blonde, blue, and braided heads swung in his direction.

I've been made.

His mystery woman straightened her dress, stepped away from her friends, and began sashaying in his direction with long, purposeful strides. Neo raised his glass to his lips and took a long draft, ready for whatever came next.

Would she motion for him to follow her to a dark corner of the resort? Would she chastise him for watching her like a dirty Peeping Tom? A dozen scenarios passed through his mind. But the last thing Neo expected was for the same jerk, who'd had his balls kneed into his stomach, to come tumbling through the crowd, bump into her, and send her careening forward, right into his lap.

His drink spilled all over his shirt and pants, and Neo was only vaguely aware of her friends calling out, "Cali!" from what seemed like a million miles away. His breath solidified in his throat as *Cali* slowly lifted her head and stared at him with a dumbfounded look in her bright emerald eyes.

"Shit," she said, her long, dark lashes fluttering. She placed unsteady hands on the cushion on either side of his thighs, and attempted to stand up, but her feet got tangled up over his.

"Whoa, easy there." Dropping his empty glass on the sand beside the lounge, Neo caught her around the waist and eased her down beside him, the heat of her breath sending fire through his veins.

Amazing, he thought, taking in the arresting features of her heart-shaped face, her delicate nose, and a temptingly curved mouth.

Apparently realizing that she was okay, her friends began to laugh between shouts of, "Way to go, Cali" and "Atta girl", their cheers giving way to the band as it began playing again.

"Oh my god, I'm so… Oh god, I'm so sorry," she shouted over the music, flaring her hand at his crotch.

"No worries," Neo shouted back.

"Seriously, I am so, so sorry. Oh my god, I am so fucking embarrassed."

You are so fucking beautiful. He placed his mouth close to her ear, resisting the urge to flick his tongue inside it. "You don't need to be sorry about anything." *Ever.* His eyes unwittingly traveled from the creamy column of her throat to the subtle rise and fall of her breasts.

"But what about your suit, and your shoes," she added, briefly glancing down at his feet. "Whoa, you are seriously dressed up. You don't have, like, some meeting to go to later, do you? Oh no…am I going to get you fired?"

"No, no meetings tonight, just a dance performance later, but my outfit is already backstage."

"Huh? What did you say?"

Neo shook his head, realizing it would be impossible to communicate the intricacies of Megiri wedding customs over the music. "Don't worry about the suit," he said. "I've got plenty more." He did, however, only have one pair of bespoke Berluti loafers, and he was certain they were now ruined. But if what he already felt in his heart for this woman turned out to be what he thought it was, it would be well worth the five-figure loss. "I'm more worried about you. Are you alright? That guy really clipped you."

Neo swore he saw something spark in her eyes. A flicker of recognition, like a match striking—fleeting, but undeniable.

"Yeah, I'm…" Her voice faded as her eyes patrolled his face, very slowly and carefully. It was as if she were seeing him for the first time—not merely the man she'd fallen into, but someone who tugged at the edges of her guarded soul. And then she blinked, and shook her head, as if awakening from a dream. "I'll be fine," she said.

"You sure about that?"

She pursed her lips and nodded slowly. "Uh huh."

Neo could sense her anxiety as she turned away from him, scanning the crowd. She was like a bird, perched on a branch, trying to decide in which direction to fly. "I'm Neo, by the way," he said, determined to keep her on his branch—in his tree. There was no way he was letting her fly off before he knew who she was.

She blushed. "Calista. But everybody calls me Cali."

"I know. I heard your friends cheering you on from the bleachers." He held out his hand. "Nice to meet you, Calista."

"You too, Neo," she said, taking his hand. "Can I buy you another drink? I feel so bad."

Neo couldn't hold back his laughter. "You really do, don't you?"

"Yes, I do! This is all my fault! I mean, yeah, that asshole just pushed me, but if I hadn't been … uh…" She paused and glanced toward her friends, now visible again through the thinning crowd. "I mean…if I hadn't lost my balance, you wouldn't be all wet and… Well, you'd be all nice and dry and drinking your…uh… What are you drinking?"

"It's a bourbon and soda," he said through an amused smile.

"Right, bourbon and soda. Anyway, let me get you another one. Or I should at least pay for your dry cleaning. Please?"

Neo studied her, a thought formulating in his mind. "I'll tell you what, Calista. I don't need another drink or dry cleaning. but I do need a date for my brother's wedding tomorrow."

Her eyes narrowed, and she edged away from him. "You're kidding, right?"

He paused and rubbed his chin, imagining the surprise on everyone's face when he walked in with Calista on his arm. "Not one bit." There was a staid firmness in his voice.

"Mmm, are you crazy then? Because you sound a little crazy."

"What! What's crazy about needing a date for a wedding?"

"Uh, what's crazy is that you're asking me to be that date. You don't even know me!"

"Maybe not, but I'd like to."

She drew her lips back into a cynical smile.

"Look," he said, determined not to let it deter him, "if you want to just pay for my dry cleaning, you'll have to give me your number tonight so I can call you. And I only trust my neighborhood cleaners with my suits. So it'll have to wait until I'm home, and that'll just complicate things. By then, you might not feel so bad about ruining my ten-thousand-dollar suit, and won't even want to make it up to me. No, I think it'll be a lot easier if you just pay me back tomorrow afternoon."

"Ten thousand dollars for a suit? Jeeesus. Who are you, Daddy Warbucks?"

Neo shrugged, a smirk hugging the corner of his mouth. "You can call me Daddy if you'd like."

She threw her head back and laughed, the sound stirring something exotic, yet familiar deep in Neo's heart. It was like a choir of angels, and he wanted to hear their chorus again and again. "So, what do you say? Your number and an expensive dry-cleaning bill, or one date, free of charge?"

Her laughter subsided, and she eyed him suspiciously. "Well, I gotta hand it to ya, you did make the first option sound pretty shitty." Her gaze, now curious, slid down his body, then back to his face, leaving a trail of heat in its wake. "A guy like you doesn't have a date to his own brother's wedding?" she asked, skeptically.

"A guy like me? And exactly what kind of guy do you think I am?"

"I don't know." She shrugged. "The kind of guy who could get any woman he wants in here."

"Calista, you're only right about that if you say yes."

Her eyes widened, her cheeks turned instantly red, and she bit into the corner of her bottom lip.

Good. She was feeling it, too. "So, do we have a date?"

She looked over at her friends, then back at Neo, cocked her head, and closed one eye, clearly pondering her options. "Sure, why not?" she finally said, just when Neo thought she would decline his offer.

"Perfect!" he beamed, unable to hide his relief. "The wedding is at three tomorrow afternoon. I'll send a car for you at two?"

"Uh, okay..." She glanced at her friends again, then back at him. "But—"

"Are you staying at the hotel?"

She nodded. "I'm staying at... um Moon...Moon-some-thing...uhh..."

Does she really not know where she's staying, or is she trying to ditch me already?

She snapped her fingers. "Moonstruck Villa! That's the one."

"Moonstruck Villa. Got it." *And thank God.* "You won't regret it, I promise," he said, the excitement bubbling in his voice.

"Well, hold on a minute, cowboy. What do you expect me to wear to this wedding?"

"What do you mean? A dress, I guess… Am I missing something?"

"You think I just flew down here for the weekend with my ten-thousand-dollar dress in my bag?"

"Oh." *You idiot.* "Probably not, huh?"

"Probably not, is right. I packed for a girls' trip, not some fancy-shmancy wedding."

"Okay, fair point." Neo scanned her athletic figure, his belly tightening with need. "I know a place in town where you can find a dress. How about we go tomorrow, and you can pick something out. My treat."

"Your treat?"

Neo smiled. "I'll pick you up in the morning. Around eight? I'll bring breakfast, and then we can drive into town together."

Calista laughed and traced a finger around the rim of her lips as she tried to catch the strands of hair the wind had blown across her face.

The sexy gesture made his stomach tighten. He swallowed hard.

"So, let me get this straight. Instead of letting me buy you a drink, or even pay for your dry cleaning after ruining your ridiculously expensive suit, you want to bring me breakfast, buy me a dress, and take me on a date to your brother's wedding?"

"Mmm, yeah, you've got it straight. You game?"

"Sure. Why not?" she said again with a shrug.

"Trust me, it'll be fun."

"Well, I don't know if I should trust you, but it'll be interesting, at least," she said, her tone laced with amusement.

From the corner of his eyes, Neo saw the belly-dancing friend standing at the edge of the dance floor, eying him up. She looked like a mother hen searching for her chick that had wandered too far and for too long.

"Oh shit! There's Manjit," Calista announced, as she rose to her feet.

Neo stood up. "I'll let you get back to your girls then. I'll see you tomorrow, Calista."

"Uh, yep, see you tomorrow," she said, awkwardly giving him two thumbs up. Then she stood for a moment, holding her thumbs in front of her, squinting at them with a puzzled look on her face, as if wondering what on earth she was doing.

"Good night, Calista," Neo said, giving her a reassuring wink.

Calista folded her thumbs into her fists, gave him a sailor's salute, then sauntered over to Manjit.

Neo watched the women disappear into the crowd. If someone had told him half-an-hour ago that he would meet a woman who would rock his heart off its axis, he would have laughed in their face. But as it turned out, they would have had the last laugh. He checked his watch. He could have stayed here watching her all night, even tried his luck with her on the dance floor, but that would have to wait until tomorrow night. It was time he got back to the rehearsal dinner. No doubt Akilah was wondering where he'd disappeared to.

Feeling as light as a feather, Neo walked past the bar toward the gravel path that had led him here tonight. Then after a moment's contemplation, he went back, described the women to the bartender, and told him to put their bill on his tab.

"Of course, Mr. Giannopoulos," the man said.

Flying high on the promise of Calista, Neo left Pelican Pier, certain that he had just met the woman of his dreams.

NEO WAS STILL SOARING as his driver passed through Jewel Beach's security gate. He'd been unable to get Calista out of his head all night—the vision of her dancing in her yellow cotton dress under the moonlight leaving no doubt that last night's chance encounter was only the beginning of their story. Sure, beautiful, sexy women had captured, and even held Neo's attention, but none had ever invaded his dreams. *None*, until Calista.

As they cruised along a narrow lane, Neo closed his eyes and recalled his dream of walking along the beach with her, their fingers intertwined while waves lapped at their feet. Her wind-tossed hair had brushed his arms, and he'd loved the way her hips felt against his thighs as he'd pulled her close and kissed her. Her breath had been sweet on his lips, and when she'd put her arms around his neck, her fingers tangling in his hair, he'd moaned loudly enough to wake himself.

Neo looked out the window as the car came to a stop behind one of JBR's ubiquitous yellow golf carts. He spotted the blue and white wooden sign with the words, Moonstruck Villa, hanging from a post. The white, clapboard house with glass louvers and blue shutters was nestled behind a fence of green hedges, its blue roof dotted with red flamboyant flowers that had fallen from the tree on the villa's front lawn.

Once out of the car, he strode eagerly up the paved walkway, flanked by rows of pink and white lilies, took the three steps up to the covered porch, and knocked on the door.

Several moments passed in silence as he waited, his anxiety growing, and after hearing no movement inside, he knocked again.

Neo felt an eternity pass him by. His skin felt hot, and his heart raced as he knocked again, and again, each time with a bit more force. Just when he began to fear that Calista had played him for a fool, the door flew open.

"What?" she barked.

Neo's heart flew to his throat as she stood before him in a T-shirt and a pair of white pajama shorts.

"Oh—uh… Hey," he stammered, at once startled and aroused by the sight of her. "Are you almost ready?" he asked, worried that he'd misremembered what time they were supposed to meet.

Calista tilted her head back, and with one eye opened, peered at him through a curtain of black, disheveled hair. "Ready for what? Who are you, and what the hell are you talking about?"

About the Author

Inspired by the strong heroines and flawed alpha heroes in the stories she read as a young girl, *New York Times* and *USA Today* Bestselling Author, Ana E Ross writes steamy and sophisticated, multicultural contemporary romance novels. Her drama-filled stories feature charming, powerful, larger-than-life billionaires and strong, independent women who fight and love with equal passion.

Born and raised in Nevis, Ana now lives in the Northeast, U.S., and loves traveling, tennis, yoga, meditation, everything Italian, and spending time with her daughter.

www.anaeross.com